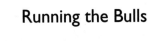

Running the Bulls

Other Books by Cathie Pelletier

Widow's Walk (Fiddlehead Poetry Books, University of New Brunswick, 1976)

The Funeral Makers (Macmillan, 1986)

Once Upon a Time on the Banks (Viking, 1989)

The Weight of Winter (Viking, 1991)

The Bubble Reputation (Crown, 1993)

A Marriage Made at Woodstock (Crown, 1994)

Beaming Sonny Home (Crown, 1996)

A Country Music Christmas (Editor, Crown, 1996)

The Christmas Note (with Skeeter Davis, Nashville Books, 1997)

As K. C. McKinnon

Dancing at the Harvest Moon (Doubleday, 1997)

Candles on Bay Street (Doubleday, 1998)

Running the Bulls

a novel by Cathie Pelletier

University Press of New England | Hanover and London

Published by University Press of New England,

One Court Street, Lebanon, NH 03766

www.upne.com

© 2005 by Cathie Pelletier

Printed in the United States of America

5 4 3 2 1

Library of Congress Cataloging-in-Publication Data

Pelletier, Cathie.
    Running the bulls : a novel / by Cathie Pelletier.
        p.   cm. — (Hardscrabble books)
    ISBN-13: 978-1-58465-487-2 (alk. paper)
    ISBN-10: 1-58465-487-2 (alk. paper)
    1. Retired teachers—Fiction. 2. College teachers—Fiction. 3. Older men—Fiction.
4. Adultery—Fiction. 5. Secrecy—Fiction. 6. Maine—Fiction. I. Title. II. Series.
    PS3566.E42R86   2005
    813'.54—dc22   2005011117

I REALLY DON'T WANT TO KNOW
By HOWARD BARNES, and DON ROBERTSON
© 1954 (Renewed) CHAPPELL & CO.
All Rights Reserved   Used by Permission
Warner Brothers Publications U.S. Inc., Miami, Florida 33014

THE BILBAO SONG
By KURT WEILL, EUGEN BERTHOLD,
and JOHNNY MERCER
© 1961 (Renewed) WEILL BRECHT HARMS CO INC.
and KURT WEILL FOUNDATION FOR MUSIC INC.
All Rights Administered by WB MUSIC CORP.
All Rights Reserved   Used by Permission
Warner Brothers Publications U.S. Inc., Miami, Florida 33014

"It's All in the Game" written by Carl Sigman and Charles Dawes.
copyright 1951 MAJORSONGS CO. (ASCAP) / Administered by Bug
All Rights Reserved. Used by Permission.

Grateful acknowledgment is made for quotations from Ernest Hemingway, *The Sun Also Rises:* Reprinted with permission of Scribner, an imprint of Simon & Schuster Adult Publishing Group, from THE SUN ALSO RISES by Ernest Hemingway. Copyright 1926 by Charles Scribner's Sons. Copyright renewed 1954 by Ernest Hemingway.

THIS BOOK IS DEDICATED TO:

Mama.
Ethel Tressa O'Leary Pelletier (1918–2000)
Even the air feels different without you.

Tom Viorikic, my husband, and the best decision I made in my life.

Louis A. Pelletier, my father, a man I so admire and love.

AND IN MEMORY OF:

Randy Vanwarmer (1955–2004)
One of the world's best singers and songwriters,
and one of the very best friends.

Acknowledgments

A special word of thanks to the following:
Gabrielle Tana, who always reads,
Deborah Joy Corey, my soul sister,
Wesley and Diane McNair, for believing,
Cherry Danker, who holds the fort at Portage, Maine.

Carl Hileman; David Logan; Sherry Sullivan; Doug Liman; Terry
Kay; Phyllis Jalbert; Darko and Lori Copkov; Julia Pierrepont, III;
Patsi Bale Cox; Tanya Tucker; Doug Kershaw; Bob and Joy Zimmer-
man; Zoran Popovic; Randy Ford; Dr. Paul Gahlinger; Jackie Cheat-
wood; Nick Shelton; Bob McDill, for some of the best songs ever
written; and, of course, Ann Warner, of Falmouth, Maine.

Cally Gurley, and the Maine Women Writers Collection, at the
University of New England, in Portland, Maine.

In Toronto, Canada: Christina Copkov, Romano DaSilva and
Tomislav Copkov.

In Montreal, Canada: Suzanne and Jean Luc Flippo, and Christo-
pher, Johnathan and Lauren Flippo.

Thank you, John Hafford, my dear friend and distant cousin, for
the cover art. And, Jessica Masse, who is John's own muse. (The
artwork of trees and sky on the cover is from a photo taken not far
from my hometown of Allagash, Maine.)

A special thank you to my editor, John Landrigan, for believing.
And to the folks at University Press of New England.

And finally, goodbye to the rescued animals who owned my
heart for so many years: Moon Cat, who lived to be twenty-two;
Dixon, who had to have a rhinoplasty, and who trusted the world
completely; Manx, who came missing part of his tail; and two very
fine, dignified dogs, Jake and Fred, a.k.a. "Anxious," who taught me
much about how to say goodbye.

"Une generation perdue . . . "
—Proprietor, Hotel Pernollet, in Belley, France,
to Gertrude Stein, about the mechanic
who was working on her car

"You are all a lost generation."
—Gertrude Stein, later, in conversation
with Ernest Hemingway

SUMMER, 1998

Bixley, Maine

one | **BULLS**

When Howard Woods awoke on what would become the most fated day of his life, he squinted his eyes at the bedside clock. Still only 3 A.M. He had been dreaming again. He could feel the moist sweat on the sheet beneath his stomach, the damp of his own pajama top. He turned over onto his back then, even though this meant he would snore off and on until morning, with Ellen poking at his ribs to quiet him. But if Ellen were deep into her own sleep, she wouldn't hear him. Howard stretched an arm over to touch her, to assess the situation, but Ellen's side of the bed was empty.

This was nothing unusual since Ellen Woods had always admitted to being a night person. Many times over the years Howard would wake to find her standing at the window, silver in moonlight, silent. Other times, he'd hear her prowling about in the rooms of the house, like some kind of midnight burglar. *My night owl,* Howard Woods called Ellen. Even when the two were still teaching at Bixley Community College—Ellen history and Howard literature—even then Ellen was often up at night, restless. "Come back to bed," Howard would say to her. And then, with sleep pulling him down, with the alarm clock waiting to maliciously uncoil, he would drift back to his own dreams, knowing he could snore freely if the urge should come upon him. Yet, at breakfast, while he ate his oatmeal and drank his coffee and read a swatch of the morning paper, Ellen was the one who had enough energy to ransack the house for Howard's quarterly tests, the ones he had finished correcting the night before. And Ellen was the one to gather up the dishes and leave them in the sink so that she could find them soaking after school, instead of clogged with egg yolk and jelly. Ellen was the one who said, "It's there, Howie, next to the chair in the study, that's where you left your briefcase." And when the children were still with them, Greta, Howard Jr., and John, she would putter about the house, finding their shoes, their socks, their sweaters, their books, and then seeing that all three ate a hearty breakfast. Ellen did this, even though Howard might have awakened the night before to find her standing at the window, head tilted, her eyes fixed on the garden. Or perhaps she was staring at a darkened tree, the house next door, some clouds. Who knew? Ellen was a night owl with energy to burn the next day, and Howard had come to accept that his wife was a little strange, at least nocturnally.

So how could he know, how could Howard Woods *imagine* that a year and six days into his retirement Ellen would finally tell him what she'd been staring at those moonlit nights, or nights of snowflakes trembling their way over Patterson Street, nights of terrified rainfall, the gutters and downspouts full to bursting. But that's what happened. Howard opened his eyes to see his wife in her usual stance at the window. Then he had fallen back to sleep. It was another dream of the classroom, another lecture he was trying desperately to deliver, about how *Macbeth*, Shakespeare's shortest play, was really a *study in fear*. He was telling this to a dream class of college students who were not only unwilling to listen, they were incapable of hearing him, for in the dream *none of them had ears!* It was a dream of retirement, no doubt about it, a dream of emasculation, a dream of finding one's way in the world after almost thirty years of chalk and test papers and classroom talks. And it was a recurring dream, one that he'd started having just days after their retirement party at the K of C Hall. But it was a dream he would not dream to the end, at least not on that night, for he felt Ellen's hand on his arm, and this catapulted him, if not wide awake, then into some kind of waiting room to his conscious mind.

"What is it?" Howard muttered. He kicked a foot at the top sheet, as if struggling to unwrap himself from the madness of the dream. The lecture he'd been trying to deliver had involved the three witches that Macbeth and Banquo encounter on that deserted heath. The witches and their prophecy. *Double, double, toil and trouble.*

"Howie, wake up," Ellen was saying, as she gently shook his arm.

Howard fought to pry his eyes into a believable, wide-awake look, but too much of the dream was still in them. Poor Macbeth, compelled to cross that same barren heath every time someone picked up the play and read it anew, cursed forever by academics and indifferent students to meet up, perpetually, with those three nasty hags and watch the course of his life spiral downward. *Fire burn and cauldron bubble.*

"Come on, Howie. It's important."

Howard's conscious mind was telling him that this was no longer about Macbeth and his witches, that something must be wrong, just as something had been wrong on all those nights, years ago, when Greta had come down with appendicitis, or Howard Jr. had been up sleepwalking again, or John had had another nonstop nosebleed.

"I need to tell you this," Ellen said, "before I lose my nerve."

Howard sat up against his pillow. The narrow slats of the window blind had been left open and now Ellen's face was ribboned with moonlight. Even her eyes were a shimmering silver, like those highlights in her red hair that had appeared slowly, over four decades of marriage. A sexy kind of silver that Howard had always liked.

"What's going on?" he asked. He could feel her fingers firmly on his arm and knew he was no longer dreaming. Ellen's fingers, sure and steady and cool to the touch, burning into the warmth of his skin. His wife's fingers, in the middle of the night. "What the hell are you talking about?"

"I'm talking about guilt, Howie," Ellen said at last, "and how it can eat at your soul. I think men know how to handle guilt. That's how they spread their seed. I think nature gives them a little something extra in their genes that fights guilt off, the way cells fight bacteria."

"Ellen," was all Howard said, and he knew then that he didn't like the feel of her fingers on his arm. They were roots, suddenly, roots that had sprouted well during all those nights he'd seen her standing at the window, meditating, pondering, whatever the hell it was she did over there. *Double, double, toil and trouble.* He wished the fingers belonged to someone else. Greta maybe, who was now married and living in Miami, with three daughters of her own. Or Howard Jr., who was a lawyer in Philadelphia, and also had two girls. Or John, the baby of the family, who had been the pilot of an F-15 fighter during Desert Storm, but was living in the same town as his parents, an executive now with Sounder Aeronautics, living just fifteen miles from Patterson Street, with his wife, Patty, and their son, Elliot. Howie wished Ellen's fingers would melt, would fall away from his arm and into a pool of silvery moonlight. But they didn't. They squeezed harder. He felt his heart lurch. His mind was still reeling itself toward total consciousness. *Guilt.* What did guilt mean? Had she wrecked the car, bounced a check, ironed a hole in his favorite golf shirt? *Guilt.*

"I'm talking about *me,*" Ellen said at last. "I'm talking about me, and Ben Collins, and guilt, and how the three of us have lived a lie, a little ménage à trois of a lie."

This information brought Howard wide awake. *Ben Collins. Ben Collins.* He was trying to place him, for he knew most certainly that he was acquainted with Ben Collins. Ben Collins! He had taught Ancient History at Bixley Community College, years ago, filling in for Samuel Frist, who was on sabbatical. When Frist returned from Greece the next year, with far too many slides of the Parthenon and a suspicious Hellenic accent, Ben had packed up his family and moved on, downstate somewhere. Yes, Howard had even played golf with Ben Collins, and remembered him as a not-too-shabby player. And then there had been all those school functions where they had run into each other, Ben with his wife, and Howie with Ellen. Sometimes, they went with other teachers and spouses for an after-the-game beer, bundled in heavy coats during basketball season and huddled around the fireplace at Red's Tavern. But then, Ellen had known Ben well. They were in the same department. *Ellen had known Ben very well.*

"Ben Collins?" Howard said, and it seemed that by just speaking the name, something broke, something fragile as glass. Howard reached out now and snapped on the night light. The silver disappeared, flew back to the moon, most likely. *Ben Collins.* He stared at Ellen's face, the straight bridge of her nose, the pretty cheekbones. He waited.

"It started just a few months after he was hired to teach at the college," Ellen said, distant, as if she were talking to someone else, her history class maybe, that old sea of faces that had risen before her eyes for almost thirty years. She might as well be staring out the window again, peering into the garden. But she wasn't. She was staring right at Howard Woods, her husband. "Ben and I were both trying to quit smoking, and we both had free periods at the same time. So, in the teacher's lounge, well, we became friends. And I want you to know that, Howie. I want you to understand that we were friends first, Ben and I. If we hadn't been, the affair never could have happened."

This threw Howard forward in the bed. He had been listening like some kind of blind, sleepy mole to what she was saying: *Guilt. Seed. Cells. Bacteria.* He hadn't quite figured out the scenario since, in his half-sleep, it sounded like some kind of surreal Botany class. But he knew in his gut that it was worse than a middle-of-the-night nosebleed. Only when she said the word *affair* could his brain register the full impact. It was because he knew Ellen so well, maybe, that he was kept frozen in suspense, unwilling to understand until she spread it all before him, unwrapped the ugly blanket of her deceit. Ben Collins! Howard leapt from the bed and groped on the chair for his pants.

"The bastard!" he said, poking with his right foot at the waist opening in his pants while he balanced himself on the left.

"It was a long time ago, Howie," Ellen was pleading now. "And it was over quickly. I wish I could have told you then. For over twenty years I've felt terrible."

But Howard didn't care to hear Ellen's pity for herself.

"So, Lady Macbeth," he snarled. "Driven mad by your conscience, are you?"

"Lady Macbeth?" It was Ellen's turn to be confused. "For heaven's sake, Howie, listen to me."

"The dirty bastard!" Howard shouted. Since his right foot couldn't find a leg slot in the pants, Howard switched feet. "I'm gonna kill him, I'm gonna kill him!" He repeated this new phrase as though it were a poem, a mantra for the retired male. "He'll never lay his hands on my wife again because I'm gonna kill him!"

Then, trousers in hand, belt dangling, Howard sat down on the edge of the bed, winded. For Christ's sake, he was sixty-three years old and yet here he was, expending energy like some kind of teenaged wolf. He would take his time, like the mature, retired adult that he was. He would put his pants on the proper way, one leg at a time, followed by his shoes. Then, he would get a butcher's knife from the kitchen—that big shiny thing Ellen used on the Thanksgiving turkey—he would find his car keys, and he would drive to Ben Collins's house—wherever the hell *that* was—and he would stab the son-of-a-bitch until the cows came home.

Howard slid his pale legs into his pants, the right one first, then the left. He pulled the pants up around his waist, zipped them, then tightened and buckled his belt. He looked over at Ellen.

"I'm gonna kill him," Howard said again. He was instantly pleased to hear the calm now in his voice. Even Macbeth, that henpecked thane of Cawdor, hadn't managed *that* in that face of adversity.

"You're too late, Howie," Ellen said. She was back at the window now, spying on the last of the spring daffodils, petals frosted with moonlight. Or maybe she was remembering the pretty spot where the kids had had their swing set, until it fell apart with age. "Ben's already dead."

Howard's little blue Ford turned left at the traffic light by the library, and then cruised slowly toward John's street. Spring had come and gone in Bixley, Maine, and now summer was in the air— it being the first day of June—with lots of leafing and budding and flowering. Lilac bushes up and down the streets had little purple blooms on them, and lawns were turning green as indoor turf. A splash of dawn was hitting the eastern sky, down where the big drive-in screen used to loll, all those summer evenings when the kids were little and he and Ellen had taken them with snacks and blankets and pillows to see whatever movie had caught their fancy that week.

All the lights were still out at John's house, but Howard knew the house would be asleep. He had just glanced at his watch and saw that it was a quarter of five. John's station wagon was dozing in the drive, its ass pointed toward the street, its eyes shut tight, thanks to those automatic lids. Howard pulled up behind it and cut the Ford's engine. He wanted to go up to the door instantly and ring the bell. He was reminded of all those middle-of-the-night nosebleeds when the faucet between John's eyes had spewed red until the early hours of morning, while he, Howard, had stood holding a cloth to his son's face, holding the boy's tilted head, and muttering to himself, "Clot, dammit, clot, clot, clot." Surely, if he knocked on the door now, John the adult would understand. "It's payback time, buddy," Howard would tell him.

But Howard couldn't bring himself to do it. Instead, he sat staring at the bicycle that he and Ellen had dipped into their retirement money to buy for Elliot, their only grandson. It leaned against the front steps of the house, the red paint turning from deep burgundy to a bright apple color as the sun rose over Bixley and life began to stir, to rekindle itself inside bathrooms and kitchens up and down the street. Inside John's own house Howard saw light finally burst forth, a tiny supernova in the bathroom. Then, one in the kitchen, as the window turned a warm yellow. Still, Howard waited.

Finally, just before seven o'clock, John opened the front door and stepped out. Howard heard him and looked up, away from that morning's *USA Today*. He had read all about how Alabama was returning its worse prisoners to chain gangs; how Massachusetts needed to clean up the pollution around Cape Cod; how Americans spend over $293 million a year trying to eradicate cockroaches; how some guy in Los Angeles was planning to run the bulls in Pamplona, carrying a huge banner as a statement against animal cruelty; and how the White House was still holding its own against the Whitewater allegations. Howard folded the paper back into its original form. John obviously hadn't seen him there, parked behind the station wagon as if he were part of a sad wagon train headed for divorce, instead of the Oregon Trail. Howard watched as John searched the front porch and then began scanning the walkway, looking for something.

Howard whirred his window down. "You looking for this?" he asked, and waved the morning paper at John, who glanced up, startled to hear a voice. When he realized it was Howard, he appeared even more startled.

"Dad?" he said. "What the hell's going on?" He was wearing only pajama bottoms, and as he came down the walk Howard couldn't help but feel a fatherly pride at his son's physique, the well-muscled arms, the kind of washboard stomach that most men work out hours a day in the hopes of attaining. This was his son, John, the one who had flown that F-15 fighter, while back home all Howard and Ellen could do was sit on the edge of their sofa and watch the bombing on television. "It looks like Fourth of July fireworks," Ellen had said, as Bernie Shaw's voice transmitted news from a hotel room in Baghdad. Howie and Ellen had been pulled into a world they knew nothing about when John volunteered for Desert Storm, a world of precision-guided missiles, night vision, infrared navigation and target designation systems, laser and electro-optic guided bombs, target sensors, all devices that would allow for round-the-clock bombing. Back then, Howard had thought it the most terrible thing that could happen to him as a human being, having his son at war. And in his role as *father*, it still was.

Howard got out of the car and then leaned back against it, the paper tucked up under his right arm.

"It was delivered about five-thirty," he said. He handed the paper to John, who took it. "I didn't think you'd mind."

"You been sitting out here since five-thirty?" John asked. Then, a look swept over his face. "Something has happened to Mom!" Funny, but Howard recognized that look as the same one that had filtered across Ellen's face, when Marlin Fitzwater broke the news to an astonished American public: *The liberation of Kuwait has begun.* In all their years of marriage they had probably never been closer than at that moment—January 16, 1991, at 6:40 P.M. in Bixley, Maine—when one of their children was in grave jeopardy. He and Ellen had sat together on the sofa, her hand gripping his, watching as American planes zoomed in over Baghdad, F-117A Stealth Fighters, modernized B-52 bombers, F\A-18 Hornet Fighters, Apache attack helicopters, SuperCobra helicopters, and, of course, those F-15 fighters, one of which was being piloted by the boy with the childhood nosebleeds. He and Ellen had sat with their strange new vocabulary floating between them, wondering, each time, "Is that plane our son? Is that John Woods?" It was the look of losing someone you love dearly, someone you cannot imagine life without.

"Your mother is fine," said Howard. "Oh, she's just fine and dandy." He stared at his feet. He had forgotten to wear socks. He smiled as he pulled up his pants leg and showed John. "No socks," he announced.

"Have you been on some kind of bender, Dad?" John asked, looking down at the sockless feet. He then leaned forward to smell Howard's breath, but Howard waved him back.

"I haven't brushed my teeth," he said. "A bender would smell better right now. Believe me."

"Then *what?*" asked John. "What the hell's going on?" Howard ran his finger down the blue paint of his car. A Ford Probe GT. A lemon, and even Bixley's Performance Ford admitted that it was. The transmission had gone twice in two years. Once, the muffler had dropped off in morning traffic. The windows shot up and down at random, as though ghosts were pushing the goddamn buttons. Howard was being kidded by the guys at Eddy's Service Station for having bought a lemon in the first place. He thought then of Ellen. He thought of the woman he had chosen to be his wife, for better or worse, a warranty for a lifetime.

"A goddamn lemon," said Howard.

"What?" asked John. He was looking back at the house, most likely wondering if Patty was awake and witnessing the scene out in their driveway.

"The Ford Probe's a lemon," said Howard. "Don't buy one, son."

"Dad, listen," John said, kindly. He leaned against the car, put his arm around Howard's shoulders. Big sturdy arms. Like his grandfather, thought Howard. He felt like weeping in that instant at the sight of his son, tall, brave, honest. How had he pulled it off? How had he raised such a fine boy? And he had done it amidst the deceit of his wife, John's mother, Ellen. He hoped he wouldn't cry, not in front of John.

"I know you didn't come over here to talk to me about cars," John said. "What is it? What's going on? Mom said retirement hasn't been easy for you. It'll take time, Dad. Hell, I wish I could retire, spend more time with Patty and Elliot. Mom says you've been moping around the house, not getting any exercise at all."

"Ha!" said Howard, and made a fist. He held it up for John to see. "Ha!" he said again. Just the mention of her name, of her pretend concern for him. Oh, she wanted him out of the house all right, running his flabby ass off up and down Patterson Street just so that she could avail herself of another neighborhood stud. Carl Warner! Two houses down from theirs, who thought himself a ladies' man and drove a Mercedes. By God, she was probably doing old Carl, and Howard didn't even know it! And now, retired, well, no wonder he was cramping her style. No wonder she wanted him out exercising his calf muscles.

"Goddamn lemon," said Howard, and struck his balled fist against the Probe.

"Jesus, Dad," said John. "It's just a car."

Next door, a man came out for his own morning paper. He saw John and waved. John waved back, and then turned to face Howard. "Come on in the house, Dad," John said. "Patty will get us some breakfast. And then maybe you'll tell me what the hell is going on." He motioned up the walk, then went on ahead, slowly, with Howard following as though he were on some kind of tether.

"Wait," said Howard. He went to the Probe and groped around in the back seat and came out with his suitcase.

"Holy cow," said John. "It's *this* serious?" Howard made a pointless gesture at the suitcase.

"Just a few things to tide me over," he explained. "But I forgot to pack socks."

Patty was in the kitchen, and still in her robe. She looked up at Howard in surprise, then over at the clock.

"Dad!" she said. "Is everything okay? Is Mom okay?"

Howard nodded, and said nothing, so Patty looked to John, who simply shrugged.

"From what I can make out," said John, "he's really pissed off that Ford sold him a lemon. And he's been waiting out in the yard since dawn to tell me about it."

John motioned for Howard to take off his jacket. Howard did so, and handed it to his son. No one spoke. Howard could hear water boiling in a kettle, and then the kettle's voice rising to a whine before Patty unplugged it. There was already a smell of muffins in the air, or some kind of bagel, or cake, and it reminded him that he was quite hungry.

"It's Ellen," he said finally. He would tell them. He would explain, and then he would feed his famished soul. "She threw me out."

"Mom *threw you out?*" John asked. He gave Howard that stunned look, the one animals have as they plod toward their own slaughter.

"Well, actually," said Howard, "I told your mother to get out of our home and she refused to leave. So, here I am." With his right arm he gestured pitifully at the length of himself. John and Patty exchanged a quick look, but Howard caught it. He had always caught John with those furtive looks. Like the time twelve-year-old John and his buddy Micky Pilcher played poker with Howard and a couple of fellow teachers, using their own marked deck until Howard, bankrupt and in debt to Micky for fifty dollars, saw something adrift in John's eyes. The boy, at thirty-three, still had a face like an open slate. Guileless. A man you'd follow into battle, or would want to follow *you* into battle.

"Why?" John was asking this cautiously now, carefully, frightful of the answer. "Why would you ask Mom to leave?"

"Why?" Howard wondered. "Because she cheated on me. That's why."

John seemed to go pale at this declaration. He spun around, began rattling about in the cupboard for some plates, but Patty, who'd been listening quietly, just nodded. Then, she smiled at Howard, gestured for him to take a chair at the table.

"How would you like your eggs, Dad?" she asked.

John came into the den where Howard was lounging on the sofa, having a second cup of coffee. He sat down, guardedly, in the chair facing Howard, and stretched his legs out before him. Howard smiled. It reminded him of another time, this quiet determination he could see in his son's demeanor. It reminded him of the time John had been caught smoking pot in the boys' bathroom at Bixley High. He had been expelled, and he had come home to wait for his father in the den, sitting stiffly in a chair, quiet, determined to defend himself, his legs thrust out before him.

"Now, Dad," said John. "I've called my office. I told them I'll be in later. Don't you think it's time you let me know what's going on?" Howard cleared his throat. He had been staring at the picture of Ellen and him on the mantle, a photo taken three Christmases ago, when the entire nuclear family had gathered in the house on Patterson Street to celebrate, with eggnog and brandy and deviled eggs, their good fortune in health and family and career. In the picture their faces were still alive with the endorphins that were pumping that day, bringing with them the joy of family, of togetherness, of continuity. The littlest grandchild, Howard Jr.'s two-month-old daughter, was blanketed in her mother's arms. Looking at the photo, Howard could now see Ben Collins, nestled there in the gray coils of Ellen's cerebrum, that trunk where old memories are kept. Everything seemed like a lie to him now.

"Remember Ben Collins?" Howard asked, and as John filed through the Rolodex of names in his memory bank, Howard pulled up an image of Ben. He had been good-looking, manly, in the way John was—not that Howard wasn't manly, he just wasn't, well, *rugged*. Ben was handsome in that rugged way that women like, that *Marlboro Man* kind of way, at least before the Marlboro Man died of lung cancer. Ben was rugged, and he had a great golf swing, a real natural. Tears came to Howard's eyes and he fought them back.

"Oh yeah," John said finally. "Mr. Collins. He taught history."

"Bastard," Howard said. "Your mother had an affair with him."

"Jesus," said John, that stunned animal look returning to his face. Then the animal look went away and another one replaced it. "Jesus," he said again, anger rising around the word. Howard held up a finger of caution.

"Don't waste your energy," he advised. "The bastard's already dead." John took this into consideration.

"Jesus," he said again. Howard nodded, appreciating the sympathy.

"Nice little mess to find myself in," he said. "Me dreaming about goddamn test papers, all night long, grading and regrading, over and over again. Or giving lectures that have no endings. I tell you, I never worked that hard when I was actually teaching. And then she goes and deals me out *this* hand."

The two sat on sofa and chair, father and son, silence crusting itself between them as they considered this new event in their lives. Patty's head appeared in the doorway.

"I'm off to the theater," she said. "We're getting the makeup and costumes ready for the play next month." John stood to kiss her goodbye, and this gave Howard a particular pain. A husband kissing a wife goodbye. "What do you say I pick up Chinese on the way home tonight?" Patty asked. "Will you be joining us for dinner, Dad?" Howard's eyes had teared at the sight of the kiss and now they were growing more cloudy. He put his head down, only to raise it again instantly. In doing so, he caught John lip-syncing words to Patty, trying to tell her before she left what the scoop was.

"Ellen cheated on me," said Howard, "with a man named Ben Collins. Twenty some years ago. He taught history with her at the college. They gave up cigarettes together and, apparently, at least according to Ellen, this act bonds people, like soldiers going into battle together. It lasted about ten months. He just died—the bastard!—and I guess that was a signal to Ellen that it was safe to tell me. Who knows *why* she told me? Guilt. She said men have something in their genes that protects them from guilt so that they can spread their seed. Cells and bacteria. We don't have guilt, Ellen says, but women do, at least she certainly does, and she wants me to forgive her." He was rambling and he knew it, yet he couldn't stop. It was a strange sensation, like being in one of those slow-motion car wrecks. Time was slowing itself down for him, and for a change. Because the truth was, it seemed like only yesterday that Howard Edward Woods had accepted his first teaching position at Bixley Community College. He and Ellen had planned long and hard as a couple. When they'd both graduated from college, back in 1957, Howard had dropped out to sell life insurance while Ellen went on to graduate school first. They had been married just a month then, and it was impossible for both of them to go to school at the same time. They needed finances in order to build stable ground beneath their dreams. A year later, just as Ellen finished her M.A. in history, she discovered she was pregnant with Greta. They had planned it that way through long talks that they shared late into the night, in that first little house they had managed to finance, Ellen's soft head resting on his arm, the two of them lying in the darkness as they laid out the course of their lives. It was Howard's way, to plan carefully and with great foresight. Then Ellen had stayed home with Greta, until Howard Jr. and John had made their own appearances into the world. Howard had supported the family all this time, as he waited for his own chance to go back to school. That happened just after he turned thirty-two years old. When he finally got his own master's degree in English, he was still just thirty-four, and a job had opened up under his nose, at Bixley Community College. By this time, the two oldest kids were in grade school, and John was big enough to leave with a trusted babysitter. So it was Ellen's turn to walk into her own classroom, when a job teaching history also became available at Bixley Community. Now she, too, could settle down to a lifetime of instruction. Well planned. Every damn bit of it. Then, one day, Howard woke up—or one *night*, rather—his pajamas and sheets soaked with so much sweat they could have been dunked in that goddamn cauldron the witches had in *Macbeth*, he woke to find that he was a retired man of sixty-three years, gray hairs abounding where once a lively chestnut brown had lived, yellow growing over the pupils of his eyes, a paunch that would make a kangaroo proud, and a stiffness in his back whenever he swung a golf club. Time had sped the bejeezus out of his life, but now, in his greatest misery, time was slowing down again. Now, now that he found himself up to his knees in a puddle of angst he had not even imagined in his teens—when he could have handled it by just being young and stupid and filled to the gills with testosterone—now, here was Time, attaching a freeze-frame button to Howard Woods's misery.

"Bummer," said Patty, and Howard remembered that he had a son, and a daughter-in-law, and that he was in their home, fifteen miles away from his own home. *Bummer*, indeed.

"Yeah, well, what you gonna do?" asked Howard, and clapped his hands together softly. It was the line he had always said in re-

sponse to why the Boston Red Sox seemed incapable of ever win-
ning a World Series, cursed for eternity for trading Babe Ruth. It
was the same hand clap he reserved for the poor Red Sox.

Patty came over and touched his shoulder, gently. She squatted
before him. Howard felt as though *he* had just been caught smoking
pot in the boys' room at Bixley High. Patty looked at him sincerely.

"It happened a long time ago," she said. "And it only lasted a
little while. I'm sure it didn't mean anything. At least she told you.
If she didn't love you, she would have kept it to herself. It's a time
for forgiveness, Dad." She kissed his cheek softly, and he realized
for the first time that he had a stubble of beard sprouting there,
what he called his *Dick Nixon Shadow*. "I'll see the two of you
tonight," Patty added. "You'll know me. I'll be the one with the bag
of fortune cookies." Howard tried to smile, but couldn't. "Forgiveness, Dad," Patty said again. Another kiss to John and she was gone.

Howard listened as the door slammed behind her. *Forgiveness.* He
looked at John, who had been staring at him all this time, waiting.

"Do you suppose," Howard asked his son, "that nature gave
women *forgiveness* in their genes? Because I don't feel it, son. I
don't feel it one little bit."

John looked over at the Christmas photo on the fireplace mantle.
Minutes slid away between them, the grandfather clock keeping
track with *ticks* and *tocks, ticks* and *tocks.* Finally, John stood, rocked
on the balls of his feet, just as Howard did in times of stress.

"Still," said John, "I think you should forgive her."

"You're kidding," said Howard. John said nothing. *Tick tock.
Tick tock.*

"No," he said finally. "I'm not kidding. You've got to think of this
family, Dad. You've got to think of us." So Howard did that. He
thought about his family. *Tick, tock.*

"I'm not gonna do it," he said. "You're the baby of the family, for
Chrissakes, and you're thirty-three years old. Yet you say I need to
stay with a philandering woman for the *sake of the family?* I don't
think so, son."

Howard stood, walked over to the fireplace where he could better see the photograph. He wiped a finger across the surface of the glass, leaving behind a pathway through a light layer of dust. It reminded Howard of a how a jet leaves its breath in the sky, a sign that it's been there, if only for a short time. He had truly believed his son would die in the skies over Iraq.

"She's hardly a philandering woman," John said now, still defending his mother. He went to the sofa and threw himself down on it. In his growing up years, John was always throwing himself on the sofa at Patterson Street, whenever something wasn't going well with the world. A football game lost, a quarrel with a girlfriend, a summer job denied him.

"How long did you say this went on?" he asked.

"Ten months," said Howard. There was another long, excruciating pause.

"Even so," John said. "You've got to think of the family."

"Why do I have to think of a family that doesn't even *live with me anymore?*" Howard wanted to know.

"Because," said John. "She's my mother." He threw a sofa pillow across the room. It struck the varnished wood beyond the rug and slid into a huge ceramic vase that seemed to be sprouting peacock feathers.

"Throw all the pillows you want," said Howard. "I'm not forgiving her." John sat up, put his head in his hands, breathed deeply. Then he sighed a heavy, tired sigh. A stranger peering in the window, seeing them both sitting there with such defiance nested between them, might think John the father, Howard the son.

"What are you going to do?"

"I'm filing for divorce," said Howard, and that's when he realized the course his retirement years would take—just as Macbeth's life had taken its own pitiful course after meeting up with the witches on that frozen heath—right there, right in the midst of that blurb of time in his son's den. That was it, then. He was getting a divorce, at the age of sixty-three, when most men get gallstones.

John pulled at a piece of thread on his shirt sleeve for an inordinately long period of time—*tick tock*—but Howard held fast. Finally, John looked at him.

"Then what?" he said.

"What do you mean, then what?" asked Howard.

"I mean, what are you going to do once you're divorced?" Time was moving fast again. Time was speeding up, asking for answers to questions that Howard hadn't yet confronted. Then, remembering something he'd read in that morning's paper, he *knew* what he was going to do. What he had almost done in his youth, in those green days before he fell in love with Ellen O'Malley and gave it all up. It had been a sublime dream of his, a great, great passion—well, he had at least *considered* it, briefly, just after he read his first Hemingway novel.

"I'm going to run the bulls," Howard said. Christ, it had a ring to it!

"*What?*"

"I'm going to run the bulls." He wondered if he would meet up with the animal rights man from Los Angeles, maybe touch elbows with him during the run, compliment him on his streaming banner. Later, they could have dinner at some restaurant called *Mi Casa—Su Casa,* or something cleverly Spanish, two sweaty but victorious expatriates, enjoying some Yank chitchat over a bottle of sangria: *How 'bout them Red Sox—how 'bout them Dodgers?*

John cleared his throat.

"What bulls?"

"The bulls in Pamplona."

John simply stared, that animal-to-slaughter look returning. Howard wondered what the look had been on his son's face during all those air sorties, when John was floating like a silent hawk in the skies over Iraq. Now John stood, began rocking on the balls of his feet.

"You aren't by any chance talking about Pamplona, Spain, are you, Dad?"

Howard nodded his head vigorously.

"I'm gonna run the bulls!" he said. He felt instantly rugged. He was being tested, finally, the way his own father had been tested in World War II, in North Africa. The way his son, John, had been tested in Iraq. Howard would be tested in *Spain*.

Tick, tock. Tick, tock. Tick tock.

"Jesus," said John.

two | **BUFFALO**

Throughout the afternoon, while John was at his job as an executive for Sounder Aeronautics, and Patty was at her job as theatrical technician, and Eliot was at his job as a second grader at Bixley Elementary School, Howard moped around their house, looking at family scrapbooks, rubbing a finger across the dusty family photo on the fireplace mantle, and had no job at all. John called twice to check on him, and to encourage him to talk things out with Ellen.

"It'll blow over," said John. Behind his voice Howard could hear other voices, busy with the chores of life, employed, engaged, occupied, *busy.* Howard heard those background voices and he hated them for their importance.

"What would you do if it were *your* wife?" Howard asked, his eyes squarely on Ellen's smiling face in the Christmas photo. He noticed that his arm was securely around her shoulder, the territorial mark of the male, his scent getting on her sweater, no doubt, his smell warding off other would-be suitors. And there Ellen was, as entrenched in her deceit as a fire hydrant. "Tell me that, son," Howard insisted. "What would you do if it were Patty?"

John didn't answer right away, as was his custom. Voices rose and fell at Sounder Aeronautics as Howard waited.

"Come on, Dad, for crying out loud," John said at last. "This isn't about Patty. This isn't about my wife. It's about my *mother.*"

"I rest my case," Howard said, and hung up. With John's voice now cut off, along with those other ghostly voices at Sounder Aeronautics, the house fell into paralyzing silence. Howard flicked on the TV, tried to concentrate on *The Price Is Right,* a show in which contestants were guessing the prices of common household products. Two women were up against a single man, a gentleman in his sixties, retired no doubt. But he proved a good adversary for the girls. Most likely the guy had been retired for *more* than a year because, the truth was, Howard Woods would have done pitifully had he been a contestant on the show. In the second year of retirement, he wondered, is that when this esoteric knowledge would come to him? Idle, tired of his slack face in the mirror, sick of his own miserable company, would he, Howard Woods, yearn to know the price of an electric can opener, a can of spray starch, a bottle of Windex?

The phone rang again, its bleat breaking the silence so quickly that Howard nearly dropped the remote control. He assumed it was John phoning back to say, "Okay, you're right. If it were Patty I might not be as forgiving as I think *you* should be." And so, without waiting for the answering machine to click on, Howard grabbed the phone up in its second ring. It was Ellen.

"Howie," she said. Her voice was tiny, grown small with sadness, and it hurt him to think of her that way. He felt an instant urge to rescue her from whatever was troubling her, until he remembered *what* was troubling her. "Howie, can we discuss this? Please? If I had known—and I *should have* known—that you were going to react like this, I never would have, well, I don't know what I would've done. It was hearing the news of Ben's death, I guess, that made me think it was time. Death is so final, Howie. It's so much worse than *this.*" She waited.

Howard waited, too. Then he said, very coldly, "What do you want, Ellen?"

"I want you to come home," she told him.

"Well, I'm not." he said, "I'm not coming home."

"Then at least come to dinner. I'll fix chicken cacciatore, the way you like it. We need to talk, Howie."

Again, Howard said nothing. A group of carousing youngsters biked by on the street outside, and the sweet sound of their laughter pierced into him. He missed his family, his kids, his goddamn seed, if you will, dispersed now like dandelion spores. He missed the sound of Ellen's voice. He missed her.

"What time?" he asked.

"Seven," she said. Then, "Is that okay?" He felt an undeniable power in this, in being the one who had to be asked for forgiveness. And there was something about his being invited for dinner, to his own house, for chicken cacciatore, that especially excited him. This anger, this short separation, had sparked something primitive in Howard Woods, had jarred him out of forty-one years of wedded illusion. He and Ellen had done everything as a team for so long. They had taught school together, even retired together. But then Ellen started matriculating outside the notion of team. She had started playing tennis twice a week with her good friend Molly Ferguson. And now she was taking ballet lessons, ballet lessons, for Chrissakes, as if she were Zelda Fitzgerald. And then, just last week, she had come home to tell Howard that she and Molly were discovering the ancient art of making clay pots. And he was welcome to join them! Howard thought not.

"Okay," he told her. "I'll be there at seven." Then he hung up. He had never hung up on Ellen Ann O'Malley Woods in his entire forty-five years of knowing her. Electricity ran up the guilty arm, sheer adrenaline mixed with raging power at having finally done the act, in his retirement years, at the age of sixty-three, when he still couldn't tell Bob Barker the price of an eight-ounce jar of Cheez-Whiz, or a gallon of bleach, or a goddamn Waring food processor.

"I'm not beat yet," Howard said aloud. The room had fallen back into silence, and he wanted it vibrant with his victory. He looked at his watch. Five-thirty. He decided to shower, then smooth his slacks with a damp cloth. They'd become wrinkled from all that time he'd spent in the Probe—the little blue lemon!—waiting for John's household to wake up. And it didn't seem worthwhile to struggle with a fresh pair from his suitcase. They would be even more wrinkled anyway. He could try ironing them, but he knew little about the attributes of steam irons. What would one cost? Ten dollars? Two hundred? Besides, who would know where Patty kept the iron. Theater people weren't operating on the same plane as regular folks.

In the shower, he felt strangely alive again, renewed, as randy as the first time he'd ever seen Ellen O'Malley, at a college dance, when he had gone with Stella Mapleton as his date and Ellen had walked in with Tyson Baker, a football quarterback. That's the first time Howard had ever laid eyes on her, her auburn hair glittering with red highlights, her bluish-green eyes, that creamy skin. The next time he saw her was at the Christmas dance. She was alone and so was he. He was eighteen, she was seventeen, and they were both freshman. The year was 1953, and the song that kept playing was "Rags to Riches." What a year that had been! A year of good grades from his professors, a year of good tunes on the radio, good movies at the local theater. A year of duck-tail haircuts and Oxford loafers. And dungarees and tee-shirts, a revolutionary style brought back to the states by World War II soldiers. It was a time when the whole country was sleepwalking behind Eisenhower, believing no wrong could come from promises of *peace and prosperity*, because the enemy was clearly defined in the Communist threat, in the Great Red Menace. Who would've known back then? Nineteen fifty-three. A truce had already been signed that very year, ending the Korean War and setting up the demilitarized zone over at the 38th parallel, a long way from Maine, a long way from the university world Howard had embraced. He told himself he had been too young for Korea anyway, and that had been mostly true. It was all over by the time he turned seventeen. But still it gnawed at him. He felt untested, one of those fortunate-unfortunate young men who remain caught between great wars. Caught between apathy and heroics. It would shape him for the rest of his life: *Born too late to be Audie Murphy, and born too early to be Abbie Hoffman.* So, when the war ended—they called it the *conflict* back then—he went back to concentrating on his grades, and singing along to "Secret Love," by Doris Day, and going for a fourth time to see "From Here To Eternity," with the surf washing up alongside Burt Lancaster's rugged groin, Hawaiian sand all over Deborah Kerr's magnificent legs. And Donna Reed as a *prostitute!* Could it get any better than *that?* That was the year Arthur Miller's play *The Crucible,* shaming the antics of McCarthyism, was a hit on Broadway, just months before the Senate would censure Joe McCarthy for good, and sensible people could breathe easy again. Six months after that Christmas dance, a peace conference would be held at Geneva, Switzerland, ending French rule in Vietnam. So, how could Howard have known, with his thoughts and eyes glued fast to the 1954 Ford Thunderbirds already on the market—how could *anyone* have known—that not even a year would pass before U.S. military advisers would begin filtering into that part of the world, over by the *17th* parallel this time, with fervent plans to train the South Vietnamese army? How could anyone have foreseen the hula hoop, let alone the fact that John Kennedy would go to Dallas with a smile on his handsome face, and a pretty little wife beside him in a pink suit and a pillbox hat? With fourteen and a half million Allied soldiers dead from World War II, and over thirteen million civilians destroyed—120,000 Japanese alone died beneath the mushroom blasts over Nagasaki and Hiroshima—who could have foreseen 58,000 more U.S. soldiers scattered dead among the rice paddies of Vietnam, or imagined the long black memorial wall in Washington, D.C., to remember them by? Who would've dreamed that man would really stand upon the craggy surface of the moon, next to the Sea of Tranquillity, let alone watch as the Challenger blew into bits of cascading silver? That the Berlin Wall would go *up,* much less come *down,* and Communism would crumble like a stale cookie. Who ever dreamed that Ronald Reagan, who was brave and bold in 1953 as Marshall Frame Johnson in *Law and Order*—yes, *Frame* Johnson, that was his name!—who would believe that Frame Johnson would eventually become governor of California? And who would've ever believed that Ellen Ann O'-Malley, after swearing to her God to honor and cherish her husband until death do them part, would, less than two decades after Howard Woods placed a gold band on the third finger of her left hand, cheat on him with Ben Collins? Then, Howard remembered what he had put aside during his new rush of power: He remembered Ben Collins.

He got out of the shower humming "I Really Don't Want To Know." He couldn't remember if it had been a hit in 1953 or 1954, only that he and Ellen had loved it dearly. Howard thought about this. Was that some kind of clue for them and they'd missed it? The words hadn't applied to them then. They were newly in love with each other, and the idea of other arms, other lips, was as vague as Frame Johnson, *dba Ronald Reagan,* ever becoming governor of a civilized state, let alone leader of the most powerful country in the world. And that's when he was struck with the most horrible thought yet. Had Ben kissed Ellen's breasts? Of course, during the span of ten long months he would have discovered her breasts, there on her chest! The very notion almost brought Howard to his knees. Funny, but all day long he had thought about Ellen's cheating in purely philosophical terms. He had thought about it in terms of ideas: honor, truth, commitment, fidelity, family. He had not yet thought of it in terms of *lips, breasts, thighs, nipples, and orgasms,* the stuff song lyrics are made of. *Orgasms.* Christ, but that last thought compelled Howard to lean back against the bathroom mirror and shake, shake all over, the way Elvis had shook in his zoot suit, in "All Shook Up," which was the number one song in the country, the week of April 12, 1957, when Howard Woods and Ellen Ann O'Malley *cordially* invited friends and family *to witness this union before God.* Ellen having an orgasm with someone else! *How many arms have held you? And hated to let you go? How many, how many, I wonder, but I really don't want to know.* Why had she told him? Some things you should *never* know, and Howard suspected that this was what the Ford Motor Company was onto when they declined to tell him he was buying an exquisite lemon in the Probe GT. Damn Ellen to hell for not letting him live out the rest of his miserable, retired life in a measure of peace! He gathered himself together. He'd just have to deal with it, that was all. He'd do as she asked. They'd talk.

John was just getting out of his station wagon as Howard opened the front door and stepped out onto the porch, wearing his damp but unwrinkled slacks.

"Hey," said John. "You look like you're in a hurry." Then he noticed that Howard was carrying the suitcase. John smiled.

"I hope this means you're going home," he told Howard, "and not to some seedy motel." Howard sighed, ran a couple fingers through his hair. At least he still *had* hair.

"I guess we're going to talk," he said at last. "Over some chicken cacciatore. I'm going to ask a few questions and she's gonna give me a few answers, and well, who knows?"

"Good," said John, and patted Howard lovingly on the arm. "Now you're talking like a sensible man."

"Yeah, well," said Howard, remembering the poor Red Sox and their own emasculation. "What you gonna do?" he asked.

"If you need a place in the future," John offered magnanimously, and Howard could tell that his son hoped the offer would be unnecessary, "you'll always have one here, in the spare bedroom." Howard nodded, and the two stood silently on the front porch, rocking on the balls of their feet and watching as cars careened up and down the street.

"Give Patty and Eliot a hug for me," Howard said at last. Then he shook hands with John, loaded his brown suitcase into the Probe, and wheeled away in the direction of Patterson Street.

Their hydrangea bush would be flowering soon, Howard noticed. And there was Ellen's little gray Celica, in its usual space in the big two-car garage. For years he had pulled into the garage and parked next to whatever car was Ellen's at that moment in time. But now, he braked sharply in the drive. He left the suitcase on the floor of the car, in the back seat, where it couldn't be seen. Then, he strolled cautiously to his own front door. He couldn't remember ever ringing his own doorbell, and as he did so the sound of it from *outside* his house was so alien to his ears that he stood entranced, listening, knowing how it must be sounding to Ellen's ears, that *inside* sound.

It would be impossible to know if Ellen had dressed especially for the dinner date with her husband. In all their years of married life Howard had never seen her look less than beautiful. She was the kind of woman who could throw on one of his old flannel shirts, a pair of faded jeans, stuff her hair beneath a bandanna, and still be as alluring as if she'd meant it, had worked laboriously at it. When she opened their front door she was wearing a black skirt and a green sweater, one he'd seen her wear before, but now it seemed even more green and fluffy. And the wearing of it had turned her blue-green eyes full green. She smiled.

"You rang the doorbell?"

Howard nodded.

"Why not?" he asked.

"Come on in, Howie. For heaven sakes, this is your *home.*"

He said nothing, at least not yet. He had said quite enough that morning, had called her a *whore,* a word that stung her so in the hearing of it that he was almost sorry. Almost, but not quite. Instead, seeing the damage and hurt that could come from one single word, he'd said it again, and again, and again, until she told him she would not leave. "*You* leave," she had said. "This is my home. It's where I belong." And that's what he had done. He had taken his battered suitcase and, sockless, he had gone to John's and Patty's house in his blue lemon.

Howard stepped past her and headed to the bar. He found himself a bottle of Bacardi and was pouring a healthy serving into his glass when Ellen appeared in the doorway.

"You're not having your usual Tom Collins?" she asked. Howard shook his head. He was surprised at how quickly anger was fighting to replace the nostalgia he had felt earlier—a slice of Eisenhower's *peace and prosperity* pie—while the hot strings of water beat away at him in the shower.

"I won't have my usual Tom Collins," he told her, "since you're not having your usual *Ben* Collins." This shocked Ellen. She stood for a few explosive seconds, staring at him, wondering what she should do.

Then she said, "The chicken cacciatore is ready. We'll eat in the kitchen."

Howard followed her into the kitchen, instantly sorry. His whole psyche was a mixture of anger and love, sorrow and nostalgia. And hatred, hatred for Ben Collins and his rugged looks, that perfect Jack Nicklaus swing. *The bastard.* He sat at his usual place, at the head of the table, as Ellen poured them each a glass of red wine. Then she brought lovely salads, with artichoke hearts and Greek olives, knowing he favored them.

"I baked fresh bread," she said, and produced a basket of warm, homemade bread. Howard's mouth watered, but he maintained a certain dignity, at least regarding the artichokes and olives and bread. He could tell Ellen was tired, had most likely not slept since she awoke that morning before dawn and decided to tell him the truth. Well, let her be tired. Cheating was a demanding pastime. More so than the making of ancient clay pots. More demanding than ballet lessons.

Ellen sat at her own place at the table and lifted her glass of wine. She tilted it at him, toasting.

"I hope this will be a new beginning," she said.

Howard had brought his Bacardi to the table and he drank from it instead, ignoring the wine before him, in one of Ellen's best crystal glasses. He knew this would sting her, for she liked things to be just so at special dinners. Bacardi and chicken cacciatore was not how she'd planned it. He took another liberal gulp of the Bacardi, then put his glass down with a thud. He had wanted to bite into the salad and bread, relish those artichoke hearts and huge Greek olives, but something kept him from it, something primitive, maybe, something *male*.

"I want some answers," he said. And he looked into Ellen's eyes for the first time since early that morning. He saw that they were red and puffy. Did she ever love Ben Collins? Was she grieving for him now?

"What do you want to know?" Ellen said wearily. She put her glass of wine back in its place near her plate.

"Did you love him?" asked Howard.

Ellen didn't answer right away. She picked up her glass again and this time, instead of drinking from it, she swirled the wine around and around.

"Looking back on it, from a sensible perspective," she said finally, "the answer is definitely no. But when it was happening there was a certain excitement, I suppose, that I might have misinterpreted as love. It was the year I turned forty and I don't know if maybe—"

"Oh *please*," said Howard. "Spare me the psychology." He hated her for her blasted honesty! Ellen O'Malley Woods needed to study public relations with the Ford Motor Company if she intended to stay in business as Howard's wife.

"Why don't you eat your salad?" Ellen told him, gently. "The chicken is almost ready." Howard picked up his fork, as if by rote, then remembered and thunked it back down by his plate. He looked over at her, her lovely Irish-American face rising above the green sweater, as though the sweater were a field of billowing shamrocks from the old country. Her eyes so green they seemed unreal. He wished he could hold her without feeling like a—what was that word from the Middle English, Shakespeare's and Chaucer's word?—*cuckold*. But he couldn't. He could not.

"Did you tell him you loved him?"

"A few times," she said, quickly, as though she might lie if she thought her answer through. And he could tell by Ellen's face that she was determined to speak the truth, once and for all, get it over with.

"The bastard!" said Howard.

"It didn't mean anything. Ben loved his wife. And he knew I loved you. I guess we were just acting like silly teenagers. We were wrong, Howie. I knew it then, and I know it even more now."

"Bastard," Howard said again. "How did you find out he died? And lucky for him that he did." He pointed dramatically upward, at the tiny light fixture over their heads, as though it were a symbol for heaven, a stopover pad. Ellen frowned, but she didn't reprimand him. This was part of that new role of power that Howard Woods had stumbled into, and finally. Maybe the day would come when he would thank Ben Collins, visit his grave with a potted geranium or something, but he doubted it. If he found out where Ben Collins was to be interred, Howard Woods was more likely to go there with a black Magic Marker and write *bastard* all over his headstone.

"Molly told me," Ellen said. "She read his obituary in the Portland paper and she called me." Ah, yes, Molly, her new soul mate. Howard had never known if he should like Molly or not. In the fifteen years since she had moved to Bixley from Portland, had taken up teaching art at the college, Molly had been Ellen's best friend. But he had always felt a certain reserve toward her. Now he knew why he had withheld his approval: Molly had been in on the scandal.

"Molly knew?" he asked, evenly, his teeth clamping down, top to bottom, in sheer tension. Ellen nodded.

"Not at the time," she said, "I didn't even know her then. But a couple years after we became friends I confided in her. I guess I needed someone to talk to, to bare my soul to. I wanted to talk to *you*, but I was afraid you'd, well, I was afraid you'd do just exactly what you're doing now." He felt like slapping her, for the first time in all the years of his knowing her. She had told Molly. She was playing tennis with Molly. She was taking ballet with Molly. She was making goddamned Incan pots with Molly. And he, her husband, was left to flutter alone in the winds of retirement.

"I hate you," he said to her, and he saw the tears rush instantly to her eyes. He didn't feel sorrow this time. Not this time. *Molly* knew.

"Who else knew?" he asked, his teeth barely unlocking to form the words.

"No one," Ellen said. "I swear to you, Howie, not even Mother, that time I visited her for a week. She never found out."

Howard stopped his mind from reeling, pulled his thoughts away from pottery and Ben's rugged looks, and Molly's smugness each time he met her, to concentrate on this statement. Ellen's mother? Her mother lived in Buffalo. Why would her mother know anyway? Ellen and her mother were never close, not emotionally, not in that *Hey, Mom, guess what? I'm fucking Ben Collins!* kind of way.

"Your mother?" Howard asked. His teeth had become veritable weapons in the cave of his mouth. Barbed stalactites. He feared he might bite Ellen if she said the wrong thing. But she did anyway.

"That week I went to Buffalo to visit Mother," Ellen said, reluctantly, as if she knew aforethought what rewards her honesty would bring her. "That was the same summer you offered to fill in for Grady Mullins and couldn't go to Buffalo with me." Howard realized that he was staring at her now with a steady vengeance, but he couldn't help himself. His whole heart and soul wanted her to be saying something else right then, wanted her to lie to him, to lie like a rug, to lie like Ford Motor Company. "So Ben came to Buffalo, too. We drove. I didn't use my airline ticket. He got a motel room. Mother never even suspected."

Ellen stopped, her face white as ivory above her field-of-shamrocks sweater, her sad green eyes watching him the way she had watched those F-15 fighter planes, flying low over Baghdad, eyes afraid to lose someone they dearly loved. She had taken Ben Collins to Buffalo for a week! Howard remembered that summer well. Grady Mullins, a fellow instructor in the English department, had come down with a cancer of the colon. Since Grady was clinging to the tapestry of life by a single thread, Good Samaritan Howard Woods had offered to teach the English Comp class in his stead. By God, he, Howard Woods, had driven Ellen to the airport! Had *picked her up* from the airport!

"The airport," Howard said softly, and Ellen nodded.

"I pretended I was going to fly," she said. "Then, I waited until you had driven away. A week later, Ben dropped me off at the airport an hour before the flight was to arrive, so I'd be waiting there."

Was she getting pleasure from this? If not, why the hell was she cleansing her entire soul to *him?* Do this to *Molly,* he wanted to shout at her. Share your dirty laundry with your goddamn tennis-playing, pirouetting, pot-making pal!

Instead of shouting, Howard felt his right arm fly up, like some kind of Las Vegas one-armed bandit, watched as it swept the wine and water glasses off the table in one fell swoop. Glass broke in a deafening crescendo.

"Howard!" Ellen screamed. "Stop this!"

Howard pushed his chair back from the table and stood, glaring down at her.

"You *are* a whore," he said, his words barely audible.

"You wanted the truth," Ellen shouted up at him, "and that's what you're getting! I'm tired of deception!" Then, she put her face into her hands and began to weep. Howard grabbed her by the shoulders, forced her to look up at him. She did, tears now plummeting down her face.

"Did you?" he shouted.

"Did I *what?*"

"Did you enjoy it, with *him?*"

Ellen pushed his hands away, sobbing.

"Yes!" she screamed. "I did enjoy it! Big deal! It's not the end of your life, Howard!" He felt his arm rising again and realized that he might strike her this time. So he brought the strength of it down on the kitchen counter. He watched in fascination as a bowl of candies rose into the air, then dropped to the floor and scattered in a blend of chocolate kisses and shards of glass.

"You crazy fool," Ellen whispered. She knelt down beside the broken wine glasses and began gathering the crystal pieces. The whole room seemed alive with smell and color: fresh bread, chicken, the potpourri of cinnamon sticks and cloves, the set of blue canisters under the cupboard. And there was sound, too, the music of Ellen's sobs mixed with the tinkle of broken glass as she collected it in her trembling hand. Howard wanted to remember them, those smells and sounds and colors of the kitchen he had known for so many years on Patterson Street, because it would be a cold day in hell—and speaking of hell, he hoped Ben was down there right at that very minute, trying to round up a decent game of golf—it would be a cold day in Hades before Howard Woods ever stepped a foot back into *Ellen's* house.

Lights had come on all over the neighborhood by the time Howard finally pulled back into John's drive and got out of the Probe, the wretched suitcase in his right hand. Feeling a great kinship to Quasimodo, he begrudgingly shuffled up the walk and rang the bell. John's doorbell sounded like Howard's did, to *outside* ears, anyway, and Howard imagined his son rising up from that favorite black recliner, his muscled arms reaching out for the door knob. He wondered what John was going to say this time, but it was Patty who opened the door.

"Dad," she said, and stepped back so that Howard could come in.

Eliot, who was in his pajamas, looked up from some show on television to see his grandfather standing in the room. They'd only had time for a short chat that morning, and Howard had promised Eliot that they would go canoeing the very next weekend.

"Grandpa!" Eliot shouted, and raced toward Howard with great exuberance. Howard scooped him up, and Eliot's little arms immediately encircled his grandfather's neck.

John, who had been sleeping on the sofa, opened his eyes. He saw Howard standing there in the den, Eliot clinging like a small monkey from around his neck. John's eyes dropped down from Howard's face, down the length of his arm, to the suitcase that he carried. Then they ran back up Howard's arm and stared straight into Howard's own eyes.

"You look like you've been hit by a bus," John said softly. Howard shrugged. Patty appeared at his elbow, touched him gently.

"If you're hungry," she said, "there's cold chop suey in the kitchen." Howard nodded, thankfully.

"Grandpa, you have no socks on," Eliot squealed. He pointed at Howard's feet. "Look, Daddy. How come I have to wear socks if Grandpa doesn't?"

"Eliot, take your grandfather to the kitchen and put the chop suey into the microwave for him," Patty said. Christ, had he grown that pitiful, that his grandson had become his keeper?

Howard looked down at John, his pilot son, Ellen's son, their last born, their *baby*. He knew that John was waiting for some sort of explanation, but he had none. Not yet, anyway.

"I'm starving," Howard said to John, who merely closed his eyes.

In the kitchen Howard lifted Eliot up and sat him on the counter. He stood watching as Eliot scraped cold Chinese food from a Styrofoam container onto a clean plate, then plopped it into the microwave. His tiny fingers sprinted across the numbers on the menu, a regular little Mozart, a little microwave prodigy. Howard waited as his grandson programmed the cooking time for three minutes.

"I'm gonna go watch my movie now, Grandpa," Eliot said. "When it beeps, take it out. If you need anything else, ask Mommy." Howard lifted the boy down off the counter, and Eliot was gone in an instant, back to the television.

He stood alone in his son's kitchen, on a street fifteen miles from the kitchen he had left behind on Patterson Street. Howard Woods stood there silently, waiting for three more minutes of his life to tick away. He wondered if Ellen had managed to wipe up all the broken glass, wondered if the glasses themselves had been part of her Waterford crystal collection, a thing she prized. She had bought them in County Cork, on a visit back to her father's birthplace. He hoped she hadn't cut herself. Before him, on the counter, several fortune cookies sat happily on a plate, portentous and smug. Howard studied them carefully before he finally selected one. He broke it open as though it were a clam, then pulled the narrow strip of paper from its belly. *Confucius say, Study the past, if you would divine the future.*

"Bastard," said Howard. He scrunched the fortune in his hand, then tossed it aside on the counter.

He went back into the den. Eliot was engrossed in his movie, and Patty seemed to have disappeared. John was still on the sofa, but this time his eyes were open. He was staring at the Christmas photo on the mantle. Howard patted the tip of John's left foot. John looked up at him, cautiously.

"The deceit is worse than I thought," Howard announced. "It stretches all the way to Buffalo."

John stared, thinking.

Howard rocked hard on the balls of his feet, and waited. He heard the microwave beep that his chop suey was now ready. *Study the past, if you would divine the future.*

"What does this mean in the larger picture?" John asked, quietly, so that Eliot wouldn't hear. Howard could now smell the chop suey, floating out to him from the kitchen. He was as hungry as a retired man, a jobless cuckold, could get.

"It means I'm back to Plan A," said Howard. "It's Pamplona, or Bust."

three

THE SKILLFUL DODGER

The next day, after a quick shave and a few exhausting pushups, Howard Woods walked into Books Etc., one of the stores in the new mall just off Davenport Road, and asked for the travel section. He was surprised to find Billy Mathews working in the store. He had taught Billy the year before retirement, American Literature the first semester, and Masterpieces of English Literature the second. Billy had been a memorable student only in that he was so remarkably *unmemorable*. Just before that second semester ended, right about the time Oliver Twist was about to ask for more gruel, Billy had dropped out of school for good.

"Travel's back in Section Three, against the wall," Billy said, and pointed. "See the sign that says Rest Room? It's just before you get to that." Howard looked. There it was, written in plastic letters above the bookshelves: *Section 3: Travel.* He thanked Billy for his help.

"I can come show you, Mr. Woods," said Billy, but Howard held up a hand, stopping him.

"Thanks, Billy, but I can find it on my own." He turned again toward the travel section. A blindfolded bat could see the plastic letters.

"Going on a trip?" he heard Billy ask. Howard looked back over his shoulder, smiled.

"Sort of," he said.

"Out of the country?" Billy wondered.

"Yup," said Howard. He was now halfway down the store's length. He could even see the sign for the rest room up ahead. One might think of clear sailing, but Billy was unrelenting.

"We got some new guides in for Paris, France," Billy announced, causing other customers to look up from their reading, at Howard, as though he were some kind of French ambassador. Howard stopped. He turned to face Billy, who was leaning over the sale table, twenty feet behind him.

"Thanks, Billy," Howard said, trying to keep his voice to a respectable bookstore level. He knew it wasn't the same as being in a library, or a hospital, but bookstores did demand their own dignified quiet. "But I'm not going to Paris."

Howard found the travel section and stood before it, browsing through the alphabet, skipping over some countries, stopping to read the spines of others: *Austria, Belgium, Great Britain, Japan, Mexico, Norway, Portugal, Spain*. He took the Berlitz guide for Spain down from the shelf. He had no interest in *Spain on Twenty Dollars A Day*, for he had no intention of watching his pesos. He would throw pesos off the first goddamn Spanish bridge—see *puente*—he came to, if he so desired. He thumbed quickly through the index, glancing up once or twice to see if Billy were salivating behind his back, wishing to be of even further service. How had Billy Mathews ever managed to secure a job at a bookstore in the first place? Shouldn't one have *reading* skills for that? But then, Billy's job seemed to be nothing more than leaning on the sales table and tormenting customers. Howard found what he was looking for: *Pamplona, Fiesta de St. Fermin, page 87*. He thumbed over quickly and read the brief paragraph: *The Fiesta de San Fermin begins with daily bullfights preceded each morning by the famous Enclosing of the Bulls, when they are driven through the streets behind crowds of skillfully dodging men and boys who are called Sanfermines. Starting on July 6th, the fiesta lasts until the 14th. The Running of the Bulls was described in Hemingway's novel,* The Sun Also

Rises. *The Fiesta de San Fermin is named in honor of St. Fermin, its first bishop.*

Howard went back and reread that beautiful line: *they are driven through the streets behind crowds of skillfully dodging men and boys.* Jesus, he couldn't help it, he felt a surge in his groin, something that Neanderthals probably felt, and military minds came to understand: the adrenaline of the hunt, the skillful dodging of the chase, the pure mark of manhood. He had no stomach for the bullfights themselves, even thought them barbaric. But the chase, the chase was the thing!

Billy was suddenly at Howard's elbow, like some kind of UFO, a bogey at five o'clock.

"Find it okay?" asked Billy, and Howard nodded. He flipped quickly from page 87 and went immediately to page 32, something about the Prado, in Madrid. He stood reading about the surfeit of El Grecos and Goyas which the museum had to offer, waiting for Billy to go away. To evaporate.

"Spain, huh?" said Billy, with a certain familiarity in his voice. Howard remembered Billy as the kind of student who would be hard pressed to find *Canada*. Now here he was, bandying the word Spain about as though he were bored with those hilly, inaccessible Pyrenees. Howard put the book back on the shelf and took down *The Berlitz Guide to Norway.*

"Just browsing," he said.

"Norway, huh?" said Billy, inching closer. "Mrs. Woods going with you?" Howard slid the guidebook back into its designated slot and then turned to face the young man.

"Billy," he said, "in the entire year that I taught you, two different and completely fascinating subjects, I don't remember you asking me a single question, not one. Now, you seem incapable of *not asking.*"

Howard waited as his former student considered what had just been said. Then, Billy tilted his head at Howard, smiled a crooked smile. In his eyes was that lightbulb look Howard remembered from Masterpieces of English Lit, a kind of forty-watt glare, just before it burns out for good.

"I guess you might say I blossomed since then," Billy answered. Then he beamed, pleased with his own joke.

Howard nodded. "Listen, Billy," he said, "there *is* something you can do for me."

Billy's face came to life. His whole frame grew taller, rose up for the occasion. Howard had no doubt that if Billy had had a dog's tail attached to his butt, it would be wagging vigorously at that moment. It would be causing more wind than the blades of a helicopter.

"What's that, Mr. Woods?" Billy asked.

"Would you go over to the fiction section for me?" asked Howard. "See if you can find a book called *The Sun Also Rises?*"

"We're supposed to ask who wrote the book before we go looking for it," said Billy. He seemed proud of this rule, as if he had been through an intense basic training and now was fully qualified for the job.

"Ernest Hemingway," said Howard, when he realized that Billy was serious.

Without further instruction, Billy lurched off. Then, he stopped and looked back at Howard, his eyebrows knitting themselves into a question, a cloud forming over his eyes.

"The sun also *what?*" asked Billy.

Howard sighed. It had been one of the five novels they had studied in American Literature.

"Rises," said Howard. He pointed at the ceiling. Billy nodded happily and then disappeared. Not wasting another moment of valuable time, Howard grabbed the *Berlitz Guide to Spain* from off the shelf—it included two cassettes to aid him in learning Spanish—and bolted for the checkout counter. It seemed the first *skillful dodging* he would have to do, on the road to Pamplona, would take place right in his own back yard, in Bixley, Maine.

The girl at the checkout seemed surprised to witness Howard running. Was it not allowed in bookstores? She gave him a sharp, questioning stare as he patted his hip pocket to see if he had, indeed, remembered his wallet.

"Billy says you taught him English," she told Howard, as she accepted the Berlitz guide from him. "That's cool," she added.

"I believe Billy was somewhat proficient in English when I met him," Howard replied. What the hell was happening to today's youth? It seemed as if four or five of them needed to congregate in order to come up with a single good thought.

"Anything else?" the clerk wondered. Howard shook his head.

"Cash or charge?"

"Which is faster?" he asked, glancing over his shoulder to see if Billy had remembered that it was the *sun* that also rises, and not bread dough.

"Cash," she said, "of course."

Howard knew that this young woman thought him incurably dumb. He dug into his wallet and fished out a twenty. If tipping would speed her up, he would have offered her a dollar, for she took forever, the velocity of the young, operating beneath a brain that was running on automatic pilot. Finally, she gave him the bag, after tossing his receipt inside.

"Are you interested in our Savings Plan?" she asked. "I was supposed to ask you that before I rang up the sale."

Howard looked down the aisle and saw what was probably the top of Billy's head, brownish thick hair gliding atop Aisle Four like a wooden boat as it made its way toward the front of the store. Billy must have looked for Howard in Section Three, and now he was on an all-out search of the store to find him.

"You pay ten dollars for the card," the girl was now saying, "but each time you buy a book you get ten percent off. It's pretty cool."

"No," said Howard, "I'm not interested. Listen, tell Billy I had to run, okay? Tell him I'll be in again and we can chat."

Then, Howard stepped out into the flow of mall traffic, that wave of shoppers that soon swallowed him up in its ranks.

"¿Como está usted?" Howard asked John, when they met in the den at six o'clock for a cocktail before dinner. Patty was still at the theater, working on the costuming for *Cyrano de Bergerac*—apparently there was more to it than just a long nose—and so John had promised to cook dinner.

"Come on, Dad," said John, "enough is enough. When are you going to quit acting like a kid and go on home?"

"¿Habla mucho Español?" Howard wished to know. Apparently, from what he'd read, the Spanish question mark was upside down to English readers. Howard imagined himself standing on his head, at the airport in Madrid, asking questions of passersby.

"Mom is all torn up about this," John said. "She won't say much to me, but she's told Patty."

"Are we speaking of Ellen O'Malley, the former Ellen Woods?" asked Howard. "Good. Let her be torn up. Let her be *gored* by this, if you will. That's certainly how I feel." He sloshed the rum around in his glass, clinking the ice. Then he took another drink.

John looked over at the bottle sitting on his bar, the one Howard had picked up on his way back from the bookstore.

"Bacardi, huh?" John asked. "And on the rocks, no less." Howard shrugged, a *why not?* shrug. He had been a Tom Collins man in his heyday, but, as he had suggested to Ellen O'Malley, what man could drink a Tom Collins and keep his mind off Ben, all at the same time? Besides, Bacardi was the best he could do until he got his hands on some pernod. Or was it called *absinthe?* That was the drink of matadors, by God. *Driven through the streets behind crowds of skillfully dodging men and boys.* Howard smiled, leaned back on the sofa, put his feet up on the ottoman.

"What's so funny?" asked John.

"Oh, nothing," Howard said, furtively. "Nada."

"Come on, what's up your sleeve?" John persisted. "What's going on in that retired brain of yours?"

Howard smiled again, mysteriously this time. He felt almost smug. After years of being the one whose job it was to pry the truth from his son, now *he* was hoarding facts. He, Howard, had always been a good and obedient son to his own father, and maybe that was part of his problem. He had never given the elder Woods any worry. The truth was that the old man would have kicked his ass to kingdom come had Howard disobeyed him. He wondered if courage and valor are forced, out of necessity, to skip generations. That was often true of artists and writers. How many famous creators gave birth to famous creators? There were the Bruegels, the father and a couple of sons. A few writers, yes—the Dumas boys came to mind, the old man and the illegitimate boy. Howard couldn't think of any composers. And singers, well, he was able to come up with Frank and Nancy Sinatra, but surely *that* combo wouldn't qualify, given the fact that Nancy couldn't sing.

"You ever hear of St. Fermin?" Howard asked.

"No," said John, "I can't say that I have. Don't tell me Mother has slept with him, too?" Howard laughed at this, such a laugh that he was obliged to lean forward and whack his own knee. John caught the fever and laughed along with him.

"I think this is called a tension breaker," John noted. He went to the bar and poured himself another scotch. "Now what was this nonsense last night about Buffalo?"

Howard held up his glass for a second Bacardi.

"Remember the week Ellen went to visit Grandma by herself?" Howard asked. John thought deeply, trying to remember. "You must have been about ten years old," Howard reminded him. "I taught an English Comp class that summer."

John brightened in memory. "We ate hot dogs all week long!" he said. Howard nodded. "And played poker every night, you, me, Micky Pilcher, and your teaching buddies. Until you caught Micky with the marked deck. It was great. It was like camping out for a week. What about it?"

"Well," said Howard, "we weren't the only ones camping out. Your mother shuffled off to Buffalo with old Ben Collins."

"*What?*" asked John. "What are you talking about?"

Howard told him, told him about the useless airline ticket, bought and paid for with hard-earned teaching dollars. Told him about driving Ellen to the airport, picking her up from the airport, while all the time Ben Collins was probably parked nearby, munching on a bucket of Buffalo Wings. She was supposed to be visiting her mother, as they had done every year since their marriage, for a week, until Howard's mother-in-law passed away. And the one time he couldn't join Ellen because he was offering up his services to aid another needy human being—actually, in truth, he hadn't cared much for Grady Mullins, and even less for Ellen's mother—she had spent the week sneaking in and out of some motel room like a teenager, telling her mother lies, no doubt, about dinners with friends, movies, who knew the scope of her deception once she got started?

"Jesus," John said sadly, and shook his head. Howard was almost pleased. Now, maybe now, he would get a little well-deserved sympathy instead of this *forgiveness* crap. What kind of a defense was *that?*

"I've got an appointment tomorrow with Mike Harris."

"Your *lawyer?*" John seemed stunned at this.

"Absolutely," said Howard. "Time's a-wasting, my boy. No need to drag this out."

"Jesus," John said again, and sat on the sofa next to Howard. He looked so put out with the latest news about Buffalo, and now divorce proceedings, that Howard was almost sorry he had told him.

Eliot bounced into the room. Gator, the dog he had named after his favorite football team, the Florida Gators, paraded along at his heels.

"When do we eat?" Eliot asked.

"Soon," said John. "I've ordered Mexican."

"You told Mommy you'd cook," said Eliot.

"Eliot, please," John said, and then he sighed. Howard could tell his thoughts were more on his mother's trip to Buffalo than on dinner. His thoughts were on that meeting Howard had set with Mike Harris.

"You even promised to cook vegetables this time," Eliot said.

"Which would you rather have?" John asked. "Enchiladas from Jose's Cantina? Or corn on the cob that I've personally boiled?"

"That's easy," said Eliot. "Jose's Cantina."

"Good," said John. "I'll call you when the chow arrives. What Mommy doesn't know, won't hurt her."

Eliot disappeared, Gator wagging at his heels. Howard was reminded of Billy Mathews as he watched Gator's tail twitch out of sight.

"Hey!" Howard yelled. He could hear the sound of Eliot's footsteps, which were now treading upon the stairs. "Grandpa will tell you a good-night story before bed." He heard Eliot call back, pleased with the promise. Then he looked over at John, on the sofa next to him.

"Did you mean that?" Howard asked his son.

"Did I mean what?"

"What Patty doesn't know won't hurt her?" *Confucius say, Study the past, if you would divine the future.*

"I was talking about Mexican food, Dad, for crying out loud," John answered. "Don't get analytical on me."

"Deception starts with the little things," Howard said, sagely. "It's the first sign of a crack in the marriage. I know that now, but I didn't know it back when I could've used it. Back when my marriage was covered with cracks, like a goddamn spider's web. So I say this to you as a warning, son. Always be truthful. Always. Okay?"

John said nothing.

"Okay?" Howard prodded again.

"No hablo Español," John finally answered.

On the way home from his meeting the next day with Mike Harris, Howard listened in horror as the Probe GT whined to a halt and refused to move an inch further. He left it sitting at the curb in front of the Bixley bank and Jose's Cantina: *Mexican Foods For All Occasions*, and he called AAA to come and fetch it.

"Take the goddamn thing to Jeff's Used & Classic Cars, on Ridgemont Drive," Howard told Triple A.

Next, he called Bixley Cab and caught a ride over to Jeff Henson's place, on the outside of Bixley, what used to be a large and empty field until Jeff opened a used car garage a year earlier. Doing well with that first venture, Jeff added the classic cars as a way to foster his own love of a well-made product. Since Howard taught both of the Henson sons, he and Jeff had talked vintage cars at more than one college ball game. Howard had intended to stop at the garage for months now, each time he passed by in the rattling Probe GT, an opportunity to take a look at the models Jeff had to offer. Some of them were real beauties: a 1955 Chevy that looked like it had never been driven a single mile, much less seen any hormonal action in the back seat; a shiny silver Corvette Stingray, early 1960s; a Packard; a Kaiser-Manhattan; and a white 1935 Lincoln convertible with red leather interior. It was unlikely that Jeff would sell that many classic cars in Bixley, but then he didn't care. As he explained to Howard, during one of the many lax moments of the basketball game against Bangor School of Divinity, "As long as Maria thinks it's a business and not a hobby, she won't care how many classic cars I buy."

While he waited for Jeff to appear, Howard admired the Lincoln—they'd been born the same year—by pressing a finger into the red leather of its seats. He'd been trying for the past hour to forget his abrupt meeting with Mike Harris. He was also trying to forget about the dastardly Probe GT—may he never enter into Bixley Performance Ford again, since all they wanted was to sell him another lemon—when Jeff came outside to greet him.

"Hey, Howard," he said. "I was wondering when I was gonna see you in here. What can I do for you?"

Howard shook his head. "I want to get rid of a Ford Probe GT," he said.

"One of their lemons?" asked Jeff. It seemed the whole world knew about the problems Ford was having with their Probes, at least everyone but Howard, and how many more Probe *owners?*

"Will you take it off my hands?" Howard asked, and Jeff nodded, which was good of him, considering that the tow truck was pulling into the lot at that very moment, the Probe's shiny blue ass high in the air.

"What can I put you into?" asked Jeff. "I just got a Toyota Camry in, and it's only about two years old."

But Howard was remembering the scene in his lawyer's office as he stared down at the Lincoln's red seats. It seemed, at least according to Mike Harris, that the divorce would go off without a hitch. "Pardon the pun there," Mike had said, and laughed, batting Howard on the back as though divorce were a game of golf. "If Ellen's agreeable, there should be no problem. Marital dissolution papers are the best route to take. You just split everything fifty-fifty down the middle." And then Howard had signed a few pieces of paper, let Mike pump his right hand, and that was it. "I'll be sending Ellen a registered letter," Mike said. "I'll call you. I'll keep you posted." As Howard drove away, he wasn't sure what he had expected: violins playing in the wings, the receptionist weeping tears instead of filing her nails, sympathy flowers delivered from old friends? The execution of the thing had been cold and quick. And much too fast. Howard had hoped Mike would tell him to go home first, wait a month or two, mull it over, be certain of his heart *and* his mind. But, apparently, with so many divorces being processed every day, one had to be quick on one's feet. Well, so be it. Howard could take it. But the Ford Probe was apparently torn up by the whole thing because it broke down, finally, whimpering to a stop and refusing to carry Howard anywhere, anymore, not now that he'd finally gone and filed for a divorce, from that nice lady with the red highlights in her silvery hair, the one who always kept the car so clean.

"Are you in a Toyota frame of mind?" Jeff was asking, and Howard suddenly remembered that he was now on foot. He needed wheels.

"I'm looking for something kind of, well, classy and sporty," Howard told Jeff. "You know, a middle-age-crazy kind of car."

Jeff thought for a minute, then smiled.

"I've got just the thing," he said. "Follow me."

Jeff Henson took Howard around to the back, past more modern cars, most likely ones traded in, like the Probe was about to be. They stopped before a 1962 Aston Martin DB, a black convertible, a stunning sight. In the summer sunshine it shone like a chunk of smooth ebony. Howard whistled.

"Remember the old James Bond movies?" Jeff asked, and Howard nodded. Who could forget those cameo roles played out by the little sports car, back when 007 was having problems of his own, with spies as well as with women. Howard nearly swooned. What a car, looking more as if an Italian had designed it rather than a Scottish chap, broad at the shoulders, narrow at the waist, perfectly fit at the rear.

"They're coming back big time," said Jeff. "But the new models, the DB7, cost a pretty penny, over a hundred and thirty thousand dollars, and only about two hundred of them out there for sale. But this one, this one's got personality."

Howard had paced the circumference of the car and now he stood looking at its grille, which stared back with a kind of tight smirk. He imagined himself flying, wind in his hair, shards of his old life strewn along the highway behind him. It was a Hemingway kind of car.

"I want it," said Howard.

Howard pulled the Aston Martin into John's empty drive and just sat in it, drinking in the smell of the leather, the contour of the seat beneath his ass cheeks. He had left the top down as he flew out of Jeff's parking lot, and now strands of his hair were mussed. But Howard didn't mind. He simply patted them back down as best he could and reminded himself to start carrying a brush in the glove compartment. No problema. He felt as if he'd always driven the Aston Martin, Pussy Galore clinging for dear life in the passenger seat as he took a turn at ninety miles an hour and lived to tell of it. With just such a scene in mind, he leaned back against the uphol-stery and closed his eyes. Feeling the heavy pull of his lids, he tried to remember how long it had been since he'd had a decent sleep. But he knew, didn't he? It had been three small days ago. And here he was, about to become divorced, driving around in a 1962 Aston Martin convertible, just a month and a week away from skillfully dodging the bulls at Pamplona. John could bitch and moan all he liked but Howard had already phoned Bixley Travel Agency and bought a round-trip ticket to Spain. Considering the dangerous task that lay ahead, he hoped he would actually be able to use the return portion of the ticket. He was assured that his travel packet would contain all the essentials. Rental car information. Maps. Hotel Confirmation. Suggested dining spots. The works. Apparently, running the bulls was more complicated than getting a divorce. But everything was fast these days. Howard remembered Johnny Carson, someone he missed almost as much as he missed Ellen, talking about drive-through funeral services in California. "Honk if you think he's in heaven," Johnny had advised. Howard wondered if Ben Collins had had such a service. He could imagine himself as a drive-through mourner at Ben's funeral, at the wheel of the Aston Martin DB, honking a few times, spitting a few angry pebbles out behind his tires. Ben Collins was dead. Funny thing. Howard wondered if Ben knew the pain he was causing, so many years after the action, causing pain even after his disappearance from the earth. Would he care, if he did know? Was pain a man-made notion that required a physical body? Howard had never embraced the hereafter, not like Ellen did. He tended to look upon himself and his fellow man as, well, walking fertilizer, until the fertilizer would be put to good use one day, deep in the earth, nourishing the roots of a tree, or a field of wild mustard. Considering his own mortality, Howard fell sound asleep.

He woke to honking, and opened his eyes to find John's big hog of a station wagon bearing down on him, overshadowing the little convertible. John got out from behind the wheel, Eliot bounding from the passenger seat with his schoolbag.

"Wow, Grandpa!" Eliot was saying, as Howard sat up behind the wheel and smoothed his thin hair back in place. "Neat car!"

Eliot opened the passenger door and piled in, bouncing happily in the seat. John approached slowly on the driver's side, his eyes taking in every inch of the car.

"You're too old to be middle-age crazy," John told Howard softly.

"Guess you can say I blossomed since retirement," Howard offered, remembering poor Billy Mathews. He grinned up at John. Eliot had found the button to the glove compartment and was now searching among the papers in there.

"Grandpa, take me for a ride," Eliot begged. "Is it okay, Dad?"

"It's up to Grandpa," said John. "If he has no other pressing engagements."

"No," said Howard, "nothing pressing. Oh, I have to pick up my airline ticket to Spain, but I got plenty of time to do that."

John shook his head, a gesture of surrender. He gave the Aston Martin one more full look before going back to the station wagon, which he pulled up to the curb in front of the house, freeing Howard's path. Then, briefcase under his arm, John headed for his front door.

"Sure you don't want to come?" Howard said to John's retreating back. "We can stuff you in here somewhere." Howard ground the gear into reverse. It would take some getting used to, this manual shifting concept. The last car he owned that wasn't automatic was the Thunderbird he had bought back in college.

"I'm sure," said John. "Besides, you need room for Ms. Galore."

"Hasta la vista!" Howard told his son. He released the clutch and the little convertible lurched backward out of the driveway.

"Bye, Dad!" Eliot shouted. John waved without looking up.

"Don't let Grandpa do anything else stupid," he warned Eliot.

Then, with some more grinding, and after finally getting the gears shifted into first, Howard and his grandson sped away into the wind.

"Listen, Jake," he leaned forward on the bar. "Don't you ever get the feeling that all your life is going by and you're not taking advantage of it?"
—Robert Cohn, to Jake Barnes, *The Sun Also Rises*

four | **DECEIT**

On Saturday, knowing that Ellen had not yet received the marital dissolution papers from Mike Harris, Howard almost phoned and asked if he could come home. There was something about a Saturday that pushed him toward nostalgia. In the summers, true, Ellen usually pestered him to mow the lawn, clean the garage, turn off the golf tournament, read a book, trim the hedge, wash the outside windows, walk with her along the Bixley River. And in the winters she pestered him to shovel the walk, fill the bird feeders, turn off the basketball game, read a book, bring in another armload of firewood, order firewood, split firewood into kindling, put up the Christmas lights, take down the Christmas lights. Saturdays were never easy, not with Ellen, but nonetheless they had marked Howard's years as a domestic male like notches on the barrel of a gun. And the truth was that for the two hours the basketball game was running, or the four hours a golf tournament took to unfold, Ellen only occasionally popped into the living room to beseech him to "do something constructive." As if watching Greg Norman hit a three-hundred-yard drive or Michael Jordan fly like a goddamn bird through the air wasn't *constructive.* "Yeah, yeah," Howard would mutter, "in a minute." And then Ellen would be gone and his mind would be back on the game, as if she had never spoken to him at all. And that had been the secret—*don't take Ellen's nagging personally*—that had held his marriage together so nicely for four decades. Saturdays had been splendid, memorable days at the house on Patterson Street, when Howard wasn't actually out playing golf, or fly-fishing, or canoeing the Bixley River, which was what he planned to do with Eliot that very day. He had promised the boy. But Eliot was now at a friend's house, enjoying a surprise birthday party that only the moms had known about until an hour before party time. Apparently, little kids and retired cuckolds couldn't be trusted with such big secrets.

On the first Saturday of Howard's estrangement, with a fierce loneliness pulling at his gut, he decided to do something wholly uncharacteristic, a way to mark the beginnings of his new life. So, humming a little Sinatra as he worked, he loaded his laundry into a wicker basket that Patty had left sitting in an upstairs bathroom. Then he hoisted the basket up onto his shoulder and carried it down to the laundry room, where, in a reasonably short period of time, he turned everything in it a light shade of pink. He stood looking down in horror at his favorite white golf shirt, his favorite khaki slacks, pink socks, even pink underwear.

"Christ," Howard said, as he shoved everything into the dryer, certain that immense heat would cause the pink to evaporate. Ellen had always done the laundry. Not that Howard was one of those husbands who insisted on playing the traditional male role to his wife's female part. Although he was not considered an extravagant cook, an occasional meatloaf that had a certain dignity to it was known to come out of the oven bearing his seal. Granted, this was only when Ellen was out of town, or gone for the evening, but it had happened more than a few times in his years of marriage. Not every man could say the same. And Howard sometimes helped with the dinner dishes, if Ellen were especially tired. Occasionally, he even went out of his way to make up their bed, if he rose after Ellen on Sundays. And sometimes he visited the big IGA, if Ellen was sick with a cold or something more serious, to pick up potatoes or a loaf of Italian bread from the deli. A couple of times he had even gone inside a convenience store to buy Ellen a big blue box of Kotex, right in front of the salesclerk and other shoppers. No, Howard was quite sure that it couldn't be said he was a husband of the Eisenhower era. He had slipped those surly bonds of his 1950s upbringing to become a thoroughly modern man. Once, he had even wept while watching an old black-and-white war movie on television. But, nonetheless, he *didn't do laundry*. Not even during that week when Ellen had been galloping around Buffalo with Ben Collins. He and the kids had piled their dirty clothes into hampers and baskets, onto closet floors and available chairs, letting it grow to mountain size for Ellen to tend to when she returned. Howard was glad now that he hadn't done the laundry that week, and that's what he was thinking as he loaded the machine with lighter clothes. He remembered to put all whites together, a knowledge he had gleaned from detergent commercials that had leaked their way into his subliminal mind after years of continual bombardment. But his thoughts were so consumed with Ellen's deception that he had not seen the red shirt creep into the batch of innocent whites. Even a retarded, myopic bull would've noticed this red sweatshirt, the one from his retirement party, the one with white lettering: *The Best Is Yet To Come*. But it was in there all right, turning the water to blood. Thinking of it all now, Howard's sweatshirt should have declared: *Study The Past If You Would Divine The Future*.

When drying the pink clothing didn't remove the stain but only seemed to welcome it in further, Howard unloaded everything from the dryer, shoved it all back into the washer, poured several cups of Clorox bleach into the tub, and then set the whole mess churning again.

"Fire burn and caldron bubble," he muttered, as he stood watching the water slowly turning red again. He wondered if putting the clothing out in the sun to dry would be better, the solar energy acting as a kind of natural bleach. Or maybe he should have put the bundle out of its misery by shoveling it all into the garbage, burying it like a dog's treasure in the backyard. He had considered calling Ellen—he had a good excuse, after all, his golfing clothes were among the spoils—but he refrained. Maybe Patty, when she and Eliot came home from the birthday party, would have an idea about what to do. Even theater types needed clean clothing, but theirs was probably all a shade of pink anyway, even the men's. Or he could ask John, when *he* got home from his Saturday racquetball with the guys from work. From what Howard could tell, John and Patty were hardly ever home together. And if Eliot had a school function, or even a social one such as a birthday party, the question was not, "How do we, his parents, work this into both our schedules?" but "Which one of us is free to take him?" During the few days that Howard had been living in their house, they had not once seated themselves at the dining room table for a sit-down family dinner. He had always assumed that the modern family, what with women now out there in the workplace, was very much like his and Ellen's family. But Patty seemed more concerned with the theater than with the laundry. And John knew by heart the phone numbers from every restaurant in Bixley that had a delivery service. Howard now had to admit that maybe his wife had been carrying more of the domestic load than he. Maybe that's what had kept his own family life rolling along smoothly. He felt a wave of guilt over this, that very emotion Ellen didn't think men capable of feeling. But then he remembered her deception. Perhaps it was her own guilt that had obliged her to carry that extra load. In an instant Howard rued the day he had ever lifted a finger to make a single meatloaf, much less the half dozen or so he had created in those years of his marriage. He let the lid of the washer slam down on itself.

Upstairs in the bathroom, Howard went in search of John's aftershave, opening one cabinet door, then another. Patty seemed to own every facial cream and body lotion on the planet, not to mention facial masks, and moisturizers, and cleansers. *Avocado. Peach. Cucumber. Lemon.* Who the hell invented all those concoctions, much less went out and bought them? When had the family medicine cabinet become a salad bar? All Howard had ever seen Ellen use, for all the years of their marriage, was a simple white jar of Pond's Cold Cream. He pushed aside a basket of strawberry soaps, and that's when he saw the single Kotex pad, lying on its back on the bottom of a shelf. He thought again of that day—Christ, it must have been almost thirty years earlier—when he had trudged home from the convenience store with that horrid blue box under his arm. A bedridden Ellen, suffering from severe menstrual cramps, had pestered him to buy it for her until he finally gave in.

The shaving lotion now forgotten, Howard picked up the pad and held it in his hand, balanced it on his palm. He wondered if it was filled with goose down, light and dreamy as it was. He had forgotten about these little white pillows, a common sight in his bathroom at one time. But then Ellen had gone through menopause, in her late forties, and the pillows had disappeared from Howard's life. He hadn't seen one for years, and it saddened him to realize this. It saddened him that his old age, and Ellen's old age, was now so easily defined. It had been marked with many symbols, many road signs, all warnings they had obviously missed. But perhaps Ellen, waking in the night to yet another hot flash, had known. A *hot flash* was, after all, a *bulletin*. Maybe Ellen had known, had been prepared, but why hadn't nature given Howard Woods a bulletin or two of his own? Why had nature left him to flounder thusly? Sure, he'd read that men go through menopause too, but he had never believed it. Now he knew his own menopause, his own change of life, by another name: *retirement*. Howard returned the soft white pad back to the shelf where he found it. Then he closed the cabinet door, left the little pillow lying there, something for the tiny ghosts of his old life to rest their heads upon.

It was early afternoon when John returned home, his hair still wet from an after-the-game shower, and agreed to a late lunch at some outdoor cafe with his father. It would be an opportunity for Howard to finally show off the Aston Martin to his son. It was no F-15, but it could hold its own. Howard suggested the restaurant with the outdoor dining area, Blanchard's, where they could sit and watch Saturday shoppers strolling along. At first, John wanted to go to Red's Tavern, but Howard balked.

"Not on a nice day like this," he protested. "Look at that sunshine. I didn't get to canoe today, but at least we can sit outside."

John finally agreed and climbed glumly into the passenger seat of the Aston Martin, his long legs folded and his knees rising in front of him as though he were some kind of praying mantis. Howard cut the little car out of the drive and they headed in the direction of Blanchard's.

"Summer's definitely here," said Howard, the wind eating up his words and flowing like a cool stream of water through his thinning hair.

John just nodded, and remained glum.

"Want me to put up the top?" Howard shouted, and now John shrugged.

"Naw," he said. "I just wish we were going to Red's and not Blanchard's. Too many of the people I work with hang out at Blanchard's. It's right next door to Sounder Aeronautics."

Howard pulled the little Aston into the parking lot, next to a towering Buick, and killed the engine. He turned to look at John.

"Good," Howard said. "It's about time I met some of your friends. I was thinking the other day, son. You and I really don't know each other as well as we should. We've been living separate lives, me with Ellen, you with Patty and Eliot."

"Isn't that the way it's supposed to be?" John asked. He opened his door and unloaded his long legs.

"But we should know each other as *adults*," Howard kept on. "It's always a foursome when we get together. This divorce thing may be a blessing in disguise."

John simply shook his head at this notion, and then followed Howard into the busy restaurant. The hostess seated them outside on the patio and a waitress appeared with menus. They ordered beers, which arrived in frosted mugs that had *Blanchards!* written all over them in small orange letters.

"Hard to forget where you are, isn't it?" asked Howard. He nodded at the lettering. "There are geniuses loose in marketing as I speak."

"It probably comes in handy if you're drunk." John smiled.

Howard took in the atmosphere around him, people seated at the patio tables, voices engaged in segments of life, the trees bursting green along the street.

"This could be one of those Hemingway cafés," Howard said. "You know, the Napolitain, or the Café Select. On the Boulevard Montparnasse."

John shook his head again—it was becoming his favorite response to Howard's new life interests, along with foot rocking—and said nothing for a time. Then, he looked directly at Howard.

"Are you really going through with this insanity?" he asked.

"What insanity?"

"You know damn well," John said. "Divorcing Mom. Running with cattle."

Howard nodded vigorously. "I've never been more serious about anything in my life."

"Let's face it, Dad. You're no Hemingway, and look where this kind of macho behavior got *him*. Alone in his bedroom with a pistol." John then sighed his heavy sigh, one that Howard had heard regularly for the past six days that he'd been living in John's and Patty's house.

"I believe it was a shotgun," Howard corrected.

"Dad, come on," John said, irritated now. "Face facts. I mean, you're not exactly Hulk Hogan. You're gonna end up a lonely old man with a bull's horn up his rectum. And that's if you're lucky."

The waitress came for their orders. They both decided upon the Blanchard Lunch Special, croissant sandwiches, potato salad, and a dill pickle. Howard leaned back in his chair, let the sweet warm sun hit squarely upon his face. He had begun a running schedule just the day before and now his legs felt stiff and sore from his first time out. He had done a mile by walking a quarter of it, jogging a quarter, walking a quarter, jogging the last quarter. His golfing buddy,

Pete Morton, had given him that schedule to go by. "After a week," Pete had said, "try running a third of a mile, walking a third, then running the last third. Do it half and half the next week. Before you know it, you'll be doing a 10K." Howard smiled, remembering Pete's prophesy. If it came true—and Howard had no doubt that it would—he'd be ready for the Encasing of the Bulls come July. Next on his list was finding a rugged wine flask, one of those big leather gourds that were always turning up in *The Sun Also Rises.* Something gore-proof, if that was possible.

"Gore-tex," said Howard, and smiled appreciatively at his own joke.

"What?" John asked.

"Nothing," said Howard. "I was just remembering something Pete Morton said. He and I are playing golf on Monday."

"I think you're making a big mistake," John said now. He had been watching the passersby with a thoughtful interest, but Howard knew where his son's mind had really been. "The bulls are bad enough, but this divorce thing is about the craziest idea I've heard of yet. You and mom are in your sixties, for crying out loud. Isn't that kind of late to go to Plan B?"

Howard held up his orange-lettered beer glass. "But there's still a fire in the basement," he bragged, and then hoped that it was true. A gas-log fireplace, at least.

"I tell you what, Dad," John said finally, after their sandwiches had arrived and Howard had given John his own pickle, a habit between them born of many deli sandwiches in their lifetimes. Howard had hated sour things even as a child. *Symbolic,* or so Ellen liked to say.

"I always thought you were a smart man," John continued. "But this is stupid action, is what it is. This is letting your emotions run away with your intellect. It's not good. It's not good in battle, and it's not good in life."

Howard felt the sting. *Not good in battle.* John would know, wouldn't he, having flown that plane into the missile-ridden skies over Baghdad. But, damn it, not every man gets the opportunity to prove himself behind the controls of a multi-million-dollar airplane, in a moment of world unrest. That was a matter of being in the right place at the right time, of standing at the edge of all that *double, double, toil and trouble.* But some men are busy *teaching* Macbeth, not *being* Macbeth. Damn John Woods for inheriting his mother's honesty. May he never seek a career with the Ford Motor Company.

"I think it takes a modicum of testicles to run the goddamn bulls," Howard said, surprised at how quickly his anger shone through.

But John was undeterred. "You're going to lose those testicles, ace," he said. "Little Spanish kids will be tossing them back and forth. Souvenirs from the *loco gringo.*"

Howard thought of protesting this in some large way. But before he could, an attractive young woman leaned over the outdoor patio fence and patted John on the back. John looked as if he'd been shot with pellets.

"Well, well," the woman said, "look who I find here. I thought you were going out of town for the weekend." John quickly stood, his beer nearly spilling in the process. Watching him, Howard remembered that day in the living room, the day his son was being reprimanded for smoking pot.

"Vanessa," John said. A quick redness had already spread across his face, even before he began to rock on the balls of his feet. Howard smiled at this young woman. He would guess she was in her late twenties, athletic, a real looker, the kind of butt that turned Howard's head whenever he and Ellen were out strolling along, at those times when he pretended to be looking at cars parked along the street, but would instead swipe a glance at some classic buttocks, circa 1960s and 1970s. Let Ellen call him a dirty old man, if she ever caught him.

Howard stood and extended his right hand. Otherwise, John would go on pretending that his father wasn't there. Just some retired guy who had given him a dill pickle.

"Howard Woods," Howard said, smiling.

"My father," John added, and now it was Vanessa's turn to blush, and then stammer a bit, and then rock on the balls of her own feet.

"Very nice to meet you, sir," Vanessa was now saying, but having a speck of trouble looking him in the eye. And now John was trying to shuffle her away.

"See you at work," John told her. Information was throwing itself at Howard, data about human beings, and human nature, and pheromones, and all that subtle stuff as he tried to come up with an answer. What was it Ellen had said? *I think men know how to handle guilt. That's how they spread their seed.* But John had already spread his seed. John already had Eliot, and yet the uneasy feeling that had crept over Howard seemed to have something to do with his grandson, didn't it? And with Patty, his daughter-in-law. Howard fought for a quick answer, a deciphering of those damn *symbols* he saw unfolding in front of his face, symbols he'd been too blind to read in his days as a happily married mole. And then Vanessa was gone, strolling off down the sidewalk, her beautiful ass swaying behind her, long auburn hair flying in the wind. If it had not been for the situation that was dangling in his face, Howard would have watched her go with all the longing of a lecher. But something was stopping him.

Howard and John sat back down in their chairs.

"Maybe I'll have dessert," John said, casually. He stared hard at the menu, strict concentration on his face. Howard, in turn, stared at John. Finally, John gave up and tossed the menu onto the table.

"What?" he asked, without looking at Howard's eyes. But a *skillful dodger* John Woods was not. How had this boy ever hidden anything from the enemy? Because he was so high above them, that's why, Howard decided. You don't look anyone in the eye when you're flying an F-15 fighter thousands of feet above the earth. Not even God.

The waitress appeared and wanted to know if they'd like another round. John quickly agreed. He looked nervously at Howard, who still said nothing.

"*What?*" John said again. He waited.

"You little son of a bitch," said Howard.

People drifted along the street, their voices rising up in clouds of excitement. The waitress brought the order and then left. Howard said nothing. A huge bus pulled up outside and hoards of senior citizens filed off like contented cattle, *Portsmouth Square Dance Club* emblazoned on their identical tee-shirts. A waitress rushed forward and led them all to a back room, their cloud of noise following them. Still, Howard waited.

Finally, John Woods turned to face him, to look deep into his father's eyes as he tried to stare Howard down with a *what's-up?* look. Howard knew this look. He knew this boy.

"Qué pasa?" John said, playfully, trying this time to elicit a smile from his father.

"You little son of a bitch," Howard said again. He could never remember, in all the years that he had been a parent, ever being this angry at his son John, the boy he thought he had lost forever in the dark skies over a strange and foreign land. "You little bastard," Howard said, and reached for the check.

They didn't speak on the ride home. When they had left the restaurant Howard took the time to put the top up. There was something too joyous in having the wind pelt one's face, something too trivial in letting words rush out of one's mouth in currents of air. For James Bond, maybe, it would be okay. After all, Pussy Galore was nobody's sister, mother, daughter, *daughter-in-law*. She was just, well, *Pussy*. But an Aston Martin convertible was not the vehicle to be written into the script between Howard Woods and his son at that moment in their lives. He thought about Patty then, and Eliot. How would this effect their lives? How could a happy, nuclear family blow up so goddamned fast? As if reading his father's thoughts, John spoke.

"You're making a mountain out of a mole hill," John said evenly. "As usual." Howard hit the brake. A car behind him honked angrily, and then flew past as the little convertible pulled up to the curb two streets away from John's house. Howard shut the engine off and then turned to look at his son.

"Am I?" he asked. "How so?"

John sighed his signature sigh and then turned to study the house he was now parked in front of, as though he were some kind of aluminum siding salesman. Howard waited again. This had always been his M.O. in the years of being John's father: Wait until the boy can no longer stand the silence. But this time John was on to him. Before Howard had time to analyze any data at all, John Woods threw a fist out and slammed it into the dashboard in front of him.

"Damn you!" he said to Howard, who sat silent and shocked at this action. "Do you have any idea what it was like over there?" No, Howard didn't, but that was only because John had refused to speak of it. "Do you know what it's like to be so fucking scared that you shit your pants?" Howard shook his head. Not even in the teacher's lounge at Bixley Community College had he been so compelled. And *that* would have been the place for it.

"That's no excuse," Howard said, evenly, doing his best to remind everyone concerned who was the father here.

"Yes, it is," John insisted. "It's a damn *good* excuse. At least, it's the only excuse I got. You come back from that kind of experience and you're changed, Dad. There's nothing that can bring back those kinds of highs. It's like standing back and watching a boring film pass before your eyes, until you realize that it's your life you're watching. And you're gonna be watching it for a long, long time."

"So you go after a little strange stuff for *excitement?*" Howard asked. He noticed that an elderly woman had come out onto her front porch and was now shading her eyes with one hand, trying to determine who was camped on her sidewalk. "You think a new piece of ass is gonna bring back the highs for you? Some soldier you are."

This angered John more than Howard realized it would. He threw another fist into the dashboard, and now, when he turned to look at Howard, there was something in his eyes above the anger. Pain was there, too.

"This isn't about us, Dad," John said. "This isn't about who's tougher, or braver, or stronger. This isn't about *us,* so stop with that competition thing. This is about *me!*" The dashboard took a third punch. Howard saw the elderly lady make a run from her porch, back inside her house. He imagined her on the phone to the police. *The young man seems to be beating up the old man's car, officer.*

Howard started the Aston Martin and sped away from the curb. At John's house he pulled in behind the station wagon, which sat next to Patty's Volvo, and parked. Howard barely had time to cut the car's engine when the front door opened and Patty bounded out, a burlap sack bouncing from one hand. She waved at the Aston Martin as she opened the door to her car and tossed the sack onto the front seat. Howard rolled his window down.

"Glad you're back," Patty said. "I've got to get to the theater and wrestle some more with Cyrano's nose. Eliot's watching TV."

With that, Patty slid behind the wheel of her car. The door slammed and then the sound of the engine. As she backed out past the Aston Martin, she waved once more. Then she was gone, speeding off down the street. Howard watched as the Volvo cut the corner and disappeared. How the hell did they expect a family to hold itself together this way, without skeletal bones, without any glue whatsoever? What was happening to the world? From what Howard could discern the animals on *Wild Kingdom* had better home lives than the modern family.

John stared ahead, saying nothing.

"I know it looks bad," he said finally, "But it's not what it appears to be, Dad. I've been wanting to talk to you about it, but it's really hard for me."

Hearing these words from his son, Howard threw off a tiny sneer. It sounded so much like the early morning speech Ellen had delivered, less than a week ago, that it was like listening to a replay. Or to the latest episode of some crazy talk show, those national soap boxes.

"However you look at it," said Howard, "it's cheating. And we both know what side of the family you got *that* from, don't we? It's in your damn DNA."

"Fuck off," said John. He put his face down in one hand, rested it there, as though he might fall asleep.

"Don't talk to me like that," said Howard.

"No, don't *you* talk to *me* like you just did," John retaliated. "You have no right to judge me. No right whatsoever. I'm an adult who is living his life apart from yours."

Howard considered this. "Then why do you want me to forgive Ellen in order to keep our family *together,* as you so sweetly put it?"

John simply waved Howard off as he opened the car door.

"Thanks, as usual," John said. "Thanks for listening to your son without having to share your own fears and longings."

"Is that an insult?" Howard asked.

John just smiled his *you don't have a clue* smile.

"I'll see you," he said tiredly. He got out and slammed the door. The little car rocked like a boat.

"That's an understatement," said Howard, as he opened his own door and got out. "Or have you forgotten that I'm temporarily living with you?"

In the morning, Howard woke ill-rested and groggy. He had heard John often in the night, footfalls pacing back and forth in the den below. He would have gone down to check on his son, to see if it was another one of those infernal childhood nosebleeds, but he knew it was useless. It wasn't John's nose that was bleeding. It was his heart. Guilt was seeping out of him, keeping him awake, the same prodding finger that used to poke Ellen out of her own warm marriage bed, night after night, until it got the better of her. *Out, out, damned spot!* What could Howard say to his youngest child? That he had temporarily lost pride in him? That he could no longer sleep in a house filled to the rafters with deceit, just as he couldn't stay at his own house for the same architectural reason? This was the boy who had gone to war, the boy who was honored by his country for bravery in battle. And yet he was handling a splash of boredom in his domestic life with espionage, with treason, with betrayal? Everyday life was where the real battles lay, Howard knew, and now he felt that not just Ellen, his beloved Ellen, but John, flesh of his flesh, had also failed life's greatest test.

Patty was still asleep and John had coffee making when Howard thumped the battered and weary suitcase down beside Eliot's schoolbag, on the floor by the kitchen table. At least the suitcase still seemed to be *employed*.

"You're up early," John said. "Want some eggs?"

"I'm moving out," Howard announced. John was quiet for a time, the only sounds floating between father and son that of the coffee machine, sucking water through grounds. Then the coffee finished and John poured them each a cup. Howard hesitated, but he couldn't resist the smell of fresh coffee, so early, and after such a restless night. He accepted the cup and took a few careful sips. John did the same, rocking slowly on the balls of his feet, keeping a close eye on his father.

"If it weren't for this thing with Mom," John said, "you wouldn't be acting like this. You're taking everything personally." Howard considered this.

"Let's see," he said. "Ben Collins fucked my wife. Yup, I think I'll take it personally."

"I mean about me," said John, "but, as usual, let's talk about *you*."

"At least I rank among the innocents," Howard noted. "And my team thinks it deserves a tad more of the pity pie."

"It's not about another woman," John said softly, peering over his shoulder, making sure Patty had not yet risen. Seeing this, Howard nodded his disapproval. He supposed that this was customary with espionage, with subterfuge, with deceit.

"You bad guys always have to be careful that the good guys don't hear you," Howard said. "What a way to live." He shook his head sadly. John ignored this by pouring himself more coffee.

"It's about trying to survive, Dad," he said. "It's about trying not to be afraid any more. It's about trying to find a reason for your life, beyond what you were taught it should be. It isn't that I don't love Patty. It's that I don't love myself. And when that happens, you need alternatives."

"I'll be at the Holiday Inn," Howard said flatly. "You know, that place with the family Bible." He put down his half-finished cup of coffee and took up the war-torn suitcase. "In case another member of my family loses his or her moral direction and wants to talk about it," he added.

"Yeah, well, be careful what you read," John muttered, as Howard and his suitcase sidled toward the front door. "Families weren't so perfect in the Bible, either."

"Listen, Robert, going to another country doesn't make any difference. I've tried all that. You can't get away from yourself by moving from one place to another."
—Jake Barnes, to Robert Cohn, *The Sun Also Rises*

five | **THE EXPATRIATE**

The Holiday Inn was on the corner of Fifth and Rayburn Streets, but smelled as though it should have been sitting next to the Bixley dump. Tobacco smoke twenty years old was now embedded in the tattered carpeting, which had so many small, black craters burned into it by careless cigarettes that at first Howard thought the round spots a part of the original design. As he waited for the receptionist to appear from wherever the hell she was, he glanced about the front lobby, at the two artificial indoor trees looking faded and haggard in their plastic pots, at the coffee urn set up in one corner, beneath a sign that said *Help Yourself Complimentary Breakfast, 7 to 9 A.M.*

In its heyday, the Holiday Inn had been a magnificent idea when it arrived in town, flaunting itself like some big-city showgirl. It had its very own lounge, one that sported plush sofas and chairs, and was considered a fine place for white-collar folks to gather for a Friday afternoon Happy Hour drink. Many of the teachers from Bixley Community College, as well as from the high school, could be seen there often, munching on microwave egg rolls and little weenies floating in some sort of reddish sauce. And, of course, listening to Larry "Mr. Mellow" Ferguson play the piano and sing songs by everyone from Sinatra to Captain & Tennille and John

Denver. At least, it used to be like that. But these days Larry was belting out "Like a Virgin," by Madonna; and a couple of Waspish and horrible renditions of rap songs; and "Knockin' on Heaven's Door," the Guns and Roses version. "Hey, at least it was *originally* by Dylan," Larry always leaned into the microphone and informed his small crowd of listeners when the manager wasn't around. This manager, a tense young woman sent by the home office to save what was left of the floundering establishment, was perpetually on the cusp of firing Larry Ferguson, or *Mr. Time Warp,* as she had personally nicknamed him. Wally, the bartender, had shared this tidbit with the regulars who sat at his bar. "She told Larry he has to catch up with the times," Wally whispered to Howard and Pete, during one Happy Hour a few days earlier, when the two had stopped in for a cold one after a game of golf. "Or Larry's ass is spring grass." It seemed as if everyone was whispering at the Holiday Inn now, as if in fear that the very rafters—probably rotted to the core with years of steam from countless weenies—would come crashing down on their heads otherwise. But Larry himself had been confessing the problem to his audience. On those Friday and Saturday nights when the tables would be a third full, and the piano man perspiring more than ever, he would lean close to the microphone. "If I don't bring in a younger crowd," Larry would whisper to his retired and semiretired listeners, the sweat beading up on his brow and catching the bluish spotlight that seemed to come from some hole in the roof, "My ass is spring grass." Then, peering over his shoulder for *Eva Braun,* his own nickname for the manager, he'd defy her by launching into "Crocodile Rock," in honor of the good ole days. This always brought Ellen and Howard and the other schoolteachers to their feet. You could jive to Elton John, just as if he were Bill Haley, and Larry Ferguson knew it.

The Holiday Inn had been a part of Howard's life for a long time. Once a year, for years, Howie and Ellen had penned a song request on a napkin and then asked the waitress to take it up to Larry. And once a year, for years, Larry had feigned surprise at reading the request. "Let's see," Larry would say, the sweat beads on his forehead shaping themselves into a thin, blue-gemmed tiara under the spotlight. "This is another anniversary night for Howard and Ellen Woods. Now, what could they possibly want to hear?" Then, he would pretend to read on the napkin: "Somebody please help me, I'm trapped! And it's signed, Howard Woods!" The crowd would snicker in appreciation, and Howard would wave a hand at Larry, pretending to be embarrassed by the whole thing, and the waitress would bring the celebrating couple a drink on the Holiday Inn. And then, Larry would finally play "All in the Game," by Tommy Edwards, knowing the words well. *Many a tear has to fall, but it's all in the game.* Larry had played that song on Ellen and Howard's anniversary for almost twenty years, ever since the Holiday Inn had opened its doors. The first notes on the piano would be Howard's cue to whisk Ellen to her feet and waltz her onto the little dance floor. It used to be you could go to the Holiday Inn, eat eggrolls and weenies on a real glass plate, drink a good martini, and feel like a million bucks. But after Eva Braun arrived there were no more complimentary drinks, no matter how regular the regulars had been over the years, and no matter what the occasion. Expenses were being cut back, or so she had informed the piano man, the bartender, and the waitresses. "And no more free drinks for you between sets," she'd told Larry, who by then had learned to guard his ass as though it were a piece of his front lawn. The same went for Wally. "Only water is free. Everything else you people pay for."

"We got two rooms left, a double and a king," Howard heard someone say. He turned and saw that the receptionist had finally materialized behind the reception desk, where she was supposed to be all along. She smelled thickly of smoke, and Howard realized that she must have sneaked into some back area for a cigarette. He stared at the *No Smoking* sign over her head. Why do people who smoke think they can fool people who don't smoke? Howard had always wondered. "You want one?" she asked, her breath finally reaching him with its sour tobacco odor. At first he thought she had meant a Winston or a Marlboro, until he remembered where he was.

"Well, now that you mention it, I *am* here for a room," Howard said. What had happened with civility? With good manners? With a business treating its customers as though they were, well, *important to the company?* Maybe politeness was being cut back these days, too. After all, it takes less time to be rude. "Is one of those rooms Non-Smoking, by any chance?" The receptionist banged a few keys on her computer board and stared at the monitor as though she were looking into some crystal ball. Or maybe she envisioned herself on the *Enterprise,* gazing forth into other worlds. The new Holiday Inn just starting up on Mars, perhaps. A moon of Jupiter. It *was* just a matter of time, after all. Howard rocked on the balls of his feet while he waited for a reply.

"Yup," she finally said. "The room with the king, right next to the ice machine. What credit card will you be using?"

Howard had no doubt that Room 17, next to the ice machine at the front of the building, and with a king-sized bed that looked more like a sad shrimp boat, might be considered a nonsmoking room by a heavy smoker. He, however, smelled the aftermath of countless cigarettes the moment he opened the door. Smoke clung to the curtains, the thin towels, the worn bedspread, to every fiber of the shoddy rug. He saw nothing that reminded him of the welcoming room that had been there in 1978, when he and Ellen spent one of their anniversaries in a king-size bed. It had been a splendid room, he remembered, not fancy but brightly new and still proud of itself. A bucket of champagne had been sent ahead and was waiting for them, *Compliments of Larry, Wally, and the Gang in the Lounge.* And there was a vase of flowers on the desk, from the Holiday Inn itself. And a coupon for a complimentary breakfast in the dining room, two free drinks in the lounge, all part of the big Get-Away Weekend offered by the motel.

Howard stood in the doorway of the small bathroom and stared down at the single bottle of shampoo *and* conditioner, two chunks of manna in one. Next to it lay the fragile shoeshine cloth, the ubiquitous plastic-shower-cap-in-a-box. Did *anyone* really use those caps? Howard picked the box up and studied it. *Place on your head before showering,* the instructions advised. Had confused Japanese businessmen used them as condoms, thus necessitating instructions? He lifted the cover of the commode and saw that the seat was protected by a narrow strip of paper that a mosquito could break if it sat its ass down. Two large chunks of the white enamel around the inner lid had been chipped away, leaving dark blotches that hinted of seagull droppings. Maybe it was not the very *same* room with the king-size bed in which he and Ellen had celebrated their Silver Anniversary, the big 25th, when he had given her a small diamond necklace. But it was certainly one like it. And therefore, it was symbolic as hell. As Howard Woods situated his suitcase on the floor beneath the clothes rack—he took note of his own ironing board and iron—he knew in his retired heart that he had come full circle.

At four o'clock Howard left his room and walked down the corridor, with its shabby rug and dizzying design, to the big double door that said *Lounge.* It being a Sunday, only a few diehards were in the place, most likely travelers passing through town, since Howard saw no one familiar. He slid onto a stool at the end of the bar and waited for Wally to discover him there. The red seats of the chairs and sofas, so plush in their heyday they were like plopping down on fat strawberries at the end of a weary week, were now threadbare from all those white-collar rear ends: bankers, salesmen, lawyers, nurses, postal workers. Howard stared down the row of empty bar stools. The upholstery had grown so thin that the cheap bluish fabric beneath was now exposed, like painful nerve endings. And, adding insult to injury, the stools had grown lopsided, causing all those white-collar butts to now tilt, even slide a bit from left to right. Before, the plushness had whispered subliminally to the customer that perhaps he should *stay awhile.* Nowadays, the slanted stools only seemed to shout, *Hey, buddy, let's down that drink and keep moving!* Even the decor of the bar—Howard had once thought it Far Eastern and alluring—had grown sickly, too much gilded effect for the approaching millennium. The help-yourself weenies and egg rolls had given way to salsa and tortilla chips, which one could eat from a community bowl with one's own hands.

Some things hadn't changed, simply aged, and those were the pictures and signs behind the bar. One was a black and white 8 × 10 of William Cohen, Maine's own son, now Secretary of Defense in Washington. Back in Bill's hungry days he had walked from one end of Maine to another, a regular vagabond, stopping in to shake hands with Wally and sign a photo for the wall. Next to Bill Cohen was a yellowing publicity shot of Lola Falana. *To Wally, Thanks for coming*, it said. *Love, Lola*. Wally had gotten it while at a club in New York City, but unless a customer asked, it appeared as if Lola had sat on one of the plump strawberry-red stools right there at the Holiday Inn in Bixley. Wally liked it that way. "She was the Queen of Las Vegas," Wally always said. "It's good for business." Wally said this long after only his most sincere regulars could remember who the hell Lola *was*.

Next to Lola's picture was Wally's handmade sign: *Home of the World's Best Martini!* It was pretty damn close to being true, too. At least, as Howard saw it, no one north of Boston could outsmart Wally on the semantics of a perfectly executed martini. This fame had prompted Wally to outdo himself, perpetually, so that he had become a walking encyclopedia on the history of the drink, so much so that he, too, was in danger of losing his job. Eva Braun had forbidden him to fraternize any more than was necessary with the regulars.

"She told me that while I'm talking to customers, they're not drinking," Wally whispered to Howard, as he put a martini in front of him. Howard shook his head with sympathetic understanding.

"What a bitch," he said.

"She said she'd rather see the customers drinking double scotches than martinis, since they don't take as long to make," Wally added, a worried glance tossed over his shoulder. Howard shook his head again.

"There's no courtesy left for customers anymore," Howard said. He wondered if he should inform Wally about his own induction into the Corporate Hall of Lies and Rudeness, thanks to the Ford Motor Company. But just then Wally shot him a swift look of terror before he fled to the other end of the bar where he began digging in the beer cooler. Howard looked up to see a slightly built woman in a crisp business suit, standing in the doorway and peering into the lounge. Seeing Wally hard at work, she disappeared.

As Howard sat munching on tortilla chips and sipping his martini, he remembered the grand opening of the Holiday Inn, back in 1976, a splendid thing for Bixley. He and Ellen had been greatly pleased to finally have an uptown place to come to for drinks and dancing. Before the Holiday Inn had pranced into town with its big green letters and its little red weenies, the white-collar teaching crowd had had to find comfort in the local and noisy taverns. The Holiday Inn had been an answer to their social prayers. As Howard waved for a second martini, he suddenly remembered that he and Ellen had even shared a drink there, during one Happy Hour, with Ben Collins and his mousy little wife. What had been her name? Sheila? Sharon? Susan? He wondered now if Wifey had known all along, if Ben's own conscience had pulled him awake at night, pulled him from his own toasty marriage bed. Or maybe she'd found out all by herself: a gas receipt from that trip to Buffalo, a motel bill, a smear of red lipstick around that damned *white collar.* Howard felt anger rising in him again at just the thought of Buffalo. He turned on his lopsided stool and stared at the room before him. The same table was there, a couple of matchbooks crammed under two of the legs, hoping for some kind of equilibrium. The chairs pulled up to it were shoddy. Even from the bar Howard could see the small, telltale black craters on the rug. He wondered if one of those cigarette burns had been caused by Ben's little mouse of a wife, that very night all four had sat around that table, listening to Mr. Mellow. Did she smoke? Was she pretty? Did she drink too much? Were her breasts large or small? In truth, Howard couldn't remember her particulars at all, and yet they'd been compatriots and hadn't known it. They'd been foot soldiers in the same war. They had spent time together, on a social afternoon now more than twenty years old. Did Ben and Ellen pity the two of them, the Mole and the Mouse, for their ignorance? Had they kicked feet beneath the table, telling each other to *look at the idiots?* Funny, but Howard *could* remember that it was snowing that day, fat flakes covering the sidewalk as they parked their cars in the Holiday Inn lot and then made their way through an inch of fresh white, toward the smell of eggrolls and weenies. He had even balled up a handful of thick, wet snow and tossed the ball of it at Ben Collins. What the mind recalls in times of stress! And Ben had tossed a snowball back—the dirty bastard—and then they'd all gone inside, stomping snow from their boots, their laughter crisp and clear on the chilly air, the Holiday Inn itself still a virgin. They thought they'd be teachers in their prime forever, didn't they? Thought they'd be looked upon with reverence from students passing them in the long, drab hallways. Forever. Students meeting up with them in grocery stores, red-faced to learn that their professors actually *ate food,* which meant they must *shit* now and then. Students who were running to plump middle age themselves. Howard had always imagined that he and Ellen would remain in their prime, perpetually teaching literature and history. Why spend all that time in college seeking an advanced degree otherwise, if it was just to be wrested from you one day? Forever. Like some image on a vase that Keats could write his odes around. Forever and ever. But Howard knew the truth. Regardless of how well the teaching world had treated Ben and his Mouse, or how well it had treated Howard and Ellen, all four horses' heads had finally sprinted past retirement. They were, as the Belle of Amherst knew so well, now pointing toward eternity.

Shit.

"Hey," Pete said, as he slid onto the stool beside Howard. "Did you get a tee time for tomorrow?" Howard nodded. He had. Nine-thirty. Plenty of time for him to satiate himself at the *Help Yourself Complimentary Breakfast Bar*—which probably meant peeling back the paper cup of a stale bran muffin and shuffling some corn flakes into a Styrofoam bowl—before he would drive out to the Bixley Golf Range and join Pete for tee-off. Howard shoved the basket of chips and bowl of salsa over to Pete.

"Where's the weenies?" Pete asked. He looked back over his shoulder in the general direction of the buffet bar, where the little blue flame had risen up under the miniature hot dogs, for all those years.

"There haven't been any weenies in here for almost a year," said Howard. "You been hanging out at Red's Tavern too much."

"No more eggrolls?" Pete seemed about to cry. Howard shook his head.

"Nada," he said. Pete fingered through the broken chips in the basket.

"What'd you do?" he asked. "Eat all the unbroken ones?" Howard nodded.

"That's the general idea," he said. "The company that makes those bags of chips counts on you throwing out the broken ones so that you'll have to buy more. They probably had a meeting with their chip designers over that. *Make sure half of 'em break, boys.*"

Pete smiled.

"So you're still on that *corporate America is ruining us* stuff?" he asked.

"Well, it is," said Howard.

Wally appeared with Pete's martini and put it in front of him. He was gone just as quickly. Pete stared after the bartender, astonished.

"What lit the fire in *his* pants?" he asked. Howard looked down the bar at Wally, who was cowering behind the draft beer dispenser. Before he could answer—and, yes, the answer itself would include *corporate America*—Pete Morton held his delicate glass aloft and aimed it at Wally, who pretended not to see.

"Oh, perhaps it's made of whiskey," Pete chanted loudly. "And perhaps it's made of gin. Perhaps there's orange bitters and a lemon peel within. Perhaps it's called martini, and perhaps it's called, again, the name that spread Manhattan's fame among the sons of men." Pete waited, a wide smile on his face, for Wally to respond. Nothing. Bottles clinked from Wally's end of the bar, indicating that he was very, very busy.

"Pete," said Howard, hoping to stop him. But Pete was on a roll. After all, Wally Davis had been making Pete Morton martinis for over twenty years, had taught him every damn poem, every song, every shanty that saw fit to mention the talents of the martini. This is what had made Wally the "Martini King" in the first place. But, sadly, as Wally had come to know all too well, the trouble with being king is that you're always in danger of a good beheading.

"Pete," Howard tried again.

"Okay," said Pete. "Then how 'bout this one?" Again, he pointed his martini at Wally. "There is something about a martini, a tingle remarkably pleasant," Pete recited loudly. "A yellow, a mellow martini, I wish I had one at present. There is something about a martini, Ere the dining and dancing begin, And to tell you the truth, it's not the vermouth, I think that perhaps it's the gin!"

Wally now seemed on the verge of hyperventilating. Bottles sang out from the cooler as he began stocking it to the hilt with Budweisers.

"Is Wally pissed at me?" Pete asked. "What's going on?"

"It's a long story," said Howard. "Wally will whisper it to you sometime, but not now." He nodded his chin toward the lounge door. Eva Braun was hovering there again, like some damn Nazi. Then she was gone.

"Who the hell was that?" Pete asked.

Howard shrugged.

"Another woman who has changed the course of our lives," he said. He took a generous sip of his own martini.

"*Who?*" asked Pete.

"Corporate America," said Howard. "In a skirt."

It was after ten when Howard finally crawled into bed. He soon found that sleep was impossible, given that room 17 was in the direct line of fire from the lights of the Holiday Inn sign. No wonder it was vacant. After staring at the ceiling, from which thumps seemed to be emanating downward, and after listening to the ice machine make even more ice—who the hell needs *ice* in the middle of the night?—he gave up. He snapped on the bedside light and looked around for something to read. He had picked up a *Golf Digest* the day before, along with a copy of *The Sun Also Rises*, but realized now that the book and the magazine were still in the back seat of the convertible. He was in no mood to dress and go out into the night to fetch them. So he pulled at the drawer on his night stand, just to see what might lie inside. It refused to open at first, and Howard assumed it was glued shut; or perhaps it was a *false* door, a sham assembled to appear functional. He would put nothing past a major hotel chain. But when he applied as much force as a retired and sleepless man can muster in the middle of the night, next door to the ice machine, the blasted thing flew open in his hand. He peered inside and saw that the Gideons had left their usual calling card, a small Bible, purplish, the color of a plum. Other than the typical propaganda flyers and leaflets from the Holiday Inn's corporate office, it was all Howard could find to read.

He took the Bible out, propped the pillows up behind him, and opened it. He tried to remember data from those Sunday school lessons when he was a boy. Just where was it in the Good Book that bad things like adultery happened? The Ten Commandments would be a good place to start, but Howard couldn't remember where they were. To his dismay, he noted that some rude guest had ripped out all the pages of Genesis, a deconstructionist, no doubt. Only remnants and shards were left to tell of the creation of the world, that first ray of light, the first leafy trees, the coming of the oceans, the fishes and animals, and then Adam and Eve themselves.

Howard flipped onward, through the other Biblical books. He suspected that adultery came up often in those times: all that red wine, and yet no television. As Howard turned on his side, hoping for more reading light, he heard what sounded like a soft hiss let loose from the mattress itself. He imagined marauding bugs of all sorts hidden out, guerilla-style, in the hills and coils of the metal springs. He would no doubt wake in the morning to find himself become Gregor Samsa, the Kafka character, a traveling salesman who turned into a six-foot-long cockroach. But at least he would fit right in. Earlier, he had noticed a couple cockroaches strolling along the length of Wally's bar, as though it were a plein-aire promenade. The Montmartre.

"Aha!" Howard said, for he had discovered a concordance at the back of the book. There it was, there was the evil word itself: *adultery, violation of marriage.* Damn right. Violation, with a capital V. He eagerly read the first listing:

> *Penalty is death, Lev. 20:10*

Howard paused. No, death wasn't somehow right. For Ben, yes, absolutely, you bet. Skewer the bastard, and then leave him in the hot sun, his eyes pried open with golf tees. But not for Ellen O'Malley. Howard reached for the lampshade over the ceramic lamp on the night stand—the base was a large yellow pineapple—and tilted the shade so it would share a parcel more light. Then, he scanned onward.

> *Spiritual, Jer. 3:8&9*
> *With the Egyptians, Ezek. 16:26*
> *In the heart, Mat. 5:27*

With the Egyptians? Somebody had committed adultery with the Egyptians? It sounded like a Biblical orgy. Howard went back to *In the heart* and read the words again. This one was Jimmy Carter's tailor-made sin. Lusting in the heart. Yet surely lust-but-don't-touch should be allowed, or at least given only a few seconds in the penalty box. It was the kind of thing Howard himself did all the time. Poor Jimmy Carter. Poor bastard. There are some things you should keep to yourself, no doubt about it. Just ask Performance Ford.

Howard tilted the lampshade yet again. Beneath the extra light, the pineapple base glowed a burnished yellow, the color of rotted fruit.

Causes loss of inheritance, I Cor. 6:9
God will judge, Heb. 13:4

Howard reread the last listing. *God will judge.* He sighed, closed
the Bible and placed it back in its drawer, where it would wait until
the next pilgrim came searching for answers. Ellen would bank on
that last one, believing in God as she did. But Howard Woods had
grown to think, over the four decades of his marriage, that a husband has a right to judge just a tad himself. He thought of Ben
Collins again, a steady habit of his lately. Had Ben ever found himself in some motel room, late at night? Had he ever opened the
Bible and scanned down through the listing under *adulterer?* Had
he ever been repentant of what he'd done with another man's wife,
and that man a fellow educator? A man with whom he had golfed,
had thrown a snowball, had shared a plate of weenies.

"Bastard," said Howard. He snapped off the light and the big shiny
pineapple disappeared, the way fruit in Ellen's refrigerator did the
second the door was closed. The sign from the all-night gas station
across the street blinked red, then white, then red, casting a mottled
scene across the canvas of ceiling. He thought of Jake Barnes in his
own set of rooms, that little flat in Paris, on the Boulevard St. Michel.
It was to this flat that Lady Brett had once turned up in the predawn
hours, drunk and giddy, as Count Mippipopolous waited with his
chauffeur in a limousine just up the street. Jake had kissed her good-
night, and she had shivered, standing there on the stairs leading up
to his flat. "You don't have to go," Jake had said. But she did. "Yes," she
told him, before she started back down the stairs. Women like Brett
always *do* have to go somewhere, anywhere. Even as one novel
finishes, you have the sense that they're off to another adventure,
sad though it may be. This is the curse, the tragedy of women like
Brett Ashley: They're too big for real life. That night on the stairs in
Paris, Brett had made her way down past the angry concierge and
back up the street as Jake watched from his window. Brett, with her
man's cap pulled low on her short hair. Lady Brett, walking out of his
life once again, walking toward her own future without Jake Barnes.

Howard felt instantly engulfed in sadness. He tried not to think of Paris as it was in the 1920s, for it was gone now, lost to him forever. Now there were only ghosts drinking in those smoky little bars, ghosts parading on the crowded sidewalks, ghosts catching late-night dinners at the Senlis. Phantoms. Instead, he watched the flickering light from the gas station as it played across the ceiling. He imagined Ellen, awash with the powdery smell of her nightly bath, all curled up, all tucked in, all ready for sleep, and wearing that lacy little nightshirt she always slept in. Ellen, over on Patterson Street. He wondered now if she still rose in those late night hours to stare out into the moonlit garden and ponder her guilt, now that Ben Collins had skipped the light fantastic.

Clink, clunk.

Howard did yet another quick flip in bed, turning his back to the door and the mechanical ice falling on command. But now he was facing the light of the Holiday Inn sign, an insulting glare that the thin Holiday Inn curtains could not obstruct. He heard his mattress emit yet another soft, low hiss as it settled beneath him. He closed his eyes and tried to imagine himself beating the pants off Pete the following day. But all he could see, on the golf green in his mind, was Ellen's beautiful face, hovering just above the sixth hole, where that clump of willow trees grew, the hole that always tested Howard most. Ellen's soft, lovely face. And then, unable to stop it, Ben's handsome face appeared suddenly next to Ellen's, right on the damn golf course! Did the guy have no shame? How would Howard Woods ever excel on the sixth hole now?

Clink. Clink. Clunk.

As the new cubes of ice were falling, Howard buried his head into the pillow, padding each ear. How could tiny squares of frozen water be so loud? Why hadn't every single person on the Titanic *heard* the iceberg? Howard tried not to think of Ellen rising from her warm bed at 7 A.M. to make coffee, its rich, thick smell permeating the whole house, the sound of toast popping, the fridge door opening and closing with its own sucking noises. He tried not to think of these sights and sounds as he fought his way toward sleep.

After all, if Howard Woods did so, he would have to juxtapose those wonderful breakfast images of Ellen with an image of himself fighting some pudgy, out-of-state salesman—a six-foot cockroach in a gray-striped business suit—for the last stale croissant at the complimentary breakfast bar.

Clunk.

six | **LANDFILLS**

"When'd you start wearing pink?" Pete Morton wanted to know. He was waiting for Howard by leaning against the side of his car and smoking a cigar. Pete had given up cigarettes three years earlier, when it had become difficult to play a game of golf without gasping for air. Howard thought then that he was free of Pete's secondhand smoke, but now Pete was back with cigars substituted for cigarettes, as if shortening the word itself would somehow make the action less carcinogenic.

Howard looked down at his formerly white golf shirt, and his formerly khaki pants. He shrugged.

"It takes a *real* man to play golf in pink," he said. Pete was extinguishing his cigar in the ashtray of his car, where he could light it up again during the break after the first nine holes.

"Maybe," said Pete. "But it takes a better man to *play* golf with someone who's dressed in pink."

"When one is retired," Howard noted, "one can do unorthodox things."

"I'll buy that," said Pete.

They shouldered their golf bags and headed to the first hole.

"Heads or tails?" Pete asked, pulling a quarter from his pants pocket. He balanced it precariously on his thumb and waited for Howard to answer.

"We've been playing golf for over twenty years," Howard said, annoyed. "And yet you still ask me heads or tails." Pete's fingers were now in place, ready to flip the coin up into the air. He gave Howard a quick look.

"You could change your mind," he said, "one of these days."

"I doubt it," said Howard. "I'm a creature of habit."

"I'm waiting," Pete said, stubbornly. "Come on now, heads or tails."

Howard frowned. He sighed one of John's deep sighs. He rocked on the balls of his feet. Still, Pete waited.

"Heads," said Howard. "Goddamn it, Pete, you know it's heads."

"I don't know any such thing," said Pete, as the quarter flipped six inches into the air. He reached out and caught it, slapped it onto the back of his hand. *Tails.*

"Looks like I'm up first," Pete said, and winked. This was the time, before they even tackled the very first hole, that Howard always asked himself *why* he played golf with Pete Morton. Playing golf was supposed to be a means of relaxation, not anguish.

"You have my blessings," Howard said, and gestured down the fairway.

As Pete was taking aim, Howard stood back and surveyed the hills and sweeps of the Bixley Golf Course. It had been constructed atop a landfill, a forty-foot-high heap of rotting garbage. This meant that all sorts of items eventually made their way to the surface and broke through to annoy even casual players. Howard had once seen a television documentary about how hundreds of recreation areas around the country—parks, golf courses, ski slopes and the like—had only a few inches of green grass separating them from the trash of landfills. And, often, a buildup of dangerous gases was also lurking down there, waiting, like something out of *The Twilight Zone.* But this was America's method of ridding itself of two hundred and nine million tons of yearly waste. Over his years of playing on Bixley's golf course, Howard had seen a multitude of pop-up waste items: a rubber hose, a bowling ball, blood bags, syringes, tires, a wig, a car bumper, shoes, and once even an old TV set. But it could be worse, for the documentary had shown that some of those landfill recreational spots even blow up, thanks to the methane underground.

It was on the fourth fairway that Howard broke down and disclosed Ellen's infidelity to Pete Morton. Pete had been about to shoot. He was polite enough, even for a serious golfer, to take a minute to console Howard.

"How'd you find out?" Pete asked. He seemed a bit uncomfortable. In all their years of being friends, Pete Morton had never hesitated a moment in telling Howard all about the women he had had affairs with while on the road as a salesman for the Keaton Electronics Company. Howard had heard about breast size, tightness, multiple orgasms, toe fetishes, you name it. And yet, when it came to talking about their own wives, when it came to sexual ideas concerning Ellen Woods or Carolyn Morton, Pete was reduced to a high school boy.

"Ellen *told* me," said Howard. "She even spent a week with him in Buffalo."

"Not exactly the romance capital of the world," said Pete. He had glanced up to see a foursome approaching from down the green, and now he seemed anxious to move on. "It was a mistake for her to tell you, that's one thing."

Howard protested this notion. How could it be a mistake to finally tell the truth?

"Because look where it got you both," Pete explained. "You're at the Holiday Inn and Ellen's home alone."

Howard took a deep breath. He looked skyward, to where turkey vultures had caught an unseen thermal and were now twirling about in it, their silhouettes like dark half moons. Black, smirking smiles. What the hell did he expect from Pete Morton, who, if he starting confessing now, would never be able to list for Carolyn all the women he had slept with over the years, from Bixley to Boston to Birmingham to Bozeman, and that was just in the "B" section of his address book. All those pop-up women he had thrown away, once he left their city behind. Why the hell had he, Howard, even bothered? Because he needed someone to talk to, that's why. Someone other than his own son. A compadre who would pat him on the back and say, "Jeeze, buddy, what a rap she dealt you." Pete was not that person.

Voices rose up behind them as the foursome approached the fourth green.

"I filed for divorce," Howard now said. Pete seemed shocked. There was something about divorce that still frightened Howard's generation. After all, they had been raised believing marriage was eternal, like death and taxes. You hung in there for the sake of the children. Happiness was dished over to a back burner of the stove. When one of their own finally broke ranks and ran, well, it scared the hell out of the rest.

"Jesus H. Christ," said Pete. "Are you kidding me? That's pretty radical, isn't it? I mean, it's not like she's having an affair *now*. It was all those years ago. The guy's dead."

They didn't speak again until they approached the sixth hole tee.

"What if it was Carolyn who had cheated?" asked Howard. Pete looked quickly at Howard's face, astonished.

"Are you nuts?" Pete asked. "Carolyn won't even have sex with *me*."

"You gents mind if we play through?" a voice asked. Howard looked up to see that the same foursome were all leaning on their clubs, like lopsided, silver-legged birds, waiting their turns. Pete shook his head, declining their offer. He readied his club and peered down the fairway. He was immediately more relaxed, Howard could tell, now that he didn't have to make eye contact.

"Marriage is like this landfill, Howie," Pete said. He cozied the club gently up against the ball, calculating his swing. "You gotta expect a little shit to rise to the surface now and then." Pete swung, connected to the ball with a deadening *thunk*.

"That's awfully romantic," Howard said. "Marriage as a garbage dump."

Pete said nothing, his eye glued to the ball as it grew smaller, a tiny white comet retreating. Howard watched the ball, too, in spite of himself. Sure, his wife had cheated on him, in Buffalo no less, and that was important. But he was a golfer, too, damn it. The ball bounced a few times, then lay still. Pete's face brightened with that same sixth-hole smile that Howard had come to despise.

"Two hundred and fifty yards, smack dab down the middle of the fairway" Pete whispered, as if in awe of himself. "Jesus, you gotta love it cause it don't get much better," he added.

Howard took his own turn, calculating carefully, then swinging. *Tink.* The ball rose into a silly arc and then curved off toward a patch of willow trees just a hundred yards away. Howard watched as it hit with a silent *splat,* and then rolled pleasantly in under the trees. A little game of hide-and-seek. It seemed a metaphor for his entire life, this veering from the track.

"I bet it's nice and shady in under there," Pete said, in mock sympathy.

Howard could tell already that it was going to be one of those days.

At the eighth hole, a bubbling ooze was seeping up from a sun-baked strip of ground that could not sustain grass, no matter how hard Bertie, the groundskeeper, tried to get it to grow. After sending a sample in to some lab, Bertie had been told that the oozing blob was caused by alga feeding on the iron-rich liquid just beneath the surface.

Howard shook his head as he stared down at the ooze.

"We ought to complain about this," he said. But it was what he *always* said at the eighth hole, just as he always picked *heads* at the first hole. Just as he always went for the willow trees at the sixth hole. He was what he always admitted he was, a creature of habit. He kicked at a graying set of dentures that had partially worked its way through the thick, wet rug, as if taking one last gulp of air, another bite out of life before going back under with the sandals, and old lampshades, and empty Pepto Bismol bottles.

"There's enough gas down there to blow us to Timbuktu," Pete said. He nodded at the wet blob, pure amber in color. With the toe of his golf shoe, he kicked at a rusted toy car that had driven itself up to the surface and was now idling there in the warm sun. It looked to Howard to be a 1959 Ford Galaxy. *The dirty bastards.* Good thing they didn't have the Lemon Law in 1959. As Pete took aim at the ball, Howard put his foot firmly on the roof of the car and pushed it back down into the slimy muck. Water and ooze crept in slowly, covering the spot where the little Ford had parked itself.

"We need a new golf course," Pete was now saying. He swung and the ball flew. "A real one, for Christ's sake. We should write a letter to Ralph Nader, or some watchdog group who gives a shit."

"Yeah, well," Howard said, as he lined up his ball, and then stared with deep concentration down the fairway. Creatures of habit and watchdogs. Maybe the two didn't mix. And besides, where were the watchdog groups that kept husbands and wives from cheating? "Let's hope it holds. We got ten more holes."

It had been another golf victory for Pete Morton. As Howard sat at the Holiday Inn after the game, sipping on a cold beer, he had to wonder *why.* Pete really wasn't a better player, not when it came to concentration and execution. So how come Pete always won? At least, most of the time he did. Howard had come to suspect that it was tied in to confidence, something undefinable in the DNA. Pete had been a high school and college jock, and the physical body never forgets that, not even after the middle-age paunch begins to appear, and the muscles slacken, and the old ticker wears itself out in just five minutes of basketball lay-ups. There's still a memory of greatness that lingers, even after the greatness is gone. Therefore, there must also linger a memory of being the guy who took an extra science lab because he didn't make the team, as Howard had done. *That* memory never goes away either, even if it's replaced one day by corporate or academic success. The nerdy guy always re-members how it felt to sit in the stands, perpetually. This is how corporate assholes are born in the first place, at least as Howard Woods saw it.

Howard pushed his beer aside and ordered his first Bacardi rum of the night. He had already come to think of the Holiday Inn lounge as his own kind of Hemingway hangout. It was a good place to sit and ponder the course of one's life. He had decided that he *liked* the smokiness embedded in the rug, the curtains, the threadbare stools. It felt more, well, *European.*

On his way through the lobby after the golf game, Howard had noticed a sign announcing a Seniors Dance. *Singles Only!* the sign warned. As he sipped on his rum, he thought about this *senior* notion. It was like being back in high school again. *Seniors will have their class pictures taken on Friday. The seniors will be going by bus to the ball game. The seniors are sponsoring a Halloween dance.* Jesus, he was a *senior* again. It was like being demoted, after years of struggling to grow up. And then, it was a different group today than in his father's generation. For Chrissakes, Jane Fonda was over sixty! Paul Newman over seventy! Liz Taylor was well into her sixth decade when she took off on a motorcycle with a shaggy-haired construction worker. A woman in Italy had given birth, *birth,* at the age of sixty-something! People were living longer and looking better, sometimes thanks to cosmetic surgery, and sometimes thanks to an energetic lifestyle. "There needs to be a plan for post-retirement these days," Howard had told Pete, during one of their perpetual golf games. "People need to start thinking about a *second career* at age sixty-two, not a bag of prunes and a good retirement community. I'm too young to go willingly to pasture." But Pete was not in agreement. "Nature doesn't intend for Tony Randall to father a kid when he's in his mid-seventies," Pete had argued. "And that's because nature doesn't want a young male who should be out spreading his genes spending all his time at home, spoon-feeding his toothless old pappy." Howard thought differently, damn it. Howard thought *young,* and who could blame him for that? But a *Seniors Dance?* What next? If this had, indeed, been high school, he would be racking his brain at that very moment, trying to figure out who he'd ask to the dance. Then a thought flashed through his mind, another snapping of the old neurons. *He was single again!* He could go to the damn dance. He could get a date, a woman in her forties or fifties, if the dance chaperones allowed *seniors* to bring *freshmen.* Maybe that blonde who worked at the bank, the one who was always leaning low to show off her beige-colored cleavage. Howard could take her to the Seniors Dance and twirl her about the floor, the envy of all the retired males who were stuck, perpetually, with their senior wives. Chang and Eng. Til death did them part. Howard could make up for high school, damn it, when he always had to pick from the leftovers, which had been very unpleasant considering that he, too, was one.

That's why Ellen, in college, had surprised him so. Ellen was no leftover. She just happened to prefer brains to brawn. *Ellen.*

"Hey, Howie, where's Ellen?"

Howard looked up to see Larry "Mr. Mellow" Ferguson, the singer-pianist, leaning on the end of the bar.

"Home, I guess," Howard told him. He took another drink of his rum.

"Many a tear has to fall," Larry suddenly sang. "But it's all, in the game." He smiled a wide smile at Howard.

"Cut it out, Larry," Wally told him. He put a glass of water down in front of Mr. Mellow. "The lawn mower catches you singing for free and your ass is mowed grass, remember?" Larry cast a worried look over his shoulder.

"I was only asking about Ellen," he whispered.

"We're getting divorced," said Howard, quite firmly. He suddenly remembered Robert Cohn's own divorce, before he met and married Frances, his divorce from *the first girl who was nice to him.* Hemingway had written the words hard and tough for poor Cohn, could have been a bit easier, considering how many times the author himself would marry and divorce. *As [Cohn] had been thinking for months about leaving his wife and had not done it because it would be too cruel to deprive her of himself, her departure was a very healthful shock.* Poor Robert, poor steer. "We're getting divorced," Howard added, "but it's a healthful shock."

Mr. Mellow thought about this for a few seconds.

"What the fuck does that mean?" he asked. Howard just shrugged, since he only imagined what it meant. That while Cohn was stunned his wife had left him, had run off with a miniature-painter, he had nonetheless *wanted* the marriage to end.

Larry picked up his glass of water and moved over onto the lop-sided stool next to Howard.

"Balls," said Larry. "What a trip. And I thought *I* had problems." Then, he quickly brightened, as if Howard's forty-plus years of marriage had required no more of a moratorium than that. "Hey, you going to the Seniors Dance?"

Howard shrugged. Maybe he was, maybe he wasn't.

"There's this broad been coming in here for the past month," said Larry, his eyes running constantly from Howard and Wally, over to the door where Eva Braun might appear. It struck Howard that this must be how men appear before they are electrocuted, always looking over their shoulder for the *zap*. "She's going to the dance. She told me so. I think she was hinting. I think she wants to get in my pants."

Wally frowned at the thought. Howard frowned a millisecond behind Wally.

"What a nasty place to end up," Wally said. "The inner sanctum of *your* pants." Then, he added, "Myra Butler's her name. She's Rick Butler's widow."

Larry took this news in eagerly. He ran a finger over the top of his brown hair, as if making sure it was still there. To Howard at least, it appeared as if Larry's hairpiece had rooted too far over on the left side of his head. Mr. Mellow was dangerously close to looking like a televangelist.

"Did you, you know, tell her?" Larry was now asking Wally. Wally threw his bar towel down and plunged both hands into the basin of sudsy water. Two glasses came out looking a bit soap-streaked but passably clean.

"Tell her what, Larry?" he asked.

"You know," Larry said, "about *it.*"

"Are you insane?" Wally wanted to know.

"I kinda wish you would," said Larry. "Then, if she's still interested in me, well, I'd know for sure."

"Are you a lunatic?" Wally asked. "How do I bring something like that up to one of my customers?" Wally turned his back and began arranging clean glasses on the shelf over the bar.

"Man oh man," said Larry, "it's a tough thing to break to a potential girlfriend. Makes me wish I was still married to Betty. You know, for better or worse."

"Maybe you should print yourself a card, like mutes have," Howard suggested. "You could just hand it to a woman, and then wait."

"Lawn mower!" Wally suddenly hissed under his breath, a part of the ventriloquist act he had perfected ever since the new management had taken over. Larry shot off his stool, pushed his free glass of water away, as if declining even *it,* and went back to his piano. In no time, a shaky version of Sting's "Fields of Gold," was emanating from the piano. Howard glanced at the door. Eva Braun. As entrenched as a hawk on a tree limb. He took a last big drink of his rum and then motioned to Wally for another. Before Wally could deliver it, Eva Braun was gone again, mysterious bird of prey that she had become.

"Poor Larry," said Wally, as he put the fresh drink down on the bar. Howard nodded, but said nothing. He stirred his newest drink with the small plastic pole Wally had stuck in the glass, propped up with a chunk of lime. There was not much Howard *could* say. Larry had been having some serious problems with impotency, ever since his younger girlfriend, an aspiring singer, had dumped him six months earlier. Apparently, he had been nothing more to her than piano accompaniment for her self-penned songs, until she met a strapping guitarist her own age. Filled with despair, and after weeks of sulking secrecy, Larry had finally confided to his fellow males that he had been rendered impotent. That should have been bad enough. But now he was like a born-again Christian: He couldn't keep his mouth shut about it. He seemed to think the guys in the bar would enjoy learning all about the malady, in case it struck *them* down one day. He was dead wrong, but that didn't deter him. And new discoveries apparently weren't helping any. Viagra, as described by Mr. Mellow, was "like giving my dick a breath mint." It did nothing but cause Larry's stomach to growl while the more important organ remained quiet. And so his doctor had prescribed for Mr. Mellow a vacuum pump, one that would *pump* him to erection on those lucky nights when he managed to talk some lonely woman in his audience into going home with him. The pump was always on Larry's mind. He had even pulled it out of its little duffle bag one night, during slack moments of a Happy Hour, and showed it to Howard, cautious as always that Eva Braun didn't catch him and wrest the thing out of his hands. The pump, to Larry, was what the Colt 45 was to John Wayne, in all those old Westerns. He never went anywhere without it. Just thinking of Larry's pump had given Howard such a sympathetic pain in his scrotum that he was compelled to cross his legs, hold his breath, and nod in a dream-like daze as Larry explained the mechanics of the thing.

"See this?" Larry had asked Howard, the first time he showed him the magical pump. "It's a hand pump and cylinder, tension rings, personal lubricant, instruction manual. And look at this. It even comes with a videotape, in its own carrying case. You ever need one, Howard, you let me know. I get a hundred bucks for every new customer I bring to the pump."

To Howard, the pump looked very much like the plastic cylinders he and Ellen used for drive-through deposits at the bank. He always waited until Larry was out of hearing before he asked the sixty-four-thousand-dollar question: "Tension rings?"

Howard's only answer from the boys in the lounge was shrugged shoulders and looks of pure terror. But Larry Ferguson's External Vacuum Therapy System gave new meaning to the language of Howard's generation, that old sexual use of the verb *to pump*. "I'd like to pump *her*," Pete used to say, as some younger woman sashayed past. But now Pete, too, fell silent in the shadow of Larry's new apparatus. Instead, like Howard, he simply stared at the thing as though it might one day jump from Larry's hands and attack any man who still had a functioning dick attached to him. No doubt about it, the pump was a penis's worst nightmare.

Larry had just hit his stride with "Fields of Gold," when John Woods suddenly appeared on the stool next to Howard. This surprised Howard. He was at first very pleased to see his son, grateful for the company, but then he remembered their last meeting. An image flashed through his mind of the young woman with the great ass, the firm breasts, and too much familiarity in her eyes when she looked at John Woods.

"Hey, stranger," said John. Howard said nothing. Instead, he stared at the faded picture of Lola Falana, hanging precariously from its piece of yellowed tape. *Study the past, if you would divine the future.*

"Beer," John said to Wally, who nodded. When the beer arrived, John took his glass and tapped it against Howard's rum. "How about a truce?" he asked. At this, Howard gave in. He clinked his rum to John's beer. There would be plenty of time in the days and weeks ahead to talk some sense into his son. But now was not the time. The truth was that Howard needed John desperately right then. Who else could he talk to? Wally "the Martini King?" Pete "Mr. Golf" Morton? Larry "The Pump" Ferguson? Freddy "The Mattress Mogul" Wilson, who was currently on vacation in the Bahamas with his newest sales clerk?

"Ok," said Howard. "Truce. But just for a while, and then it's war again until you come to your senses." John didn't like this, Howard could tell, but he let it drift away.

"So what's *really* bothering you, dad?" John asked. This caught Howard off guard. He thought it was as plain as the surgically altered nose on most people's faces. Ellen had cheated on him. But apparently John begged to differ. "This isn't about Mom's having an affair back in the Dark Ages," John added. "So what's it really about?"

Howard said nothing for a time. He was thinking of how fast William Cohen had aged since those days when he walked the length of Maine, asking for votes. Even the picture of him shaking hands with Wally seemed to be an artifact. The tape holding it up was as yellow and dusty as Lola Falana's own adhesive strip. What's it *really* about?

"It's about your mother and Ben Collins," said Howard. "At least, that's numero uno."

"What's number two?" asked John.

"I need to pay my dues, son," Howard said suddenly, and it surprised him. He watched as Wally made someone at the other end of the bar a splendid martini. Paying dues. Proving one's manhood. Men had always been doing that. But it was also about *heart,* wasn't it? *Passion?* It was Hemingway's own sympathy with the Loyalist cause that had carried him to Spain and his first war. It had carried him toward the sad, irreversible knowledge that if liberty is lost *anywhere* in the world, then liberty is in danger *everywhere* in the world. This was why John Woods had gone to Kuwait, wasn't it? Howard thought of Byron, outfitting an entire ship that he would then sail to Greece to help fight for their independence, Shelley freshly dead. Was it merely a way for the poet to overcome that misshapen foot? After all, and as Howard had often told his own students, George Gordon Bryon wasn't one of the swashbuckling heroes he often wrote about. He was short, chubby, and a born limper.

"I can pay my dues in Spain," Howard added, and heard John's stool twitch, as if in disapproval. He tried not to think of how Lord Byron had died fever-stricken in Greece, thirty-five years old. Leeches had sucked the blood out of him as if it were his last, fluid poem.

Howard finally looked over at John, who, in turn, looked around the shabby lounge, at the stools tilting beneath asses, the table legs hoisted up with matchbook covers, the broken chips floating in the bowl of half-eaten salsa.

"You're paying your dues *here,*" John noted.

"It's called success, my boy," Howard said now. "And it has always eluded me, like some prostitute who keeps turning the street corner just ahead."

"Aw, come on, Dad. You were successful. Hell, you've taught hundreds of students, maybe thousands."

Howard shook his head.

"I don't know," he said. "I read in a magazine once about a cat in Scotland, a mouser. During its lifetime it caught and killed twenty-eight thousand mice. Was that cat *happy?* Happier than the cats who ate Purina and never caught a single fucking mouse? I don't know, son. What *is* success? I guess it all comes down to that." The rum was making the pit of his stomach warm and fuzzy.

"It all comes down to catching *mice?*" John asked. "Jesus."

"I know I'll never be a shaker and a mover," Howard went on, sadly. "I'll never be the kind of guy who soars, like a kite. But I *would* like to grab on to the *tail* of the kite."

"If you run the bulls in Pamplona, I guarantee you'll fly higher than any kite," John said. Howard ignored this.

"Mind you, I'm not asking to see what the kite sees," he added. "I'm just asking to go where the kite goes."

"Jesus," said John again. "It's worse than I thought. I figured you were just upset over retiring, maybe losing a few brown hairs. I didn't realize it's been about mice and kites all this time."

Silence sat, lopsided, between them.

Then, "Who *counted* those twenty-eight thousand mice?" John asked.

We went down the stairs to the café on the ground floor. I had discovered that was the best way to get rid of friends. Once you had a drink, all you had to say was, "Well, I've got to get back ..."
—Jake Barnes, *The Sun Also Rises*

seven | **THE PHONE CALL**

"We're snuggled in between Big Beautiful Woman and Nails, Nails, Nails," the travel agent told Howard, when she phoned to alert him that his packet for Pamplona was ready and waiting. As Howard headed the little Aston Martin out toward the mall, he tried not to visualize where the place lay. It sounded like some sort of painful initiation involving cleavage and clawing. At Patterson Street, the exit to his old life, it seemed as if the little car made its own decision to bear right. Howard simply rode with it, the wheel moving in his hands of its own accord as it turned smoothly past Mrs. Fennel's white house on the corner. At first, he was surprised at how quiet things were on Patterson. Had his former life always been so serene, so easily defined? Lawns were neatly mown, the first cuttings of the year, and now, with the top rolled back, the fresh scent of grass wafted through the open car.

At Ellen's house—as he had begun to call the place—the shades were drawn, although it was well past breakfast. Howard slowed the car just enough to get a good look. The newspaper was still lying where the paperboy had thrown it in the early hours of morning. That wasn't so unusual, considering Howard had always been the one to trudge out in his slippers each day and retrieve the paper. Before the house fell backwards in his wake, he noticed that Ellen had left the garage door open again. There was her little gray Celica, its butt peering out at passersby in a most suggestive way.

Howard gunned the Aston and sped to the end of Patterson, circled around the cul-de-sac, and sped back. The garage door seemed to laugh at him this time by, a black, open mouth. If Howard had told Ellen once, he'd told her a million times to close that damn door, whether she was at home or not. It was nothing more than an open invitation to robbery, and he didn't care to hear from her how low Bixley's crime rate was. This was America, for Christ's sake. Violence was now a part of the American dream, a few slices of the pie. Howard's—no, *Ellen's*—house disappeared behind Marjorie Cantor's overgrown lilac bush as Howard braked for the stop sign at the end of Patterson. How much time does it take for the human thumb to push down gently on an automatic button that says *Close*. Just tell Howard that.

By the time he got to the mall, Howard was still feeling a modicum of tension over the garage door. It didn't matter that the divorce papers, if Ellen agreed to sign them, stipulated that she would keep the house, a house on which they had finally made their last payment after thirty years of licking stamps each month and pasting them on envelopes. In compensation for half of what the house was worth, Howard would settle for the money they had hoarded as their life savings. Sixty-five thousand dollars. This might put Ellen short on ready funds, but that wasn't his problem. She should have thought about that the day she let Ben Collins unhook her bra. Let her sell a few clay pots, make some extra coins that way. Let her find work as a ballet dancer. Her retirement pay should sustain her, but it was *her* problem now. He pulled the little car into a parking spot between an older model Buick, and a big green Wagoneer. That's what Howard liked most about the Aston Martin. It was like maneuvering a Chiclet. You could park it on an area the size of a bathroom rug and still have room to step out, stand back, and admire the little beast.

The Bixley mall was busy for an early morning weekday but Howard didn't mind. These days he almost seemed to find comfort in what Hardy had called *the madding crowd*. The men, women, boys and girls that he met, on his way to the spot between Cleavage and Clawing, seemed like warm strands of water coming at him. A soft blanket of humanity, not too close to smother him, but close enough to remind him that he wasn't quite alone. Without Ellen at his side, Howard Woods had begun to look solitude square in the face. And the face that looked back at him bore a grimace, not a smile. Then, there it was, in black letters painted onto glass, Bixley Travel Agency.

"Eloise?" Howard asked, as he stepped through the glass doors and into an office so small a mouse's fart would have blown it to smithereens. The woman behind a desk that seemed built of Styrofoam looked up at him and smiled.

"You must be Mr. Woods," she said. Howard nodded. He judged her to be in the mid-thirty range and so immediately eliminated her as a possible date for the Seniors Dance. "Don't lose this," Eloise warned, as she handed him a manila envelope, her fake fingernails so long and so red that Howard was almost afraid to reach out and take the thing from her grasp. There was no doubt where Eloise had recently spent a lunch break. What Howard saw gripping his travel packet were *Nails, Nails, Nails*. "That first page has some important phone numbers and addresses on it, such as the U.S. Embassy in Madrid, so be extra careful that you don't misplace it," she instructed him. Her voice was unnaturally loud, and Howard soon realized this was probably in deference to his age. Eloise was deliberately cranking up the volume for this *senior*. The very idea irritated him. Did she think him incapable of hearing, for Christ's sake? Does the younger generation believe that when one retires one must turn in the ear drums, as well as the keys to the office?

"The good news is that no inoculations are required when entering or leaving Spain," Eloise said, a little smile appearing around lips that were also red. "So you needn't, you know, worry about that." She gave him a quick little look. Did she think his withered ass would turn to parchment and crumble at the first prick of a needle? Howard tried to respond—he was going to Pamplona to *run the bulls,* for Christ's sake—and this was when he realized that Eloise didn't desire any response from him. She plowed onward with what was obviously her memorized travel spiel, with Pamplona substituted for, say, Dublin, or Lisbon, or Sydney. For Howard to reply was to interrupt the speech and perhaps cause her to lose the way. "The second section contains your ticket and hotel info, as well as a map. And the third has historical and local facts and places that you might want to visit, including museums, bars and restaurants. If you have any questions at all before you leave, don't hesitate to call me."

"Thanks," Howard said, for she seemed to be finished. He accepted the packet from her hand, avoiding the inch-long nails, and opened it. It was all neatly arranged and quite simple, just as Eloise had predicted. The ticket had a *Mr. Howard Woods* booked on an American flight from Bangor's International Airport, on the third of July, to Boston, where he would connect to a British Airways flight to London's Heathrow. From there, it was straight on in to Bilbao Airport, in Espana.

"Your car rental info is right there," Eloise noted. She reached out with a red talon and tapped the sheet of paper in question. Did she think him blind as well as deaf? "With a route all laid out for you from Bilbao to Pamplona."

"Yes, I see it," he said. How could he *not?*

"Don't lose it," Eloise warned again, as if Howard might at that very moment let the ticket drop from a hand that had simply *forgotten* it held something. Her next move would be to *pin* the damn thing to the inside of his jacket, the way his mother had pinned his childhood mittens. "We've got you in a standard room with three single beds, at the Tryp Sancho Ramirez."

This surprised Howard. He was to share a room with two other people? He had thought he'd have his own room, or better yet, a room at some hotel like the Montoya. He suddenly remembered

Jake Barnes, asking old Montoya about the rooms. *Did you give Mr. Campbell the room on the plaza?* And then Montoya, smiling in his embarrassed, deprecating way, nodding and saying, *Yes, all the rooms we looked at.* By God, that's how it should be done! With a few words, a few gestures. Save all the big emotion for the running of the bulls, and the fights, and then the drinking afterward. Howard had even told Eloise that his first choice was the Montoya Hotel. Now, she seemed to read his mind, one-celled as it was, and as only a travel agent can. She looked down at the notes on her desk, Howard's file, as if it were some kind of "tourist profile," such as police keep for criminals.

"That hotel you asked about," she said, and struggled to read her own writing. "The Montoya?" Howard nodded, waited. "It doesn't exist, Mr. Woods. It may have, you know, years ago, but it doesn't anymore. But you'll like the Tryp Sancho Ramirez. It's very modern. And the room is only fourteen thousand eight hundred pesetas."

She waited for him to respond, but he didn't. Music started up next door, at *Nails, Nails, Nails,* a local radio station that was currently airing a commercial for the store. *Are you tired of looking at nails that are chipped or bitten or just too brittle? Then get on down to Nails, Nails, Nails, because boy, boy, boy do they have a deal for you!*

"That's only about eighty-five dollars," Eloise comforted.

"But I'd really like a room of my own," Howard said, trying not to think of Virginia Woolf and those other whining biddies. Suddenly he was a child, a boy tired of bunking in the same room with a younger brother or sister. A strange sense of helplessness overtook him just then. Eloise gave him a weary look. He could almost hear her later, telling the other travel agents the story. *You think that's funny, wait til you hear what a customer just asked me. He wanted his own room. Ha ha ha.*

"This is in July, Mr. Woods," Eloise said. Howard could hear the forced patience in her tone. He feared she would thrust a complimentary calendar into his hand, something else he could lose. "July in *Pamplona, Spain.* You're lucky to get a straw mat on the sidewalk in front of the Hotel Crap."

Considering that, Howard turned and discovered the glass door only six inches from his nose. If Eloise's nails got any longer, she would be forced to keep the door open. He imagined them growing so long that one day they would be wrapping around trees in the parking lot, trellising. His nose so close to the glass, Howard saw that the letters for *Bixley Travel Agency* were now backward. It threw him for a moment, as if it were symbolic of how his life had suddenly ended up. *Backward.* He turned and looked at Eloise, who was just examining a chip in the polish of her index fingernail. He felt compelled to explain himself. *See, my wife, Ellen, slept with this guy named Ben Collins, and now, well, it's no life being a steer.*

"Forget something?" Eloise wondered. Before she could warn him again not to lose anything, including his dignity, Howard stepped through the glass door and was gone.

Howard cut a wide arc as he approached Books Etc., not wishing to run into Billy Mathews, which is exactly what his detour did for him.

"Hey, Mr. Woods!" It was Billy's voice. Howard stopped and peered across the mall at the bookstore. Had Billy Mathews, hanging out too long in the science section of Books Etc., slowly morphed into some kind of human Hubble telescope? "Right here, Mr. Woods."

Howard looked around. To his right was a small grove of indoor palm trees, a tiny *park*, if you will. Some design genius had been busy. The idea was to suggest to the casual shopper that a tropical paradise had rooted inside the mall. An illusion, of sorts. An oasis in a Maine desert. Around the palm trees were tall, tropical-looking flowers, what Ellen had once pointed out as Birds of Paradise. Below the trees and flowers lay a tiny fishpond in which red, tropical-looking fish pirouetted just below murky, tropical-looking water. Near the pond, and bolted down in case a shopper tried to steal it, was a green metallic bench. On the bench, his ass cheeks perfectly situated over the metallic slats, sat Billy Mathews, holding in his hands, of all things, a book. Beside him sat a McDonald's soft-drink cup, its straw at half-mast.

"Billy," said Howard. "Imagine running into you again." Billy beamed, as if this were some kind of compliment. He put the book face down on the bench and picked up the McDonald's cup. Howard watched as dark liquid was sucked up through the straw. He hoped it hadn't come from the pond.

"I'm on my fifteen-minute break," said Billy, putting the drink back down. "I get two breaks a day, besides lunch." Howard considered this. Two breaks a day. Billy was a lucky man, since most people go their whole day through without a single break. Just ask Howard Woods.

"Well, nice to see you again, Billy," Howard nodded. "You take care." With that, he tried to step back into the path of mall traffic, but Billy was too fast for him.

"Wait! Mr. Woods!" Howard couldn't pretend he hadn't heard, could he? After all, Billy was just a note short of a bellow. Howard stopped, turned, looked back at paradise. From his seat on the bench, Billy had a palm frond growing up out of his head. He smiled at Howard. Waited. Finally, Howard gave up and trotted back.

"What is it, Billy?" he asked. He tried to sound kindly, patient, the way a teacher should sound. But dammit, Billy Mathews needed to be reminded of one little fact: *Howard Woods was no longer his fucking teacher!*

"I been reading this book," said Billy. He picked up the face-down book and showed Howard the cover. To Howard's utter amazement the boy was several pages into *The Sun Also Rises.*

Billy waited, as if for a pat on the head.

"Well, well," said Howard. The book was new, its spine intact, its cover shiny, the kind of covers that publishers now like to put on older novels, hoping to reach a younger market. Howard imagined Hollywood just then, and a remake of the movie. Harrison Ford would be Jake Barnes. Madonna as Lady Brett. Billy Crystal as Robert Cohn. Antonio Banderas as Pedro Romero, the Spanish bullfighter who becomes Brett's lover. Howard could see these four heads now, all positioned on the cover according to star status, a bull ring behind them, a bull snorting at their backs, the dust of the arena in a passionate swirl over their heads.

"I found it for you the other day," said Billy, happy to have been of service, even if it was useless service. "But you had already left the store, and so, well, I figured I'd just buy it for myself. Employees get twenty percent off on paperbacks."

"Well, well," said Howard, as he searched for a better response. He reached for the book and opened it. "Papa Hemingway. Imagine." He looked down at the page Billy had dog-earred to mark his place. *Do you know that in about thirty-five years more we'll be dead? What the hell, Robert, I said, What the hell.*

"So what do you think so far?" Howard asked. He simply couldn't help himself. It was a literary car wreck, all right, and Howard felt compelled to slow down for it. Billy stood, deposited his soft drink cup in a nearby trash can that had been cleverly hidden within some Birds of Paradise. He turned to Howard, who was just passing the book back to him. Billy took it in his hands, rubbed a finger over the shiny cover—van Gogh's *Crows in a Wheatfield*—as he thought about his answer. Howard had never seen him this pensive when he was actually *required* to read *The Sun Also Rises* for a grade.

"I think they're just very, very sad people," Billy said finally. "But then, I'm only on page seven." Howard nodded in sympathy.

"Keep in mind that it might get worse," he said. "Well, nice to see you, Billy." Howard started to turn.

"Wait a sec, Mr. Woods," Billy implored. Howard racked his brain. How was it Jake had gotten rid of Robert Cohn? Oh yes, he had taken him down to a bar, had a drink, and then said, "Well, listen, I got to get back." Jake Barnes knew how to get rid of pests, but what could Howard do? Take Billy to McDonald's for another coke? Squander the boy's last break of the day just to be shed of him?

"What is it, Billy?" Howard asked, waiting.

"I'd like to talk to you about the book, you know, see what you think, see what I think. Maybe we could meet here in the mall.

There's a café just around the corner, near the video store." Howard forced a smile.

"Listen, Billy," he said, "I'm leaving the country soon, for a time." It sounded so very, well, *expatriate,* and he liked the tone of it. *Leaving the country soon for a time.*

"You going to Norway?" asked Billy.

"Norway?"

"Yeah, I know you were looking at that Norway book."

"I'm really too busy, Billy, to sit and discuss books," said Howard. "But maybe sometime next year." And with that Howard turned on his heel, made a dash past the palms and red fish and lush flowers, left Billy alone to ponder Papa Hemingway.

On the drive home Howard stopped at Red's Tavern to pick up one of Red's famous chicken sandwiches, to go. He would eat it alone in his room, at the Hotel Holiday Shit, hardly a place for old Señor Montoya to roam the premises. But it would have to do until Howard returned from Pamplona, a reborn man with a new plan. He was sure this would happen. It was a *literary theme,* for Christ's sake. You go, you see, you change. His sandwich sitting beside him on the car seat, as if it were his date to the senior's dance, Howard pulled out of Red's parking lot and turned toward the Holiday Inn. He had decided not to cruise down Patterson Street again, at least not today, maybe not ever. Wind ripped at his thin hair as he shifted the little car into third, let her build herself up to a nice speed. On the floor mat of the passenger seat, weighted down by his own copy of *The Sun Also Rises,* lest he *lose* the blasted thing, was his travel packet to Pamplona. He was going. He was seeing. He was doing it.

"That old Bilbao moon, I won't forget it soon," Howard sang. Wind ripped at the sides of his mouth, the words streaming out like water. "That old Bilbao moon, just like a big balloon." What had become of Andy Williams? Was he still dating Ethel Kennedy, his fellow senior? Was Ethel wearing Andy's ring, finally, her husband dead long enough that America could finally allow it? "That old Bilbao moon would rise above the dune, while Tony's Beach Saloon rocked with an old-time tune." Howard's eyes welled suddenly with tears. Did he miss Andy Williams that much? He wiped the warm tears away quickly, steering with one hand. "No paint was on the door, the grass grew through the floor, of Tony's two by four, on the Bilbao shore, but there were friends galore, and there was beer to pour, and moonlight on the shore, that old Bilbao shore."

Howard slowed the Aston Martin down to an easy crawl. He simply could not stop the tears from seeping out of his eyes. He didn't *want* to cry, had no inclination at all. This warm liquid seemed to be washing up out of him from a place he had no control over. *There were friends galore, and there was beer to pour.* The truth was that his whole generation was slowing disappearing, one by one, being picked off by snipers in a war they had no control over. What had happened to Mack Fortin, who retired from the college five years earlier? Bill Foote, the year before? Carolyn Stubbs? Rod Blakely? Where the hell had they gone? Were they all wrapped in cocoons somewhere, dangling from attics and basements, no longer useful to anyone, not even themselves? Where the hell was Andy Williams, that's what Howard would like to know.

The chicken sandwich from Red's Tavern half eaten, Howard opened a second bottle of the beer that room service had delivered to his door. He had even availed himself of a bucket of ice from the constant supply just outside. He was about fifty minutes away from Happy Hour and his first rum of the day, so the beer would tide him over nicely. He opened the package from Eloise and spread it out before him on his little brown table. He took up the historical page first and scanned it. *One of the reasons that the history of the ancient kingdom of Navarre is so rich is that it is crossed by The Pilgrim Way, Camino de Santiago. The region's capital, Pamplona, a quiet and pleasant city, is world-famous for the Running of Bulls. To find fashionable ambience at a later hour, try a part of town known as Barrio de San Juan, especially* Avenida de Bayona *and surroundings.*

Fashionable ambience.

Howard took another swig of the beer. Damn it, it all sounded so exciting. Maybe this was a secret those brave explorers knew: You can avoid the unpleasant circumstances of your everyday life by heading out on some dangerous mission, a sea route to India, a passage through the Bering Strait, a little jaunt to the moon. Howard was thinking of what he might encounter *after* he ran the bulls—Everest wasn't that high—when the phone bleated him out of his reverie. It was Ellen.

"What would you like me to do with your mail, Howard?" she said. "Do you want it forwarded to the Holiday Inn?"

Howard, not *Howie.* And certainly not *sweetheart.* He took a deep breath, surprised as he was to hear her voice.

"That will be fine," he said, curtly. "Thank you."

"You're welcome," Ellen said. "I'm happy to do it. But since I found divorce papers from Mike Harris among my *own* mail, I assume that you intend to live elsewhere than this house. Therefore, could you possibly have your address officially changed at the post office?"

Howard didn't know what to say. He had assumed she'd break down and phone him eventually. As he thumbed through those papers in Mike Harris's office, he had noticed the blank line where Ellen was to put her name. He could even envision her, sitting at the kitchen table with that morning's mail, her fingers twirled about the handle of a coffee cup—*World's Best Grandma*—wearing that fuzzy pink bathrobe she often wore after her shower. She would open the envelope and stare at it, speechless, mouth open, eyes misting. The second she knew what it was, the instant she saw the word *divorce,* she would rip the thing to pieces, maybe even spilling coffee on her fuzzy robe in the process. Then, she would rush to the green wall phone near the refrigerator and call Howard, weeping, begging for their old life back again. So then, if this were the case, why did he want to thrust the knife a bit deeper into her heart? Because he *had to,* that was the only answer he could find. He had to show her how serious and hurtful her act had been. It had forced him to lie awake at night, wondering if every single event in their past had been a sham. The birthday cake she baked for him, that same year of her infidelity, for instance. Was she thinking of Ben Collins as she sifted the flour, cracked the eggs, chopped the walnuts? And if he was now suspicious of such tiny events, then what of the big ones that were still to come: the children graduating and marrying and having children of their own. Had Ben sneaked into her mind on those important days, too? Ellen had ruined the past is what she'd done, no tiny feat.

But, nonetheless, Howard still felt positive she would contact him, for there was no doubt she knew where he was, considering John and Patty had mouths. But to call him about changing his address at the post office so that she would never have to see his name written on a envelope again? *I'm happy to do it.* That was a bit much.

"I'll take care of it," Howard said. He waited for her to say something else, something sensible, damn it, like *Howie, you need to stop this nonsense and come home,* so that he could say, *No way, Ellen, no damn way,* and then hang up on her again. His breathing was much too loud now, as if he were about to hyperventilate.

"Thank you, Howard," Ellen said. "I appreciate the consideration. There's just one more thing. Eliot's birthday is coming up, and since we used to take him to lunch on his birthday, well, how can we arrange it this year?"

"What do you mean?" Howard asked. Somehow, and foolishly he now realized, he had assumed they would still take their only grandson out for a birthday lunch. For *his* sake, not *theirs.* Some rituals were unbreakable. Weren't they?

"If you don't mind," said Ellen, "I'll take him to lunch and perhaps you can take him to dinner. That way, it won't be awkward for him, or for us."

"Sure," said Howard, "whatever is best." Before he could even ask how she was doing, if he had even *wanted* to ask, and he didn't, Ellen said a quick goodbye and then hung up. *Every action has an equal and opposite reaction.* Howard suddenly remembered that line from his old high school physics class. *If you push on something, it will push back on you.* It was the second of Sir Issac Newton's laws of physics. Or was it the third? Howard had never been very good at physics, a fact that was now showing up in his personal life.

The phone had grown warm against his face, but he held it for a few more seconds. It was as if the dead silence that floated to him all the way from Ellen's house had its own kind of heartbeat, a living thing that deserved to be kept alive, at least for a little time. But then, to his dismay, the dial tone suddenly clicked on, the connection broken. Howard put the phone back in its cradle and looked at his watch. Only thirty more minutes until *La Hora Feliz.*

eight | **THE DANCE**

It was a week later that Howard stopped by John's house to pick up those items of his that Patty had gathered in his wake. He had heard nothing from Ellen, nor had he asked about her. She had continued to send his mail on to the Holiday Inn, and that's all that mattered to him. He would do a change of address card when he knew just where he would be living for the rest of his life. He felt quite certain it wouldn't be at the Holiday Inn near the ice machine, but how to be sure? As Howard turned into John's drive, he saw John sitting on the front porch with a cold beer. This was surprising. After all, it was just past eight o'clock in the morning. That was early to be drinking beer, not to mention that John was known for never missing a day's work, not even when he felt ill. Howard pulled the little Aston Martin into a puddle of shade cast off by the immense elm at the edge of the drive and cut the engine. He got out and straightened the legs of his pants, smoothed away the wrinkles. How the hell had James Bond kept his trousers in such good condition? Each time Howard crawled out of that tiny car, his pants looked like they'd been in a street brawl.

Howard could feel John's eyes upon him the full distance up to the porch.

"Hola!" John said. He held up the beer. "Cerveza, Señor Woods?"

Howard climbed the steps of the porch and stood peering down at his son. John was still in his tee-shirt and a pair of jeans.

"Why aren't you at work?" Howard asked. A fatherly scold was there in his voice, but he couldn't help it. Some things die hard.

"Am I grounded?" John wondered. Then he smiled, that big smile that had won him so many friends through high school and college.

"I'm simply asking as a concerned person," Howard lied, "and not as your father."

"Well, concerned person," said John. "Sit a spell. Put your feet up." He gestured to the chair next to him, a rocker. Howard sat in it, set it to rocking with his foot.

"You shore do look mighty comfy, Pa," said John. He took another swig of his beer. Howard inspected him closely.

"Are you on some kind of drug?" he asked. John smiled again.

"The elixir of life, Father," he replied. "Pure, sweet life, and the last time I checked, it was legal." Howard frowned.

"Patty called to say she found my razor blades and other things," he said.

"Can we trust you with razor blades?" John asked. When Howard said nothing, John gestured at the house.

"It's all in a bag, just inside the door."

"And where is Patty?" asked Howard, caution lining his words. John gestured again, this time at the street.

"Gone for her power walk," he said. He raised the beer again.

Howard nodded, said nothing. So, they'd had a little fight, had they? Well, it could mend, as long as John kept away from what's-her-name, the filly with the full mane of hair and the firm flanks.

Howard went on inside the house just as Eliot came flying down the stairs, his school bag bouncing off his back. This surprised Howard more.

"Why aren't you already at school?" he asked, after the boy had stopped long enough to give his grandfather a worthy hug. Eliot shrugged.

"I'm not good at getting up early," he said. He smiled at Howard, a miniature version of his father's own captivating smile, then headed for the front door.

"Hey, listen, I'll drive you, pal," Howard offered. "I got the *little car* with me. You'd like that, wouldn't you?"

Eliot grinned back at him.

"Dad says you look like Magilla Gorilla in that little car," he said.

"Your dad is just jealous," said Howard. "Now, how about that lift? Just let me get this stuff your mom left for me." Howard had already found the bag: *razor blades, a tie, two magazines, a shirt, a Spanish dictionary.* But by the time he turned back to his grandson, Eliot was already halfway out the door.

"No thanks, Grandpa," the boy shouted back to Howard. "I'm riding with David and his mom. David is always late too. See you for my birthday. Grandma says she'll drop me off at the restaurant."

The door slammed. The boy was gone. Howard stood at the front window and watched as Eliot's school bag, the tiny body hurrying beneath it, disappeared up the street. He opened the door and came outside to find John reading the paper. John looked up, saw the paper bag in Howard's arms.

"Oh good," said John. "I see you found your school bag."

Howard just nodded. He stared down the street, still able to hear the sound of Eliot's voice as the boy met up with David, at David's white house on the corner, and then the roar of a car's engine. Soon, a light gray BMW eased past John's house. The horn tooted. Howard saw small white hands waving like surrender flags from behind the car windows. Eliot, waving. John looked up from his newspaper and waved back.

Howard went down the steps, the bag still secure in his arms, and headed for the Aston Martin.

"Y'all come back now, ya hear?" John shouted from the porch.

That did it.

Howard stopped, spun on his heel, and tread back up the walk. He leaned forward so that no neighbor who happened to be having late morning coffee on some screened-in patio would hear him.

"You need to get a grip," Howard said, softly, but with a pinch of anger.

Then, he turned and headed back to where his little car was waiting for him, like the small, black shell of a turtle.

"Hasta la vista!" said John.

Before Howard could crawl back into the sensible safety of the Aston Martin, Patty came power-walking up the sidewalk, her clasped fists rising up and down in the air, up and down. *Bam. Bam. Bam.* It looked to Howard as it she were engaged in some sort of boxing match with an invisible foe. Lots of upper cuts.

"Hi, Dad," Patty said, when she saw Howard. He smiled. He had always liked Patty. Once her fists were lowered, she looked so young and cute, even vulnerable in those pink jogging duds, which were now wet with sweat. Her long dark hair was trussed up in a thick ponytail. Patty leaned against the car in order to stretch her leg muscles.

"I won't hug you," she told Howard. "I'm all sweat."

"I'll take a rain check," Howard said.

"By the way, can you keep Eliot on Saturday night?" Patty asked. "I've got rehearsals. And Grandma Ellen is going to some dance." The muscles around Howard's mouth did a series of dance moves themselves.

"What dance?" he asked.

"Some dance they're having in the ballroom at the Holiday Inn," said Patty. "Guess that's like having it at *your* house, huh?" She smiled as she reached down to the pouch she carried around her waist and took out a timer watch. She snapped a few buttons and then stared hard at the numbers on the watch's face. Howard glanced over at John, who appeared engrossed in his paper.

"I'd love to watch Eliot," said Howard. "You know that." Patty looked up, as if she had forgotten that she'd even asked Howard a question. She held the timer up for Howard to see.

"I'm getting faster," Patty said, triumphant. "I think that's a good thing."

"Trouble is," Howard continued, "I was planning on going to that same dance myself." Patty simply shrugged.

"No problem, Dad," she said. "We'll find someone. David's mom is probably cool." As Howard watched, Patty went on up the walk, her pink running tights disappearing into the house like a swirl of cotton candy. There was not so much as a nod to her husband, who still lounged in his chair, with his newspaper and beer.

"Did you know your mother is going to a dance Saturday night?" Howard shouted up at the porch. John lifted his head, considered this statement.

"Why shouldn't she?" he asked. "Thanks to you, she's a single woman in every way but on paper." This angered Howard more than he could say. John went back to reading. Howard waited a few seconds.

"Why can't *you* keep Eliot?" he asked. Maybe it was none of his business, but he couldn't help himself. John looked up.

"I got plans," he said. "You know, with the guys." Then he winked. Howard spun around, furious, and opened the door of the Aston.

"Hasta la vista!" John shouted again, in case Howard hadn't heard the first time.

As Howard drove away from his son's house, he caught a glimpse of John Woods in the rearview mirror. He had gone back to reading the paper, a shank of dark hair falling down on his forehead. His son, Howard's son, *backward.* And then the lilac bush at David's house loomed out of nowhere and John Woods disappeared in a cloud of purple blossoms and green leaves.

Saturday, the day of the dance, seemed like the longest day Howard had lived through yet. It was long in the same way the days of childhood are long, stretched to their full length by sheer expectation. He had lain for most of the day upon his rickety bed at the Holiday Inn and read *The Sun Also Rises.* The Hemingway boys were already in Burguete, up in the lovely mountains of Spain, fishing in the Irati river and saying clever things back and forth like, *Were you ever in love with her? Sure. For how long? Off and on for a hell of a long time.* And this was on a drunken fishing trip, guys and wine and wiggly worms. How could anyone say Hemingway was anti-women? He was really just an old softie with a grizzled exterior. Howard was just starting chapter 13, with the arrival of Michael's letter to Jake, saying that *Brett passed out on the train* when his alarm clock went off. He looked at it for a couple seconds before he reached over and silenced it. Had the world always known sadness? Were people always hurting each other, since the very beginning? He looked back at the clock. Six-thirty. Time to shower, shave, and get ready for his first singles dance in almost forty-five years.

"Hey, look, everybody!" Pete Morton shouted from his lopsided bar stool. "Here comes Dances with Bulls!"

Howard heard a ripple of laughter as he let his eyes adjust to the smoky dimness of the Holiday Inn Lounge. There they all were, the *guys*, if you will. Pete. Wally. And, of course, Larry, who was passing around a photograph. It had arrived just that day, it seems, from good ole Freddy "The Mattress Mogul" Wilson, who was still on vacation in the Bahamas.

"You can be a real wise-ass, you know that?" Howard asked Pete. Pete grinned that silly grin he should have given up in his twenties, a grin as lopsided as the bar stool beneath his ass.

"How'd you like to be Freddy for about five minutes?" Larry asked. He was brandishing the photo as if it were something rare and wonderful. Howard took it from Larry's beefy hand and studied it closely. Freddy had on a purple shirt that was emblazoned with big yellow flowers. What made sensible men and women don such garments the moment they step a foot upon the sands of an island? Freddy had been going to Quick Tan, the tanning bed out at the mall, for weeks before he actually felt the hot sun of Nassau. Weeks. Now, his teeth jumped out from his tanned face like big white tiles set in brown earth. On Freddy's large, tanned head sat a Panama hat one size too small. On his tanned, plump arm was the young brunette sales clerk he had hired just the month before.

"I shoulda gone into mattresses instead of music," Larry said, enviously. He had been peering over Howard's shoulder all this time, his breath warm on Howard's neck. "He looks good, don't he?" Larry added. It sounded more like an accusation than a compliment. Howard nodded, but the truth was that Freddy Wilson's face, with sixty-five years of wear and tear, and sporting a couple of drastic face lifts, had come to resemble a leather purse from another time, something a Flapper might have carried next to her racoon coat. Overall, Freddy himself reminded Howard of a tired alligator trapped in a skintight suit. Howard handed the photograph back to Larry.

"So, how's it hanging?" Pete Morton asked. Howard heard, but ignored him. Instead, he gestured to Wally that he was in dire need of his rum. Wally poured a Baccardi on ice and set it down in front of Howard.

"I expect that dance is gonna be packed," Wally said, "especially if they send a courtesy van to the nursing home. My ass'll be busy all night."

Howard sipped his drink. He could feel Pete Morton's eyes burning holes the size of golf balls into him. He said nothing. *A courtesy van from the nursing home?* How had it grown so rotten, so fast? Weren't they all well-functioning men just a short time ago? Their bladders were as durable as good wine flasks, their teeth were all intact, their penises were still rising happily, saluting anything and everything that moved. And most of the women they married still carried their wombs with them, like pocketbooks. Now, well, it seemed to Howard that his generation had become a junkyard of useless parts. Bladders were deflated, teeth were artificial, hairs were falling daily, and penises were being pumped to attention like sad, old tires. Would anyone even *care* if they signed their donor cards?

"Well?" he heard Pete Morton ask. Howard turned and looked at him. *Dances with Bulls.* Leave it to the bastard to come up with something so funny it would stick. And this one would stick, oh yes, Howard could tell. He even wished he, himself, had thought of it first, had beaten Pete to the draw. That would have taken away some of the sting.

"Well, *what?*" asked Howard. He took a generous gulp of the rum and felt it beat its way down his throat. By the second drink, the fists of the alcohol would be tinier, almost soothing. By the third, those fists would be downright caressing. Howard was drinking more than he had back in his college days. But, well, things are different when one is a *senior.*

"Why ain't you talking to me?" Pete wondered.

Howard sighed.

"Among all those unfortunate women you bedded," he said to Pete, "was there not *one* teacher of English grammar?" Pete thought for a few seconds, serious, as if he were taking inventory for a tax auditor.

"I don't think so," he said. "Ellen taught *history,* didn't she?" Howard ignored the comment.

"Shouldn't we go?" Larry asked. "It starts at eight."

"Yeah, let's go," Pete said, and looked at his watch.

Howard put his drink down on the bar and gave Pete Morton his full attention.

"It's a singles dance, for crying out loud," Howard said. "*You* can't go. You're married!" Pete held a finger up to his lips.

"Ssh," Pete whispered. "Carolyn's gone to Boston. Her hysterical sister is finally having a hysterectomy."

"That doesn't make you single," Howard insisted. Pete looked up at him, that sad look coming to his face, the one that probably got him laid behind the stadium all through his high school football days.

"So who's gonna tell on me?" Pete asked, sincerely. "You?"

"Maybe," said Howard.

"You're not divorced yet," Pete reminded Howard. "Besides, if you guys don't take me with you, neither of you will get laid."

Howard suddenly felt sick to his stomach. How was this happening? How had he been spit through some kind of time warp, spit back to a place he had once hated. He had failed miserably at

Boy Meets Girl. He had despised the whole experience before he met and fell madly in love with Ellen. He had loathed it because, unlike Pete Morton, he'd never been good at it. Howard even suspected that some men and women marry people they don't even like, just so they'll always have someone to go to the dance with. Someone to eat with. Someone to sleep with. But Howard Woods had been lucky. Howard Woods had met and married Ellen. And now, he was being tested again. *Senior Meets Senior-ette.* He could almost hear the personnel over at the nursing home: *Be sure to have her back by ten o'clock, Mr. Woods, in time for her medication.*

"You ready, boys?" Howard heard Larry ask. Larry had the night off since a dee-jay would be employed in the ballroom, and not much would be going on in the lounge in the way of dancing. Larry stood, straightened his tie. He looked good in the dark blue suit he was wearing, even if the buttons on the jacket seemed ready to pop. Pete put his drink down on the bar and also stood. Ever the jock, Pete had on khakis and a white shirt. He reached into his pocket and pulled out a crumpled tie, shook it out to its full length, then went to work fitting it around his neck.

"There," Pete said, when he'd finished. "How's *that* look?"

Howard could never stay mad at Pete. That's the way it had always been: The cool guys always draw the other guys back, sooner or later. They reel them in like lost fish. Howard sighed as he reached over and grabbed Pete's tie, undid it, then tied it correctly, straightened it.

"You're helpless, you know that?" he asked. Pete smiled and planted a mock punch on Howard's arm.

"Okay, Team Viagra, let's head out!" Pete shouted. "The opposite sex awaits."

As Howard tipped back the last of his rum, he caught a glimpse of himself in the mirror behind the bar, flanked on each side by Larry and Pete. He felt a sudden embarrassment for the three of them. They looked, well, trapped. Just to the right of Howard's head was poor Lola Falana, her firm young breasts spilling out of the top of her dress. And William Cohen, whose photograph was so positioned that his eyes seemed forever locked on Lola's boobs. Trapped. Forever. Grecian urns in Maine.

Howard put his glass down and followed Pete Morgan to the door of the lounge. He looked forward to the next rum, the one with the pleasant and soothing fists.

As Howard Woods saw it, whoever had the audacity to still refer to the large hangar inside the Holiday Inn as a *ballroom* should be given a ribbon for creativity. The once haughty ballroom, the very spot where William Cohen had been served a chicken stew dinner to help sustain him on his walk across Maine, now looked like the indoor courtyard of some third-rate French bordello. From the tall windows overlooking the parking lot, faded red-velvet curtains sagged from bent and tarnished rods. Scarlett O'Hara might have found enough material to make herself a decent pair of pantaloons, but Howard doubted a *gown* could be coaxed from the thread-bare panels. The rug on the ballroom floor had far too many diamonds in the pattern. If one stared at it for more than a few seconds, those diamonds began to spin and twirl, as if the floor were one huge disco ball. Faded murals along the walls depicted proud scenes from Bixley's history: the founding fathers landing at Discovery Point, on the Bixley River, 1843, looking more like tired Fuller Brush salesmen than pioneers; several scruffy soldiers marching off to join the Civil War, circa 1860; the opening of Bixley Community College, in 1939; the creation of the nature park, in 1965; and, well, that was pretty much it.

Howard studied the faded painting of the college. Other than the addition of the gymnasium and several more classroom buildings, the place hadn't changed much at all. He reached out his hand, put a finger on the brick-red paint at the upper end of Bixley Hall. That's where his office had been—still was, with someone else now using the sturdy old desk, filling the rickety drawers with test papers, saturating the window with fern-like plants. Someone else, ready to teach *Macbeth* all over again. Poor Macbeth, poor weary bastard. Howard couldn't help but stare at the tiny likeness of Bixley Hall, as if he might find *himself* there, a small glob of flesh-colored paint, peering out through the yellow globs that stood for windows. He'd spent a lot of his life behind those windows. *A lot of his life.* And then, even though he had been trying hard to avoid it, he looked directly at the little yellow window that was the teacher's lounge. This is where Ellen and Ben Collins had given up their cigarettes together. Had they kissed in that room? Had they done things even worse?

"You'll find alcoholic and nonalcoholic refreshments at the table over there," said a young voice from behind him. Howard turned to see a girl, no more than twenty, who had obviously been hired to act as hostess. She was nicely dressed, a red pantsuit clinging to the youthful curves of her body. And she seemed to take her job very seriously. There was even a desk for her, set up just inside the entrance, which was where Pete was now waiting, two drinks already in hand. "There are also cheeses, vegetables, and dips on the table." She pointed, the way a stewardess points at the emergency exits. "And it's all for fifteen dollars," she continued, "unless you've prepaid." She waited, her eyes intent on Howard, who finally realized that she wanted him to produce his ticket or pay her the cover charge.

"Sorry," he said. He shuffled a hand around among the bills in his pocket and came out with a twenty. The hostess took it and quickly gave him his change. Then, before Howard could protest, or even question her intent, she grabbed his hand and stamped the top of it, firmly. Howard looked down at the letters now emblazoned on his hand in purple ink: *Senior Dance Summer 1998* it announced.

"Here," said Pete. He handed Howard a rum. "Next one's on you."

Howard could see Larry Ferguson's head bobbing away over in the corner. Larry was already surrounded by a small gaggle of women, the Bixley Bowling Babes, who came every Thursday night after the game to hear Mr. Mellow in the lounge. Larry claimed to have already bedded half of the team. Now that the pump was in his life, his plans were to go back for the second half, this time with a little more compassion since he needed it in return.

"Let's mingle," suggested Pete. Howard followed him, nodding at faces he either knew well, knew briefly, or didn't know at all, faces that were sometimes tired, or expectant, or sad, or blissfully happy. It apparently did take *all types* to run the world. And all those types had paid fifteen dollars to attend the Senior Singles Dance.

"Ooh, looking good, looking good," Pete whispered, as if to Howard, but it was really meant for a woman who was just passing by. Her short blonde hair was stylish, her white dress impeccable, her lips a full red. She had taken good care of herself over the years. Like Ellen, this woman would always be beautiful. Howard could tell by the arrogant way in which she held her head that she had been in charge back in high school, was probably captain of the cheerleaders. And she was in charge *now*, having two female followers tagging just behind her, neither of them even close to looking as good as she. But that's the way it was supposed to be. Some things never change.

All Howard—who was Pete's follower—wanted was to get through the crowd of people, past the blonde and her pale cronies. His mission was to pretend interest in the plates of veggies at the snack table so that he might scan the room. So far he hadn't seen Ellen.

"Yes sir," Pete added, and this time he said it directly to the blonde. "Looking *damn* good."

The blonde appeared bored. She shot Pete a look of pure disdain.

"Why don't you tell it to the Marines?" she suggested. Pete considered this.

"I *am* the Marines," he said. "Or at least I used to be."

This made the blonde smile. She gave him a more in-depth look as she continued to push her way through the crowd. Suddenly, Pete did a double take. The blonde did a double take. They turned and faced each other. A few seconds hung like smoke in the air. Then Pete's face broke into a massive smile. The blonde smiled too and shook her head. She had the kind of lacquered hair that never moved.

"I'll be damned," the blonde said. "Pete Morgan." He nodded.

"I'll be damned right back," Pete said, "Abigail Reed."

"You dog," said Abigail. "I wondered if I'd see you here."

"You haven't changed a bit," said Pete, "not since we dated."

"You either," said Abigail.

"Would you two excuse me?" Howard asked, and pushed on past them. He had no intention of watching as Pete and Abigail rediscovered their high school selves.

After nearly an hour of grating dee-jay music, carrot sticks, olives, and thin strips of cheese on Wheat Thins, Howard could still find no sign of Ellen. Had she changed her mind about coming? He was amazed at how expectant his insides had grown, the kind of fluttering he had known back in those days before Ellen agreed to wear his class ring. He would have thought that, at his age, all the butterflies had long migrated. He had even left the snack table for a time and taken up his vigil from one of the metallic folding chairs along the wall. He saw plenty of other seniors, but no Ellen, and no Molly. Then he had even positioned himself for a time near the door to the ladies' room, remembering how often he used to complain about Ellen's frequent trips to the bathroom, when the two were out for a night of dancing. No Ellen. Plenty of chitchat floated by as "the girls" went inside to pee, fluff their hair, and reapply their lipstick. Howard was amazed at the differences in *before* and *after*. There was more in the dynamics of the ladies room than met the male eye. And perfume! Tons of it wafted out each time the door opened and closed, clouds thick enough to intoxicate the masses. Howard was so sick of smelling sugar in the air that he wished he had some kind of fox hole to dig down into, the way World War I soldiers had avoided mustard gas. And then, when he least expected it, there she was.

At first he was simply struck with her soft and quiet beauty, youthful and vibrant, a dire contrast to the calculated appearance of Pete's friend, Abigail Reed. Even a stranger could tell by Ellen's demeanor that she was completely unconscious of her looks. Or, at least, they weren't the most important thing about her. And her smile seemed genuine, especially compared to those superficial smiles that were flashing like Kodak bulbs across the dance floor as men and women met, danced, drank, and ate Wheat Thins. And yet, there was a sadness on Ellen's face, or did Howard imagine this, wish for it? As he watched, she slipped out of her white cotton sweater and draped it across the back of one of the folding chairs. Then she and Molly made their way, side by side, to the food and beverage table, where they immediately asked for glasses of white wine. At least, that's what the bartender poured and presented to them. They seemed content to talk to each other and weren't constantly scouring the room with their eyes, as Howard had seen many of the other women do in the past hour.

Howard pulled back behind two men who were talking golf so that Ellen and Molly wouldn't see him. He watched, wondering why *she* had no interest in searching the room for *him*. He imagined that she and Molly were discussing one of their classes, pots or ballet, for they were busily chatting. That's when Howard spotted Larry, just a few feet away, in deep discussion with a woman who looked to be in her late fifties.

"The tension ring is *very* important," Larry was saying. "It's important for about thirty minutes." As Howard watched, the woman slipped away from Larry and disappeared into the crowd. Larry sidled over to Howard, leaned in close.

"I don't get these chicks," Larry whispered. "When was the last time *she* saw thirty minutes of good, stiff, you-know-what?"

"I think you should be less forthcoming, Larry," Howard suggested.

Someone, some teenaged chaperone, had dimmed the lights and now the music grew softer and more romantic. Howard wondered if he should ask Ellen to dance. He went to the beverage and snack table for yet another rum, thinking it would give him more courage. Then, he stopped by the dee-jay's booth and requested "All in the Game." By the time Howard got back to his look-out behind the golfers, Ellen was gone. Frantic, he searched the faces along the wall, then returned to the door of the ladies room. He was standing there, like a useless tampon, waiting, when the song began. *Many a tear has to fall, but it's all in the game.* He felt electric tentacles of pain shoot throughout his gut, his chest, his arms. Currents of longing. He needed to find her.

Just then Pete Morgan appeared with Abigail Reed hanging onto his arm for support. It was easy to tell that she was already drunk. When she saw Howard, she beamed.

"Imagine this dog never tracking me down, once his divorce was final," Abigail said. "And there I am in windy Chicago, still carrying a crush for him." She whacked Pete on the arm and giggled. Pete, in turn, looked and Howard and shrugged.

"Woof, woof," Pete said, and winked. "Did you find Ellen?"

Howard shook his head. It was none of Pete's business.

"I gotta pee," Abigail confessed. Like Brett Ashley on the train, Abigail Reed looked about to pass out cold. She pushed up on her tiptoes to kiss Pete's face, and then sashayed into the ladies room. Pete turned to Howard, a desperate look on his face.

"Quick," Pete said, "before she gets back. Give me the key to your room."

"Are you insane?" Howard asked. "Get your own room." Does adolescence never go away? he wondered. Does it lurk in a corner of the brain, like a computer virus?

"Come on, for crying out loud," said Pete. "I'm talking an hour or two, tops."

Howard sighed as he plopped the keys into Pete's sweaty palm.

"Don't do anything exotic with my pillows," he said. Then, his mind back on Ellen, he wove his way in and out of the dancers until he found himself on the other side of the room. He assumed she had met up with someone from her teaching days and was chatting up a storm somewhere. Each time he saw reddish hair with a silvery shine to it, he examined the face just below. Not Ellen. Not Ellen. Not Ellen. *Once in a while he won't call. But it's all, in the game.* And then he saw her, in one of the last places he thought to look. Ellen was on the dance floor.

Dancing.

Howard stood for some time and watched the spectacle unfold. He knew the man who was dipping his wife, oh yes. Floyd Prentiss. Good old Floyd. Floyd had taught Psychology at the college, and, like many psychologists, was in personal need of serious counseling. Howard smirked to see how intently Floyd was peering down at Ellen's face. Surely he didn't think he had a chance with Ellen O'Malley Woods. What bothered Howard was how Ellen was smiling back at Floyd. *Many a tear has to fall.*

Howard made his way back to the beverage table where he immediately ordered another rum. When the young bartender peered at him closely, Howard was taken aback.

"What?" he asked.

The bartender seemed embarrassed.

"It's just that, well, I need to make sure you aren't drinking too much, sir."

"Give me a goddamn drink," said Howard. When the young man made no move to do so, Howard leaned forward. "I'm riding in the nursing home courtesy van," he whispered. "I just don't want these girls to know." With this, the young man smiled and nodded that he understood. After all, every guy wants the babes to think he has his own wheels. It's in the male DNA. He quickly poured Howard a generous rum.

By the time Howard and his drink maneuvered their way back across the room, through the throng of sweaty dancers, there was no sign of Ellen at all. He even checked the metallic chair that had held her sweater, soft, white cloud that it was. The sweater was gone. Ellen was gone. Worse than this, Floyd Prentiss was also gone.

.   .   .

The only light Ellen had left on was the porch light. Its small yellow beam seemed useless against the black night, a blob of yellow paint such as the ones in the mural. Was anyone's life real? Howard wondered, as he sat at the curb in the Aston Martin and waited for his wife to come home from the dance. All around him, in the houses up and down the street, he watched as yellow lights winked out, first downstairs, then upstairs, his former neighbors settling down for the night. He found his suit jacket in the passenger seat and spread it over his arms. In no time, he was dozing.

Howard heard the sound of the car first, and opened his eyes to see round white lights appear at the end of the street. As the car drew closer, he saw that it was Ellen's gray Celica. It cut into the drive and eased up to the garage door, which had already been told to rise by Ellen's remote. Howard thought of tension rings just then, and Larry's sad pump. Things rising on command. He tossed off his jacket and sat up just in time to see the red taillights pull into the garage, the door of which then began to close. No thirty minutes here, just seconds. Before the door came fully down, Howard saw Ellen's delicate feet step out on the cement floor of the garage, her flat white shoes. She was home, all right. Cinderella, back from the ball.

He rang the doorbell, gently at first, and then he laid into it, as though it were an elevator buzzer and he'd been waiting all day to go up or down. Ellen opened the door a crack at first, as much as the chain guard would allow. When she saw it was Howard, she undid the chain and opened the door wider.

"What is it, Howard?" She asked. "Is something wrong?"

"You bet there's something wrong," said Howard. He pushed the door wide open and strode on in. He headed first for the bar where he found a bottle of rum. He poured a tall glass of it, no ice. He took a nice gulp as Ellen came up behind him.

"My God, you're drunk," she said, softly. He spun around and glared at her.

"So now you're fucking Floyd Prentiss?" he snarled. "What are you and old Floyd giving up? Cigars?"

Ellen's face went white, which made her blue eyes even more spectacular.

"Get out of here, Howard," she said. "Now."

Undeterred, Howard headed for the sofa. By God, his name was next to hers on the mortgage papers, right where they had signed for the house, over thirty years earlier. It was still half his until the divorce was final. He was about to share this thought with Ellen when he saw the photograph on the coffee table. There it was, the same damn picture as at John's house, the Woods family having what they thought was just another merry Christmas. Howard grabbed it up in a flash and threw it against the wall. Glass broke. The frame bounced out onto the floor. He looked up to see Ellen on her way to the telephone. Howard cut her off. He grabbed the phone's cord and yanked hard. It held fast. He yanked again. Same thing. Funny, but in all those Hollywood movies Howard had watched, a phone cord always ripped easily out of the wall the minute a star yanked on it. And it didn't seem to matter if it was big strong Mel Gibson, or scrawny little Woody Allen. Howard gave up and tossed the phone down onto the floor. It hit with a thud, then lay still, its receiver off the cradle, its dial tone crying out for help.

"You were gonna call the cops?" Howard asked. He was as insulted as he was surprised.

"I was calling John," Ellen said. "But I *will* call the cops if you don't leave."

Howard stared at Ellen, at her pale face, her bottom lip trembling just a bit as she fought back tears. He could not remember her ever looking so beautiful, not even when she was in her twenties, not even how she looked that first night they had ever made love. Howard had rented them a room in Boston. He had been nervous when he signed the registration card, thinking the clerk would know he was lying. Mr. and Mrs. Howard J. Woods. He was twenty-five years old and scared as hell. It was April 2, 1957, and they were to be married in less than two weeks. Somehow, considering that, it seemed all right. And Ellen had been nervous, too. But love covers up for so much. Love unbuttons blouses with ease, unzips pants with the steady hand of a professional. They had been so much in love. So much.

"Why?" Howard shouted at her now. "Why did you do it?"

Ellen seemed to have passed a point of caring. She threw a hand out and slapped his face, hard. Howard stepped back. He waited a second, enjoying the stunned look that had come to Ellen's own face. She put a hand to her mouth.

"Why," Howard asked again, "did you cheat on me with Ben Collins?"

Ellen was crying now.

"Passion!" she screamed. "Don't you know what passion even means?"

Passion. This was the wrong thing to say to Howard Woods. This was red to a bull. Jesus, but he'd come to hate people with passion. People who are kites, always flying high, always dropping their kite tails for the followers to grab. Howard glared at Ellen.

"You want a little passion, sister?" he asked. "Well, pucker up, 'cause here it comes!"

Howard reached out to grab Ellen's arm, but she pulled away from him and ran for the den. He caught her just as she tried to open the sliding glass door that led to the patio. He pulled her toward him then, into his arms, feeling the instant warmth of her body. He had missed her so much. He knew he should tell her this, should say the words aloud, if only his anger would let him. Would set him free. He put a hand under her chin, tried to tilt her head back for a kiss, but Ellen dodged his lips by turning her face. He kissed her hair instead, hair that smelled clean and sweet, the way Ellen's hair always smelled. With his free hand, he found her breast, round and soft beneath her cotton blouse. Ellen's soft, warm breasts. She had nursed all three children, having read horror stories about baby formulas. Howard had grown accustomed back then to seeing dark, wet spots on Ellen's blouses. In a flash, jealousy burned into him, bringing those images that he hadn't been able to wipe from his mind. Ellen and Ben Collins, a goddamn kite, if ever there was one.

"Is this what Ben did?" he shouted at her. His hand began to knead her other breast, rougher now. Ellen pushed him away.

"Howard, stop this," he heard her say. "You're drunk."

So Howard did. He stopped, his hands falling away, useless hands now. The hands of a retired man. Hands without a job, other than to swing a golf club, lift a fork of food up to his mouth, maneuver the remote control for the TV set. Hands without Plan B. He looked at Ellen and saw tears running down the sides of her face. She wasn't openly crying. The tears were coming from somewhere down deep, somewhere unstoppable, a place that was so hurt by his actions of the past few days that it would take lots of time to heal itself. He wanted desperately to say something about how much he loved her, to explain how much it hurt to think she had betrayed him. How much it *hurt*. He wanted to say it kindly, softly, to let her know he was in pain, and, therefore, he was in trouble. But he didn't say any of that.

"I'm sorry, Ellen," Howard said. But he knew it was too late. He knew *her*. He knew he had just crossed one of those invisible lines that each and every person paints around themselves in order to live. Emotional boundaries.

"I can't take your self-righteous punishment any more," Ellen said softly. Howard could only nod, for he understood. If the shoe were on the other foot, he'd feel the same way, too. But the shoe wasn't on the other foot. And that was the problem.

Ellen said nothing more as she followed him to the door. Howard stepped outside onto the porch. He paused there without turning to face her, hoping words would finally come to him. They didn't. They came, instead, to Ellen.

"If you can't truly forgive, Howard," he heard her say, "don't come back to this house again."

Howard heard the door close and lock behind him. The deadbolt this time. He stood staring out at the street. In the stream of porch light he could see the bed of irises that came up every spring, unasked. Ellen had planted them ages ago. He saw the cement turtle, a gift he had bought for her birthday, ten or more years earlier. And there was the weathered birdhouse hanging from a lower branch of the elm. John had put that up while he was still in grade school. A lot of families had been hatched in that wooden box. And what was Howard's own house, what were all those houses of his neighbors, but *wooden boxes?*

Behind him, the porch light went out. Howard felt an intense loneliness to see its warm yellow beam disappear. He made his way in the darkness past the bed of irises, and the cement turtle, careful not to hit his head on the hanging birdhouse. His little car was still waiting for him at the curb. The cool night air had seeped in through the crevices around the canvas top and now Howard shivered as he slid behind the wheel. He found his jacket, rumpled on the seat, and put it on. Somehow, he couldn't bring himself to start the car, not yet. Instead, he sat staring at the house on Patterson Street. When the yellow glob of downstairs light went out, he waited, still. He waited for at least an hour after the upstairs light went out, the yellow glob that had been *their* bedroom. Then, he found the strength to turn the key in the ignition.

By the time Howard Woods arrived back at the Holiday Inn, the huge parking lot was almost empty. Pete Morton's car was gone. The dance was long over.

"If it were done when 'tis done,
then 'twere well it were done quickly ..."
—Lady Macbeth, *Macbeth*

nine | **CHANGES**

Ellen Woods didn't bother to mail the marriage dissolution papers to Mike Harris. Apparently, or as Howard Woods saw it, she so distrusted the United States Postal Service to deliver the divorce agreement back to Harris & Harte that she drove them over to the law firm herself. On Monday morning Howard had innocently called Mike's office to inquire as to whether the divorce decree had, indeed, been returned. His hope was that he would then get up the courage and decency to tell Mike to just put those papers aside for the time being. "Maybe I'm being a bit too rash," that's what he intended to tell his lawyer. But before he could utter even one word of those sentiments he was informed by Harris that the divorce papers were already signed and returned. In person. Courtesy of Ellen Woods, née O'Malley. Howard felt such a tingle in his legs, a bolt of electricity right behind his knee caps, that he quickly sat down on the edge of the bed, his Holiday Inn pallet. The springs hissed just to receive him.

"The receptionist said she dropped them off this morning," Mike Harris was now saying. "Didn't say a word, just turned and walked out." Howard was certain that his heart was going to explode inside his chest, splatter the pineapple lamp, the flimsy curtains, the worn rug.

"She must have said *something*," he insisted. He imagined the blasted receptionist sitting, as usual, with her silly head up her ass, missing important clues that Ellen had no doubt tossed all about the office. "Was she at all upset?"

He heard Mike sigh, all the way from Harris & Harte, a lawyerly sigh that could cost anywhere from fifty dollars upward.

"Look, do you want to talk to Gloria yourself?" Mike asked. "I'm not Oprah, for Christ's sake."

"Gloria?" For an instant Howard feared that Ellen had hired Gloria Allred, that short, little power lawyer who was always on TV with some wronged female at her side. He flopped onto his back, to even more hissing from the springs. From this new vantage point, he noticed a large crack inching across the ceiling. The way his luck was running, all the furniture in the room above him was likely to come crashing through the floor one night, brittle chairs and cheap lampshades, all bouncing off the top of his head. And there would be no padding there on his head, no hairy cushioning. Just that morning Howard had noticed that his little bald spot, like the worn patch on an inner tube, had grown somewhat larger, like a pinkish open mouth, laughing at him.

"Gloria, my receptionist," said Mike. He sounded as if he were trying to maintain his patience. Funny, but Mike had been patient enough while Howard sat and filled out the divorce papers. Patient to the tune of two hundred bucks an hour.

"No," said Howard. "I don't want to talk to Gloria. What does this mean?"

"Well, it means all you need to do now is come back and sign these things yourself," said Mike. He was almost humming. Do divorce lawyers rejoice over divorce, Howard wondered. "Then it's just a matter of filing it, and you're a free man, dude."

Howard hung up. The ceiling with its crack seemed to go swirling around. He feared gravity might let go its hold on him, let him fly off into space, a retired, divorced man, about as useful as space junk. This was not how he had imagined things turning out, not even close. Ellen would plead until, his ears eroded from the blast of it all, he would break. He would forgive her. He would take her back. He would go home.

Provided.

He would want full details of every moment that had passed between her and Ben Collins, every kiss, every caress, every whisper, every lick. All of it.

The bastard.

The dirty, dirty, *dirty* bastard.

And now, this. It would appear, even to a retired cuckold, that he'd pushed it a tad too far, the trip to her house on Saturday night being the *coup de grâce*. He imagined a long line of dominos, toppling, each one taking the one in front of it down, a mindless, unstoppable stream of action. Anxiety now set up housekeeping in Howard's interior. Muscles ached and pounded and beat away at his chest plate. Ellen had signed the divorce papers and returned them, bright and early, like that smart little pig who got up at dawn to outwit the wolf. Howard had imagined those papers as a weird kind of souvenir, something he and Ellen would keep and be amused with for years, a tangible symbol of how close they had come to losing each other. Now it was a reality. It was happening. So be it.

The morning held more surprises, like a toilet that suddenly backs up and, at its own inclination, begins to spew shit all over the place. Ellen had been busier than just dropping papers off at a legal firm. She went so far as to write a letter to Howard Woods, which Patty Woods was kind enough to deliver for her. Patty knocked several times on the motel door, ice clanking down from the ice machine as if in accompaniment, before Howard managed to get a towel to stay wrapped about his waist long enough to answer. When he saw it was Patty, and not Larry or Wally playing some preadolescent trick on him, Howard asked for time to get dressed.

"I'm still dripping from the shower," he told her before he closed the door and pulled on his pinkish golfing pants. Patty was leaning against the ice machine when Howard finally opened the door and let her in. At first, she seemed amused by the room as she walked slowly about, examining things.

"It's not home," said Howard, as he arranged a stack of books on the desk, "but it'll do." Patty smiled, nodded.

"It reminds me of my old room back at college," she said. "And how much I wish I were still there, my whole life ahead of me."

Howard said nothing. He had assumed this was why she had come, to talk about the sadness that had washed up in her own marriage, another toilet backing up, another landfill exploding. But he was wrong. She had come with a letter from Ellen. An *epistle.* Howard motioned her to the only Holiday Inn chair, a lumpy thing sitting in a spray of sunshine that had broken through the grimy window. He tore open the letter. Ellen's neat handwriting was immediately recognizable, an old-fashioned kind of cursive you rarely see these days, swooping tails on the S's, fancy loops and curls on all the capital letters. She cut to the chase. *I would like for you to remove your belongings from my home no later than Saturday, June 27th. If this isn't done, I will be forced to ask the authorities to intervene. Until then, you are forbidden to enter this house for any reason. I have spoken to counsel and find that I am within my rights to ask this of you. Thank you. Ellen O. Woods.*

Howard folded the letter and slid it back inside the envelope. He looked at Patty, who smiled weakly.

"Do you know what it says?" Howard asked. She nodded. No words were spoken for some time as Howard stared at the grime on the window, a gray film that seemed to be caught between the two plates of glass, uncleanable now. Trapped. Out on the street a brownish bird, what he assumed was a sparrow of some kind, flew up from the sidewalk and disappeared into the upper part of the huge Holiday Inn sign. Howard had seen the sparrow before, busy, bustling, and assumed there must be eggs by now in its nest. A new family, waiting to be born. Then he remembered that he had company. He looked back at Patty and tried to smile, to put on a brave face for this daughter-in-law that he loved as his own child. She smiled back. She had picked up his copy of *The Sun Also Rises* and was thumbing through it, waiting, perhaps hoping, for Howard to finally speak. But he couldn't. He was simply too dumbfounded. How did it get to *this*, and this *fast?* is what he kept asking himself.

"She also wants to let you know that she'll be taking Eliot to Chuck E. Cheese for his birthday lunch," said Patty. "And that you're to pick him up for dinner at our house."

Howard nodded that he understood. Message delivered. He walked over to the mirror and peered into it. What he had left of his hair was still wet, and now it sat like a grayish rag on his head. He combed the strands over to one side, studied them a bit, then smiled. He laughed out loud, an almost gleeful burst of joy. Patty came and stood next to him, peered into the mirror herself, as if hoping to see what was entertaining him so. But how do you tell someone still in his or her thirties how outrageously funny it is to see an aging man who looks just like your father, a gray rag sitting atop his head, peering at you from within your own mirror? You can't. So you don't. Instead, Howard turned to Patty and gave her his second smile that day.

"You theater people know anything about hair color?" he asked.

The girl at the drug store wanted to show him every product on the market that would change the natural color of a man's hair for just a few dollars. Howard wasn't interested.

"I'm looking for Greek Formula," he told her. She stared, a snippy smile appearing at the corners of her mouth.

"Would we be talking about *Grecian* Formula, by any chance?" she wondered. He felt like slapping her.

"Whatever," he said. It was the kind of hair color that Larry Ferguson used, the first in the group to fall by the wayside. And then Wally had taken it up. Howard even suspected that this magical box was the true reason Pete Morton wasn't sprouting any gray hairs, but Pete would be too proud to admit it. Howard was last to fall, but he was ready. His only concern was that he not look like other men in their sixties, men like Larry, and Freddy the Mattress Mogul, and Floyd Prentiss—*the bastard*—who colored their hair one solid color, as if they were painting a chest of drawers. Men who looked as if a black beret crouched atop their wilting heads.

"Here," the clerk said, and handed him a box that said *Grecian 5*. The color was Medium Brown. "This is what you need. It targets only the gray areas. It'll look more natural." She was trying very hard not to study the hairs on Howard's head as she said this. "Shannon will ring you up, over there." She pointed at the cash register and then disappeared, as if he had only dreamed her.

When Howard pulled the little Aston Martin into John's drive, he was humming. There was a panic lying just beneath the hum, it was true. But at least to the ears of the outer world he was humming. He saw Patty's car already there, pulled up close to the garage door. Good. She had done just as she promised. She had gone straight home to wait for him. She opened the door on his first ring. He held up the brown paper sack that contained his purchase. Patty gave it a quick look.

"I hope you didn't get blond," she said.

"Medium Brown," said Howard. "The sales clerk helped me. Think you can work your magic in time for my golf game? We tee off at one o'clock." Patty stepped back, allowing him passage.

"This way to the alchemy room," she said, and pointed to the kitchen.

Howard went straight to the chair Patty had positioned in front of the sink. He had many questions for her, and none of them had to do with alchemy.

"What did Ellen say?" he asked, as Patty put a towel about his neck and shoulders. She had already donned the thin plastic gloves that came with the formula. As Patty worked the dark liquid through Howard's hair, she thought about his question.

"On the one hand, she wishes now she'd never told you," Patty said. Howard thought about this. How the hell could there be *any other* hand? Patty soon answered his question. "On the other hand," she went on, "Ellen says that people often get married in their youth and then fall asleep. When they wake up years later and open their eyes, they realize they don't even know that person they fell asleep with."

This infuriated Howard. Ellen probably knew Ben Collins all right, when she woke up next to *him*, in some seedy bed in Buffalo. What was happening to people? Did Cro-Magnon brides and grooms wake up one day to realize that they didn't want to hunt and gather as a team any more? No, and that's because Cro-Magnons didn't have Phil Donahue, and Sally Jessy, and Rosie, and Maury, all those psycho-babble gurus like Deepak Chopra telling them how to get in touch with their inner feelings. Inner feelings were meant to stay inside, damn it. That's why they're called *inner* in the first place.

"What else?" Howard asked. He heard the bottle in Patty's hand squirt viciously and felt a cold dab of the hair coloring hit the side of his temple.

"Oops," said Patty, and wiped it off with a towel. "That was about it. She wants to be alone for a while, so she can think."

"I see," said Howard, as brown formula, the color of shit, ran down the side of his face.

"Well, what's it gonna be?" Pete Morton wanted to know. He stood waiting, the quarter poised on his thumb. It was just a few minutes past one and a perfect day to play, considering that only one other twosome was on the golf course. "Heads or tails?" Howard took a deep breath. He rearranged the new hat he wore on his head. He looked at Pete.

"It's gonna be heads, Pete," Howard said evenly. "But then, you already knew that."

It wasn't until after they'd played the sixth hole and Pete had knocked the ball, *thunk,* a couple hundred yards or more straight down the fairway, and Howard had sent it, *tink*, into the patch of willow trees, that Pete brought up the new hat. They were standing side by side, two grown men, basking in the same old victory, the same old failure.

"I bet it's nice and shady under there," Pete said, his eye on the willow trees where Howard's ball had neatly disappeared. As usual, Howard said nothing. They started a slow walk toward the clump of trees, where Howard would be forced to kneel and dig the damn ball out from under the green branches with his club as Pete watched. This was usually when Pete began his little "it's all psychological," pep talk, the one that always informed Howard that the willow trees were *in his head*. But on this day, Pete broke with custom.

"I can't stand it any more," he said. "Why the hat?" Howard got back on his feet, slapped the green grass from off the knees of his slacks, and slipped the ball into his pocket.

"I just needed something to keep the sun out of my eyes," he said to Pete.

"But a *cowboy* hat?" Pete asked.

"It was the only one at Baker's Merchandise that fit," Howard answered. That wasn't really true. But the other hats were so, well, *old-fashioned*, the kind of hats aging men wore in movies, men curved over wooden canes, men inching along sidewalks like slow-moving spiders, hoping to catch a bus, gray felt hats pulled low above their yellowed eyes. The cowboy hat was, well, the kind of hat *cowboys* wore.

They were at the eighth hole, overlooking the algae blob, and Howard had already said, "We should complain about this." And Pete had already used the side of his shoe to push a red toothbrush, its white bristles fat and worn, back down into the slime and ooze. It was then that the hat came up again. In fact, it was when the hat came *off*. Howard had just noticed that the little 1959 Galaxy car was back, had driven itself up again to the surface of the muck, its painted yellow headlights half-hidden in greenish algae. He felt an instant sympathy for it, for what it *used to be*, a shiny new idea, once, years ago. And the painted yellow lights reminded him again of the mural on the ballroom wall, back at the Holiday Inn, a frozen memory of warmth, once. Surely, with the proper cleanser that rust would come off. The thing was probably a collector's item by now. After all, car companies don't make *real* cars anymore, cars with personality and looks. Eliot! Howard imagined his grandson opening a birthday box to discover a fully restored classic toy car. It was one small way the Ford Motor Company could pay him back for all their harassment. And that's why he had bent over and pulled the little Ford Galaxy up out of the muck. And that's when Pete had pulled Howard's cowboy hat off his head.

Nothing was said for what seemed like very long seconds. *Tick tock. Tick tock.*

Then, "Holy shit," said Pete. "What the fuck happened to you?"

Howard was almost too angry to speak. He grabbed the cowboy hat back from Pete's hand and repositioned it on his head. He felt a warm blush moving like a cloud across his face. Would Pete Morton ever grow up? Ever learn how to act like an adult? So Howard asked him both of these questions. Pete thought for a minute.

"*You're* the one with orange hair, and wearing a cowboy hat," Pete said.

"It isn't orange," said Howard.

"Yes, it is," said Pete. "When the sun hits it just so, it's got an orange tint."

Howard sighed. His hair was very, very *Brown,* this was true. There was nothing *Medium* about the brown, and there was certainly nothing *natural* about it, considering the formula had decided to attack every hair on his head and not just "target the grays." And when Howard Woods found the time to dash off a letter to the company that had manufactured *Grecian 5,* he would inform them of this. As well as the fact that when light, artificial or otherwise, struck his hair in a certain way, it did look as if the strands might be on fire. He heard Pete suppressing a laugh behind his back.

Howard turned and looked toward the clubhouse, that distant glob of white paint, all the way down at the eighteenth hole. Fuck it. He was done for the day. He'd simply had enough. Without a word, he turned to face Pete Morton, and then, his eyes staring hard at Pete's, he swung his golf club around and around in the air above his head. Pete ducked just as Howard let the club go. They both watched, fascinated, as the club flew gracefully through the air like a dark boomerang, cutting a fine arc as it went. It struck the top of some elm trees thirty feet away. Then, silently, the club made its way down through the arms of the tree, taking its time, all slow motion. Small branches and leaves broke away and came down with it. Finally, the club hit the ground at the base of the tree with a *thunk,* and lay there, exhausted. Sun caught the silver and it sparkled. Pete looked back at Howard.

"You know, Dances with Bulls," Pete said, "that's the best drive I've seen you make in years."

"The brown is way too dark," Howard told the same salesclerk who had sold him the infernal box of formula in the first place. "And when the sun hits it, it has an orange tint." He was whispering, embarrassed that other shoppers might hear. And he was again wearing his cowboy hat.

"I don't understand," the clerk said. She was blatantly staring at the feathers in the brim of the hat. "Why would it do that?" Howard wished she'd lower her damn voice.

"Because," he whispered. "The color you gave me didn't work."

He removed the cowboy hat and showed her his hair. She stared, her bottom lip doing a bit of a quiver. Since she now appeared ready to run, Howard quickly put the hat back on. Maybe she thought his next move would be to unzip his pants and expose himself, orange-tinted pubic hairs and all.

"You obviously left it on too long," she said, her voice high enough to crack a Pepsi bottle. "It's a five-minute formula. Didn't you read the box?"

Howard thought about this. No, he had *not* read the box. He had read *Macbeth,* by God. He had read Hemingway and a host of other great writers. He had even read Samuel Pepys's boring diary, ridiculous old free-loading, gossipy leech that *he* was. But no, by Christ, he had not read the goddamn *Grecian 5* box!

"No," he admitted. "I didn't."

"Well, no wonder it didn't work," the clerk said, smug again. "So what happened? Did you fall asleep with it on?"

Howard couldn't help himself. He wanted to explain, to perhaps vindicate himself. Otherwise, she would think he had dabbed dye on his head just in time to nod off in a senile snooze, the box still in his hand, his mouth wet with drool. All he had set out to do was to hide a few straggly gray hairs. Was that such a crime?

"My daughter-in-law is in theater," he heard himself telling the clerk. Had he grown so pitiful that her opinion of him was suddenly important? Yes, he had. "And she got to telling me all about Cyrano de Bergerac, and then Eliot came in for a sandwich which Patty made for him, and then Patty's mother called, and while she was talking on the phone I started reading my new *Golf Digest* and, well, we sort of forgot about the time."

He *had* fallen asleep, there in the chair, and Patty let him snore, thinking a nap would be good for a retired cuckhold about to become divorced.

The clerk stared at him, as if waiting for his full confession. Howard gave up. Let her think him rude, ruder than any of the other senior shoppers. He turned his back on her and began searching through the boxes himself. *Grecian Liquid, clear, colorless. Grecian Cream, grooms and conditions hair. Grecian Plus, foam that thickens and conditions gray, thinning hair.* When had it become an *empire*, this hair business?

"Maybe you ought to go to a specialist," the clerk suggested.

Howard remembered seeing a small beauty salon out at the mall, a few shops down from the Bixley Travel Agency. This was a safe distance from the salon in town where Ellen and Molly frequently sat under hair dryers, flipping through the pages of *Women's Wear*

Daily. And, if Howard remembered correctly, the mall shop had a sign on their door that said: *Walk-ins Welcome.* The little Aston Martin spun away from the drugstore, just ahead of rush-hour traffic.

Ten minutes later, and still wearing the protective cowboy hat, Howard was peering through the glass panel window of The Hair Cyndi-Cut. Seeing that all the stylists were busy with customers, he decided to wait outside the door until a chair became free. Passersby stared at him, or so he imagined. If he thought his life as a *cuckhold* was embarrassing, that was only because he had not yet become a *walk-in.* Finally, he saw that a chair was becoming available, a young woman digging into her purse for a credit card. The stylist looked through the glass at Howard and nodded. She was ready for him. Howard took off his cowboy hat—he was still too much the Eisenhower generation to step inside any room wearing a hat—and held it against his chest. But before he could lift a foot, a hand gently touched his arm. Billy Mathews.

"Billy," said Howard.

At first, Billy simply stared at Howard's hair, assessing. Howard could almost see the brain process in the works, a few dull snaps along the neurons, a few listless sparks. Then, it was as if Billy understood. He smiled.

"Did you just get back from Norway?" Billy asked. Howard was about to ask "what the fuck are you talking about, Billy Mathews?" when he remembered. *The Berlitz Guide to Norway.* Howard nodded.

"I did, Billy," he said. "As you can see, I was there for their big national celebration." He pointed up at his hair. More wattage burst forth in Billy's eyes.

"Was it fun?" Billy asked. He had in his hand that perpetual McDonald's cup, the straw sticking like a periscope up through the plastic lid.

"Billy, I'm about to go inside here," Howard gestured at the chair, the stylist. "And get my hair *American* again."

Billy nodded that he understood.

"When you come out," said Billy, "can we talk? I don't quite get the thing with Jake and Brett. I mean, why do they sit in bars and talk a lot? Why don't they ever act like, you know, boyfriend and girlfriend? I think that's really all they want to be."

Howard put his cowboy hat back on his head, lest someone he used to teach with, some graying academic, pass by and see him there. He looked again at Billy's pale blue eyes.

"Billy, I'm no longer your teacher," Howard said, gently. "The class is over. The grade has been turned in." And, if Howard remembered correctly, he had been gracious to give the boy a D, instead of failing him.

Billy's face seemed to hang like a sad moon before Howard's own.

"Hey, cowboy!" someone shouted. "Park your horse and get in here!"

Howard looked up to see the stylist, hovering at her empty chair, a hand now on her hip, impatient. She had short, frozen spikes of hair sprouting all over her head.

"See you, Billy," said Howard. "Take care."

Howard clutched his hat and stepped inside the salon. He went willingly to the stylist as she swung the chair around to accept him. A small badge pinned to her shirt said, *Hello, I'm Cyndi*. A shiny silver bead gleamed from the left nostril of her nose. She picked up a plastic black sheet and shook off dead curls from the previous customer. Then, she looked closely at Howard's hair.

"Whoa, look at this!" Cyndi said, loud enough that all the other girls stopped cutting and curling and combing and coloring in order to listen. "Incoming wounded!"

ten | **MORE CHANGES**

It was Wednesday afternoon that Howard drove toward Patterson Street in a rumbling rental truck, Pete Morton bouncing around in the passenger seat. Howard had already backed the orange monstrosity up to the service door at the Holiday Inn, where Wally had tossed out a couple dozen empty boxes.

"If you need more," Wally said, "I'm expecting a delivery tomorrow."

Howard had thanked him, and then he and Pete Morgan had climbed into the cab of the truck and, gears grinding, had headed for Patterson.

"A van would have been big enough," said Pete. "I mean, she's keeping the furniture, right?"

Howard tried not to think about this: *the bed they had slept in for all those years, a nick in the wood on his side of the headboard; that sofa that seemed to reach up and pull one's tired body down into the plushness of it; the kitchen table where John had dropped his pocket knife in the third grade and knocked away a small chunk of wood; the lamp Ellen had bought at an antiques store in Connecticut, a clipper ship of some kind that they'd always intended to have appraised; the coat rack Howard Jr. had made in shop.* He could go on and on if he got to reminiscing about the material things inside the house. But he had agreed in the divorce papers that the house and its contents would remain with Ellen, his personal belongings would come with him. On paper, it was just a string of words, meaningless. Now, those words had turned into a string of brown boxes.

At the corner of Patterson, Howard slowed the big truck as he shifted from third into second. Pete rolled his window down and rested his crooked arm in the open space. He looked over at Howard.

"I mean, this is a Norman Schwartzkopf kind of truck," Pete said.

As they passed the massive lilac bush at Marjorie Cantor's house, Howard shifted back into third. He wanted a big truck, dammit. He wanted Ellen to see in a *big way* what was taking place. He had called the night before to inform her that he would be arriving the next day to get his things, as her letter had instructed him. She was polite. She was cool. She was brief. "That's fine, yes, that's fine," was all she had said. Now, Howard envisioned the big orange rental truck as a military maneuver all its own. When Ellen saw him packing his personal things, his clothing, books, mementoes, into brown boxes that said *Smirnoff* and *Cutty Sark* and *Jack Daniels,* when she realized he was really moving out, the knowledge would shake her up. Funny, but in the beginning the power of the fight had lain in Howard's hands, at Howard's camp, his to dole out as he wished. But now, he sensed a change in the air, something Stormin' Norman probably also knew, a knowledge that the sands of war had suddenly shifted. They had shifted all right, and now Howard Woods had gone from being a general who could hang up on his wife, to a nomad who didn't even own a ratty tent. A funny thing, the war of divorce.

"By the way," Pete added. "I like your new hair. It takes a week off your age, maybe even two weeks."

Howard ignored him. He honestly didn't care if anyone noticed that a few dignified grays were now tactfully scattered here and there among his *natural medium brown* hair. Let Pete joke all he wished. Howard *did* look younger, and what's more, he *felt* younger too. He had even made an appointment with Cyndi, for the very week he returned from Spain. "Remember," Cyndi had lectured him, the silver bead in her nostril catching the overhead light. "Roots are the enemy."

Howard tooted at some kids who were hovering dangerously close to the street, the chrome of their bikes gleaming beneath them. He could see his old driveway just ahead, so he shifted down to second, and then to first.

"You know," Pete said, thoughtfully, "if I'm gonna use your room now and then, I wish you'd move away from the ice machine."

Again, Howard said nothing. He had no intention of letting Pete Morton use his room ever again, and this was even before he found the tan bikini panties under his pillow, looking more like a band-aid than an article of clothing. His true intention was to move out of the Holiday Inn soon, very soon. Whether he would be moving back to his home on Patterson Street or not remained to be seen. He would know more once he looked into Ellen's green eyes and determined for himself what was lurking there.

Howard parked the truck close to the garage doors, which Ellen had actually remembered to close. He would be blocking her car inside, true, but he doubted she would go anywhere while such a dramatic event was taking place. After all, her husband for over four decades was moving out, the way Howard Jr. had moved out when he went to law school. The way Greta had moved out to take that job down in Miami. The way John had moved out to enlist in the Air Force.

Howard pulled the heavy parking brake on and then opened his door.

"Wait here until I talk to her first," he said to Pete, who waved a hand, understanding the need for privacy.

"Do what you gotta do, pal," said Pete. He reached inside his jacket pocket for the remains of that morning's cigar.

Howard walked to the house with what he hoped was a confident stride. He knocked on the garage door but there was no answer. He turned the knob. Locked. The house itself was quiet, no radio playing, no sound of laughter from the back patio, no whirr of a vacuum cleaner. He turned toward the gray cement stones leading across the lawn to the front door. Ellen had made that walkway herself, during one of her summer vacations from school. From the corner of his eye, Howard could see a cloud of cigar smoke wafting from the passenger window of the truck. He felt Pete's eyes on his back with every step he took. At the front door a note was taped to the outside knob. Howard pulled it away and opened it up. There was Ellen's old-fashioned handwriting again, those swooping tails on the S's, those fancy loops and curls. He'd been seeing a lot of this writing lately. *Howard. The key to the garage is under the front door mat. I've packed all your things for you. You'll find the boxes in the garage. I'm at ballet class, but if there should be a problem, you may reach me on my cell phone.* And she had kindly listed a phone number for him.

With Pete's eyes burning boulder-size holes into Howard's back, he folded the note and slipped it into his pants pocket. He leaned down to the mat beneath his feet, lifted its corner, and found the key waiting for him. Ellen with a cell phone? One of those contraptions she was forever complaining about when they buzzed loudly in quiet restaurants, in bookstores, at the library? What she called "the end to civilization as we know it?"

Ellen had a cell phone?

Howard heard the truck door slam and Pete grunt as he jumped down from the passenger seat. Wanting to see for himself what awaited him, before Pete Morgan could add his five cents worth, Howard quickly unlocked the garage door and stepped inside. What he saw overwhelmed him. There before his eyes was cardboard box after cardboard box, one piled on top of the other, all the way up to the ceiling of the garage and filling the entire space that used to hold Howard's little blue Ford Probe. His life, his guts, all packed neatly and piled out in Ellen's garage for him to gather up and disappear with into the world. *If you push on something, it will push back on you.* Howard heard Pete whistle softly from behind his shoulder. He hoped there was a lesson in this somewhere for his golfing buddy, hoped that something good would come from Howard's pain. Maybe the brown mountain before them would compel Pete Morton to toss out that little black book of which he was so proud.

"Holy shit," said Pete. "You mean I really gotta help you move? I figured you'd come over here, pack a golf club or two, and she'd start crying." He whistled again, soft and low. Howard could do little but read the names on the sides of the boxes as he searched for something to say: *Murray's Clay Pot Kit, the Bread Company, Amazon Books, Lilly's Glassware,* and so on. Not a single *Smirnoff* or a *Cutty Sark* or *Jack Daniels* among the pile. So much for the opposite roads their lives had taken.

Howard turned and walked out to the street, stood there looking up and down the length of Patterson at the separate houses his neighbors had built for themselves, those wooden boxes in which to contain the years of their lives. The Masons, the Taylors, the Bradfords, the Davidsons. He could name every house on each side of the street if pressed to do so. It was as if they had *all* moved to that housing development at the same time, all hoping to raise their families in a pool of sensibility, as far from the riotous sixties as they could get while they struggled to keep the ideals of their parents alive. They had prospered as a team, the Kings, the Hartmans, the Turners, the Whites, names that might have come over on the Mayflower, the kind of folks who settled Jamestown, or climbed into Conestoga wagons and bounced West, sensible and adventuresome WASPs that they were. They had been part of a *team,* those Eisenhower teens had, the dollars and cents on their paychecks growing thicker as their hairs grew thinner, an inground pool here, a gazebo there, AstroTurf here, a second family car there. That's what Patterson Street had always meant to Howard Woods. Mornings when he came out to fetch his paper, the grass still limp with dew, he always took a few seconds to pay penance to the street where his kids had first walked to school, first pedaled their tricycles and bicycles, and then spun the tires of their first cars before disappearing out into the world. There was something about

Patterson Street that had given Howard the illusion that he was still safe in the 1950s, on a street such as the one he had grown up on, in those days when he was just coming to his young manhood. Those were the times when one could hear hammers tapping out all over America as the earnest and well-meaning built homes away from cities, those halfway houses between civilization and the primordial sea, between safety in numbers and no safety at all. Their own little purgatory, the 'burbs. And Howard had loved that notion, had loved his safe house, his safe job, his safe wife. Let others think what they would, but to Howard Woods the 1950s had been a sweet, almost idyllic time for him to grow up. It was all so easily defined back then: Democrats beat up on Republicans, who beat up on Communists, who beat up on the poor and downtrodden, who then beat up on each other. Nowadays, it was tough to tell a Democrat from a Republican from a Communist. But back then, in America, there was a new idea called the middle class, and Howard had found himself smack dab in the center of it, thanks to the fact that his father had managed to start his own construction company. And what a time to be building in the United States of America, when those soldiers who had been at war came back to set up housekeeping! Sure, it was also a time when your own neighbor might be a Commie spy, coming and going from the new ranch-style home with the latest model of Chevy gleaming in the yard, just to throw off suspicion. Who wants to borrow a cup of sugar from a Commie? So if the bastard's got a strange last name, or a stranger accent, just tell him the house on the corner is no longer for sale. And keep your kids away from his kids, because Communism comes hand in hand with indoctrination. It's catching. It rubs off. And if it does, well, you might as well pack up your Commie ass and move to Russia. That was the nature of the 1950s. If you weren't for America 100% then, by God, you were against her. Sure, that decade had its modern critics but Howard wasn't fooled by that. He knew damn well that if it hadn't been for the fifties there wouldn't have been any sixties! Any dolt could see that it was back in those Cold War years, those days before color television, in those times of lynchings and McCarthy's witch hunts, that the ideas took firm root for the seedlings that would crop up a decade later. This was where the feminist movement got its boost, in the dazed faces of all those suburban housewives, in all those old black-and-white TV commercials, women with aprons lashed around their waists and tied securely at the back in Little Bo Peep bows. Women who stood vacant over TV dinners and waited for the doorbell to ring and that briefcase to appear, the man they married firmly attached to the handle of it. Women who slipped off their Donna Reed high heels at the end of a day and soaked their swollen feet behind a closed and locked bathroom door. Were they unhappy? Were they anticipating the Valium and the Xanax, and all those other antidepressants that were still to come? Maybe. But Howard hadn't forgotten the lesson Americans had learned from Khrushchev and Nixon: There are no modern kitchens in Commie Land, no new dishwashers, no new electric stoves and ovens, so before you sell a sketch of the atomic bomb to the Reds, you better shake the little missus out of her stupor and ask if she really *really* wants to cook dinner where there's no electric can opener.

Ellen had a cell phone.

Howard turned and walked back into the garage. Pete was sitting on the inside step that led up to the kitchen, just finishing the last of his cigar. Howard looked down at Pete. Neither man spoke of the incident, for this was their own code, just as Hemingway's men had a code and stuck by it. Men of Howard's generation weren't the Alan Aldas who wanted to appear on a television show and discuss their deepest angst. This was their own code, and they both knew it.

"I'll lift and carry," Howard said to Pete. "You pack 'em into the truck."

It had taken them almost two hours to load all the boxes into the back of the big rental truck. At least, it had taken Howard that long. Pete had found one excuse after another to avoid work, cigar breaks being at the top of the list. And several times, declaring he could function no more without water, Pete had knelt by the outdoor spigot where Howard usually attached the garden hose and drank from the flow, his lips wrapped around the faucet like some kind of mutant horse. Howard's impulse had been to run over and kick Pete's ass, but then, the moving was *his* fault, not Pete's. All Howard could do was carry away the contents of his life, pack them neatly into the back of the rental truck, and then drive away from the suburbs, toward the nasty cluster of billboards and businesses downtown.

Now, aching and tired, Howard was sitting atop one of the lopsided stools in the Holiday Inn lounge as Larry sang "Candle in the Wind" to the Happy Hour crowd. It was the song Elton John had written about Norma Jean Baker, also known as Marilyn Monroe, and it was causing Howard Woods a great deal of pain. It wasn't that he missed Norma Jean, or gave a hoot about her tragic life. It was because the sadness in the tone of the thing reminded him of his own sadness. But that was the general concept behind Happy Hour: Render everyone so miserable and depressed they'll drink barrels of booze.

Wally came by and put a postcard down on the bar in front of Howard. It was from Freddy Wilson, the Mattress Mogul. The picture on the front was of a seedy-looking pinkish hotel in the Bahamas. *This is where Howard Hughes lived for a time,* Freddy had written on the back. Apparently, Freddy had beaten the postcard back to Bixley. According to Wally, the Mattress Mogul, like some kind of Elvis impersonator, had "just left the premises."

"That's his cigar," said Wally, and pointed to the still smoking butt in the ashtray at the end of the bar. And then Wally went to clean the ashtray, fearing, no doubt, another assault from Eva Braun.

"Hey, Dances with Bulls!" Pete shouted from a nearby table. Howard sighed. Minutes after they'd arrived at the lounge, Pete had spotted two plump, fiftyish women sitting by themselves for a Happy Hour drink. It had taken him just seconds to ingratiate himself, and now he was perched in a chair between them, hitting on the more attractive of the two. Howard knew that this was the exact verb that was taking place since Pete had said so. "I'm gonna go hit on those girls," Pete had declared, as he took his martini and strutted off. As far as Howard was concerned, the only *hitting* Pete Morton should do at his age was that of a baseball to a grandson. And now, Pete was trying to enlist Howard into the insanity. Howard turned on his stool, away from Pete and the women, to listen to the last of Larry's song.

"Hey, soldier, when do you ship out?" he heard Pete shout from behind him. Howard picked up his rum, downed it, and motioned to Wally that he wanted another one. Just as Wally put the fresh drink down on the bar, Howard felt a soft tap on his shoulder. He spun around on his stool, ready to inform Pete Morton that it was time for him to grow up, and that's when he looked into the face of a woman with eyes so blue they defied sensible genetics.

"Loretta," she said, and held a hand out to Howard, who took it. She had probably been a natural blonde once, but now her hair was a Hollywood blonde, and this made her eyes that much more unreal.

"I've never seen eyes so blue," Howard admitted. He simply couldn't quit looking at them.

"Contact lenses," Loretta leaned in close and confessed. "But don't tell." Perfume hit Howard's nostrils and a sweet, sickly taste appeared in his mouth. He had always hated too much perfume. "Why don't you come join us?" Loretta added. "Your friend tells us you're about to go to Spain, and that you may not be coming back." Loretta smiled at this. So, they were having a little joke about his running of the bulls, were they?

Howard looked over at Pete, a cigar butt peeping from the corner of his mouth, as if he'd just swallowed something with a stubby brown tail. Pete held up his martini glass and toasted Howard from a distance. Howard looked back at the fake blue eyes before him.

"Pete's a funny guy, all right," Howard said. "And now that the penicillin seems to be working, it's good to see him dating again."

By seven o'clock that evening Howard had dialed both Ellen's home phone and her brand new cell phone several times, but no answer. The rums had come in a steady stream, some being charged to his own tab, some from acquaintances who drifted in and out of the bar all afternoon as Happy Hour turned into Happy Evening. Pete had finally gone home to his wife, and the azure-eyed Loretta had gone to a birthday party, taking her friend with her. Now the people in the lounge had become a dream-like kind of people, the mood in Howard's brain switching from sad to pleasant, then more pleasant, then very pleasant. Fuck Ellen O'Malley Woods! Fuck her, and the horse she rode in on. Ben Collins would be a good name for that horse. Fuck them both. He had even dialed up her home phone yet again to tell her this. And yet again, her answering machine had clicked on. This time, instead of just hanging up so that she wouldn't know it was Howard calling, he had taken the time to leave a message.

"Fuck you and your horse Ben Collins!" Howard had said, noticing for the first time a sudden thickness to his tongue. "Fuck Buffalo and your friend Molly!" He hung up and then instantly called back. "And fuck those fucking pots you've been making! And your cell phone! And your fucking ballet classes!" Then, he slammed the receiver down. There, that ought to prove to Ellen that he had accepted the idea of divorce like a gentleman.

On his way back from the men's room, where it seemed the rum would never stop pouring out of the end of his dick, he stopped to request "Never Been to Spain" again. Larry Ferguson nodded, nervous suddenly, as if anxious for Howard to go sit down. Howard found this odd. He'd been requesting the song every half hour, and Larry was playing it almost that fast. Three Dog Night had been one of John's favorite groups. How did Howard know, back in those years when he was listening to "Never Been to Spain" blasting from behind his son's locked bedroom door, that it would one day be his own theme song? He couldn't. Life was such a hoot, and Howard Woods was beginning to prefer it that way.

At the bar, he discovered a rather attractive young woman in a smart red suit sitting on the stool next to his. Wally had just put a Bloody Mary down in front of her.

"Is it a double?" she asked Wally, who nodded his head, terrified. Howard smiled what he hoped was a sexy smile as he slid back onto his stool. He lifted his rum, held it up as a toast. The woman looked over at him. He guessed she was in her thirties.

"Here's to divorce," said Howard. "The legal alternative to murder."

At this, the woman smiled. She clinked her Bloody against Howard's rum, and then they both drank. Howard wished Pete was still around to see him *hitting* on a woman so young. Pete should save his energy for moments like this, and not for the Abigails of the past. Not for fake blue eyes.

"I'm Donna," the young woman said. She put her hand out and Howard took it. "You're one of the regulars, aren't you?" Howard lifted her fingers up to his lips and kissed them. A glob of spit stayed on the hand, and so, gentleman that he was, he wiped it away with his shirt sleeve. He heard Wally drop something from behind the bar. It crashed and broke. Larry suddenly couldn't remember the words to the song, or so it seemed, for he quit singing.

"You're a good-looking young lady," Howard said then.

"You're not so bad looking yourself," Donna replied, and it seemed to Howard that she honestly meant it. She tilted her head then and looked closely at him. Was she being seductive? Was this a female signal, a transmitting beacon? Howard grinned. He couldn't help himself. Jesus, it was good to be alive. Why shouldn't he be talking to this woman? He was almost divorced. He was certainly retired. And he still had between his legs the pump nature had given him. Why the hell not?

"Here's to life," Howard said, and they toasted again, taking long drinks. Then, as fast as it had come, the smile was gone on Donna's face.

"My boyfriend just broke up with me," she said, lip trembling. "He's gone back to his wife and kids." At this last disclosure, she burst into tears. Wally appeared instantly, like someone shot from a circus gun, the Human Cannonball, a stack of napkins in his hand. He put them down in front of Donna, who grabbed one. Howard took a second napkin and held it out before her, waiting, a kind of backup for when the first one grew wet and soggy.

"Do you know what the problem is with men?" she asked. Howard shook his head. He didn't. "They spend ninety-five percent of their time thinking about their penises." Howard considered this. That was a lot of time. How did he ever manage to read *The Iliad* twice, not to mention Shakespeare, Chaucer, and Dickens?

"I haven't thought of my penis since I got back from the mens' room," Howard told her. Donna smiled at the joke. It seemed to placate her.

"Okay, ninety percent," she said.

"I just moved all my stuff out of my wife's house," Howard confessed then. It felt amazingly good to be confiding in a stranger, someone who didn't know Ellen, who could remain, if not on Howard's side, then at least neutral. Donna blew her nose now on the napkin and tossed it down on the bar. Wally fetched it up instantly, disposed of it in the trash barrel.

"Bring me another double Bloody," Donna told him.

"Put that on my tab," said Howard.

"Oh, don't be silly," Donna laughed. "I'm not one of those broads who sit in bars hoping men will buy them drinks. Besides, mine are all free. I manage this big white elephant." And that's when the disco ball in Howard's head slowed its spinning. He suddenly realized why Wally had become like some pathetic Step 'N Fetch It, why Larry had launched right into "Crocodile Rock." This was Eva Braun sitting next to him, two of her three sheets already flapping in the wind! Good Christ, but Howard Woods was hitting on corporate America in a skirt!

"I came to this shitpile town to save this dump from extinction, and what do I get for it?" Donna said. "Deceit and lies."

"I know all about that, sister," said Howard, sympathy now seeping from his pores, along with rum.

"For five years he's been getting a divorce," Donna said now. "He promised."

Howard slammed his glass down on the bar.

"You heard the woman!" he shouted to Wally, who appeared to be frozen in front of the cooler. "Another double Bloody!"

Larry Ferguson had to get used to the sight of a sweaty Howard dancing with Donna Riley, aka Eva Braun, before he could even play "All in the Game." But Howard did what he used to do on all those anniversary celebrations over the years. He requested his and Ellen's favorite song. *Many a tear has to fall.* His shirt had dark wet moons under both arms but he didn't care as he pulled Donna up close to him. She had taken off her red suit jacket earlier, a corporate red all right, a dress-for-power color. All evening Howard had watched the movement of breasts beneath her white blouse, as if they were sleek, white dolphins swimming just beneath waves of silk. Now, he could feel those breasts against his chest as he and Donna danced, slow, sensual, pelvis to pelvis. Twice, she had lifted herself up, unsteadily, on the tips of her feet, to kiss Howard on the lips. And he had kissed back, even allowing some of his tongue to wander into the arena of her mouth. He had stopped caring that Wally and Larry were watching every move he made, every move *she* made. As far as Howard was concerned, there was just the two of them, just him and this firm young woman who was going places in the corporate world. Now and then, he looked over toward the blue beads on Larry's forehead to request another song. "Never Been to Spain" had become the most popular one of the night.

"Let's get out of here," Donna finally whispered, and Howard nodded. *Let's do that,* he wanted to say, but words were not important just then. They were on the same wavelength, he and Donna Riley, their two broken hearts joined on that night, in that seedy lounge, to make one good solid heart.

Between the two of them, and what with holding each an extra drink which they'd brought from the bar, it took Howard and

Donna Riley twenty minutes to get to his room. Part of the delay had been in Howard's insisting they stop at the pay phone where he again dialed Ellen's answering machine. This time, laughing too hard to say anything himself, he had handed the phone to Donna and motioned for her to speak. She had done so, pretending into the receiver that she and Howard were having wild sex. *Oh, Howie, baby, oh that feels good, that feels so good, do it again, Howard, oh baby!* And then, seeing Howard doubled over in hysterics, she had hung up. Howard couldn't remember when he had so much fun. But that was before Donna put her two Bloody Marys down on the floor and again took off her red jacket.

"Come on, bulley bulley," Donna said, beckoning to Howard. "Look what I've got." She then flapped the red jacket back and forth as Howard thrust fingers out from each side of his head, implying that horns grew there.

"Olé!" Howard shouted, as he charged the red jacket. But Donna whipped it out of his reach. "Olé!" he shouted again, as he turned and came charging back. For five boisterous minutes Howard had charged Donna's red jacket, there in the long hallway of the Holiday Inn. Twice, sleepy guests had complained by opening their doors and threatening to call the manager. This caused even more mirth as Howard covered his head with Donna's jacket and listened while she explained, between fits of giggles, that *she* was the manager.

When they finally found Howard's door, the unlocking of it had presented another kind of obstacle. Howard put both of his drinks down on the hallway floor and fished the card that was his key out of his pocket.

"How the hell am I supposed to open my door with *this?*" Howard had asked, as he held the card key up and peered through the holes in it. "This should get you a book at the library, not open your door."

It was Donna's turn to try, and she did so, giggling when she couldn't hit the slot. That was when Howard looked down the long corridor to see Wally and Larry, both peering around the corner, watching like voyeurs. The card finally clicked in the door.

"Fucking A!" Donna said, jubilant. She pushed the door open and then went with it, landing with a *splat* on the floor inside. Howard managed to help her up onto the bed before he went back outside to fetch their drinks. That's when he peered again down the corridor. There they were, Larry and Wally, their faces like two shiny moons glistening at the other end of the hall.

"Howdy, boys!" Howard shouted. He heard Donna laugh from within the room. He slammed and locked the door, still grinning to know that he had just become a legend in the lounge.

Donna sat up on the king-size bed and patted her hand atop the mattress.

"How do you sleep on this?" she asked. "I wasn't here a week before I had a new box spring and a Sealy Posturepedic delivered to my room." This made her laugh again, a giggle that seemed to be part hiccups, and part belch. "I charged it to the bastards who own this place." She reached for a Bloody Mary and tried her best to get the straw to go into her open mouth. But, as the key had done earlier, the straw kept hitting outside the slot. The more the straw turned away from Donna's mouth, the more she giggled. Howard finally staggered over and helped guide the straw home. Donna sucked on it loudly. This struck them as insanely funny and they laughed together, the camaraderie of drunks. But then, this had been their M.O. all night long. This was what had bonded them, along with their broken hearts: They had the same sense of humor.

"God, that was funny!" said Donna. She began unbuttoning her white silk blouse, oblivious to the spots of tomato juice that dotted the front. Howard sat in the lumpy chair and watched, ice clinking in his glass of rum as he swirled it. He imagined this action a sexy one, swirling one's drink as a woman undressed. That was until he spilled the rum on the front of his own shirt. Seeing this, Donna giggled again. She took her blouse off and threw it at him. It hit his chest and lay there, silk clinging to sweat. Jennifer Kranston flashed into Howard's mind just then. Ah, yes, Jennifer! She had been one of the first students he'd ever taught. She was young, but so was he back then. He was young and married. He had wanted Jennifer

Kranston every damn time she glided into the classroom. But he had denied himself that lovely student. He was her professor, after all. And, like Donna's ex-boyfriend, he had a wife and kids.

When Donna unhooked her bra and let her breasts fall free, Howard moved from the chair and onto the bed next to her. She was not a beauty, not like Jennifer, or Ellen. But she had become suddenly soft, and vulnerable, which is saying a lot for corporate America. Howard put his lips against the warm skin of her neck as his hand came up and touched her breast. He kneaded it gently and Donna moaned.

"God, I am so horny," she whispered. This almost stopped him. It seemed too much too soon, an admission that Ellen would never have risen to. Not even with Ben Collins. "I was supposed to go to Boston this weekend, to visit Anthony," Donna added. She stood, wavering a bit, and unzipped her skirt. Her breast was pulled from Howard's hand then and he let it go. What was it about this breast? In his drunken stupor Howard had been trying to put a finger on it, so it speak. And then, naked and soft and seeming to need him so, Donna stepped directly in front of his face. She lifted one of her breasts and guided the nipple into his mouth. Howard bit it gently, and then took both of her breasts into his hands.

"You look wonderful," he said to her, and she seemed to like this. She smiled as she leaned toward him and kissed his forehead. She slipped her panties down and kicked them away with one foot. Still standing before him, she reached for one of his hands and pulled it down between her legs. She quickly separated his middle finger from the others and then urged him to push it into her. He did so, and she groaned. It was all so different to Howard. Women had not been like this in his day, at least not the women *he* knew and dated. Where did these newer girls learn such things? He imagined Donna studying these maneuvers at some corporate seminar, a new strategy on how to fuck the American consumer. *First, trainees, you separate the fingers . . . watch closely now as Paula Simms, our marketing director, demonstrates.* But, dammit, Howard Woods had come of age in the early 1950s, when the Kinsey Report was still dripping its controversial ink. When Howard first got a copy of the report and read the entire thing from cover to cover he was changed forever. He could no longer look at Ralph and Agnes Craig, who lived next door in the beige ranch-style, in the same way ever again. He couldn't even look at his own parents the same way. His conclusion back then was that there should be a law about people over thirty having sex like that. But hey, it was the 1950s. Maybe there *was* a law.

"Wait for me," Howard said to Donna. He took off his shirt and then his pants, tossed them both onto the lumpy chair in the corner. Wearing only his boxers, he pulled her down onto the bed and again took her left breast in his hand. He lowered his mouth to it. What was it about this breast? He tried not to think this thought, for he could feel the stiffness of his penis, its intensity against the warmth of her leg. He had already learned, somewhere in his midforties, not to deny the penis its urgency. But the more he squeezed and kissed Donna's breasts, the more they felt as if small, hard balls were rolling about just below the skin. And then he knew. The breasts weren't real! He was holding two sacs filled with some liquid. So this is what Pete Morgan had been complaining about, all those mornings and afternoons on the golf course, about those women he had met and bedded in middle America. *It's like holding a couple bags of putty,* Pete always said. *I tell you, a tit just isn't a tit anymore.* But Howard had paid little attention to Pete's lamentations, assuming he, himself, would never know what two bags of putty felt like, happily married to Ellen as he was.

Donna reached down and began fumbling with Howard's boxer shorts.

"Get these off," she whispered. "Hurry."

Howard kicked the boxers off. She reached down and put her hand on his penis, began stroking it.

"Nice," she said. How could he help it? He was proud of himself in that instance, when he dared pause to think of it. *Yes sir, the good old pump nature had given him. Nice, indeed.* Suddenly, Donna was up on all fours, her head tossed back to look at him.

"Put it in," she said. Howard could only stare. *Doggy-style?* He hardly knew this woman. It had taken Ellen and him years to build away from the missionary style and toward something more, well, *secular*.

"Hurry up," Donna ordered, the corporate side of her suddenly returning. Howard was afraid she might bark, or even bite, considering the style of sex she was demanding. He crawled up behind her and peered over her shoulder. She was swaying back and forth then, a soft humming noise coming from her throat. He put one hand on her waist and inched in closer. He reached down and lifted his penis with the other hand. At least *it* didn't seem intimidated by this young woman. He leaned forward on his knees as he entered her. She opened her mouth just then and let the hum escape, like it was some kind of chant, a mantra maybe. Ice rained down suddenly outside the door. *Clink clank clunk.* Howard shut his eyes. He tried to block out both the ice and Donna's incessant hum, which was now beginning to sound like an outboard motor. The quick sex had somehow quelled the merriment of the alcohol. *How had it gotten this bad this fast between Ellen and him?* that's what kept running through his mind as he pushed forward, Donna pushing back to meet him, a hum with each thrust.

Suddenly, there came a great hiss, one which Howard knew didn't originate in Donna Riley's throat. He had heard a milder form of this hissing before. But where? Donna hummed again, as if answering even his thoughts. And then he remembered! In that instant, as if knowing he was onto it, the box spring crashed through and onto the floor with a thud. Howard was pulled free of Donna and thrown up over her head, as if they were two dogs being separated by some invisible animal control officer. His forehead hit the headboard with a dead *thud.*

For a few long seconds there was only silence as they both realized fully what had happened. *Clink clank clunk.* The ice machine seemed more busy than usual. And then Donna laughed again, a long bleating laugh. But this time, Howard sensed a sadness in the laugh. It was the kind of laugh he had always reserved for Charlie

Chaplin. Sure, the Little Tramp was funny, but how can you fully laugh at someone so hungry they boil and eat a shoe? Donna laughed that kind of pitying laugh. She arched her back, her elbows poking into his stomach, and he realized then that she was pinned beneath him. He did his best to lift his head from the headboard and flop over onto his back. The coils of the mattress hissed again as they accepted the weight of him. Donna pushed steamy, wet hair back from her face and looked over at him.

"Howie, you ought to order yourself a new Sealy," she said. "And move away from the ice machine." Howard only nodded. He wondered if he could charge a new mattress to the bastards who owned the place, as Donna had done, and especially now that it appeared he would be living there forever. Now that he was flat on his back, he was coming to realize just how drunk the two of them were. Donna turned on her side then, away from him. In no time small snores were floating over to Howard, coming from the same throat that had produced the infernal hum. He closed his eyes. It seemed if he didn't, he might cry, and that might wake the young woman who slept soundly at his side. He wouldn't want that. Tomorrow would bring with it a sad reckoning, and she would need her strength to meet it head-on. *He's gone back to his wife and kids.* Funny, but that's exactly where Howard Woods wished he, too, could go.

When Howard opened his eyes, it was almost dawn. He had forgotten to pin the curtains and now light was leaking in through the perpetual part in the center, a thin stream of pink and yellow sky. He could see that the sparrow was already busy coming and going from its nest in the Holiday Inn sign. Donna Riley was gone. The only proof that she had even been there were the two glasses sitting beneath the pineapple lamp, tomato juice and lipstick smeared around their rims. Howard brought a finger up to touch his right temple. There seemed to be a small bell beneath the skin there, one that was being steadily rung. He hoped his face wasn't bruised, remembering that he had not tried to break his fall against the head board. He stared up at the ceiling, more distant now that the box spring was flat on the floor. *How had it gotten this bad, this fast?* He decided he would wait for sunrise before he dragged himself up and into the shower. As he looked down at his white arms, his hairy white legs, a terrified notion hit him. What if he saw, engraved and swollen in his skin, a dozen or so tattoos? He had read about sailors, drunk to the gills, engaging in all sorts of self-mutilations. He lifted his arm, afraid he might see a big corporate-red heart with EVA BRAUN written inside it, next to MOM. But his pale skin was still unblemished, except for the marks and ravages of time. He turned his head to watch the sparrow.

"Ellen has a cell phone," Howard said aloud.

"I've been through hell, Jake. It's been simply hell."
—Robert Cohn, *The Sun Also Rises*

eleven | **REALITY**

It looked like a slow lunchtime at Chuck E. Cheese, and Howard was thankful. The last thing his throbbing head needed was even more kids jumping into a pile of colored balls, or zapping space invaders, or hurling softballs at target holes. While he waited outside in the parking lot for Eliot and Ellen to arrive, he took his travel packet out of the envelope and opened it up. *Only 80 miles east of Bilbao, across Euskal Herria, as the Basques call their mountainous region, is Burguete, a town that has long depended on tourists and is most eager for more.* Howard wasn't surprised to read this. This was where Hemingway had stopped to do some trout fishing before he himself ran the bulls, back in 1924. And that's how Jake Barnes had come to go fishing there with Bill Gorton, in *The Sun Also Rises*. Reading these words, Howard now wished he had allotted time for a quick trip to Burguete. Hell, why not take the time? He could rent a rod somewhere and do a little trout fishing. And since he'd been unable to find the Hotel Montoya, he would seek out the Basque hotel where Papa had stayed, that charming place three thousand feet above sea level, the little house with the low ceilings and oak-paneled dining room. Howard had read that chapter of the novel just days before. It was so chilly that high up in the mountains, even for a June evening, that Bill Gorton played the piano to keep warm. What was it they had eaten? *The girl brought in a big bowl of hot vegetable soup and the wine. We had fried trout afterward, and some sort of stew, and a big bowl full of wild strawberries.* Howard felt quite certain that Ellen would love that little hotel, knowing her penchant for places quaint and cozy. That's why he had driven out to Bixley Travel Agency, on his way to Chuck E. Cheese, and purchased an airline ticket for *Mrs. Ellen Woods,* who would be flying on American's flight 5743, from Bangor's International Airport, on the third of July, to Boston, where she would connect to a British Airways flight to London's Heathrow. From there, it was straight on in to Bilbao Airport, in España. And luck was with him, for on all the flights the seat next to *Mr. Howard Woods* was available.

Howard felt his stomach growl before he heard it. He closed the travel packet and looked at his watch. What was keeping them? And that's when he saw Ellen. She must have driven in and parked while he was absorbed in the hot vegetable soup, the fried trout, the wild strawberries. Now, she and Eliot were striding across the parking lot, Ellen's blue sweater draped gracefully from her shoulders, Eliot keeping pace at her side. Ellen was wearing sunglasses, and a yellow blouse, a soft pastel color. Howard felt such emotion rush up inside him just then. He had loved this woman for so many years. At the front door, Eliot stopped to tie his shoe while Ellen waited, looking down at the top of her grandson's head, a smile on her face. She was wearing the faded blue jeans that still made her ass look the way it did back in college. At least to Howard it did. Ellen always denied this, but he knew she liked hearing it. He should have said it more often. He *would* say it more often. He watched as they disappeared inside, and then he opened his car door.

Once his eyes adjusted to the inside light, Howard spotted them instantly, at a table over by the stage. Ellen was just draping her sweater around the back of her chair, and Eliot was studying the menu. Howard took a deep breath and then walked toward them. Eliot saw him first, his little face registering instant surprise.

"Grandpa!" he shouted.

"Howdy, campers," said Howard. Ellen looked up then, her own kind of surprise filtering across her face, one followed by a quick flash of anger.

"You're having pizza with us!" Eliot added. "Cool!" Howard patted the boy's head and then quickly pulled out a chair, sat down. Ellen seemed about to say something, perhaps even summon a bouncer who would then bounce Howard out onto the sidewalk. But Eliot, bless him, prevented her from doing so just by his own innocence.

"This is great!" said Eliot, his face guileless and happy. "I was only pretending that I didn't care, but I did. I wanted to spend my birthday with you both." And with that, the boy bounded out of his chair and hugged Howard tightly, his small arms encircling his neck. Then, he went to Ellen and did the same. At least it made Ellen smile. She reached for her purse and took out a roll of quarters, gave it to Eliot.

"Now go slowly," she said, "or you'll be busted in no time." Eliot nodded a promise.

"I want pepperoni on my pizza," he said, and then he was gone. Howard could see the top of the boy's head as he went from one machine to another, deciding at last on a game of Asteroids. The waitress appeared and Ellen ordered what they always ordered, a large pizza, half vegetarian, half pepperoni and cheese. When the waitress left, Ellen simply stared at Howard. She had always done this when she was furious with him. And he imagined that she was now as furious as she would ever get.

"How are you doing?" he asked.

Ellen waited for a time before she answered.

"You must have had quite a night," she said. Howard thought about this, then nodded.

"I did," he said. "It was tough seeing my whole life packed up in boxes."

"It took me some time to erase the phone messages," Ellen said then. "I had no idea you knew all the words to The Bilbao Song."

Howard grimaced. He had sung the song on her answering machine? He didn't even remember it. "And it's nice that you took the time to teach it to the younger generation. What was her name? Donna, I believe."

He had let Donna sing the song, too?

The waitress put a Diet Coke in front of him and Howard almost hugged her, thankful for a moment's break. Ellen picked up her own Diet Coke and sipped at it. Howard noticed that she had no trouble finding the straw. He felt warm shame fill him just then. The waitress left.

"I'm sorry for turning up like this," Howard said. "But I wanted to see you." He waited. Game machines rang out from around the room, asteroids being fired upon, gophers eating their way up through tunnels, Pac men gobbling fruit, froggers frogging. The laughter of the children made Howard's head ring.

"I see you've got a nasty bump," said Ellen. "I trust there won't be some kind of lawsuit accompanying it. You know, statutory rape, for instance."

Howard felt a smidgeon of his own anger rise up then.

"I didn't ask for this," he said. "I was just settling down to retirement when you drop a bomb on me, in the middle of the night."

And then, as if someone had poured ice water all over him, moments from the night before flashed back to Howard Woods. He had not only let Donna leave messages on Ellen's machine, he had *insisted* she do so. What was that last one, the one she left as they made their way to Howard's room, before they played "Here, bulley, bulley," in the corridor, Donna's corporate red jacket enough to entice any self-respecting bull. Ice water, tons of it, rushed through Howard at that moment. *Oh, Howie, baby, oh that feels good, that feels so good, do it again, Howard, oh baby!*

It had seemed so damn funny at the time.

Eliot rushed back to the table just then and grabbed his drink. His face was flushed from the intensity of the game.

"I just beat my high score," he told Howard, who smiled at his grandson. He was such a handsome little boy, but even better, he was *kind*. There was something inherently good in Eliot, as if the best of his parent's genes had gotten together when they created him.

Before Eliot could go back to his game, the stage curtains suddenly pulled open and the house band at Chuck E. Cheese began a song. Eliot smiled and slid into his chair to listen. The waitress put a large hot pizza down on the table in front of them. They had done this so many times with Eliot, he and Ellen had. Howard had grown to hate every one of the mechanical singers in the Chuck E. Cheese band, but he had taken Eliot there for every special occasion, a good grade in school, a spring vacation getaway, Christmas, Valentine's Day, many times. The boy never seemed to tire of the place, so he and Ellen had always gritted their teeth and pretended to enjoy the mechanical band, and the roving host in the silly bear suit. Howard took a piece of pizza onto his plate and began to eat it. With his hangover, a thundering noise accompanied each bite he chewed. The Chuck E. Cheese band was blasting out Willie Nelson's "On the Road Again," and now Howard excused himself, pretending he had to use the bathroom.

Inside the men's room door, he leaned against the wall, waiting for the big mechanical bear, and the big mechanical rabbit, and the mechanical girl with the pigtails and freckles, and the mechanical boy who looked to be suffering from kind of mutative disease, to finish belting out the song. When he came back out again, Eliot was playing another game of Asteroids. Howard sat back down at the table with Ellen, who was resting her chin on one hand as she kept an eye on Eliot. He saw that her hair was a still a bit damp from the shower. Even from across the table, he could smell that natural yet perfumy smell of her skin. All around him, *zings* and *pings* and *pongs* and *whirs* rang out nonstop. It was as if someone had designed a Sartrian place called Hangover Hell, and now Howard had been sent there for eternity, to wait for Godot. He reached into his pocket and pulled out the ticket to Spain. He put it down next to Ellen's plate.

"What's this?" she asked.

"A ticket to Bilbao," he said, and smiled. "I thought that if you came with me, we could make it a retirement get-away. After I run the bulls, we can go sight-seeing."

Ellen stared at him, that sardonic look on her face.

"I've read up on that whole area," Howard said. He could feel balls of sweat rolling down the back of his neck. "There's this road called the Route of Don Quixote, named for you know who. There are even windmills along that route. Imagine."

Ellen stared at him.

"Okay," he said, as if conceding something. "If you come, I won't run the bulls." He took a deep breath.

Ellen stared.

"I want you to know that while I'm not ready to forgive you, I'm ready to forget," Howard added. He had practiced these words all morning. They had even seemed logical, almost sagacious, on the drive over to Chuck E. Cheese. Now, he had delivered them to her. He waited for her to speak, hoped she would, then was sorry that she did.

"You're amazing," Ellen said, softly. He hoped she meant this in a good way but something told him she didn't. She reached down then and picked up the ticket to Spain. She put it in Howard's shirt pocket, patted it, as if to say goodbye to it forever.

"You started this, Ellen," Howard said then. He wanted to say as much as he could before Eliot returned. "You and Ben started this."

Ellen had a soft smile on her face as she studied Howard's own features.

"Do you know how difficult it's been to be your wife *and* mother all these years?" she asked. "Find my papers, Ellen. Where are my shoes, Ellen? What's for dinner, Ellen? Did you iron my shirt, Ellen? Do we have any cornflakes, Ellen? Now I'm free Howie. So don't you worry about forgiveness."

She stood then, reaching for her sunglasses and sweater. He sensed that if he couldn't keep her a while longer that he wouldn't see her again for some time. Would she really get a restraining order against him? He hated to call her bluff on that one.

"I want to talk this out," Howard said. He was glad the guys at the bar wouldn't hear this, especially right on the heels of their respect for him, considering his conquest of the night before. And then he hated himself for even thinking this. "I still haven't signed the divorce papers," he added.

Ellen looked down at him for a few seconds, as if considering his proposal.

"I want some time to myself," she said. He could tell she was as sincere as she could be. "The blame is not all yours, I know that."

"Gee, thanks," said Howard. He had no intention of hiding the sarcasm, given her statement.

"But you took what should have been a private issue between a husband and wife and you turned it into an extravaganza. You rallied all the troops you could. I've seen a side of you I never knew existed, Howard, and it's a side I don't like."

"Ditto," he said. He stared down at the pizza on his plate.

"Life is a tough place," Ellen said then. "And that's what your problem is. Do you know why?" He shook his head, but he felt quite sure she was about to enlighten him.

"Your problem, Howie, is that you're a coward," Ellen said. She turned then, and walked away from the table. He watched as she paused at the Asteroids machine to say something to Eliot and then kiss the boy good-bye. Putting her sunglasses atop that cute Irish nose, she went out the door, with not so much as a glance back at Howard's table.

Before Howard could dissect her words, the curtains opened and the Chuck E. Cheese band was ready to sing again, this time "Tie a Yellow Ribbon." Eliot hurried back to the table to listen.

"Grandma says you're driving me home," Eliot said, excited. "Cool. I like your tiny car."

Howard noticed that Ellen hadn't bothered to pick up the check. Sure, he was annoying as a husband, not to mention a coward, but he wasn't too annoying or cowardly to foot the bill. He motioned to their waitress, who either didn't see him, or didn't *want* to see him. Howard put his Mastercard down on top of the bill and waited. He looked at Eliot, who was listening to the band.

"So how've you been, kid?" Howard asked.

Eliot drank some of his coke before he responded.

"I've been busy, Grandpa," he said. "David and I are building a Battlebot."

"A what?" asked Howard. He tried again to get the waitress's attention. She was telling some kind of wild story to another of the waitresses. Now and then she looked Howard's way, but went back to her tale. He could only hope she hadn't been at the Holiday Inn lounge the night before.

"Battlebot," said Eliot. "They're robots that you build to fight other robots. We're gonna kick butt with ours."

Howard smiled. Seeing the waitress again look his way, he waved the check in the air. She then went back to her story.

"Battlebots, huh?" Howard said. "You need any help, you just ask." Eliot considered this.

"David's dad is helping us," he said. "He's an engineer."

Howard nodded. Of course. What would a retired English professor know about artificial intelligence?

"So what else have you been up to?" Howard asked. He didn't want to pump the child—to use another meaning of that verb—but he was hoping to find out just how close the nuclear families were to blowing up, his and Eliot's.

"I been spending lots of time with Grandma now that she lives alone," said Eliot.

"That so?" said Howard, and felt instant jealousy. Before he moved into the Holiday Inn he, too, had spent lots of time with his grandson. Now he knew why. Patty and John were too damn busy in their own lives, which were spinning in opposite directions.

While Eliot trudged off to the bathroom, Howard took the check and walked over to his waitress. She seemed surprised that he needed her.

"I was on my way to your table," she said to him, defiant.

Howard couldn't help but remember the words he had just read. *The girl brought in a big bowl of hot vegetable soup and the wine. We had fried trout afterward, and some sort of stew, and a big bowl full of wild strawberries.* What had happened to the good ole days? To waitresses who came and went with bowls of soup and strawberries, nothing more on their minds than to please the guests? What was wrong with people?

"You were talking to your friend," Howard told her.

"Don't get rude with me," the young woman said loudly. Howard looked around, embarrassed. He was only trying to pay his damn bill. Was that a crime?

"What's going on here?" a voice declared from behind him. Howard swung around and looked directly up at a giant bear. It was the Chuck E. Cheese mascot, supposed to be Chuck E. himself, just as that clown with the orange hair was supposed to be Ronald McDonald. Were Americans now doomed to discuss company policy with the mascots? Howard could see the two of them, sitting down at some conference table, he with his usual rum, the bear with a warm glass of honey.

"I'm just trying to pay my bill," said Howard.

"This guy is being an asshole," the waitress told the bear.

"I am not," Howard insisted. He gave the bear a stern look. He had no intentions of backing down on this issue because, damn it, he was right. He could hear the guys in the bar now, Wally and Larry and Pete. *First he went to bed with Eva Braun, and then he wrestled a bear.*

"Listen, pal," said the bear. Howard could smell pepperoni and onions on the breath coming from behind the plastic snout. "We don't need the customers giving our waitresses shit."

"Are you people all insane?" Howard asked. He was sincere about this question. "All I want is to pay you the money I owe and then leave *her* a tip for being rude and ineffective."

"See what I mean?" the waitress asked.

The bear moved in close and peered down at Howard, the kind of threatening stance animals take in the wild. Howard realized that it must be very hot inside that furry get-up. After all, that wasn't

Chuck E. Cheese himself in there, but some pimply young man full of testosterone. Howard handed the waitress his credit card. But, damn it, he was only leaving a fifteen percent tip, whether she liked it or not.

Howard pulled into his usual Holiday Inn parking space, next to the big rental truck. He would have to call the rental company and lease the monster for a month, a kind of storage house on wheels. It would be expensive as hell, but he had no choice. Until the marital dust settled, or until he found himself a new home, where could he go with all those boxes? He was about to open the padlock on the truck so that he could crawl inside and dig around for the blue denim shirt he'd been missing in his life at the Holiday Inn, when he heard laughter. He looked up to see that Pete Morton was just coming out of the lounge. Behind him was Larry Ferguson, and Freddy "the Mattress Mogul" Wilson.

"We been looking all over the place for you," said Pete.

"Howard's been a busy man," said Larry, and winked.

Howard said nothing as he relocked the rental truck.

"Hey," said Freddy, his face brown as dirt. "How you been?" He put a hand out to Howard's and they shook, the two gold bracelets on Freddy's wrist jingling.

"If I ever need to buy a good mattress and box spring," asked Howard, "can you fix me up?" Freddy grinned, white teeth appearing in the brown field of his face.

"Can I fix you up?" asked Freddy, as if this were the silliest thing he'd heard since his wife had told him to give up the girls he hired to sell mattresses or she'd take half his empire. "I just got a new shipment in," he added, looking over his shoulder, as if maybe his wife's lawyer were spying on him. But Howard had to hand it to Freddy. He had not stopped bedding his mattress salesgirls, and he seemed to be doing very well with only half an empire.

"Get in your car and follow us over to Freddy's warehouse," said Pete. It wasn't a request, it was an order.

"Why?" asked Howard.

"Just trust me," said Pete. He looked at Freddy and they smiled, tossing a guy's look back and forth as though it were a football.

"It's a new kind of entertainment," said Freddy. He reached in his shirt pocket for his own cigar. "A little game to entertain you boys."

They rode one behind the other to Freddy's Mattress Warehouse, with Pete in the lead in his jeep, Freddy behind in his big cream Caddy, Larry in his older model Volvo, and then Howard pulling up the rear, top down on the little Aston Martin. As he watched them drive down the interstate, Howard felt a sudden sympathy for them all, himself included. They weren't afficionados, after all, the kind of boys Hemingway hung out with. Instead, they had become a kind of geriatric Rat Pack, Bixley's own answer to Frank, Dean, Sammy, and Joey.

Freddy's warehouse was an immense building piled high with mattresses of all kinds, cheap mattresses, expensive mattresses, white mattresses, blue mattresses. They were what made Freddy a mogul in the first place. Freddy waved the boys into his office at the back of the building. Once inside, he closed and locked the door. He pointed to what looked like a large video game. It came with wires attached to a helmet, a headset of some kind with thick lenses across the front, like goggles.

"There it is," said Freddy. "You're the only one who hasn't tried it, Howie. Even Wally took a break from the bar and drove out."

Howard accepted the headset from Pete.

"You ever hear of virtual reality?" asked Pete. "Well, here it is, baby."

"Virtual what?" asked Howard. The truth was that he was computer illiterate and intended to stay that way. Ellen was learning to e-mail, but mostly, they had been old-fashioned when it came to cyberspace and the information highway. Good books had always seemed three-dimensional enough to Howard.

"Virtual sex," said Freddy, again looking over his shoulder, even though he himself had locked the office door. "If this were in a bar in Boston, it'd cost you fifteen bucks a pop."

"Hurry up," said Pete. "I want to go again."

He reminded Howard of a kid waiting to ride the Ferris wheel. Well, why the hell not? He'd just come from Ellen's rejection of him, not to mention arguing with a bear, why not something to make him laugh? He fitted the helmet on his head and suddenly everything was dark. Pete put a rod of some kind in his hands.

"This is the joy stick," he heard Pete say, from somewhere out in *real* reality. "You'll see what it is once Freddy turns the thing on."

"Here goes," said Freddy's voice. Howard heard a click. And in that instant he saw before him a naked woman sitting on the edge of a bed. She wasn't a *real* woman, of course. Still, it was amazing since she looked so human. She wasn't moving, just staring toward the face of whoever might be wearing the helmet and goggles.

"Now lift your joy stick." It was Pete's voice, from that other place, that world of everyday problems. Howard did so and was stunned to see an enormous penis bob up suddenly in front of him.

"Whoa!" he said, and jumped back. He heard laughter from the boys, and wondered if the appearance of this monster had scared them at first too. Now the woman was moving in the virtual scene. Once Howard had operated the joy stick, she had lain back on the bed and opened her legs to him. A look of longing on her face, she was now reaching out to him with open arms, asking him to come to her.

"Hell of a game, ain't it?" Larry said. "Just put the airplane in the hangar and she'll put on quite a show for you. You'll also get five extra minutes playing time."

"Learn to control the penis," Howard heard Freddy say. "It's all in the wrist."

And then, Pete's voice again.

"We're gonna leave you alone now, buddy, you know, in case you end up with a free hand."

There was more laughter and then Howard heard the door to the office close. He imagined them all still standing there, watching, waiting. But he knew they were gone. Freddy had an asthma problem that could be heard from several feet away. Howard could hear him now, wheezing from the other side of the door. And Pete's voice was out there, too. And Larry's. He moved the joy stick to the left and the huge penis went with it, slowly. It must have been fifteen inches long if it was one. And it was real-looking, the true color of flesh. He wondered if a male model had supplied the graphics for it, the kind of guys who end up donating body parts to the Smithsonian. He didn't know enough about virtual reality. The girl, for instance, was she once a real model? She looked to be in her twenties, enormous breasts, full red lips. Her hair was dark and long and spread beneath her on the bed. Howard steadied the joy stick right in front of him and she again opened her arms to him. So that was it. Learn to balance and steady. He pushed forward on the stick and the large penis moved toward the young woman. This made her smile. She spread her legs wider and he could now see between them the redness of her, almost too red to be real. But then, she *wasn't* real. Howard pulled the joy stick back and this action caused the penis to loom up so quickly before his face that he jumped again. Then, he felt foolish. After all, to a spectator watching from the *real* world, he was a sixty-three year-old man standing there with a goofy-looking helmet on his head. He slowly guided the penis back down in the direction of the woman by pushing forward on the joy stick. *Is this a dagger that I see before me, the handle toward my hand?* Howard wondered what Macbeth would do at a time like this. With *this* in his possession, the poor sot could've defeated Macduff, beat him over the head out there on the heath until he expired.

This time when the young woman, luscious and fleshy, reached out for him, Howard suddenly remembered the prostitute, the one his Uncle George had taken him to when he was seventeen years old, a high school graduation present. "We're gonna make you a man, son." It had been his first encounter with sex, with a female who was also not real, at least not to Howard at the time. And yet, he had been afraid to touch her, afraid to enter her, as if a part of him might never come back out of her if he did. The prostitute, too, had seemed a fabrication, something planned as a joke by his uncle. She was like one of Macbeth's witches, created only to entertain the passers-by. Now, here was another woman lying on a bed before him, eager to have him take her, eager to offer up to him the millions of bytes it took for some godlike computer nerd, his own penis the length of a paper clip, to create her. Like the prostitute, this young woman was not a personality, not a woman with a past, a future, a woman with geraniums on her kitchen window sill, nylon stockings hanging to dry from the curtain rod in her shower, a woman with a dog, a cat, a penchant for old movies. She was simply arms, and legs, and vagina, created for his purposes, for his pleasure.

"I can't do this," Howard heard a voice say, and realized it was his own voice coming back to him from that *real* world, the planet earth, better known as The Big Landfill, back where all his problems were boiling and simmering on the surface of his life. He quickly took the helmet off and tossed it down on the chair near Freddy's desk. He hoped he hadn't hurt the young woman who lived inside, who waited until someone else came looking for her, the way Macbeth's witches waited on that cold and barren landscape. Howard opened the door to Freddy's office and stepped out in the bright sunlight. Pete and Freddy were standing there, waiting, smiles on their faces.

"I can't do that," said Howard. Pete frowned, not understanding.

"Geez, Howie," said Pete. "It's not like you gotta buy her dinner, or anything."

Howard went out into the sunshine of Bixley, away from the dark places where men have sex with imaginary women. He went flying into the fresh air and sunlight, spinning through town in the little Aston Martin. He knew now that *nothing* was real. Nothing can be counted on. His marriage wasn't real, not the way he had imagined it to be. The golf course wasn't real. Donna's breasts weren't real. Loretta's eyes weren't blue. The gold trim on the mirror behind the bar at the Holiday Inn was just paint. Even the ice in the ice machine was manufactured. It seemed the only thing left that you could depend on to be genuine, the only thing eternal, was pain. And maybe love, if you knew how to get it and hold on to it.

It was not until he pulled into the parking lot of Bixley Community College and shut off the engine that Howard realized where he had been headed. After so many years of driving out there, after so many mornings, he had gone like a rat in a maze back to some of the best days of his life. He paused for a time at the big front door before he opened it. Summer school had not yet started, and so he felt a measure of safety that he would not run into former students or colleagues. As he suspected, there were ghosts in the hallways. Ghosts were turning the pages of books long outdated. He looked in on Ellen's old room first, then the one where Ben Collins had substituted for Samuel Frist, thinking to find clues, perhaps, still embedded in the walls there. He even spent a few minutes gazing into the teacher's lounge, where the affair had sparked to flame in the first place. It didn't seem like a place to fall into lust, what with the tattered chairs and worn curtains, the walls a bleak lime color. *We were friends first, Howie, or it never would have happened.*

It was his own room that stirred him the most, *remembered him,* as if it were whispering: "Welcome back, Howie. Take off your coat and grab some chalk." It still smelled the same, a sterilized yet safe smell. On the blackboard he saw written: *For Friday. Tennyson. The Coming of Arthur.* The class must be reading *The Idylls of the King.* He turned and stared at the rows of empty seats, imagined faces from years gone by, all his best students reassembled from three decades, all wearing the fashions of the day: bell bottoms, miniskirts, polyester, denims, crew cuts, shags, French buns. And then he remembered Jennifer Kranston for the second time in less than a day, called her image up before his eyes, a Virtual Student, sitting at the desk she always chose as her own. It had been in 1969, his very first year of teaching, when he was thirty-four years old. Jennifer. *Jenny.* Who had wanted to be a poet, but who had died of a drug overdose in the early seventies. She looked up at him now, her soft brown eyes sober and staring. Howard felt a grip of emotion pull at his gut. His eyes watered.

"But o'er her meek eyes came a happy mist," he whispered, remembering his own love for "The Coming of Arthur." And then Jennifer was gone again, had only been the ghost of a memory. Howard walked down the aisle and stopped in front of the desk where she used to sit. Funny, but he had forgotten her for quite a few years now, her memory emerging less and less to confront him. Even the ghost of Hamlet's father must grow tired, weary of those cold, Danish winters, that icy suit of armor. Jennifer Kranston. Christ, but he had felt something in his groin every time she walked into the classroom. After all, he was only ten years older than she. And it was not just her love of poetry but the sway of her ass that had pulled him toward her. And those perfect, round breasts, back when you could be almost certain that breasts were *real*. Howard could tell she wanted him too. He knew this in that part of him that knows such things, that *natural* part, the one that drove even dinosaurs to mate while gnawing at each other's necks, rending flesh and smashing trees. *That* part. Jennifer wanted him, too, and would have been his had he flicked even one of his fingers. But he hadn't. And it was because of Ellen. And the kids, those babies he had chosen to create during those hot nights in bed with his wife. Howard felt overcome with sadness. It *was*, wasn't it, because of Ellen and the kids? Or had he been afraid of Jennifer, too, the way he had been afraid of the prostitute, afraid, and yet ejaculating almost instantly into her warm, anonymous hand. The way he was afraid of Donna Riley's silicone breasts, of the Virtual Woman, reaching out to him from a blur of white computer blanket. The way he was afraid of Pork Chop Hill, the Bay of Pigs, the Mekong Delta. But he had fought his skirmishes and battles and wars in the classroom, hadn't he, and he'd been damn proud of it. So he had not taken Jennifer Kranston to a motel in Buffalo, or in Bixley, or anywhere, no matter how much poetry she had memorized. And he had prided himself on that for quite some time, until Jennifer learned a new poetry, *Hell no! We won't go!*, and went off to protest another war Howard wouldn't fight, her new Afro hair grown frizzy with the electricity of life, her fingers perpetually forming a peace symbol. Until she took too much *something* one night and then died from it. Maybe it was an overdose of passion, a surfeit of *life*, all those things Howard had avoided as he plodded onward in his own safe existence.

He traced a finger along the edge of Jenny's old desk, tried to imagine how her breasts would've felt, *light*, probably, at least compared to a sack full of silicone. Or even compared to the heaviness of Ellen's own breasts, breasts that had nursed their children. He remembered how Jenny used to look at him, that inviting look, her arms loaded down with books simply to impress him, books on Shelley and Keats and Tennyson.

"But o'er her meek eyes came a happy mist," Howard said again, his finger still moving, a blind man reading Braille, still tracing the old energy of the desktop. "Like that which kept the heart of Eden green, Before the useful trouble of the rain." It was all somehow connected, wasn't it? Tennyson was certain that Camelot was unblemished and doing just fine until evil seeped in. And that evil was adultery, adultery committed by Lancelot and Guinevere. But Howard had never agreed with Tennyson. He had even told his class so, back before the adultery had happened to *him*. Passion wasn't evil, he'd maintained. Tennyson was too much a representative of that dominant Victorian social class. Too sentimental, too intellectually shallow, too narrowly patriotic. But this was at a time when American liberals had just bitten firmly into that wonderful and crazy apple of the 1960s, a full century after Tennyson's own 1860s. But Alfred's *sixties* had been a crazy time, too, a time when science was kicking the pants off religion. *Before the useful trouble of the rain.* If he had believed that, if Howard had disagreed with Tennyson, then why didn't he know what it was like to press little Jennifer Kranston onto her back in some motel room?

"Accountability," Howard whispered aloud. "We need to be accountable, that's why." But he knew that maybe that wasn't why. Maybe it was because he was a coward, after all. Afraid of passion. And now he hated Ellen Woods, hated her for having the courage of *his* convictions, for marching onto a battlefield where he, Howie Woods, had never trod. Ellen had seen the blasted elephant, no doubt about it. Ellen was a goddamn soldier. A bell rang loudly, and Howard jumped. But then, there couldn't have been a bell. It was summer. The system had surely been turned off. But he had heard a bell, hadn't he? Was it real? Or was it Memorex? For thirty years Howard Woods had jumped to bells like some well-behaved Pavlovian dog. Bells ringing to announce cheese. Bells ringing just for the hell of it. Maybe Ellen was right this time. Maybe the two of them needed a break from their marriage, from each other. He would miss her. No, goddammit, he would mourn her every day. But what else could he do? Howard lifted the top of Jennifer Kranston's desk, then let it drop with a heavy thud that echoed in the empty room, bounced at him from all angles, no bodies there now to absorb the sound waves. Empty. But even ghosts need a day off. Sometimes, ghosts even retire.

By the time Howard Woods strolled into the Holiday Inn lounge the mood among the Happy Hour regulars was downright festive. Celebratory might be the better word. To Howard's astonishment Larry Ferguson was behind the bar, fixing himself a drink, the jukebox blasting away in his stead. Wally was having a martini while entertaining two attractive women at a table over in one corner. Howard could hear him all the way across the room, giving them his beloved martini chant.

"Oh, perhaps it's made of whiskey, and perhaps it's made of gin," Wally was saying, "perhaps there's orange bitters and a lemon peel within, perhaps it's called martini, and perhaps it's called, again, the name that spread Manhattan's fame among the sons of men." The women clapped, enjoying the free show.

Howard walked over to the bar and stood there. The place looked one step away from bacchanalian frenzy.

"What's going on?" Howard asked Larry, who beamed as he poured Howard a rum.

"Free at last, free at last," Larry told him. "Thank God Almighty, we're free at last."

Howard looked over at the stage. Pete Morton was just turning on the microphone. It reverberated loudly, a deafening feedback that caused Howard to wince.

"Eva Braun quit," Larry said, putting the drink in front of Howard. "She packed up her whips and chains and left about an hour ago for Boston."

Howard had a sudden vision of Donna, up on all fours, her head tossed back, her throat humming. The truth was that he had liked her. He had liked the soft part of her that she kept covered up, down beneath the coarse red jacket and the silk blouse, the innocent part.

"Hey, Dick-in-a-Splint!" Pete shouted into the mike, at Howard. Glasses shook on the shelf behind the bar. "We don't know what you did to that poor girl, and we don't care. You have rid the lounge of its scourge and for that, sir, we salute you!"

"Darling, I've had such a hell of a time."
"Tell me about it."
"Nothing to tell . . ."
—Brett and Jake, *The Sun Also Rises*

twelve | **THE DISCOVERY**

Howard was having his morning coffee when he opened the first of his two letters from the Ford Motor Company. It appeared that while Ellen Woods didn't want him back, Ford did. The large American auto maker seemed most anxious to *probe* him yet again. *Dear Howard,* the first letter began. It seemed that he and Ford were now on a first name basis. This was good. This was an improvement. *Performance Ford would like to thank you once again for acquiring your 1995 Ford Probe from our organization. We now need to purchase several 1995 Probes before November 16, of this year in order to fulfill a special used car interest.* Did they think him daft? Did they really think he believed this nonsense? *As General Sales manager, I would like to offer you an opportunity. We will exchange your 1995 Probe for a new 1999 Probe with a monthly payment that fits your budget. Please stop by with this letter before November 16th and allow me to assess the value of your Probe.* Howard would allow his testicles to be stretched on a rack before he would do this. Did they also think him without dignity? It was signed Justin Hobbs and ended with a P.S. It would appear that big corporations also forget to include things in the bodies of the thousands of letters they mail out daily. Did they think all car owners brainless? *P.S. If you come by before November 16th, you will receive a free lube job, as well as an oil and filter change.* He scrunched the letter into a ball and tossed it into the trash can next to his bed. He had a good mind to put a rubber glove on his right hand, smear it all over with Vaseline, storm into Bixley Performance Ford, and give Justin Hobbs his own free lube job. Bastard.

The second letter was less personal than the first, more hyped. *Go ahead and throw us the keys to your 1995 Probe and catch the keys to a brand new Ford, with little to no money trading hands! That's right, Howard! Little to no money down!* Had Ford become some kind of Sugar Daddy? Howard imagined that this was the kind of language Freddy the Mattress Mogul used on his sensuous female clerks. *That's right, girls! A brand-new mattress, with little or no money trading hands!*

Howard tossed this letter into the trash can as well. He got out a sheet of Holiday Inn stationary and found a pen. *Dear Justin Hobbs, and Ford Motor Company,* he wrote. *You hurt me too deeply to make it up to me now. I wouldn't stop by Performance Ford for a free BLOW job, much less a lube. I'm sorry, but you should have thought of this back when I couldn't get you to answer my phone calls. Now, if you continue to stalk me I shall seek some kind of restraining order. Get a life. Get some closure. Sincerely, Howard J. Woods.*

He would mail it on his way to the library. His intentions were to drop by the mall first, for an hour or so. He had some quick shopping to do. After all, it was already the 29th of June, and since Ellen wouldn't run off to Spain with him, he was back to Plan A. He'd be leaving for Bilbao in four short days. He needed new tennis shoes, some khaki pants and underwear that weren't pink, a jacket, socks, the accoutrements one must have in order to be an skillful dodger. He thought it might be nice if he also wore a white shirt, around which he would wrap a red belt. That way, he would blend in well with the other Sanfermines. And a new pair of jeans, what the hell. Howard hadn't worn jeans in public for almost thirty years. He had an old, battered pair that he pulled on now and then for yard work. They were nice and soft, all broken in. He wondered if, at age sixty-three, he would live long enough to break in a new pair. But hey, the sky was the limit. With the excitement of the trip dangling again before his eyes, he was feeling his old energy seeping back. Donna would be proud of him. At least *fifty percent* of his time was now employed in thinking of bulls, and not his penis.

And Howard was thinking of his family again. With his departure day so fast approaching, he phoned John and asked if they could meet for lunch. Given his own marriage seemed to be over, Howard hoped he might still work some magic in John's. But John Woods had a full plate that day, or so he told his father.

"What about day after tomorrow, Dad?" John asked. Howard heard that important buzz of people in the background at John's office. Busy. Employed. Again, he couldn't help but feel a quick resentment. But soon, soon, he'd be busy himself, even if it *was* in extracting a bull's horn from his ass, as John had once predicted. "That'll still give me a couple days to talk you out of this foolishness," John added.

Howard addressed the envelope to Bixley Performance Ford, then sealed it. He put the letter aside and took a drink of coffee. Then he picked up the small box that was lying next to him on the bed. He had made this special purchase on his way back from the college, a few days earlier, on the heels of his meeting the virtual woman, of remembering Jennifer Kranston, of visiting his old classroom where the past lay like dustballs in the corner. He had pulled into a Radio Shack, on the spur of the moment and purchased a couple of needed items. He had even taken the time to sign up for some kind of long-distance service that would activate the thing, make it official. Now, he opened the box and took out the owner's manual.

Congratulations! You are the new owner of a dual mode cellular phone, which means you can automatically switch between digital and analog.

He had no idea what that meant, nor did he care.

It was just past eleven o'clock when Howard arrived at the library. He told the librarian exactly what he was looking for, an obituary that would've been in the newspaper during the last days of May. The librarian disappeared. In less than five minutes she was back with newspapers from the last three days of the month. Howard chose a table over by the water fountain, a more private spot, and spread open the first paper. A man named Ben Freedman had died in Bangor, but surely Ellen hadn't slept with *him*. No Ben Collins in the second issue either, but there he was, in the obituaries for the final day of May. *Benjamin Lloyd Collins, 61, of Kittery, died at home after a long illness.* The bastard! There was no photo of Ben, and that was one of the things Howard had been curious to see. *He is survived by his wife, Vera Collins, also of Kittery.* Vera. So that had been her name, not Sheila, not Shelley. He read the rest of the piece with interest. Ben had served in the Air Force, had received his higher education at Boston University, had been a professor of history, lastly at the University of Southern Maine, had been a member of the Kittery Bridge Club, had had two children, a son and daughter, and seven grandchildren. Services were held at a local funeral home, but friends were asked, in lieu of flowers, to send donations to the Cancer Society. That was it. The last chapter of Ben's life, short and sweet.

Howard looked at his watch. Pete would be just arriving at the golf course now, just taking that first cigar out of his shirt pocket, lighting it up, leaning back against his jeep to enjoy it, knowing that Howard would arrive ten minutes later. Pete went early, had always gone early, so that he could smoke his stogie in peace. Howard folded the newspapers neatly and left them on the table where he'd been sitting. He nodded a thank you to the librarian as he went out through the heavy front door. Rain clouds hung in the east, but Pete had predicted they'd get a full eighteen holes in before the shower truly hit.

As Howard swung the little black Aston Martin onto I-95 and headed south toward Portland—from there, it would be just another forty miles to Kittery—he imagined that Pete Morton was crushing the tip of his cigar in the jeep's ashtray, knowing it would be waiting for him after the game. With his right hand, Howard reached for the new cell phone on the seat beside him. As he steered with his left elbow, he punched out a phone number. He looked up to see that he had swayed dangerously over into the passing lane. He quickly veered back. How the hell did people stay on the road and talk on phones at the same time? he wondered.

A nasal voice answered on the other end of the phone line. Howard recognized it instantly as belonging to Bertie, the groundskeeper. The only thing that excited Bertie anymore was his battle against the blob that was oozing out of the ground at the eighth hole. Bertie no longer saw the golf course as a haven for golfers, but as his own private battleground. His own personal hell.

"Bertie?"

"Yeah? What?"

"This is Howard Woods," said Howard. "I need you to do me a favor. Pete Morton is out in the parking lot, just knocking the fire off his cigar."

"So?"

"So, I want you to go out and tell him I can't make it today. Can you do that, Bertie?"

"I dunno," said Bertie. There was a little pause. Howard heard Bertie take a deep breath. "I'm busy here, Howard. I'm waiting for a call from a lab out in Salt Lake. I sent them a sample. They can study the gases. Maybe tell me just what I'm up against. And I read about some fish that'll eat the fucking algae. I was just about to call the seller."

Howard imagined Don Quixote, out tilting at the amber blob on the eighth hole, the blob tilting back.

"One more thing, Bertie," Howard added. "Make sure you tell Pete Morton that I called from my new cell phone."

Howard hung up. His other major purchase of that morning was also beside him on the seat, a nifty CD player. He had even brought extra batteries. He assumed the first set would last on the trip down, but now he would be covered for the four-hour drive back north. One drawback of a classic car, unless one wanted to do modern nicks and tucks, was that it had only the most prehistoric kind of radio. Back in 1962, when the little Aston Martin DB was rolling off the production line, cassettes and CDs were not even wild dreams about to be dreamt. Even the eight-track had yet to make its appearance. What had Howard been doing in 1962? Selling life insurance. Saving for his retirement. He imagined himself back then, his hair full, still brown by nature, his briefcase stuffed with forms as he chatted up folks about the importance of insuring one's mortality. His family healthy and growing—they had two children by 1962, with John still to arrive—he had bought a Rambler, blue with a white top and gray interior, one of the most enduring economy-styled cars that automakers were offering the American consumer. It would remain the Woods family car for more than ten years, which was a good thing, considering the long, lanky legs that would appear on John and Howard Jr. Like Donna Riley, the Rambler wasn't a beauty, but she had guts and determination. She came equipped with an inline six-cylinder engine that produced 138 horsepower, enough to drag a lanky-legged family of five down to the local Dairy Queen, where they could then jump out, slam four doors, eat five hamburgers, drink five Orange Crushes, use the bathroom, and then jump back in for the ride home. Howard had even *liked* the Rambler, with its push-button, automatic transmission. How had almost forty years dropped away? How had those lanky legs disappeared into the hairy legs of adult men? Those were the days when Howard had *longed* for retirement, imagining himself on the golf course daily while enjoying a life of hard-earned riches. Nineteen sixty-two. Out in the larger world, Mickey Mantle was still tearing up baseball, his own retirement just seven years away. The Cuban Missile Crisis had the world teetering on the brink of disaster, and John Kennedy had twelve more months to live. How the hell had so many years evaporated?

Howard plopped his new CD disc—*Andy Williams*, the two-disc Collector's Edition—into his new CD player and pushed number six. *That old Bilbao Moon, I won't forget it soon, that old Bilbao moon, just like a big balloon.* He was absolutely amazed to see that Andy had cut "It's All in the Game," as if there were no end to the knives Fortuna could stick into Howard's gut. But Howard Woods knew what bullfighters probably are born knowing: *Meet the horns head on.* That's the only way one can get past the fear. *That old Bilbao moon would rise above the dune, while Tony's Beach Saloon rocked with an old-time tune.*

Twenty miles south of Portland, he met the horns of the rain head on. He pulled into the first Texaco he saw and quickly put up the canvas top, snapped it into place. He found a local phone book, dangling by a chain to the outdoor pay phone, and flipped through the battered pages, over to the entries under Collins. There they were. *Benjamin and Vera,* at *257 Spring Street.* Howard paid the attendant for the full tank of gas, and then politely answered all the questions about the Aston Martin DB that he'd grown accustomed to in the past couple weeks: *Yeah, she's a beauty, no she's not too hard on gas, yes, it's the same car as James Bond's, no, she's got more power than you'd think.* He had even kicked the back tire a couple times as he talked, since, it was the kind of thing guys do when they're talking about cars. Instead of using their hands, like women often do, guys like to use their feet. And then, top up and rain pelting hard on the roof, he had piled back into the car and spun out of the Texaco.

With less than ten thousand souls in Kittery, it wasn't hard to find someone who knew where Spring Street lay. While Howard paid for his bottle of lemonade at the local 7-11, a sleepy-eyed clerk had given him precise directions. At Spring Street, things were quiet. Howard counted the uneven numbers down as he cruised to the end of the street. There it was, on the mailbox in front of a modest house that had a *For Sale* sign in the front yard. It was a one-story house, the kind of red-brick ranch built in the fifties that is so hard to sell in the nineties. By this time, the plumbing is tired, the way a person's veins grow old and thin. The carpet and floors are wrecked, the roof is leaking, the basement has a crack running from one end to the other. It takes a modern sensibility to keep an old house up and respectful, as Howard had done for the one back on Patterson Street. But he doubted Ben Collins was the house-loving type. And now Vera would be left to sell the aftermath.

Howard pulled up into the yard and killed the engine. He saw movement behind the curtain in what must be the kitchen, a woman leaning forward, as if over a sink, to peer out at him. Why couldn't he remember a single damn thing about Vera Collins? Had she been just a virtual wife? Nothing but smoke and mirrors? Is that why he hadn't noticed? His new jeans squeaked all the way up the brick walk.

When Vera opened the door, she seemed taken aback. She gave Howard a penetrating stare, as if desperately trying to place him.

"I thought you were from the real estate agency," she said. She appeared tired, no doubt having been kept awake nightly by the sorrow of her recent loss. Her short, dark hair had traces of gray here and there. Howard remembered now, seeing them again, how large and dark her eyes were. And he remembered that Vera Collins had been tiny, petite, especially next to Ben's impressive stature.

"I hope you don't think I'm rude, Vera," Howard said, and held out his hand. "My wife and I were friends with you and Ben, a lot of years ago." Vera's eyes stayed on Howard's face. Then she smiled.

"You taught at Bixley Community," she said, "at the same time Ben did." Howard nodded as she accepted the hand he was still offering her.

"Howard Woods," he said. "I taught in the English department. My wife, Ellen Woods, she taught in the history department with Ben." Now Vera's memory had been fully kick-started. She nodded, her eyes glazed with that *thinking-back* look, that veiled peep into the past.

"We only lived there for a year," said Vera. "And my memory isn't what it used to be."

"I heard, *we* heard about Ben," Howard told her. It was the truth, damn it. And then he lied. "I happened to be in Kittery, so I thought I'd tell you how sorry we are."

A sadness came over Vera's face just then. She held the door open to him.

"For heaven's sake, come on in," she said. "How is your wife? Ellen, you say? Yes, of course, I remember now. She had reddish hair, didn't she?"

Before Howard stepped inside, he had wanted to give Vera a chance to respond either for or against the mention of Ellen's name. For if Ben's widow knew about the affair, then Howard would apologize and leave immediately. He wanted no part of hurting this innocent woman any further. But, damn it, he had so many questions. Now it was obvious by her words that Vera hadn't been told. So much for Ben's honesty. Good old Ben.

Howard stepped inside the bastard's house.

What do you say after twenty plus years to someone you never had anything in common with in the first place? Very little. Vera told him all about the children, and then the grandchildren, whom she and Ben adored. Howard understood. He loved his own offspring. He produced pictures from his wallet to prove it to her, Eliot, and the five granddaughters. Seeing the young and smiling faces that had been in Howard's hip pocket, Vera insisted that he now look at the fruit of the Collins family tree. She reached under the coffee table and came out with a fat photo album.

"This is Ronny," she said, and pointed to the face of a small boy who was missing his front teeth. "His first school picture. He's our oldest grandson. And this is Janet, and Laura, and that's Stacy. And that's Shelly, Brian, and Sean. They loved their grandpa."

Howard politely looked at each photo. It struck him how all kids, like baby chicks, look alike: the shorn bangs, the gaps for teeth, the freckled noses, the cowlicks, the ponytails, the button eyes. These could have been his own family pictures.

"Nice," he said. Vera pointed to a photo of an old man lying back in a reclining chair, a blanket tucked like a shroud beneath his arms. Howard nodded as he looked at the ravaged face of a man he suspected was her father. Howard's own father had passed away, his mother too, over a decade earlier. Losing people is tough.

"That was taken over a year ago, on Ben's sixtieth birthday," Vera said. "It was the last time the entire family gathered, what with Lynn

Marie living out in Seattle." Howard said nothing for some time. He leaned in closer for a better look. This wasn't her father? Better yet, it wasn't *Ben's* father, for it did, indeed, look like Ben Collins. But this Ben was an old man, wrapped in that blanket and waiting to die, two plastic tubes running up into his nostrils. Howard suddenly realized what Vera was saying. This was Ben!

"Those darn cigarettes," said Vera. Her voice trembled. "No matter how hard he tried, he couldn't quit. Ben loved his Winstons. Of course, now we know how the big cigarette companies put all kinds of chemicals in the tobacco. I've heard it said that cigarette smokers are more addicted than cocaine addicts." She looked at Howard. His face must have given away his shock. "You didn't know that Ben died of lung cancer?" Vera asked. Howard shook his head.

"I thought he quit smoking years ago."

"He was always trying," Vera said. She smiled at Howard then, a pretty smile, turning her almost girlish. Of course. Vera Collins! How could he have forgotten her so easily? "He used to quote Mark Twain," Vera added. "'Giving up smoking is easy, I've done it a thousand times.'" She closed the book and slid it back under the coffee table.

"I'm sorry," said Howard. Vera thought about this before she replied.

"My son, Ron, says it was a blessing in disguise," she said. Then, as if sitting were too confining for such sad thoughts, Vera stood. "The emphysema started in his late forties. By the time he was fifty-five, he could barely walk. He spent a lot of years in that recliner." She looked at Howard. "I'll make some coffee," she said.

With Vera clinking saucers and cups in the kitchen, Howard sat on the sofa and felt utterly weak with the emotion that was coursing through him. Ben Collins, not as the rugged golfer who was fixed in Howard's mind, but as a man grown old young, confined to a chair and plastic tubing. It was an amazing discovery. He could hear Vera's voice as it drifted in to him from the kitchen, talking to him now about safer things, such as how she planned to sell the house and move out to Seattle to be with her daughter and grandkids.

"Do you take cream?" Vera asked.

Howard told her that he did, indeed. And then, before Vera reappeared in the living room, Howard quickly grabbed up the fat photo album and opened it again. He flipped past pink booties and bows, ballerina dresses and baseball uniforms, braces and casts and crutches, bathing suits and beach balls—the traces of Ben's children and grandchildren unfurling their lives—flipping through the pages as if they were years. And then, there it was, the photo of Ben, curled up like a leaf in a black recliner. Howard quickly slid the picture out from under the protective plastic and slipped it into his shirt pocket. A part of him, the jealous part, wanted to show Ellen what had become of her lover. Time had reduced him to a sickly, vulnerable mortal. And not only had Ben kept on smoking, but the cancer sticks had killed him in the end. So much for their bonding in the teacher's lounge.

Vera appeared with cups of coffee and a plate of cookies. She put the tray down on the end table next to Howard. He felt a spray of guilt just then, but ignored it. Something told him he *needed* that picture, needed it now and would need it even more later on. It was the only way he would be able to erase forever that image of Ben still carved in Ellen's mind, that younger Ben, that vibrant Ben. Besides, Vera had plenty of other photos. Howard had seen them. There were so many snapshots of the ailing Ben Collins at the back of the album that it looked like the sick ward at some hospital. Ben, in the last throes of emphysema, tubes running like spider webs into his nostrils. Howard promised himself that he would mail the photo back to Vera Collins one day. *Sorry, but I accidentally took this with me, Howard Woods.*

Howard stayed long enough for a cup of coffee and a chocolate cookie with some kind of sprinkles on the top. Then he bade Vera Collins good-bye. At the door he shook her hand, promising he would tell Ellen hello, and that if they were ever in Seattle, they would give Vera a call.

The rain ending, at least for the time being, Howard sailed up I-95 with the top down. Wind ripped at his face, his hair, but he didn't care. He almost couldn't hear the song floating about in the front seat of the little car, what with the torrents of air rushing at him. *No paint was on the door, the grass grew through the floor, of Tony's two by four, on the Bilbao shore.* He couldn't explain it, but he felt like a changed man. Lazarus come back from the dead. He had put the photo of the sickly Ben Collins on the dashboard of the little car, as though it were an icon of some sort, a plastic Jesus. As he drove, Howard managed to glance at it now and then, to study the tracks that time and illness had left on Ben's face. And that's when he came to think of that face as a kind of landfill where everything was obliged to finally wash to the surface, wrinkles, age spots, carcinogens, even *deceit,* for Howard could see a sadness in Ben's eyes. Every day until he died, Ben Collins had had to look at that sweet, lovely woman he married, knowing what he was leaving her in his will: Vera Collins had become the beneficiary of a lie. But had Ben been right to take his secret with him? Look what the truth had gotten Ellen.

Howard Woods felt a certain measure of peace settle down in his heart.

"Maybe it's the beginning for me," he thought. In less than a week, after all, he'd be in Pamplona. But when he came home a changed man—how can one run with bulls and not be changed?—that's when he would go to Ellen and tell her that the past was the past. After all, we make mistakes. We're human. Would he show her the photo of poor Ben Collins? Would he even want Ellen to see the ruins of a once fine man?

Damn right he would.

It was nine-thirty and Happy Hour was long over when Howard walked into the Holiday Inn lounge. A fresher hell had broken loose while he was gone, and now Larry Ferguson seemed on the verge of tears. At first Howard thought that Donna Riley had changed her mind, had returned to her white elephant and her sure-fisted monarchy. But it was worse than that. Someone had stolen Larry's pump. He had left it where he always did, tucked away safely in its duffle bag and leaning against the inside of his keyboard, where no one would see it. But someone did, for it was gone. Vanished. Larry had looked high and low in the lounge, under the tables and chairs, behind the curtains, the jukebox, the boxes piled near the bar. And then Wally had looked high and low. And then Pete and Freddy Wilson had turned up for an after-the-golf-game drink, Freddy having filled in for Howard at the last minute. Pete and Freddy had looked high and low. Then, they had all looked high and low as a team, asking the few customers seated at tables if they minded lifting their feet as Larry's flashlight swept across the rug. But no pump. They found quarters and dimes, room keys, a couple unused condoms, hair combs and barrettes, cigarette stubs, matches, several Bic throw-away lighters, business cards, and a high school class ring. But no duffle bag containing a vacuum pump with cylinder, tension rings, and personal lubricant.

"I left it here last night," Larry said, his voice shaky. "I was going home alone anyway, so I figured what the hell. We were all celebrating, and I didn't even think to check for it. Now, it's gone. I should have taken it with me. I shouldn't have left it like that."

"Why'd you even bring that thing in here?" Pete asked him. Larry shrugged. He looked like a helpless boy.

"I just never know when I might need it," Larry said. He was staring at the two plump women who were seated at a table near the stage, watching every move Larry made, his own personal groupies. "I just never know," Larry added.

It appeared, given the circumstances, that someone had actually purloined the pump. How else was it missing? It couldn't walk, not even with those tension rings to buoy it up. But Larry didn't want to phone the police. He wanted as few people told as possible.

"I have my reputation to think of," Larry said.

"Can't you just buy a new one?" asked Howard. It seemed reasonable since Larry often mentioned how the apparatus didn't cost much. Larry shook his head.

"It's personal," Larry said. "You just can't understand until you own one."

Freddy Wilson was picking through the broken bits of chips in the chip basket, and doing his best to dip the shards in the last of the salsa.

"I lost my dog once, when I was a kid," said Freddy. "It hurts like hell."

No one said anything for some time, a kind of male moratorium. A few moments of silence for the pump.

"The show must go on," Larry said then. He went back to the stage and took his seat behind the keyboards. He rolled up his shirt sleeves, then smiled at the listeners before him.

"I wanna do this song for the lovers out there tonight," said Larry, his voice gravelly with emotion. "And you know who you are." The two women at the table near the stage smiled big, identical smiles. Then, Larry launched into "I Won't Last a Day Without You," by the Carpenters.

At the bar, the boys huddled. Wally seemed to think the guilty party was one of the two salesmen who had been in the day before for Happy Hour.

"They were drunk as coots and requesting songs nonstop," said Wally.

Pete and Freddy suspected the two women sitting like fat mushrooms at that table so close to the stage.

"Look at the smiles on their faces," Pete noted. "They always return to the scene of the crime, don't they?"

Wally shook his head. Absolutely not.

"Those are the Baily sisters," said Wally. "Larry has had them both, even at the same time. I doubt the Bailys would hide the pump. They need it."

It was too much for Howard to think about. He had his own revelations to deal with. He ordered a rum from Wally and then reached inside his shirt pocket for the picture of Ben. He pulled it out and again studied the frail arms, the tubes disappearing into the nostrils like two railroad tracks, the shock of pure white hair.

He noticed for the first time an ashtray on the table beside Ben, within reaching distance, a thin curl of smoke wafting up from the cigarette in its belly. The poor sucker had smoked right up until the end. Howard decided then that he *would* come to terms with what happened during that spring and summer so long ago, those ten weeks between Ellen and Ben Collins. It was just taking a little time, running its course. That's all. Soon Howard Woods would lean to the future, the way a plant leans toward sunlight.

But who knew the future? Before it was all over, Howard might find himself back at Bixley Performance Ford, bent over, letting someone in greasy coveralls give him a lube job.

thirteen | **THE FALL**

Within four days of its disappearance, the pump and Larry were back in touch. At least, Larry had heard from the pump. Apparently, it was at Pioneer Village, down in Massachusetts, its plastic neck in one of the exhibition stocks. Larry was sitting at the end of the bar, his head in his hands, as if his own neck was in a vise grip. Wally put a letter in front of Howard, nodded for him to take a look. The envelope was addressed to *Larry "Pump Boy" Ferguson,* in care of the Holiday Inn Lounge. Howard opened the letter and found a postcard inside, along with a Polaroid picture. He looked at the postcard first. *Greetings from Pioneer Village, Salem, Massachusetts.* On the back, in a childlike scrawl, was this message: *Dear Master. I miss you but I'm having lots of fun. Love, Bator.*

"Bator?" said Howard. Larry let loose a long sigh at the end of the bar. It sounded like air being leaked from a tire, slow and painful.

"That's a bad joke," said Wally. "He doesn't call it that at all."

"I called it Petie," said Larry.

Howard picked up the Polaroid and stared at it. It was of the stocks at Pioneer Village, the punishment exhibit set up for the public to visit. There was the pump all right, out of its duffle bag and naked for the world to see. Someone had laid the round plastic body inside the circle where a neck is supposed to rest. *Have fun at the stocks and pillory* had been the description typed on the back of the postcard, and that seemed to be what the pump was doing. Howard looked up at Wally, who was looking over at Larry.

"Shitty thing for her to do," said Howard.

"He shouldn't have called her a fucking bitch before she left here," said Wally. "I even warned him. Didn't I warn you?" He asked this of Larry, who merely shrugged. "Let her go without a word I said. But no, you had to go and call her a fucking bitch and now your pump is in the stocks."

Larry took a drink of his beer. He kept his eyes on the yellowing photo of Lola Falana behind the bar.

"Still," said Howard. "It was a shitty thing to do."

Wally softened. "It was," he said. "And she *is* a bitch."

Larry seemed to feel better. He picked up his drink and went over to the jukebox, stood looking down at the selections without playing any. Once Larry was out of eyesight, both Wally and Howard let loose the laughs they'd been suppressing. These were silent, Marcel Marceau laughs, so that Larry wouldn't hear. Wally picked up the Polaroid shot again and he and Howard both stared. So Donna Riley had a sense of humor after all? Howard was glad that the boys now understood and appreciated this. Donna was a hoot, and despite the trouble he was in, he'd had one hell of a fun night with her, until morning had dawned with its sad reality.

"Listen, I'll see you later," said Howard. "I gotta get my stuff moved into Pete's cabin."

Wally had managed to stop laughing, especially now that Larry was on his way back to the bar. He nodded at Howard.

"Don't worry, Lar," said Howard. Larry sat again at the bar, motioned for another beer. "It'll come home."

As Howard left the lounge, he winked at Wally.

Pete's cabin was one of the larger and nicer ones at Bixley Lake, which lay just two miles from the Bixley town sign. Howard had gone there many times to fish, and had always enjoyed the chance to breathe in a little nature. During the summers, the other cabins filled up on weekends as the owners brought their families out to enjoy the water and sun. But weekdays were mostly quiet, and he was thankful for that. Pete was the one who had suggested the cabin when it became obvious to even the kitchen help at the Holiday Inn that Howard was now using the rental van as a closet, and sleeping in a room that was costing him a weekly rate of two hundred and ten dollars.

"I'd have suggested the cabin sooner," Pete said, as he and Howard drove the rumbling truck all the way around the lake, through the white birches and poplars and flashes of pine, to arrive at the two-room cabin. "But I figured you'd be going home any day." So had Howard. But he said nothing as Pete backed the orange rental truck up to the cabin's front porch and shut off the engine. It snorted a few times before it fell silent. The first thing Howard heard was the chickadees. He thought of the sparrow back in the sign at the Holiday Inn and wondered if it would miss him. If it ever knew that he'd been watching it for so many days, wishing it well. He had one more night to sleep in the room beneath the huge sign. He would say goodbye to the little bird by leaving it more of the complimentary breakfast bar's croissant, on the pavement near the base of the sign. So far, the sparrow had been one of the few not to complain about the staleness.

Pete got out first and slammed his door. Howard followed. Both men stood for a minute, breathing deep, listening, staring out across the lake. Squirrels rushed through the tops of the trees, scurrying away from the sudden noise. Howard felt a small breeze waft in from the water, thick with the threat of rain. It was cool and soft on his face, and he thought of Jake and Bill Gorton, fishing so high up in those Spanish mountains. This would be a good place for him, here at the lake. He should have come straight there until the issue was resolved between Ellen and him. But how did he know, that early dawn he had driven over to John's house, his suitcase bouncing around like a dog in the back of the little blue Probe, that a month later he would still be wandering about in the desert, next to the ice machine? Howard unlocked the back door of the truck and he and Pete began the chore once more of carrying boxes. *Murray's Clay Pot Kit, the Bread Company, Amazon Books, Lilly's Glassware.*

Pete had built an addition, a small alcove off the one bedroom, and had set up a toilet in there, one of the bio-degrading kinds. This meant his cabin was one of the few with no unsightly outhouse loitering behind it. There was a tiny kitchen, a sink with water running in from a tank outside, a table, a fridge, a small woodstove, and Pete had managed to add a sensible fireplace, something Carolyn had insisted on for ambience. It was rustic, but it was comfy. Howard felt a kind of welcome from the unvarnished hardwood floors, from the modesty of the table and chairs, the bed, the reading lamp, which was oil and had a wick.

When they were finished stacking the boxes inside, Howard and Pete broke open beers and stood drinking them out on the front porch. Summer was in full swing now and canoes dotted the lake here and there, along with an occasional small boat. Warblers careened in the tops of the trees, and red squirrels scurried across the roof. Howard assumed they were picking up the rainstorm that weathermen had already predicted, and this was the cause of their excitement.

"I'd worry about you out here with no electricity," said Pete, "but you'll be gone before cold weather hits."

"Let's hope," said Howard, "but these days I place no bets."

Pete smiled as he took his remaining cigar out of his shirt pocket and lit it up. Smoke curled away from the tip, caught the breeze and then vanished on the wind.

"Well, Thoreau," said Pete, "in that case, the woodpile is around back."

When Howard and Pete joined the Happy Hour regulars, they were all in a tizzy, the way birds get excited at a feeder. Another postcard had arrived that afternoon from Larry's pump. This time, it seems, the pump had visited the Old North Church, in Boston. On the back Donna had scrawled, *one if by hand, two if by pump.* Larry had tears in his eyes as he read the card for the fiftieth time.

"Fucking whore," Larry said. "She's pushing my back to the wall on this." The picture of his pump at Pioneer Village was now taped to the mirror behind the bar, in between William Cohen and Lola Falana. Next to it was a newer Polaroid shot: the pump on the steps of the famous Boston church, waiting for Paul Revere to thunder by.

"I say we form a special commando unit, go down to Boston and get the thing back." This was from Freddy Wilson. Howard had just stopped by room 17 to drop off his jacket. He would sleep there one more night before moving out to Pete's cabin. Once that happened, he had already made a promise to himself to visit the lounge once a week, maybe less. True, he and Pete had liked popping in after a game of golf for a quick, cold beer. But in the past almost month that Howard had lived in the building, he'd seen enough of Pete, of Larry, of Wally, of Freddy, of the other regulars. He wanted his safe, married life at Patterson Street back. He wanted to mean it the next time he said, "Hey, good to see you," to any of these guys.

He ordered his rum.

Two more days and he was on his way to Pamplona.

"So, how's it feel?" asked Wally, as he gave Howard the drink.

"What's that?" asked Howard.

"You know," said Wally. "I mean, shit, none of us thought you'd really go to Spain. But you're doing it, man. I gotta tell you, Howie, I'd be scared as fuck to run with them bulls."

Howard tried not to let his total appreciation show. He had waited years for this kind of scene, had dreamed of it since he was a boy, watching all those old Hollywood flicks in which men like Audie Murphy, and John Wayne, and Gary Cooper proved themselves. Men with Remingtons strapped to their lean hips, with machine guns rat-a-tat-tatting in their hands, with airplanes buzzing beneath them, or horses sweating against their chaps. Men with just their fists, but *men,* dammit. And they were smart men, too, back in those days. In the '50s you didn't have Arnold Schwarzenegger and Sylvester Stallone, you didn't hear dialogue like "Hasta la vista, baby!" and "Yo!" You heard intelligent speech, dammit, because men were *allowed* brains back then, to go with their dicks. Hollywood knew it. And the average guy on the street knew it, too. So why hadn't they seen the signs? The warnings of what was to come? Because the signs were there, too, if you knew how to look for them. Trouble was, few people did. And guys like Howard had no way of peering into the future and witnessing what would be the emasculation of the American male. Instead, American men felt a rumbling in their groin area, a trembling of what was to come. But the minute they got a glimpse of it, the minute they realized that maybe those *suburbs* they were so proud of, maybe all that growing *industrialization* that they were part of, those sleek automobiles that were getting bigger and longer by the year, maybe it was all going to shrink one day, the suburbs running out of space, the American car growing smaller and smaller until it became Japanese. Maybe it was going to suck them down the drain, where they would all disappear for good. But Howard and his ilk had ignored those signs. Instead, if he and the average American guy got nervous, all they had to do was rush down to the movie theater and buy a ticket to see Brando one more time in *The Wild One.* Or maybe Jimmy Dean, in *Rebel Without a Cause.* Then, they could sit back and breathe easy as Marlon and Jimmy played it all out for them on the big silver screen, made that tingling they felt lessen just a bit, made them forget about the castration that was sure to come, so many years down the road. They could sit back, with one hand into a bucket of buttered popcorn, the other hand dangling from the arm they had just thrown around the back of their best girl's neck, dangling as close to that pure, lily-white breast as was possible in the 1950s. That was the Holy Grail of Howard's generation, because all that mattered back then was getting that titty into your hand, holding it as though it were a soft white snowball. It was all that mattered because Marlon and Jimmy were looking out for the

American male. Marlon and Jimmy were watching the store. How did anyone know that Marlon and Jimmy were slowly being morphed into Arnold and Sylvester? How the hell could anyone dream?

"This is on the house," said Wally. He put another rum in front of Howard. Wally was a generous man again, now that Donna Riley was gone. "You cover your ass over there, you hear me, Howie? That's a dangerous thing you're doing."

"Yeah, well, what you gonna do?" Howard asked. An image of Babe Ruth flashed through his mind. He hoped he lived to witness the Red Sox lose the World Series one more time. He would be sad, but he would be alive. And Wally was right. He was really, really going to do it. He was leaving in the morning for the drive to Bangor. From there, it was on Boston, London, and then, *that old Bilbao moon, would rise above the dune.*

"Hey, Runs without Balls!" Pete shouted. Howard turned and stared at Pete, who was now *hitting* on five women, all seated around a table by the door, and dressed in what looked like waitress uniforms from a fast food joint, purple and yellow. They reminded Howard of a flock of exotic finches. They waved in sync, five hands, five big smiles. Howard had asked Pete several times about his wife. *Doesn't Carolyn ever miss you at home?* No, Pete had said, she doesn't. There you had it. Howard knew *why* she didn't miss him, too. He turned his back to the table. His plan was to say goodbye to the boys early. In the morning, he would rise with the sparrow in the sign, he would go for a mile-long run before showering and driving to Bangor. Well, maybe not a mile. A half mile would do it. He hadn't taken up running as he had intended earlier, and as Pete had instructed him to do. But there was still time. He would run in the morning, and then walk a lot in the airport at Logan while he waited for his international flight. And then, when he got to Pamplona, he would still have two days to get over his jet lag and get in shape. That ought to be enough time. How fast can bulls run?

Wally had begun entertaining a young couple who had taken lopsided stools at the bar, new, fresh faces on whom he could ply his wares, wares that were no longer appreciated among the regulars.

"There is something about a martini, a tingle remarkably pleasant," Wally recited as he made their martinis. "A yellow, a mellow martini, I wish I had one at present."

The woman giggled and the man nodded his appreciation of such fine talent. The phone rang behind the bar. With one hand, Wally put the martini in front of the man. He answered the phone with his other hand. Larry looked up from his keyboards, anxious, as if by some wild chance it was the pump, escaped from its captor and calling from a pay phone. *Help. I'm on the roller coaster at Coney Island.* But the call was for Howard. He thanked Wally as he accepted the receiver from him. John had promised to phone if he was able to make dinner that night, so Howard expected to hear his son's voice on the other end of the line. But it wasn't John. It was Ellen. She was crying hysterically. It took Howard an eternity to calm her down enough to find out where she was. *The hospital.* Why? *Eliot was there.* Why was Eliot there? Howard felt something breaking inside him. It was starting to come together. Ellen phoning him, of all people, at the Holiday Inn lounge, of all places. Howard waved his arm at Larry, a frantic wave, telling him to stop playing. Seeing Howard's face must have been enough for Larry, for he quit instantly. Pete and Freddy also saw that something was wrong. They stopped talking. Voices filtered over from some customers at other tables, but the bar had fallen into paralyzed stillness.

"I can hear you now, Ellen," Howard said into the phone. "Tell me what's wrong." And so she did. She told him. She was phoning from the hospital where they'd taken Eliot. He'd been riding his bike on the street in front of his house. Davie was with him. A car had coming flying down the street, the driver possibly drunk. The car had lost control, had driven up onto the sidewalk. It was dark blue, at least Davie *thought* it was. It struck Eliot. It went on its way. Eliot was still alive. But barely. And then, Ellen had hung up.

Howard stood for a few seconds, phone in his hand, staring at the photos of Bill Cohen and Lola Falana behind the bar, dusty and yellow, but still holding the old energy of the day they were taken. Eliot was still alive. Wally gently took the phone from Howard's hand. Pete appeared at Howard's elbow.

"My grandson is in the hospital," Howard said, his voice trembling the way Vera's had when she talked of her husband, Ben Collins. "He was struck by a car."

"Come on," said Pete. "I'll drive you out there."

When Howard arrived at the Bixley Hospital, he rushed in through the large glass doors of the emergency entrance, only to be informed that he must wait there for a doctor to come out and speak to him.

"I'd like to see my grandson," Howard had told the young woman at reception. She shook her head, and looked generally helpless with the situation. Before she could assure Howard yet again that it would be just a minute longer, a doctor arrived. He had been summoned to the front with the news that the grandfather was waiting in reception. This is how Howard learned that his only grandson, Eliot Lane Woods, had just died.

"Your son and his wife are still with him in Intensive Care," the doctor said, his voice soft and steady. "Do you want me to take you there?" Howard looked at this man's face, a face years younger than his own, a stranger to him. He nodded. He would like to go wherever Eliot was. The doctor put a hand on Howard's shoulder.

"Come on, Mr. Woods," he said. Howard heard all this through a blurred glass, as if the world had suddenly separated itself from him. He was conscious of Pete, there at his side, asking the questions Howard couldn't think to ask. *Where's Ellen,* being the first. She was somewhere in a private room, he was told, with a nurse who was trying to console her. Another nurse came along with Howard and Pete and the doctor, down the long, shiny hallway.

"I want to see Ellen first," Howard told this woman. He felt strong, warm tears on his face and realized they were running from his eyes. Could you cry and not know it? Pete put his hand on Howard's shoulder. The hand felt warm and heavy.

"We'll find Ellen," Pete whispered. The nurse opened a door that said *Family* in small white letters on a black sign. Howard wiped his tears away. He didn't want Ellen to see him cry. The nurse and the doctor stepped aside so that Howard could enter the room. Pete came with him. Inside, Ellen was sitting in a chair by the window. Her own eyes were swollen and puffy. On her lap she held Eliot's jacket, the *Florida Gators.*

"I'll wait out here in case you need me," Pete said gently, and Howard nodded to him. Pete left the room, closing the door behind him. Good ole Pete. He was a steady friend, steady as their golf game all those many years.

Howard walked over to Ellen and stood there, looking down at the jacket. It lay on her lap like something that had once been alive, but was now lifeless. He knew he *had* to see Eliot one more time. He knelt next to Ellen and she instantly dropped her head against his shoulder.

"Oh Howie," she cried. "How will we live without him?" Howard cradled her in his arms, rocked her body, touched his lips to her hair. It felt so good to hold her, and yet he could feel the weight of grief now in her body. The lightness of her had gone away.

"I don't know, sweetheart," Howard said. It had been a lot of days since he called her that, and yet, it was what he had called her for almost forty years. "Sweetheart, I just don't know," he said again.

Another doctor stepped into the room, a man not much more than thirty, his face grim with the news. Maybe death was still somewhat new to him, given his youth. He looked at Howard.

"I'm Dr. Moirs," he said. "Do you want to join your son and daughter-in-law?" Howard nodded, but Ellen shook her head. She lifted the jacket to her face and breathed the scent of it. It was already wet with her tears.

"I want to remember him as he was," said Ellen. Howard leaned over and kissed the top of her head. Then he followed the doctor out of the room and down the long hallway. At the room that held Eliot, several nurses had gathered outside, talking in hushed tones.

When they saw Howard, they fell into silence. A nurse with tiny diamond earrings in her lobes opened the door for him. He followed Dr. Moirs into Eliot's room. Patty was sitting on a chair by the bed, her head down in her hands. There seemed to be no life left in her. How can emotion actually have weight and substance? Howard wondered. But it did. Like Ellen, whose body now seemed sodden with grief, Patty appeared to be helpless beneath some great boulder that was pressing her down, pressing the life out of her. But Howard knew Patty was alive. He also knew that the weight was unbearable, that it might even kill her.

John was lying on the bed, his lanky legs stretched out before him, Eliot in his arms. Howard stepped to the side of the bed and looked down at them, his son and grandson, his seed, his offspring, his life. Eliot's little lips were already blue. His face was badly cut, his right eye swollen. A patch of hair had been torn from his scalp. But he was still that little boy, the gentle child with the big heart who loved pepperoni pizza and a game of Asteroids. John seemed to be humming some song, the kind of childhood lullaby parents sing to their kids. When he sensed someone standing near the bed, he opened his eyes. Howard put a hand on John's leg, the only way he could say *I'm here, son.* He wanted to speak those words, but he couldn't. It felt as if his throat had broken open, split with grief, no matter how hard he was trying to be strong for John and Patty. Howard reached out then and took one of Eliot's hands in his own. There was a cut on the hand, and a purplish swelling around Eliot's little finger. Howard realized then that the finger was broken. A flash of panic overtook him. He turned to the doctor, frantic.

"His finger is broken!" Howard shouted. "Somebody needs to fix it!" He heard Patty cry out, a anguished cry that tore through the room. A nurse came and put her hand on Howard's arm.

"It's okay, Mr. Woods," the nurse said. She patted his back. "It's okay." Howard turned to John, who had bent to kiss the boy that lay in his arms. John kissed Eliot's face, his forehead, his lips, his nose. He smiled down at his son. Then, he looked up at Howard.

"There were children, you know," John said. Tears ran out of his eyes and down his face. "Beneath those bombs we dropped on Baghdad," he said, for he could tell that Howard was confused. "There were children."

It was just before midnight that Howard and Ellen stepped outside the big glass doors of the Bixley hospital emergency entrance. Patty's mother and sister had arrived earlier and they had driven Patty and John home. Pete had already gone, after telling Howard he would leave the Aston Martin in the parking lot, in case Howard needed it. By the time Ellen and Howard walked out into the night, it was pouring a cold, summer rain. Howard held Ellen's cotton sweater for her so that she could slip her arms into it. They stood back out of the rain, side by side, and watched as lightning broke the sky in the east, and then came crashing to earth somewhere in the distance. So much power. So much pain. Howard looked over at this woman he loved so well, Eliot's grandmother. He saw it clearly, recognized it, identified the monster that had grown between them like a fungus, an algae that can't be stopped: *grief.* It either joins, or it separates for good. And now they were standing with nothing but pain between them.

Howard put his arms around her then, and Ellen rested her head against his chest. He was now glad, no *exhilarated,* maybe even *exalted,* that he'd crashed the birthday lunch at Chuck E. Cheese. What had Eliot said? *I was only pretending that I didn't care, but I did. I wanted to spend my birthday with you both.* Howard wished he could ask Ellen if she needed him to come home, at least for the next few days. Home was where *he* wished to be. But he wanted now, more than ever, to do what was right, an action that would help, not hinder. The Woods family had in an instant, and thanks to a stranger whose name they might never know, become a family that would need all the help it could get. As if reading his mind, Ellen looked up into his eyes.

"No, Howie," Ellen said, and he nodded. He understood instantly. That's what so many years of marriage can do for a man and a woman. It gives them their own language, like twins who speak gibberish. *No,* was all she had to say. But he knew how she meant it. It was not that she didn't love him, or miss him, or need him. It was that the monster between the two of them had not been slain. It had only been replaced with this new monster. And now Ellen wanted to share her grief with no one, not even him, not even Eliot's grandfather. She wanted to hoard her sorrow, as if it were a family heirloom. And so she turned and walked across the parking lot to her car. Wind and rain swept along the pavement, a blanket billowing at the heels of her feet, following along with her. Howard waited, wanting to see her safely inside the gray Celica. When she backed out of the parking lot and left the hospital, he followed, the storm beating on the canvas top of his little car, wind rocking it back and forth. At Patterson Street, he waited at the curb as the garage door went up and Ellen's car disappeared inside. He waited as the door came back down. He waited as the kitchen light burst on. Howard waited, outside, in the heart of the storm, and imagined how tiny the lights of his car must look on a wind-tossed sea. Two small yellow beacons. He hoped Ellen saw them out there in the dark, gray rain, and knew that she was being watched with great affection. He waited.

The bedroom light finally came on upstairs, all warm and yellow and safe. When it went out, twenty minutes later, Howard put the little car in gear and drove off into the wind and rain. This would mark the first night they would live and sleep and dream without Eliot Woods among them. He hoped Ellen had found comfort in the fact that a friend—not a *husband*—had watched her drive home. That a friend who loved her had waited for her garage door to go up and then down, for her bedroom light to blink on and then off. He could never bring Eliot back, could never bring back her grandson for her to hold. So Howard hoped she knew.

fourteen

GRIEF

The driver who killed Eliot had not been found. He was anonymous, a *virtual* driver, careering down the information highway, hiding out somewhere in Cyberspace. It wasn't that law enforcement hadn't looked. They were searching everywhere. They just didn't have much information to help them, other than a small boy's traumatized glimpse of a car that *might have been blue.* It was almost too painful for Howard to think of Eliot, to imagine him, and so he tried hard not to. During the three days that followed Eliot's death, as he waited for the family to arrive and for the funeral services to be over, he kept busy by unpacking the many boxes and arranging his things in the tiny cabin. It was the only way he could shelve the pain. He now had shirts and slacks hanging from hangers in the makeshift closet. He had the crude bookshelf bulging with his books. He had stacked the woodbox above the brim, just because it was empty. He had gone to the local K-Mart and purchased a few pans, a few forks and knives, some dish towels. He had even bought curtains, a means to discourage the morning sun since the only window in the modest bedroom opened to the east. He had stopped by the hobby department and selected a can of cleanser and some bottles of paint for the little toy car, the

'59 Galaxy. He had shopped at the huge IGA and picked up plenty of canned foods, some fruit and bread, coffee, and a few bottles of wine.

Howard was keeping busy, but he knew he couldn't put it off forever. When he wasn't being careful, he would find himself staring at the faces of drivers he met, in those blue cars that cruised along the highway. He stared at oncoming headlights, the silver sneer of a front bumper. Was that what Eliot had seen? Was that his last picture? There, that car just turning onto Fillmore Street! Was *that* the one that had run the boy down, his bicycle crunching like aluminum foil beneath the tires? Was that the one? That woman? That man, there, in the car just pulling up to the dry cleaners? That girl, the one talking on her cell phone and not watching the street? How blue did Davie think the car was? How new? How long? The questions, if he gave in to them, were relentless, and so he forced himself to push them aside. Instead, he concentrated on putting his physical life in order. He was getting ready for the pain the way one gets ready for a long, hard winter. And all the while he worked, he was aware that Ben Collins was keeping a close eye on him from the photograph that Howard had taped to the mirror over the tiny sink. Ben was keeping an eye.

At the bottom of the box that had *Murray's Clay Pot Kit* written on its side, Howard found the battered dictionary that he'd kept for years on his desk, in his office at Bixley Community College. He was pleased to see it again, had not realized how much he missed what it represented, that place to go when one needed help with words. But since his retirement, the only thing he'd written had been his letter to the Ford Motor Company. He flipped through the tattered pages until he came to the one he was looking for. The verb *to grieve* comes from the Middle English *greven*, which is derived from the Old English *grever*, which is derived from the Latin *gravere*, to burden, which is derived of *gravis*, or heavy. Howard closed the dictionary and put it on a shelf of the bookcase with the other books. Now he knew why the lightness had gone out of Ellen, why Patty looked as if she were being pressed to death. It's been known for some time, then, that grief is a burden. It's heavy as stone.

Howard Jr. had arrived first with his family, and then Greta with hers. They had gathered, they had hugged each other, they had mourned. Apparently, Ellen hadn't told these two older children yet about the changes that had taken place in her own life, in her marriage to their father. Nor had he mentioned it, the few times over the previous month that he'd spoken to them by phone. If they were surprised to learn that Howard was now living in a camp near Bixley Lake, they kept it to themselves. The larger, more important issue was Eliot, who was dead, and his grieving parents, who were alive. That's all. Howard Jr. and his wife, Rachel, had gone to her mother's home and put up there. Greta wanted to be with her own mother, with Ellen, and so she settled into her old childhood room for a few days, the kids in the spare guest room.

On each of those past three days, Howard had gone to Ellen's door on Patterson Street to ask if she was okay. Did she need anything? And while he was there, he stayed long enough to visit his daughter and other grandchildren, girls who were not old enough to understand the mechanics of grief. And then he had gone to John's house, Patty's house, what used to be Eliot's house. No one seemed to need him there either, so he had sat up in Eliot's room, on Eliot's bed. He had fed Eliot's dog. But there was nothing else for him to do. John and Patty had made good friends in their marriage and now those closest friends moved in like a small, soothing army to see that the proper things were being done. The casket. The funeral. The burial. Howard was thankful for this. He assumed Ellen was thankful, and that John and Patty were thankful. Thankful. He had heard John say only one thing about the preparations: "His Gators tee-shirt," when the question arose as to what Eliot should wear in his casket. Howard left then. He wanted to hear no more. The family had decided that they and everyone else should remember Eliot as he was, and not the bruised and broken little boy he had become, under the tires of some unknown automobile. There would be no wake. There would be a memorial service for family and friends. They would say goodbye, they would separate again, and then they could all concentrate on the task of grieving.

So be it.

. . .

On July 6th, the day that hundreds of anxious runners gathered in
Pamplona where they would soon skillfully dodge the bulls, Howard Woods stood with the rest of his grieving family and watched
as Eliot's casket was lowered into the earth. Eliot Lane Woods, born
in 1991, on a god-awful, rainy night that had seen Howard and
Ellen skidding into the same emergency parking lot at Bixley hospital, unfurling their umbrellas, then racing up to the delivery
room so that they would be there when John walked out with that
little bundle in his arms. Their first grandson. Seven years ago, and
yet it was a lifetime. *Eliot's* lifetime. When the small casket disappeared below the edge of the burial hole, Howard heard Patty cry
out again, that cry he'd heard in the hospital the night Eliot died, a
cry she might have made with the pain of Eliot's birth. John was
there to comfort her, his big arm around her narrow shoulders. But
his own face was void now of that confidence he used to have.
Howard had to wonder if John's face would ever return to them. Or
was it gone somewhere now where they would never see it again?
That happened sometimes with death, Howard knew. He'd seen it
in his own mother, when his father had died. It was as if his father
had taken the best part of her with him.

After the funeral, they had all gathered at Ellen's house for food
and consolation. But Howard felt little comfort, the house already
becoming strange to him now that his things were no longer in it.
While the others huddled in the kitchen, trying their soldier's best
to tell the happy stories of Eliot's life, *the time he locked himself in
the basement, the time he gave his teacher a white mouse, the time he
found the hundred-dollar bill, the time he ran away from home and
came to Patterson Street,* Howard stood staring out at the birdhouse
in the backyard and wondering how sixty-some years could disappear so fast, much less seven. His lifetime. Eliot's lifetime.

Howard Jr. had to get back, a meeting the next day that couldn't
be avoided. Greta and her husband were buying a house and had papers to sign. As fast as they'd come, in a whirlwind of suitcases and
wet tears, they were gone. Back to their lives. The silence they left behind was unbearable. Howard wasn't sure if a death had really taken

place after all. Was it real, or was it Hollywood? But this is how people must live, he told himself. This is how they go on, by pretending it will never happen to them. This is where their courage lies, in avoiding the truth at all costs. His only concern now was Ellen. And so, he had gone to her again. He had told her he would come home in an instant. And again Ellen said no. "It would be because of Eliot," Ellen said. These were the words she didn't speak to him that night in the rain, standing outside the hospital. "But in a year, two years, Howie, this thing between us would raise its ugly head again, and we'd be right back where we started." He couldn't argue with her, for she was right. Ellen was always right about those subtle things that lie just below the surface. He knew in his own heart that he still didn't feel forgiveness. He still didn't feel it, no matter how hard he tried.

On the afternoon following Eliot's funeral, with his son and daughter disappeared again into the world, with John and Patty holed up in their own house not wishing to see anyone, Howard worked on the little toy car, the one he had hoped to have ready for Eliot, as a Christmas present. He did this for his own sake, so afraid was he that the grief would press him to death. And then, if it did, no one would be there for Ellen. He smiled as he poured some cleanser onto a damp cloth and wiped away the rust and grime. A 1959 Galaxy, the first year Ford ever made the model. Howard had been desperate to buy one, knowing that with his family about to happen, it would be his last splurge on a fancy car. He even remembered what the thing would cost him, a whopping $2650, but it would be worth it. She was a beauty, sleek and shiny, with those little gold balls on the fenders. And if you pretended you didn't see a Thunderbird flying past you on the highway, you could imagine that you had the sportiest model Ford could offer. She'd be a collector's dream one day, given that '59 was her debut year. He had explained all this to Ellen. The Galaxy would be his *sporty car,* and he would leave it sitting beneath a cover in the garage. Some day, one day, he would sell her for good money. She was an investment, damn it. But 1959 was the year Greta was born. Ellen was thinking ahead to two more children yet to come, to the appendixes that might need to come out, to the braces that would surely need to go

in. How could a monthly payment be made on something as friv-
olous as a *sporty car?* She was right, of course, and so Howard had
given in to marriage, fatherhood, the sensible Rambler, and impending middle age.

Howard painted the toy car the same color as the Galaxy he
never bought, a shiny red. He painted the headlights yellow, and
then added strokes of silver for the chrome. When he was finished,
he put the little car on the windowsill over the sink, where the
morning sun could dry it fully. Then, he stood back and admired
the simplicity of her, remembering how sweet she had looked as
she rolled down the highways and byways of 1959. What a notion
that had been, what a safety in those days. But Howard now knew
the truth. America was a country sound asleep, waiting for something to prod it awake, the way Ellen had prodded him awake to tell
him of Ben Collins. And when it came, it was a crash so loud that
people jumped to their feet, dazed, stunned as sheep. Howard
knew now that 1959 had been our last good sleep before the sixties.

"So what do you think, Ben?" Howard asked the photo beneath
the strip of tape. Ben's eyes were everywhere these days, like one of
those Catholic icons that appear to see everything. "She's a beauty,
isn't she?"

That night, in his narrow bed out at the cabin, with the sounds of
the lake waters lapping against the shore, Howard dreamed that it
was Richard Nixon who had been driving the car that killed his
grandson, Robert McNamara in the passenger seat. He had peered
from behind the curtains of his living-room window and watched
as the runaway vehicle veered up onto the sidewalk and then
plowed its way down Patterson Street, killing other kids. Killing
lots of kids. Howard wanted to do *something,* he wanted desperately to *act,* but his arms were broken again, useless wings that
flapped at his sides as he watched in horror, watched as though the
scene before him were taking place on a large television screen,
Walter Cronkite narrating.

Finally, Howard woke, his back moist against the wet sheet beneath him. He woke and stared at the ceiling as he fought to place the dream fragments into some kind of order. "Symbolic," he thought, like the Macbeth dream, a dream of longing and helplessness. Not to mention another war that Howard had missed because he was old enough to be safe with a wife, and three children, and a teaching job. Another war his sons were too young to be killed in. But other people's sons, 58,000 of them, had perished among the rice paddies. There was Howard's neighbor, Sam Mason, who still lived in the two-story brick on Patterson, the very street where Ellen was probably dreaming her own nightmares. Sam had lost his boy, Bradley, a nice young man, tall and good-looking, who drove a white Mustang wherever he went. That is, until Bradley went to Vietnam and stepped on a live mine, somewhere in the Mekong Delta. For years the white Mustang sat parked above Sam's garage, pooling the spring rains, catching up the autumn leaves. A zillion snowflakes had hit, then melted on, the Mustang's canvas roof before Sam finally had the heart to sell it. Everything takes time. Even for Robert MacNamara, who had finally published a book admitting that the war had been wrong. *It all takes time.*

Howard sat up, slid his legs over the side of the bed, sat there as the gray film of dawn ebbed in over the treetops. One of the loons was already awake, for he heard its cry echo from the other end of the lake. He thought of the eggs in the sparrow's nest, back at the Holiday Inn. Soon, they would crack and break open, the safety of the shell taken from them. He imagined the fledglings opening their small plum eyes to the neon glare from signs along that busy street. The first thing they would know of this strange, new world would be *Goodyear Tires, On Sale Now! Try Our Taco Salad! Develop One Roll of Film, Get One Free! Mel Gibson in Conspiracy Theory.* They would wake to the first big car sale that summer, at Gregson's Auto Sales, just across the street, their sealed eyes opening to the newest Chevrolets on the market, their small beaks coated with the dust of the parking lot, their feathers filled with exhaust. The ones who died in the nest, from sickness or hunger or predators, would never fly up far enough on their new wings to see the blue lake below, or the white birches, or the yellow stars. What had John said? "There were children beneath the bombs we dropped, there were children." But didn't John know that war was big business? McNamara certainly knew it. And *big* business meant *good* business, and good business meant *body count.* It was that simple. It had been that way since the first bloody war ever waged on the planet. It would always be that way. And some bodies were better to count than others. We'd learned that from television, too. We'd seen how the corpses of Vietnamese civilians were simply thrown onto the pile and forgotten about. And those 58,000 American bodies? They were thrown onto a long black wall in D.C., another mark for big business since lots of folks came every day to look at the names, to spend money in the cafés, the stores, the gas stations of our nation's capitol.

Finally, Howard cried. And when he did, it felt as if his insides would run out of him, right through his tear ducts, his guts, his heart, his liver, his goddamn *soul,* whatever *that* was supposed to be, for this was where it hurt. It hurt in the part of him that *lived,* that recognized himself as a husband, a father, a grandfather. The human being part of him. Not the part that told him to invest a few pitiful dollars in MacDonald's. Or the part that had aspired to teach literature for a weekly paycheck. Or even the part that had tried to have sex with Donna Riley, the same part that had created Eliot in the first place. No, it was the best part of him that hurt, the *divine* part. It was the part that made him human and godlike all at once, made him aware of sunsets, and good books, and the smile of a fine French wine. The part that tells painters to pick up their brushes and shape the world on canvas, if only to save it for a few hundred years, or even an hour. It was the part of him that kept his heart beating, like a ticking clock, the whispering part that said to him daily, "Time is running out, Howie, old chap. The goddamn bird is on the wing. So get the lead out."

But at least Howard Woods cried.

 AUTUMN, 1998

fifteen | **COMMON GROUND**

July had brought with it a record heat for Bixley. All that long month, Howard slept with the windows open at the cabin, atop sheets that were wet with perspiration. August came with a blessed cooling, followed by September, and the first signs of fall when a single maple across the lake burst into scarlet. As September inched away, he could almost feel the land pulsing beneath the floor of the cabin, getting ready, gearing up. He had lain awake many mornings, listening to that prehistoric call of the loons. He had read about this. Sixty million years ago there were loon calls echoing on the earth, in the smoky gray mists of those ancient dawns. The squirrels grew bushier as they grew busier, and in the birds he could sense a kind of anxiety. Those that were leaving had a long way to fly. But the ones who stayed behind had a long way to go before spring.

With October came the gold, the red, the orange, the yellow, as winter hovered in the air each morning. Howard had long been making fires from that stocked woodbox, the one he thought he'd never need. He had come to view the small brown cabin as a kind of shell, a sturdy nut that would keep him safe from the elements. He had grown to respect the simplicity of the oil lamp, of quiet nights without radio or television. If he wanted music in his life again, if that day ever came, he would have the trusty CD player and the trove of unused batteries. He boiled his morning coffee in a pot on the woodstove, learning after a time the perfect amount of grounds to toss into the bubbling water. He had gone so far as to talk to Pete about the possibilities of winterizing the cabin, which he would pay for himself, maybe adding a small generator into the bargain. As it was, he ate his main meal of the day, his only hot one, at the Bixley Café, a chance to hear human voices again, something he needed. He knew now why Thoreau, for all his claims of isolation, had sneaked into Concord each Sunday to have dinner with his mother. Human beings are a social breed. This is why they fall in love, as well as get into trouble. Pete had left the answer to winterizing up to Howard, since so much hung in the meaning of it. Did it suggest that he and Ellen would never reunite? Would Howard grow old in the cabin? Would he die some morning in the narrow bed, only the leftover birds of winter to mourn him? Who knew? Maybe the cabin could shelter him from the elements, from the wind, the rain, the snow, but it couldn't shelter him from life. He was one of those social human beings, after all. But human beings endure. It's in the DNA. It's as simple as that. *It all takes time.*

As Howard stepped out onto the front porch he noticed that some of the birch leaves had finally fallen in the night, during the brief rainstorm that had swept over Bixley. The ground was yellow beneath the trees that grew around the cabin, as though someone had sprinkled gold coins there while he slept. And the canvas top of the Aston Martin was a blanket of leaves, too, a natural pattern, as if carefully arranged. The first fallen leaves of the season. It was coming. Winter was pressing in. There was a greater chill in the air since just the day before and Howard wondered if that was the day he'd need to replace his running shorts with sweat pants, his tee-shirt with a sweatshirt. The next day, for sure, would be the cutoff, for the temperature was dropping quickly by the day. And then he'd need those thermal underthings that cold-weather runners wear. And he would need a cap to protect the scalp beneath his thinning hair, which was now more gray than ever. He had long ago let his natural color grow back, deciding he liked the notion of *roots*.

Howard leaned against the front of the cabin and stretched his calf muscles long and hard, feeling them pull like taut elastic bands. Stretching was essential before the brisk, five-mile run that he now took to begin each day, a run that brought him back to Bixley, then out past the Community College and the cemetery, around the high school football stadium, and then back to the lake. Five miles almost on the nose. He had slowly built up to the distance, thinking it a marathon at first, the road ahead of him seemingly endless. By September, the five-mile run was old hat. He had taught literature long enough to know that the symbolists would call it an *emotional* running, a *desperate* running. They would say that he was not running *to* something, but *away* from it. But Howard Woods was retired. He didn't have to think of the damned symbolists anymore.

Howard straightened, and shook his arms loosely, getting them ready for the stride ahead. He took a deep breath and felt the cool air tingle the insides of his nostrils. He had forgotten how intensely alive and intensely mortal one can feel in the heart of autumn. He had even dug out the old dictionary again and looked the word up. It was thought to be of Etruscan origin, but it meant what he suspected it did: *a period of maturity*. As he ran, the blue lake falling away behind him, he thought of Ellen. He had seen her occasionally during short visits he paid to the house on Patterson Street. She seemed to be doing all right. At least, she was surviving. She and Molly were still taking ballet lessons. Ellen said it was a kind of meditation for her, a way to put her mind on her body, and not on Eliot. So be it. Whatever it took. Once, Howard had seen her through the window of the Bixley Café, having a coffee with Floyd Prentiss. They seemed to be in the midst of a heavy conversation, so Howard had not bothered to stop by their table and say hello. Instead, he changed his order, telling the waitress that he now wanted it *to go*. Then, he had then taken the white sack and left the café without so much as a look back. Ellen was a grown woman. What she did was her business.

The marriage dissolution papers were still unsigned by him and right where Howard had put them, between the pages of his dictionary, which lay on the table by the oil lamp. He had looked up the word marriage and discovered it was from the Old French, *marier*. That's when Howard decided to leave the papers right there, marking the spot. The symbolists would win this one. It was exactly halfway through his dictionary and that seemed perfect, somehow, given that marriage was supposed to be a fifty-fifty venture. If the day came when Ellen wanted him to sign them, if the day came when Floyd Prentiss evolved into something more than a *kaffeeklatsch* mate, then Howard would know exactly where to go for the papers. This would save Ellen time and money, too, considering that Howard had already paid Mike Harris's fee for divorce consultation. In the meantime, Ben Collins was keeping a good watch on the dictionary, on the room, on Howard. Some mornings, Howard saw in Ben's eyes a kind of desperation, what with those tubes running like useless veins up into his nose, those eyes peering out at the world with the certainty of a doomed man. But other times, Howard saw in those same eyes a kind of acceptance. It was the latter that Howard himself wished to find.

It was just as Howard crested the top of Stony Hill Road that he saw the cruiser coming toward him, Sheriff Lee Collins behind the wheel. Howard slowed his stride and then, as the cruiser reached him, he stopped altogether. He knew what it meant without even seeing Lee's solemn face. He waited as the sheriff eased out from behind the wheel of the patrol car.

Lee didn't bother with the nuisance of formality, as in "great weather we're having, ain't it?" And Howard appreciated that.

"We found him," Lee said. Howard turned then and stared out across the empty fields that lay on each side of Stony Hill Road, gone to brown and mulch now, waiting for the snows. "Or at least, *he* found *us*." Howard looked back now at Lee's face, indicating to him that he was ready to hear the name.

"Roddy Burkette," said Lee. "We arrested him on a drug charge. In the middle of his interrogation, he broke down and confessed. He's being held at the moment, but I suspect he'll be out on bail in a day or two."

Howard simply could not respond, and so he didn't try to. With Lee still leaning against his patrol car, Howard broke back into his stride, down the rest of Stony Hill Road and out past the cemetery where Eliot was buried, and then on to the stadium at the college. He knew Lee would understand. He'd known Lee from all those college sports events, when Lee had worked security for the college, fresh to his uniform back then and eager to talk with Howard about the semantics of basketball, or baseball, or soccer, whatever the season happened to be. And Howard knew Roddy Burkette, too. This was the part he still couldn't speak to Lee. He knew Roddy Burkette. But then, so did Lee, so did a lot of folks. Roddy had been the Golden Boy in his heyday. Roddy had been the basketball star, the football star, the soccer star, again depending on the season. Roddy had bedded the best cheerleaders, had even been courted by a couple major league teams, and had produced some of the worst academic work ever to befall Bixley Community College. Roddy had been a Golden Boy who began to tarnish as soon as sports left him behind. With ligaments torn in his knees, and with his twenties running out on him, Roddy had disappeared into a blur of drugs and booze and misdemeanors. Howard had even tried to talk to him once, just before the young man dropped out of college for good. But how do you tell Brick Pollitt, that good ole boy ex-football star in *Cat on a Hot Tin Roof,* that he needs to put a few pennies into the piggy bank, that he needs to look to the future? The trouble with being a Golden Boy is in being blinded by the glare, and that was the case with Roddy Burkette. The last Howard had heard of him, he was divorced, the father of two children, and the owner of a run-down landscaping company. Roddy Burkette, in a blue car, on a rainy afternoon, nothing but time on his hands. It seemed the debris in Roddy's life had finally risen to the surface. *He* found *us,* Lee had said. *He confessed.* It all takes time.

Howard made his turn around the stadium and then headed back toward the lake and the cabin. At the cemetery, he picked his pace up, even though the run was uphill. He had not been able to visit Eliot's grave since the day the boy had been lowered into it. He no longer pretended he would try to make the visit. He'd done that for the first month or two, always slowing as he reached the gates, then finding himself utterly incapable of stepping inside. He would know when the time was right, but for now, it wasn't. And besides, what difference did it make? Graves were for the living. Eliot himself was gone, and his grandfather's memories of the boy were safe inside his head.

Roddy Burkette.

That night, Howard took up the Hemingway book again, finding his page marker right where he'd left it three months earlier, at the last chapter, nineteen, which was all of Book III. He forced himself to go back, as he always did, and reread the previous chapter, reminding himself of the tone, the landscape, the feel of the thing. But he had forgotten just how bad that chapter had been: the bullfight itself. He read quickly, trying his best to keep the emotion of it at a distance. *Then without taking a step forward, he became one with the bull, the sword was in high between the shoulders, the bull had followed the low-swung flannel, that disappeared as Romero lurched clear to the left, and it was over. The bull tried to go forward, his legs commenced to settle, he swung from side to side, hesitated, then went down on his knees, and Romero's older brother leaned forward behind him and drove a short knife into the bull's neck at the base of the horns. The first time he missed. He drove the knife in again, and the bull went over, twitching and rigid.* Howard closed the book, unable to read further. In the morning, maybe next week, he would pick it up again and finish that final chapter, the one without the bulls lying heavy and black on the sands of the arena, their limp tongues hanging lifeless from their mouths. He would read, instead, about Brett and Jake, and their ride together through

Madrid in a taxi just as the lights were coming on in the square. But not now, not tonight.

Twilight was just settling over the lake as a thin, autumn rain began to beat on the tin roof. Howard heard wind rattle in off the water. Any day now, when it rained, it would turn to snow. Thinking ahead to what he predicted would be his coldest night so far in the cabin, Howard filled the fireplace with kindling, and then heavier chunks of firewood. He would need more than just the tiny wood stove to generate heat on such a night. He had thought of dropping by Ellen's earlier in the day, to see how she was taking the news. But he had long stopped visiting without calling her first. It just didn't seem polite otherwise. And when he had phoned earlier from the café, there had been no answer. He had just finished lighting the wood when he thought he heard a car door slam. He assumed it had come from one of the nearby cabins, that the owner had driven out to do a last-of-the season check on things. But then he heard footsteps on the front porch, followed by a knock. He opened the door to see John Woods standing there.

"How are you doing, son?" Howard asked. He stepped back so that John could come inside. A wind wet with lake water followed him in.

"It was Roddy Burkette," said John. Howard pulled a chair up to the fire for his son, and another for himself.

"I know," he said. And then, "How's Patty taking it?"

"She's glad it's over," said John. "Mom is with her now."

Howard stared at the firelight.

"How are *you* taking it?" he asked then.

John shrugged. "It's too soon to tell," he said. "But if I see the son-of-a-bitch out on the street, I don't know what I'll do to him." Howard nodded. He understood. It was too soon for any of them to know if they would find a way to survive. Anger would now be their greatest comfort, and anger was a dangerous thing. They sat for some time, both staring into the fire.

"Tell me something," John said. "During Desert Storm, were you proud of me?"

"Of course I was," said Howard. "Both your mother and I were proud. And we were thankful that you managed to stay alive." In truth, they had been more than thankful. They had also been doubtful. He and Ellen had lain awake far into the night, discussing the lives beneath the bombs, discussing the waste of it all, discussing the atrocity of war. But it wasn't their fault, and it wasn't John's fault. It was the fault of governments, of men like Saddam Hussein.

"All I ever wanted was to fly airplanes," said John.

Howard smiled. John was the boy who had model airplanes dangling on strings from his bedroom ceiling by the time he was five years old.

"It was tough at first for us to look each other in the eye," John said then. "Do you remember that, Dad? War does that to people. It changes them forever."

Howard felt a great sympathy wash over him just then. He had an urge to take this man in his arms and hold him, cradle him. But they were not that kind of family, and both he and John knew it. Yes, he had heard the talk on television shows, in a paper here and there, in the cafés and restaurants, that these American pilots were like boys playing a video game, pushing buttons that caused sparks at a distance. It wasn't as bad as what the veterans of Vietnam had to put up with, nothing like that, which was all thanks to Hussein himself. They had a visible enemy in such a crazed and dangerous man. But people who were on the sidelines could sometimes be cruel. They just didn't know. They didn't realize the horrors of having a son in one of those planes, just as Howard hadn't known Sam Mason's terror in having a son in the Mekong Delta. But he had never been ashamed of John, not once.

"Do you remember what I said in the hospital?" John asked now. "The night Eliot died?" He looked up at Howard, who nodded.

"I remember," said Howard.

"Well," said John. "It was true. And it ended up being a ghost I brought home with me." Howard tried to interrupt him.

"Son, you don't have to tell me this," he said, but John held up a hand. His eyes were clear, steady. He'd lost a lot of weight in the weeks since Eliot had died, as if his grief was pulling away parts of him.

"I *do* have to tell you this," John said. "If we don't get rid of the ghosts in our lives, Dad, they'll ruin both our families, yours and mine."

"What do you mean?" Howard asked.

"I mean you need to go home and tell my mother that you forgive her for what happened over twenty years ago," John said. "And you need to mean it, Dad. That's the catch."

Howard started to explain that he was trying, that he was working toward the day that it would happen. But that's not what he said.

"I still feel shame," Howard said. "Shame that my wife would do what she did."

John studied his father's face then. Outside, wind lifted a branch and slammed it against the back of the cabin. The rain was picking up, gathering its force from out on the lake.

"You sorry son-of-a-bitch," John said, a near whisper. At first Howard thought he was mistaken, that John had said something else, expressing his anger at Roddy Burkette, maybe. After all, John had been the most obedient child, the one who always wiped his muddy shoes on the rug, who always rinsed his dish and placed it in the dishwasher, the kid who never, ever shot a sparrow or pulled a cat's tail. "You sorry son-of-a-bitch," John said again, and now there was no doubt. Howard felt indignation rise up. This was his kid, for Chrissakes. How dare he? But then John slammed his fist into his own chest, again and again, beating his breast as though it were another person receiving this punishment.

"Do you know how many times in my life I've tried to talk to you?" he shouted. Seeing this, Howard felt the indignation replace itself with worry. He simply nodded, hoping it would placate John. His grief over losing Eliot was speaking now, Howard guessed. His despair after finally putting a name and a face to the driver behind the wheel of the blue car. Howard supposed there had been times that his son had wanted to talk to him in the past. Girls, in those early days. Peer pressure. Career. His marriage. There had been lots of reasons for a son to consult his father, but John never had. And then later, after John flew those missions over Baghdad, in that sleek F-15 fighter, he had talked to no one. Patty had told Ellen about the sleepless nights, in those months following the bombs, nights of staring at the ceiling, wordless nights with nothing but moonlight between them on the bed. But this wasn't Howard's fault, was it? They came from a long line of sensible families, such as the ones along Patterson Street, the Masons, the Taylors, the Bradfords, the Davidsons, folks who might have come over on the Mayflower, settled Jamestown, climbed into Conestoga wagons and bounced West, the Hartmans, the Turners, the Whites. They could take on wild Indians, the prairies, buffalo herds, sickness, disease, the elements, good adventuresome WASPs that they were. But you couldn't expect them *to talk to each other*.

"You wanna know about shame, ace?" John asked. He looked at Howard, as if daring him to answer. "Shame is pushing a button on the cockpit of your airplane so that a laser-guided GBU-12 bomb will drop out of its belly. Shame is the pride you feel later, over a beer with your buddies, talking about *precision,* the incredible fucking *precision* of the hit. And collateral damage? That's just a lot of dead strangers, those men, women, kids the same age as Eliot. Kids younger than Eliot. And you pretend that's the end of it. But it isn't, Dad. It's just the beginning."

John paused, but Howard knew he wasn't done. He knew his son had been waiting a long time to open this floodgate.

"When I came home, I couldn't make love to Patty," John said then. In all their years of being father and son, the two had never discussed sex. Just as Howard had never discussed it with his own father. Just as the Hartmans never discussed it, or the Taylors, or the Bradfords. "It was as if Patty *knew,*" John went on. "She knew I dropped those bombs. She saw those kids on television, their arms blown away, their faces swollen with bruises. Patty knew, but Vanessa didn't. Vanessa thought I worked for Sounder Aeronautics and nothing more. The thing with Vanessa is all over now, but see how simple it is, Dad, now that you know the truth?"

Howard stared at the same spot in the fireplace where John was now staring. John, the quiet kid, his face awash with the orange glow of the flames, his thoughts far away from that spot he was occupying in the chair, in that cabin, on the outskirts of Bixley, Maine, that tiny stop along the universe. Howard remembered again that night, could pull it up at the drop of a hat—January 16, 1991, at 6:40 P.M.—when Marlin Fitzwater told the world: *The liberation of Kuwait has begun.* "It looks like fireworks," Ellen had whispered. Later, with Bernie Shaw watching the war from a hotel room in Baghdad, they heard him say, "I'm looking in the direction of the Euphrates River." Ellen had grasped Howard's hand in her own. "My God, Howie," she cried. "We're bombing the Cradle of Civilization." Howard had agreed then, but since that night he had had time to really think about it, on all those morning runs along the lake, the fields, past the cemetery and out around the stadium. Now Howard saw it more clearly. What difference did it make *where* an atrocity occurs? After all, what was the Cradle of Civilization but our oldest landfill, where human jaw bones, teeth, hip joints, work up to the surface to bake in the sun. Old poems written on papyrus. Shards of ancient pots, similar to the ones Ellen and Molly were learning to make. What difference did it make *where*?

"You need to forgive my mother," said John. "And I need to forgive myself."

Howard sat quietly, staring at the fuzzy glow of firelight, bright flickers of orange and blue. After Desert Storm, Kuwait had burned for more than a year. Howard sat and waited for John to decide what he should do next, what he *must* do next.

"I used to think we had nothing in common, you and me," John said at last. "And we didn't. But now, Dad, *now,* what we share is grief over the loss of a little boy. It's what I share with Patty. It's what I share with my mother. And it should be enough to hold us all together, until we can fix ourselves again."

John stood, zipped his jacket, turned its collar up about his throat. He searched in his pocket for gloves and then put them on. The days were getting colder so fast, so sudden. Just that morning

Howard had noticed a thin film of ice rimming the shores of the lake. He had seen specks of what he thought might be red-tailed hawks, headed South for the winter. And he had noticed that the squirrels were anxious. Something in that old primitive coding was urging them to get ready, to line the burrows with more leaves, to remember all those caches with their stored nuts. *It all takes time.*

At the door John paused, looked back at Howard.

"We're lucky men, Dad," he said. "We've finally got some common ground. Even if it is at the Bixley cemetery."

sixteen | **ENDURANCE**

Howard spent the next few days winterizing the cabin. The squirrels and what birds hadn't already migrated watched him from the tops of the trees. They seemed to understand this need of his, this urge to feather the nest, to line the burrow with some sturdy grass. A couple of guys came out from Morgan's Home Builders, the back of their pickup truck filled with insulation and a new roofing material guaranteed to withstand the wrath of winter. Pete had driven out to the cabin to give his blessing to the work, but he would trust Howard to make the actual choices. Pete's greatest concern was that Howard had let the golf season slip away without one last game. But Pete understood. He would catch Howard in the spring, for the first game of the season, and he would whip his pants off then.

"Why don't you stop by the lounge some time and say hello?" Pete said, as he piled back into his jeep and reached into the ashtray for the remainder of his latest cigar. "I think the guys miss you."

"Tell them I'll show up one day soon," said Howard. And then he watched as Pete's shiny jeep disappeared among the white trunks of the birches.

Three days later, the guys from Morgan's Home Builders were able to assure Howard Woods that he could survive in the little cabin, come hail, come snow and sleet, until spring. As long as he kept the woodbox full and the stove and fireplace burning during the coldest days and nights. Howard felt that he could do that. He had decided against the generator for now. When spring came, he would know more of what would become of the rest of his life. Maybe when the warblers returned from their warm nooks and crannies they would bring the answer with them. Right now, he had no idea what course his life would run next. But he knew a few things, on the larger scope, in the bigger picture. He knew now what Macbeth came to know too late: *Life's but a walking shadow, a poor player that frets and struts his time. So get the goddamn lead out.* He even came to pity Lady Macbeth, stung again and again by that snake of a conscience. Some mornings, Howard would wake in the predawn and lie there in the narrow bed, missing the sad cry of the loons. That's when he would think of Lady Macbeth, tormented by the memory of her victims, trying to wash away that infernal blood. And this, in turn, always made him think of Robert MacNamara. Did the former Secretary of Defense rise in the night from his own anguished nightmares? Did he, too, try to cleanse himself of the blood of all those soldiers? Howard doubted that he could. And why should he alone pay the price? It was a useless scrubbing of a blood too deeply embedded to rub out, and Lady Macbeth knew this. She knew it, and that was her pain: the knowledge that she must live and die with what she'd done. And then, with dawn lying in a pink ribbon along the horizon of lake, Howard would focus on *her,* not on her husband. After all, the play wasn't titled *Mr. Macbeth.* Or even *Lord Macbeth.* Maybe this was a little trick of Bill Shakespeare's that no one had caught onto yet. Maybe the work, that *study in fear,* was really about the little woman in the family. Howard decided to give her a first name, to know her a bit better. After all these years, and for all his teaching of her dirty works, they should be on a first name basis, as he and the Ford Motor Company now were. *Brett Macbeth?* No, it was too catchy. During one of those early mornings, he came up with the name Laura. *Laura Macbeth.* He liked it. It gave her a life suddenly, flesh and bone. It suggested a past, maybe even a reason for her scheming and her greed. What had her own childhood been like? Those were the questions counselors would ask today. Maybe those Human Resources folks, had they been around in Shakespeare's day, would have gone in and saved Laura Macbeth, put her in a better home environment. If Lady Laura Macbeth were living today, she'd hire the best divorce lawyer around. She'd hire a publicist and pour her heart out to the media. In the end, her lawyer would sue the witches and Laura would sit on the Scottish throne all by herself. It became Howard's modern version of the play.

On the day the builders finished their work, cleaned up their debris, gathered their tools, and disappeared back toward town, Howard decided it was time to do some grocery shopping at the big IGA. He would shop first, and then do his run later in the afternoon. He had just put a box of cereal and a can of coffee grounds in his cart when he turned down an aisle and bumped into Patty Woods, his daughter-in-law. Howard was astonished at how thin and haggard she had grown. Beneath her eyes were dark circles that seemed to be embedded in the skin, as if she were born with them. He had tried to stop by John's house every other day in the beginning, offering what support he could. But it seemed that Patty wanted none. It seemed that she and John were grieving at their own pace, and on their own terms. Howard didn't want to be a nuisance. Besides, he had his own grief to wake to each morning, to fall asleep to each night.

"Patty?" he said, and she turned. She smiled to see him, and then, as if uncertain, finally stepped into the circle of his arms. He felt as if he were holding a small child, a wounded girl.

"Dad," she said. "How've you been?"

"Fine, fine," said Howard. "You?" Patty shrugged.

"I'm still here."

"How is the theater group coming along?" Howard asked. "I'm sorry I missed *Cyrano de Bergerac*. I take it he hasn't had a rhinoplasty yet."

Patty had to think, as if trying to remember what group, what play, what connection. Then she remembered.

"Oh, I haven't been back to the theater," she said. "It was just too much, you know, without Eliot and all."

"Of course," said Howard. He forced a smile for her benefit, but he supposed she'd seen enough of those smiles since that day in early July, when Roddy Burkette's car had come out of nowhere.

"Dad, I gotta run," Patty said then. "I'm having company later today and well, I was just picking up some snacks."

"Sure," said Howard. He glanced down at her cart. Candy bars. A bottle of Pepsi. A box of cookies. A can of tuna fish. Cigarettes. She had started smoking? The power-walker?

"Maybe you'll take a drive out to the cabin," he said. "It's peaceful by the lake."

Patty smiled again, relief spreading over her face that she was finally being released from the conversation.

"You got a deal, Dad," she said. And with that, she spun her shopping cart around and headed for the checkout counter. Howard watched from an aisle behind her as she paid for the few items in the cart. He watched through the big glass window at the front of the store as she hurriedly loaded the shopping bag into the back seat of the Volvo. He watched as she pulled out of the parking lot and disappeared.

An hour later, and holding two bags of vegetables, fruits, milk, cheese, and baked bread from the deli, Howard rang the bell at Patty's and John's house. John's car was not in the yard, but Patty's was. Eliot's dog, Gator, was sleeping on the front porch. When he saw Howard, Gator stood and shook himself, his tail wagging a welcome. When Patty opened the door, she didn't seem surprised at all.

"I knew you wouldn't fall for company's coming," she said. "But it was the best I could think of at the time."

"Actually, you were telling the truth," said Howard. "It's just that *I'm* the company."

As Howard stepped into the house he was immediately aware of the disarray. Clothes were strewn about on chairs and across the living room. Shoes. Socks. Used towels. Dishes had been left on the coffee table, several days worth of them. Dust covered the bookshelves and the television set, which was broadcasting some talk show. The kitchen was in a worse mess, the sink piled high, smears across the fridge door, the dog's dishes spotted with dried food. And over it all hung the musty odor of cigarette smoke. Patty didn't seem to care. Maybe it had become the new order to her new life.

"I've been so busy," she said. "My mother and Ellen, they've been keeping things up. But it's been a couple days."

"Don't worry about it," said Howard. "What have you been doing to keep busy?" He wanted to get her talking a bit so that he could determine just what was going on in her head. Patty brightened then, an excitement in her eyes.

"Come and I'll show you," she said. He followed her past the clutter of the living room and into the tiny back office where she often stored her theater supplies. Now, an easel had been set up in there. She'd been busy all right. Everywhere Howard looked, he saw paint-by-number paintings. They were hanging on the walls, leaning against furniture, lying on the desk top, propped up in chairs. Dozens of them. A talk program was coming from a radio that Patty had obviously plugged into the socket under her desk. Howard couldn't see it, but he could hear it. Some male voice was giving investment advice.

"I keep the radio on all the time," Patty said. "And the television too. I like the sound of human voices, you know, as I paint."

Now Howard was beginning to see a theme in the paint-by-number paintings: just dogs on one wall, just clowns on another, just pastoral settings on the ones lying flat on the desk. It was Patty's new passion, all right.

"I like the numbers telling me what to paint and where," Patty explained, when she saw that he'd been staring. "It's so much easier that way. The first month, I painted only dogs. The second month, it was just scenes of the countryside. You know, peaceful.

Now, well, I like clown faces now. I like to see their different expressions."

"They're very nice," Howard told her.

"It was Roddy Burkette," said Patty, startling him. He nodded. He said nothing as he put a finger on one sad clown face, touched the buildup of red paint on the round ball nose. "I never met him," Patty added. "But I suppose he's hurting too, just as we are."

"I suppose," said Howard. He needed to leave. He needed to be away from the sad clown faces and the dogs who seemed lost without owners. He gave Patty a quick hug and promised he'd be back soon.

When Howard stepped out into the autumn day, he breathed deeply, bringing the fresh air down into his lungs, trying to exhale the smoke he had just left behind him. He got into the little Aston Martin and drove it quickly through the colored leaves, out around the stadium, up past the cemetery with its wrought iron gates, and then the college where he'd spent so many years of his life. From there, it was bare, open fields until he saw the lake glistening blue in the distance. He flew in among the white birch trunks where the ground was now yellow with leaves. He saw the cabin ahead, sitting still and solid among the trees, and a certain warm feeling rose up inside of him. *Home.* It might not be where his heart was, but at least it was home. And anything was better than the Holiday Inn. He had been trying his best not to think of Patty as he drove. He was still amazed at how pure her grief was. It was not tinged with anger, nor cluttered with any kind of guilt. She didn't even seem to hate Roddy Burkette, as Howard was certain *he* did. Instead, through her obsessive painting, she was quietly trying to fix the world, to remake it, to shape it into a better place. *I like the numbers telling me what to paint and where.*

Howard got out of the car and slammed the door. The echo of it rushed out on the water and then bounced off the trees on the opposite side of the lake. Pure. Peaceful. Like those pastoral settings Patty had been painting. Howard breathed the fresh air again. He decided he would not run that day. Instead, he would cook himself a hot dinner, right on the top of the woodstove. Some kind of pasta, maybe, with a marinara sauce. He would spend a quiet evening with a glass of wine. He would not dwell on the disorder at John's house, where lives seemed to have been tossed onto the backs of chairs, lives smoky with pain, crusted and dusty. He couldn't save everybody, could he? And then, he did have himself to think of. Besides, Patty's mother and Ellen were dropping by often to help out. Women knew how to nurture other women. What did Howard know, other than that you don't wash red things with white things. He had learned that the hard way and now he was a bit of an expert at the Bixley Laundromat, his tubs being sorted and washed properly. He wondered if Lady Laura Macbeth did her own laundry. Was she careful to separate all those bloody sheets and pillowcases from the white stuff?

For the next few days, with October firmly rooted now in the scuttling of leaves, and in the ice rimming the lake before the sun rose and took it away, Howard simply couldn't wipe Patty from his mind. He continued to run along his daily course, past the fields and the college and the cemetery and the stadium. Some days, he took the little Aston out for a spin, down past the sleeping golf course with its dentures and syringes, past the shopping mall, out to the Mattress Warehouse, where Freddy Wilson was mostly likely still his throne. He began to see Bixley anew, from a distance, and this time with the eyes of a wise outsider: the school's dim windows, the church spires, the faceless shoppers along the streets, the rooftops and parking lots, the grocery stores and gas stations, the neon signs where leftover eggshells lay in birdnests. And he began to think of the people who were sheltered inside those private homes, those larger nests, people who ate and slept and raised the children they had created. They were like the soft figures in an impressionist painting, just enough out of focus that they might be the people who walked along the Montmarte over a hundred years earlier, and not those modern residents of Bixley, Maine. But all one can do is *live,* as Howard was beginning to realize, a little tenet the sparrows already knew so well. Frailty comes hand in hand with endurance, so all one can do is live *in spite of everything.*

It was just as the sun came to rest on the horizon of water, before it sank beyond the lake and evening moved in, that Billy Mathews came to visit. Howard was sitting in the rocker on the front porch, watching the late-feeding birds in their frenzy to grab that last meal of the day, when he heard the rumble of a car's engine. A small green vehicle, one of those unrecognizable Japanese models, made its way down the gravel road, through the white trunks of the birches, and up to the steps of the cabin. The engine died and the door opened. This was when Howard saw that it was Billy.

"Mrs. Woods told me where to find you," Billy said. Howard was trying to imagine how he could untrap himself this time. He couldn't use Hemingway's old ploy, *Well, listen, I got to get back,* not out there in the woods. Billy came up the steps and onto the porch. He smiled as he held his hand out for Howard to shake.

"Billy," said Howard. "Imagine running into you, out here in the woods." Billy was staring out at the lake now, at the colors of the sun resting atop the water.

"This is sure nice," said Billy. "I'm used to that indoor pond we have over at the mall." Howard nodded, remembering the murky water, the Bird of Paradise flowers, the rigid benches.

"Well, welcome to Walden," he said.

"Is that the name of the lake?" Billy asked, and Howard could tell by the guileless look on the young man's face that he meant this.

"Sit down, Billy," Howard said, and Billy did, taking the empty chair beside Howard's. "I was just watching the sunset and having a glass of wine. Would you like one?"

Billy smiled a wide smile. When Howard came back outside with a glass of wine, Billy was still smiling.

"What's so funny?" asked Howard. Billy took the wine and held it in his hand. He swirled it a bit, and then looked up at Howard.

"I always imagined what this would be like," said Billy. "You know, the cool kids, the smart ones, they were always sitting with the teachers in the student lounge. Talking about stuff the rest of us didn't understand."

Howard sat down next to Billy and picked up his own glass of wine.

"Looking back on it now, Billy," he said. "I doubt any of us knew what we were talking about. We just thought we did."

A chickadee sang out from the branches overhead. Howard smiled, knowing he would have them all winter. He had already bought a twenty-five-pound bag of sunflower seeds. The chickadees and the finches and the gray jays, they'd weather the cold and the snow with him, until the buds of May. So the feeding of them was the least he could do.

"I just came to tell you that I finished it," said Billy. Howard looked at him.

"Finished what?"

"The book," said Billy. "*The Sun Also Rises.* I finished it last night."

"I see," said Howard. Billy had begun reading that book the first of June. Well, what could Howard say? He still had a chapter to go himself. But then, he'd read it a dozen times over the years. He doubted Hemingway had read it that often.

"What do you think?" asked Howard. These days, he was no longer afraid to venture into unknown territory.

"As I see it, this group of friends go on a trip and realize just how unhappy they really are," said Billy. "It's like that time our senior class went to Quebec City. Shelly Lynn fell in love with the guy who worked at the hotel, and even dropped out of school to move up there with him. But he was married and had kids and never told her that. And on that same trip, Marla was attacked by two guys who tried to rape her. I think you come back different from trips, even if you come back happy. I think trips change you forever, and that's why I don't care much if I ever travel far from Bixley. It's just not, well, *safe.* I want to find a nice girl and get married, settle down and raise a family. By then, I expect to be managing the bookstore. And I think that's all Robert Cohn and Jake Barnes ever wanted too, you know, families to belong to. They were just too far from home to do anything about it."

Billy was done. He took a deep breath. Howard realized that the young man had planned to say all this to him, had maybe even rehearsed it on the drive out to the cabin. It was as if Billy Mathews was finally taking the test he was supposed to take, back when he gave up college for good and dropped out, dropped away, disappeared until he turned up again at the bookstore. But now Howard understood that maybe Billy had gotten more from the class than any other student. More, even, than the instructor.

"What did *you* get out of the book, Mr. Woods?" Billy asked. Howard considered this. How long had it been since he'd delivered a Hemingway lecture? A few years? He had loved it, hadn't he, teaching? The thing about being a professor of any subject was that you got to stand at the front of the classroom, all those faces turned your way, all those eyes glued to your lips. It wasn't that they liked you, necessarily, or even gave a shit what you had to say. It was that you held their grade at the tips of your fingers. A professor is the king, the queen of the classroom. Even if you were the kid back in high school no one wanted to date, the scrawny kid with glasses, never picked for baseball or the cheerleading squad. It was *your* turn now to shine, your turn to benefit from all those nights of hitting the books while the hippest fraternities and sororities partied all over campus. *Your* turn. And Howard had loved every minute of it, missed it deeply, longed for the part of him that was fulfilled by it each time he stepped behind that lectern. That's when sexy young women like Jennifer Kranston, girls who wouldn't have given him the time of day back in high school, when he was their peer, now gave him those little looks, those gestures to let him know, *The answer is yes, Professor Woods, if you want it to be.*

Howard drank some of his wine. Billy was sitting, waiting, his jacket still zipped and keeping him warm on the front porch of the cabin.

"There are two kinds of people in Hemingway novels, Billy," Howard said. He could already hear the change in his voice, in the intonation of his delivery. He was Professor Woods again, and it felt good to be that person. "The first kind is the Jake Barnes and Brett Ashley kind. They're the ones who have had their faith in moral values taken away from them by World War One, so they live cynical lives, and they care only about their own emotional needs. It's how they survive. The other kind of people Hemingway wrote about are people who live basically simple lives, with emotions he saw as being quite primitive. Bullfighters, for instance, or prize fighters, especially the ones who battle circumstances outside of their control. Even the girl who brings them hot bowls of soup, in the little farmhouse so high up in the mountains of Spain, on that fishing trip that Jake and Bill Gorton took to Burguete. Remember her? Hot vegetable soup, and wine, and then fried trout. Wild strawberries. Sounds like nothing, doesn't it? And yet to this day tourists go to that same farmhouse up in those Spanish mountains, and they ask for a bowl of the same soup that Bill and Jake had. And they think about that girl. I know they think about her, Billy, they think about her and her simple but courageous life."

Billy had listened carefully to this lecture, entranced, almost childlike. He said nothing for a long time. Then he reached inside his coat and brought out his copy of the book, the one he had shown Howard that day at the mall. The cover was now worn, a bit frazzled, but van Gogh's crows still rose up from their perpetual wheatfield, their black wings destined to flap forever, just as Macbeth's witches were destined to stir the cauldron out on that barren heath. Forever. Billy looked over at Howard.

"I guess I'm that second kind of person," he said. "At least I hope I am."

Howard smiled.

"I'd say you are, Billy."

Billy studied the cover of the book in his hands. The title, the author's name.

"Ernest Hemingway," he read. He looked over at Howard, questioning.

"He was just another scared SOB," Howard said, "Just like the rest of us."

"He still alive?" Billy asked.

"No," Howard said. "No, he isn't."

"That's too bad," said Billy. Then, "What was he like?" For a second Howard wondered if Billy Mathews thought that he and Papa Hemingway were old friends or something, that maybe they'd fished for marlin off the Keys, drank large amounts of wine from leather gourds. A canoe passed far out on the lake and sent its ripples toward them. Howard watched as the small swells finally reached the shore.

"He was all man, Billy," Howard said, "and that's why the sixties threw him away. He was too barrel-chested, too mythic, too masculine for the tone of the day. He stood for ideals that no one believed in any more. Television replaced him, and jet planes, and computers. They replaced him, Billy, but they can't seem to kill him. He's the old bull that's just too wise to die. He'll be around long after the hippies, and the yuppies, the investment bankers and the corporate lawyers, the Hollywood executives and the university academics, the Iron Johns and the feminists. Know why, Billy? He might have been scared, he might have been a lot of things, but coward wasn't one of them."

Billy stood then, put his empty wine glass down by the leg of the chair. He slipped the book back inside his jacket, and then zipped it against the cold. He looked at Howard.

"Which one are you, Mr. Woods?" he asked. "Which Hemingway type are you?"

Howard said nothing for a few seconds. He watched as a loon dove far out on the lake. The other loons had already gone, but he'd noticed this late straggler just that morning, autumn nipping at its tail feathers. He hoped it would go too, soon, before the lake froze over and it had no options left. It was awful to be left without options. When the loon resurfaced, a hundred feet on down the lake, Howard looked back at Billy with his answer.

"Once upon a time, I wanted to be the first kind," he said. "Some of us, when we grow older, fall into a sort of panic. We want our lives to be larger than they really are, so that it seems the living of them was worth it. But it takes a lot of courage to lead a small life, Billy. It's the kind of courage I think I've finally found."

Billy smiled, as if pleased that he and his old teacher finally had something in common.

"You know, I always admired you, Mr. Woods," Billy said then. "You done a lot for me. I'll be seeing you then."

Howard watched as Billy went back down to his little green car and opened the door. Then, on an impulse he knew he'd never be sorry for, Howard stood up from the rocker.

"Billy?" he said. Billy Mathews was just about to slide back behind the wheel of his car, but he stopped, looked up at Howard, there in the twilight of the front porch.

"There's a book called *Walden*," said Howard. "You can buy it at the bookstore. I think there's a lot of things in there that you'll find interesting." Billy's face was instantly happy.

"Can we talk about it afterward?" Billy asked. "Like we did just now? Like the class used to do?" Howard nodded.

"You read the book and then we'll talk about it, Billy," he said.

"Thanks a lot, Mr. Woods," Billy said.

Had Howard, for the first time in his life, finally become a teacher? As he stood watching Billy's green car disappear into the dusk, back through the stand of straight white birch trunks, he thought about Papa Hemingway. So many scholars, students, even his friends had missed what was really great about the man. It was his comeback. Critics had predicted that he was washed up after he bombed with *Across the River and into the Trees*. Even his fans were embarrassed for him. But this was in 1950, and the son-of-a-bitch had gone on to win the Pulitzer and the Nobel Prize. His *comeback* had been extraordinary, remarkable, and yet people only remembered the hedonism of his fishing, his hunting, his drinking, his fucking. They forgot all about his relentless devotion to his art. Or the fact that *The Sun Also Rises* had changed the way a whole generation thought, how they walked and talked. Thousands of American college girls dreamed of being Brett. They wore their hair short like Brett's, they smoked cigarettes and drank like Brett. They spoke in clever, Brettish phrases. And thousands of young college men wanted to be Jake *before* the war. But people forgot all that by the time the fifties rolled around and critics began to stab their knives into him. Papa must have sensed the sixties in the bottoms of his feet, the way rabbits know an earthquake is coming. He had taken a shotgun and put it to his head. He had killed himself before the new ideas of a world he would have hated did it for him. That was in 1961. So he must have seen it all coming.

Before Howard went to sleep that night, he picked up his own copy of the novel and read that final chapter. Brett, her heart broken because she knew she could not keep the young bullfighter as her lover, had sent Jake a telegram, asking him to come to Madrid. Howard read on, and then he savored the last paragraph. Brett and Jake had found a taxi to carry them through the streets of Madrid, since Brett had never seen the city. *We sat close against each other. I put my arm around her and she rested against me comfortably. It was very hot and bright, and the houses looked sharply white. We turned out onto the Gran Via. "Oh, Jake," Brett said, "we could have had such a damned good time together." Ahead was a mounted policeman in khaki directing traffic. He raised his baton. The car slowed suddenly pressing Brett against me. "Yes," I said. "Isn't it pretty to think so?"*

Howard fell asleep with the book broken open across his chest. He dreamed then, the most vivid and colorful dream that he had since childhood, maybe ever. It was more a dream of life than it was a dream of the subconscious, so he was positive that it was happening. It was happening and he was caught up in it, unable to break free of the colors and sounds. It opened beautifully, film-like, to the excited noise of a fiesta and the dust of the streets rising up in brown clouds. He even felt the intense heat, so hot that perspiration ran down the back of his neck. He knew instantly that he was in Pamplona, and that the bulls were about to run through the streets. And then Howard saw them, thousands of them, coming from the nearby villages, coming from the distant cities of the world, all dressed in sparkling white shirts and waving the red neck-scarves, *los sanfermines,* those skillful dodgers. They were filling up the square in front of City Hall, the same square Howard had seen so many times in the pictures of his travel packet. Then a man, a *councilor,* jumped up onto a platform and turned to the mass of faces before him. This is when Howard realized that he was one of those faces, in that sea of men. He, Howard Woods, of Bixley, Maine, was about to run the bulls! He looked down then and saw that his shirt was pure white, spotless, and in his hand was the red neck-scarf. "People of Pamplona!" the councilor shouted. "Long live San Fermin!" Howard smiled. He had read that this would be shouted in Spanish and Basque, but the councilor was speaking English, which was very nice of him. And then noise exploded all around as a rocket soared high over the square and then burst into stars. As he stared up at the fireworks, Howard knew what John's bomb had looked like to the faces on the ground. And then a festive cry rang out from the thousands of voices around him, as if a great bell were being rung. He felt himself being pushed along with the crowd. Now there was music in the air as the street bands beat out their songs. Voices sang in unison, sweet and pure: *We ask San Fermin, as our Patron, to guide us through the Bull Run and give us his blessing.* He saw vendors along the way, reaching out to him with cups of champagne, sandwiches, sunglasses, sombreros, ice cream. He tried to take some of their offerings, but they rushed past him in a blur, on the sidelines, as he was pushed along with the wall of bodies, all those white shirts moving *en masse,* all those red scarves being waved about in the air. He was exhilarated suddenly, the heat, the music, the sweat of life unfolding as it was, like a great, unstoppable pinwheel. And then, someone shouted, "Los toros!" and Howard knew the bulls were coming. The film sped up then, much too fast for his liking, and he was pushed violently now. The crowd was changing, he could sense it, the happy faces growing stern, blossoming into anger. "Kill the bull!" someone shouted in English. And then hundreds of hands were raised into the air from out of the mass of bodies, hundreds of white shirt sleeves, the silver blades of hundreds of knives flashing in the hot sun. Howard realized then that the *sanfermines* were stabbing the bull, again and again and again. He turned to the man next to him, hoping he could help stop it. There was a banner floating above this man's head: BULLFIGHTING IS CRUEL TO ANIMALS! His tee-shirt said: *I ♥ Los Angeles*. It was the man Howard had read about in the newspaper, that fateful day Ellen told him about Ben, and he had driven to John's and waited for his son to wake up. It was the animal rights activist! "Do something!" Howard shouted to him. "Help me stop this!" The man turned toward Howard then, his banner streaming above his head, and that's when Howard realized that he no ears. Just as his students had no ears in those Macbeth lectures he'd been giving in his nightmares, ever since his retirement. Now Howard was frightened, his body tingling the way it does from the fear that comes with a nightmare. "We aren't suppose to kill it!" Howard shouted to the man on his other side. "We're just supposed to run alongside!" Now this man turned to look at Howard. His brownish hair was shoulder length, his eyebrows thick and full. He was dressed like the other *sanfermines,* the white shirt, the red belt, the neck-scarf. Howard recognized him instantly. It was Roddy Burkette. "It has to die anyway," said Roddy. "It has to die later, in the arena, so why not now?" Howard felt panic then. He had to find a way to save the bull. He elbowed through the crowd of skillful dodgers, that sea of faces, the boiling mass of hands, of knives. As they fell back, they reached out and touched his white shirt with their hands, leaving behind their bloody prints. And then, finally, Howard managed to reach the bull, so great was his desire to rescue it. He pulled away the last man who was kneeling over the animal's body, which he knew must be dying. He pulled away the last *sanfermine* from the bull, only it wasn't the bull. It was Eliot. Howard knelt and picked the boy's head up into his lap, cradled it. "Oh, Eliot," he whispered. "I wish it had been me instead of you." Eliot opened his eyes then and looked up at Howard. "I know, Grandpa," Eliot said. "But it's okay now. It's almost over. And it doesn't hurt so much, not as much as I thought it would." Howard could only nod. He held the small body of his grandson up tight to his chest, which is what he wished he could have done the day Eliot had lain in the street, dying alone in that pool of blood. Eliot. And then, in the bizarre scheme of dreams, Howard began to sing to his grandchild, not a lullabye, for dreams don't care for such sensible things. "That old Bilbao moon, I won't forget it soon," Howard sang, and in the dream he was just as good as Andy Williams. "That old Bilbao moon, just like a big balloon."

When Howard woke, he was already crying. He could still feel the warmth of Eliot's body, pressed against the sweat of his chest. Warmth, a thing that could be touched, alive, like electricity. And then the dream was shaken away from him like a cobweb, and Howard realized that the warmth was only the sweat of the dream itself, dampening his tee-shirt. And now, the warmth, the wet, was growing cold as the night air reached it. Cold, as Eliot's body must be, the sweet earth swallowing it up in its own mouth, churning it into fertilizer. Howard didn't think the cry from deep within him would ever stop. It came out of his body as if it had teeth, tearing at his gut, his flesh, his heart, ripping away any sense of shelter he had ever known. It was much worse than the night of Eliot's funeral, and he had thought *that* was as bad as it would get. And then it was over.

He went into the small bathroom where he bathed cool water onto his face, then patted it dry with a towel. The sky outside the window was just ripening with dawn. He went out to the other room and lit the oil lamp on the table. He put more wood in the stove and then, nothing but time on his hands, he stood before the photo of Ben Collins that was taped to his mirror. He hoped Ben could help him with this one, this big question. Had his life been lived for nothing? Maybe not. He had, after all, endured. The truth is that he'd been *skillfully dodging* the great issues of his life, *all his life*. He would give the goddamn symbolists their due, their crust of bread: *He'd been running the bulls for as long as he could remember*. As he peered into Ben's eyes, Howard wondered if he would visit Roddy Burkette one day, in his jail cell. Or if he couldn't visit, maybe he would find a place in his heart that would forgive Roddy, who seemed to need no help in his own self-destruction. One day. *It all takes time*.

"I'm growing up, Ben," Howard said to the tired and sick face in the photo. "By God, I'm finally gonna do it." How could he have ever dreamed that he would show Ellen the photo of Ben Collins? What had he been thinking, in those raw days of his naiveté? He had known for some time now that the photo would be his secret, and Ben's secret. He felt strangely protective of Ben Collins these days. They'd been through a lot together. Howard saw his own face then, just behind Ben's, his reflection staring at him from the mirror. He could feel the swelling already coming to his eyes. But it would be gone by daybreak. A lot of things would be gone by then. And that was the new knowledge Howard Woods must now learn to live with. It all takes time and then, then, the comeback's the thing.

seventeen | **THE COMEBACK**

Snowflakes were falling among the bare birches as Howard boiled water for his morning coffee. He threw the right amount of grounds into the bubbling water and then went into the little bedroom to dress. By the time he poured a cup of the coffee and took it out to the front porch, the snow had stopped and a pale, yellow sun had broken through. The late-straggling loon was gone. At least Howard hadn't heard it in the early hours as light came in over the lake, followed by daybreak. It would seem that the loon had looked at its options, and had chosen an arduous journey to better climes over certain death. That's what life was all about, really, the options. Canada Jays spotted him and swooped down to the ground by the front steps. They had already learned that Howard would toss them a scrap of morning bagel, or a piece of doughnut. They had come to depend upon him for this, and he felt good about that.

There on the porch of the cabin, with the sun hitting the rocking chair full blast, Howard settled down with a yellow legal pad and a fountain pen. It had been his favorite way of writing, his preferred *accoutrements*, for as long as he could remember. A good old-fashioned pad of paper, a nice sturdy pen with lots of fluid ink.

He stared at the pad thoughtfully for a time, and then he wrote the first sentence. It would come just after Brett told Jake that she didn't want to be one of those bitches that ruin children, and so she had sent the boy-bullfighter, her lover, away for good. In Howard's version, they would be drinking in the back of the taxi, Brett leaning against Jake's chest.

"I don't like it you know," she said.

"Like what?"

"The bullfight, the bloody fight. I don't like it one bit, darling, it's terrible."

I didn't answer her just then. A prostitute, a *poule*, I recognized from the Palace Hotel was just going upstairs at Botin's for her dinner. She would probably have the suckling pig and then drink some *rioja alta*. She looked up as the taxi passed and smiled. I had thought her pretty once, but now she had aged in the short time I had been away. But so had I.

"Then we won't do it," I said.

"Do what?"

"The bulls, we won't go again to Pamplona."

"It's ghastly, isn't it?"

"Yes."

"Oh, Jake, do you mean it?"

"I don't want to be one of those bastards who ruins bulls," I said.

"I'm glad we won't do it."

Brett was smoking again. Her cigarettes were an American brand and quite inferior. I knew that she would die of lung cancer if she didn't stop smoking. A lot of people were dying. More than in the war.

"Let's go back to the bar at the Hotel Montana," I said. "At least the bartender there is nice." It was difficult any more to find someone polite in food services.

"It's ghastly, isn't it?"

"We'll have a nightcap."

"Do you think we should stop drinking?" Brett asked. She looked very frightened. I thought she might cry.

"They say two glasses of red wine a day is good for the heart." I would order us a bottle of rioja alta.

"I'm going to quit smoking soon," said Brett. "Maybe New Year's. Oh, darling, wouldn't it be lovely?"

"We'll quit the wine too, one day."

"And then, Jake, we'll be just like everyone else."

"Wouldn't it be pretty to think so?" I said.

THE END.

Howard smiled. In a day or two, he would dig out his old Smith Corona typewriter and beat away at the keys, just as Papa himself had done. He would type the thing up, give it body, give it a bit of respectability. After all, Ernest Hemingway had written the novel in the mid-1920s, when he was still just a boy. What did he know of what was to come? The damn stock market hadn't even fallen yet. Gertrude Stein was happily holding court at her salon, and Fitzgerald was still dancing in the streets with Zelda, the ink not dried on *Gatsby*. How could Papa have known what the '30s and '40s would bring, much less the '50s and '60s? No wonder he wrote about cynical human beings, irresponsible men and women whose greatest quest was to turn life into one endless and glittering party. Howard saw this as his chance to help Papa out. Granted, no one would see it but the gray jays and the chickadees. But that was okay. That didn't matter. Maybe he would mail it out one day to a magazine, just to appease the Politically Correct Police who were now roaming the valleys and dells of American literature. He'd toss them a bone, sharks that they were. Papa would understand. He knew all about sharks, knew how they follow the boat, eating away at the body until nothing but the head remains. It had won him the Pulitzer Prize, this shark knowledge.

By the time Howard dressed for his run and came down the steps of the cabin, it was again snowing, light and feathery. The ground was already white, with just flashes of yellow here and there where all those autumn leaves had piled up. Winter was trying hard to happen but autumn was still holding its ground. But soon, soon, the snows would come full force.

Howard changed his run. He went straight into town this time, and on past the church to the post office. He had a couple of bills waiting for him and another letter from the Ford Motor Company. *Dear Howard. We have learned from our files that you have fully purchased your 1995 Probe. That's exciting news since a new model awaits you! But time is running out, Howard! P.S. When you stop in with this letter and take a test drive before November 25, 1998, we'll give you a certificate for a* FREE *holiday turkey!* He didn't waste his energy on balling up this one. Instead, he tossed it into the big trash barrel at the post office. Inside the barrel were other letters from Ford, the envelopes all addressed with a computer's script font, so that they would appear to be handwritten. Apparently, Howard Woods wasn't the only one who had gotten a personal love letter that day from the Ford Motor Company.

As he jogged into the parking lot of the Holiday Inn, the fresh snow was just starting to cover the big green H on the sign. A light dusting was all the weathermen had predicted, and that's what it looked like, *a dusting.* The morning sun would take it all away. By late October, it would be back and it would stay for months. Howard slowed his quick stride down to a walk. As he reached the towering sign, he stopped. He took off his gloves and put them into the pockets of his jacket. He wanted to catch his breath a bit before he went inside. It was almost four o'clock and already Pete's jeep was in the yard, along with several other vehicles. Howard knew this meant the *sanfermines,* those *afficionados,* would be leaning on their elbows at the bar. There were a few footprints barely noticeable in the light snow, signs that people had recently passed that way. And that's when Howard remembered again that day when he, and Ellen, and Ben, and Vera—now that he had a name for her—had all come to the Holiday Inn together for a drink after some school activity. It had been snowing that day, too, fat flakes covering the sidewalk as they parked their cars and then made their way toward that perpetual smell of egg rolls and weenies. And that's when

Howard had balled up a fistful of thick, wet snow, shaped it into a snowball and tossed it at Ben Collins, who had quickly tossed one back. He could almost hear their old voices ringing out, and the sounds of their boots stomping off the snow before they went inside for one of Wally's famous martinis. Those were the days when the Holiday Inn was more a virgin than a *poule*, a faded prostitute that still lurks on street corners in old novels. They thought they'd be husbands and wives forever, didn't they? Teachers, forever in their prime.

"Hey look, everybody!" Pete Morton shouted, as Howard stepped into the dimly lighted lounge. "It's Dances with Squirrels!"

Things hadn't changed much. Larry left his spot behind the keyboards to come over to the bar and shake Howard's hand.

"Jesus, Howie, it's good to see you," said Larry. "We been thinking about you. We're all real sorry, you know, the bad news." Howard nodded. He didn't want to talk about Eliot. He only wanted to think about Eliot, in the safety of his own mind, his own thoughts, his own memories, until he could come to some kind of terms with it all. The guys understood. He knew they wouldn't mention it again. They were guys.

Wally started to pour him a rum, but Howard shook his head.

"A glass of red wine," he said.

That's when Howard noticed that Bernie, the groundskeeper at the golf course, was sitting on a lopsided stool at the very end of the bar. The course had been shut down for the season, and, as usual, Bertie had nothing but time on his hands until next May. It was common knowledge that Bertie only turned up in the lounge after the last golf ball had been hit out at the course. It was Bertie's own code, and he'd stuck by it for years. He was on the telephone now, sounding more frustrated than ever.

"I *know* it's caused by algae feeding on the liquid," Bertie was saying, most likely to some laboratory he'd read about in New Zealand, since he'd gone through most of the North American labs. "I been fighting that thing for five years. What I *don't know* is how to stop it. And all it's doing right now is resting up until spring."

As Howard sipped his wine, he turned and looked across the room. How he and Ellen had loved that place in its heyday. It was the perfect retreat from college students who thought it too dull, too boring as a hangout. But it had been the ideal place for his and Ellen's crowd, with its plush sofas and chairs, a place to munch on microwave eggrolls and those perpetual weenies floating in a reddish sauce that even Bertie wouldn't try to classify. And, of course, they'd listen as Larry Ferguson banged away on his piano and sang the songs they loved to hear. Sinatra. Captain & Tennille. John Denver. How many times had Howard twirled Ellen about out there on the dance floor? *Ellen.* He'd been trying not to think of her, either.

"Hey, Howie, your new mattress is in!"

Howard looked over to where the juke box sat and saw Freddy Wilson, his skin more tanned than ever, his teeth glowing white in his brown face. Freddy was sitting at a table with a very young woman, one who would most likely sell mattresses for the Mogul before the night was over.

Howard took the stool that had been designated his, during all those many Happy Hours when he had been holed up in room number 17. Pete came and sat next to him, took out his cigar and lit it up. Howard read Pete's tee-shirt: GOD GRANT ME THE SENILITY TO FORGET THOSE PEOPLE I NEVER LIKED IN THE FIRST PLACE.

Larry came and sat on Howard's other side, the stool squeaking beneath his weight. He looked at Howard and smiled.

"So what've you been up to?" Larry asked. Howard thought about that for a moment.

"Well, like most existentialists," he said, "I've been getting up early every morning to search for values in a universe of chance." It was Larry's turn to think. Here was a man who had risen early every morning to search for his *pump.*

"Me, too," said Larry. Apparently, it had sounded like a good plan to the lounge singer. He gestured to Wally. "Another tomato juice, Wal."

On the mirror behind the bar were more Polaroid pictures of Larry's pump. Howard leaned forward in order to see them better. The pump had gotten around. New England Aquarium. Fenway Park. In one, it was sitting outside Cheers, the Boston bar made famous from television. Larry noticed that Howard was staring.

"Fucking bitch," said Larry. "But the joke was on her. She actually did me a favor. It's back."

"What is?" Howard asked. He imagined the pump arriving at Larry's door, wearing a red blazer, with a steamer trunk in tow.

"*You* know," said Larry. He threw a quick look downward at his crotch. "*It.*"

"Oh," said Howard. "I guess that's a good thing, then."

"I found me another doctor," said Larry. "Know what my problem was?" Howard shook his head. How could he possibly guess, unless it was an algae that was feeding on the iron-rich liquid just beneath the surface of Larry's scrotum.

"It was nothin' but a case of Nervous Nuts," said Pete.

"Don't be an wiseguy," said Larry. He looked at Howard. "It was stress and too much alcohol. But I'm back good as new and making up for lost time. That bitch can just keep the damn thing."

"What's that?" asked Howard, and pointed to a fresh newspaper clipping that was taped just above the yellowing publicity photo that Lola Falana had signed. *To Wally, Thanks for coming. Love, Lola.* Wally brightened.

"It was in the papers last week," he said. "I finally found out where Lola is. She's born again and living with her parents in Philly." Then he added, "She's got M.S."

A silence fell over them then, their own way of wishing Lola Falana the best, of wishing life had been kinder to her. But she was a girl with pizzazz and they all knew it. Somehow, Lola would not only survive, she would prosper.

"Man, she was something," said Pete. "Remember when her boob came out of her dress on Johnny Carson?"

Howard stood. His wine glass was still half full but he pushed it back across the bar toward Wally.

"I better run, guys," he said. "And I mean that literally."

Before Howard left the lounge, Pete had an original thought. "Hey, Runs Without Bulls!" Pete shouted. "Don't be a stranger."

Howard had almost always run in the mornings, except for the past few days, his schedule being thrown off-kilter by the workers from Morgan's Home Builders. He had no way of knowing that Ellen often visited the cemetery in the late afternoon. But he found out as he crested the top of Stony Hill Road and saw the little gray Celica pulled up and parked by the wrought iron gates. The snow had stopped again, and again the afternoon sun was breaking from behind clouds. The iron bars of the cemetery lay in shadows upon the white snow next to the Celica. When Howard saw that it was, indeed, Ellen, saw the smallness of her out by the grave that must be Eliot's, over in the upper corner of the graveyard, he picked up his pace. He was a half mile further down Stony Hill Road when he finally turned, tears in his eyes, and ran back to the cemetery. As he had hoped, it was a long enough jog that the tears were gone by the time he reached the gate.

Ellen was sitting on the snowy ground by the edge of grave. Considering Howard had not been there since that hot day in July, when they had buried Eliot, he hadn't imagined that the grass would grow so fast on his grandson's resting place. But it had. The mound must have been green all through August, for now brown spikes of grass thrust up through the thin layer of snow, grass rigid with autumn, with impending winter. But there must have been that little spurt of life before the winter cold stung the roots into submission. A smattering of floral bouquets covered the mound, two of them still quite fresh. Howard supposed this was Ellen's and Patty's doings. He also supposed that it had been women who put daisies on those ancient Neanderthal graves, a need for everlasting beauty, even in death. Ellen was staring at Eliot's name, inscribed with a deep flourish of lettering on the tombstone. She looked up as Howard approached. For a few seconds they said nothing. Howard saw that someone had left a baseball at the bottom of the headstone. He recognized it immediately. It was the one Howard had given John, signed by Carl Yazstremski that lovely summer's day, years ago, that Howard and his son had taken in a game at Fenway Park. John must have left it there for his own son, passing the treasure on. Howard looked away, a lump rising in his throat, a burning again in his eyes.

"I brought the violet," Ellen said, and pointed to a little pot with an African violet growing up out of it. He was surprised at the sound of her voice, the lilt in it. Was he forgetting, after forty long years? Can it happen that quickly? Would he eventually forget Eliot's voice, too? He hoped not. He hoped to hell he didn't. "When Eliot visited, he used to admire the purple flowers on mine."

Howard smiled at the warm memory of this. He looked down at Ellen. She seemed tinier than he remembered her, as if she were melting inside the thick black jacket, what she called her *autumn* coat. Maybe she was disappearing, alone now in the big house on Patterson Street, alone in her marriage bed, maybe she was dissolving in sadness. Like Patty was dissolving. In a short time, Howard knew in his heart, Patty Woods would be gone all together if they didn't do something to save her. He thought about Eliot then, really thought about him in a way he had not allowed himself to do yet, because the flesh and blood of the boy was too painful to remember. Eliot, small and loving, an admirer of the Florida Gators. Innocent. Eliot Lane Woods would know about *forgiveness*.

Howard reached into his jacket pocket and brought out the little car, the red Galaxy with its yellow headlights. He had carried it in his pocket every day that he ran, wondering if that was the day he'd stop and leave it for Eliot. It all takes time. He leaned down and put it on the ground of Eliot's grave, on top of the rich soil that was already churning itself toward winter, waiting, knowing in its core that there is such a thing as spring. He wanted it to stay there with his grandson, next to the flower pots and the baseball, Eliot, who was now grown wiser than all the humans he left behind. Ellen smiled to see it.

"That looks like that Galaxy you wanted," she said. "Remember? Back when Greta was just born? I always felt guilty that we couldn't afford it." She looked up at him then. "That's why I think your little James Bond car is a great idea."

"You do?" asked Howard. The truth was that he had been wavering. It had nothing to do with Ford's blatant turkey bribe, and everything to do with the notion that maybe he belonged behind the wheel of a car more befitting his age. Ellen never failed to amaze him. And this is what had kept their life together interesting for forty years.

"Sure I do," Ellen said. "You think I haven't seen you flying around town with the top down?" He smiled. He certainly *hoped* she had seen him. That had been part of the plan, after all.

"Wanna go for a ride sometime?" he asked.

"I don't want to make Pussy Galore jealous," Ellen said.

"She'll get over it," said Howard.

Evening was falling, the sun dropping, the early autumn night moving in. He could feel the cold beginning to penetrate his jacket. He took a deep breath, full of the richness of fall, the clean, cold air.

"Can I take you to dinner?" Howard asked. Ellen waited a few seconds before she answered.

"How about if I cook instead? Chicken cacciatore."

He nodded his approval.

"I'll bring the wine."

"This time, try not to throw it, okay?"

"I'll try."

Ellen reached out and touched the petals of the African violet. Surely she knew that it would freeze during the night. But it would hold its purple flowers for a couple hours, at least, and that would be enough. That would be an eternity.

"We bought him that damn bicycle," Ellen said then, as if this thought was too much to keep to herself any longer. She took a tissue from her jacket's pocket and blew her nose. The tip of it was already red with cold.

"Guilt is part of this, Ellen," Howard said. He was impressed with how wise he sounded in that instant, how brave. "Don't be tricked, sweetheart. Guilt is part of it." He felt big, uncontrollable tears well in his eyes, but he wasn't ashamed if Ellen saw them. They would be a family awash in tears before time came around with its salve and its rolls of gauze. Never a *healing*, no. But a means to keep the wound wrapped, a way to stop the flow of blood. A promise of *distance*, eventually, sweet, lovely *distance*. And *forgiveness*. After all, the greatest part of life is just that, Howard had come to realize. It begins with us forgiving our parents for forcing us to be born. With forgiving *ourselves*, for being foolish enough to take part in the first place, despite all our misgivings. For scurrying like blind moles across The Big Landfill, a place where rules are bent or broken, a kingdom where unfairness runs rampant.

He had called her sweetheart.

"What about tonight?" he said to Ellen, then. "What about dinner *tonight?*" It almost surprised him. Ellen stood, brushed the snow and dried grass from her jeans. He walked with her back to the car. She opened the door and turned to face him.

"Bring red wine, okay?" Ellen asked. "It goes better with chicken."

Howard nodded. Then he stood and watched as the gray Celica backed out onto Stony Hill Road. Ellen waved, a quick, sweet wave, and Howard waved back. Soon, the car had disappeared beyond the crest of hill. He listened to the sound of its engine, growing more and more distant, until it, too, was gone.

As Howard ran back toward the cabin, he wondered if it would happen over dinner, perhaps while they were eating their salads with the artichoke hearts, that Ellen would ask him to move back home. Or maybe *he* would be the one to ask, at the very second the cork came popping out of the wine bottle, his cue to speak. Maybe they would go out for dinner, instead, and it would happen then. He imagined an ending to their own novel, his and Ellen's. He would drive to her house again for dinner. He would ring the bell, but only once, showing a Hemingway kind of control. Ellen would open the door, look at him, tears in her eyes. *Darling, I've been so miserable,* she would say. Howard would merely nod, for he had learned how cruel and vicious words can be. He knew now how words go deep. They go like horns into the gut, the heart, the soul.

Listen, Ellen, he would say, *going to another country doesn't make any difference. I've tried all that. You can't get away from yourself by moving from one place to another.* And she would smile, and so he would take her out to see the town, not in a taxi, but in the little black Aston Martin. He would put the top down so that the cold, autumn wind could sing through her reddish hair. As they drove, all the houses of Bixley would look *sharply white,* just as they had from the taxi, that last night in Madrid, with tears stinging Brett's eyes, with Jake wanting her more than ever. Howard would take Ellen to dinner at the Café Le Bixley, where a girl would bring them hot bowls of soup, and wine. And on the way home, Ellen would put her head against his chest, and she would say something Brett-tish, like, *Oh, Howie, we could have had such a damned good time together.* But now, now, Howard would know just what to say. He wouldn't say what Jake did. He wouldn't say, *Isn't it pretty to think so?* Hell, no, he was far too wise for that now. Howard would sim-ply kiss the softness of her face. He would kiss her and then he would whisper, very gently, *We still can, Ellen, we still can.*

Maybe it would take a day, two weeks, a month, but it would be soon. That's all Howard knew. He felt it in his bones. The way Billy Mathews felt the urge to lead a small and happy life. He felt what the squirrels feel, each time ice rims the shore of the lake. It would be soon, and it was *about time.* At the age of sixty-three, Howard Woods was headed straight for his future. It would happen just like it does in a book, because lives are like that. All people have is their own stories, their own versions of what happened to them. How-ard imagined himself putting the book of his and Ellen's life to-gether high up on a shelf, the one in his old study at Patterson Street. But before he did, he would say the speech to her that he'd wanted to say for such a long, long time: *I forgive you, Ellen Ann O'Malley Woods, with your lovely green eyes, and your ability to en-dure. I forgive you, sweetheart, with all my heart and soul. Now, now, can you forgive me?*

Reading Group Guide

Questions for Discussion

1. The novel opens with a dramatic confrontation, as Ellen reveals her infidelity to Howard. Why might the author choose to begin the story at this point? How does it affect your reading of the novel?

2. How do you respond to Howard's claim that he needs to "pay his dues"? What does he mean by this? Why does he think running the bulls in Pamplona will allow him to pay his dues?

3. Howard refers frequently to Ernest Hemingway's *The Sun Also Rises*. What associations or expectations about Hemingway and his work do you bring to this book? How do those associations resonate with this novel?

4. The characters in this story frequently act contrary to their own best interests or true desires; for example, Howard initiates divorce proceedings, not because he truly wants a divorce but as a means of punishing Ellen. How do these misguided efforts shape your feelings about the characters?

5. What do you make of Howard's encounters with his former student, Billy Mathews? What do they suggest about the depth of his distress?

6. Ellen tells Howard that he is "a coward." Do you agree with that? What portrait emerges, over the course of the novel, of their married life?

7. How do you respond to Howard's encounter with Donna Riley, the hotel manager? Does his infidelity somehow balance or cancel out Ellen's?

8. What do you make of Howard's nostalgia for the 1950s? Does he really believe it was a better time? In what ways does he undermine his nostalgic visions even as he creates them?

9. The author has referred to this novel as a "coming-of-age" story about a sixty-three-year-old man. How does the description resonate with your experience of the book?

10. Critics have called Pelletier a writer with "a unique ability to be simultaneously sympathetic and wickedly funny." In what ways does *Running the Bulls* achieve such a balance?

Author's Statement

I suppose the last thing most novelists, critics, publishers, and those who work within the hallowed walls of book publishing want to hear is this: "The idea for my novel started as an idea for a movie." But that's what happened with *Running the Bulls*. I had had a busy week, in the summer of 1996, as I remember, having written for four long, straight days (while suffering from what had to be a form of pneumonia) on an eighty-page synopsis for my second McKinnon book, titled *Candles on Bay Street*. I sold the synopsis, by the way, and the book was published in 1999. But I had also been working on adapting my novel *A Marriage Made at Woodstock* for film producer George Stevens, Jr., and his son, Michael Stevens.

For me, a book or any project, no matter what the genre, often starts when I hear a character actually say something to me, or if I imagine them doing some act. Why do characters start talking or performing for an author? I have no idea, but that was a busy week, as I said. I had just finished the eighty-page synopsis when basketball players from the 1920s suddenly jumped into my head. I didn't want them to, but they jumped, as only basketball players can do. I stayed in bed, recuperating, and my husband went shopping for me. Soon my bed was covered with books about the history of basketball. I wrote twenty pages for a screenplay to be called *Cagers*, one that I intend to finish soon. (*Cagers* is the term used for basketball players of yore since they were usually inside a cage so that the spectators couldn't throw things and hit them.) Thinking that surely I would then take a rest and fully recover from the flu, I recovered just enough for Howard Woods and Ellen Woods to suddenly appear. This was on the heels of the *Candles on Bay Street* crowd, and the *Cagers* of the 1920s. (I've often said that I wish characters would have to pay rent for the time they spend tramping about in a writer's head.)

So I dashed off four or five pages of screenplay notes: "Howard is a retired prof . . . his wife wakes him one night to tell him she's had an affair years ago . . . he goes a bit crazy." I started writing dialogue and ideas and then, that sinking feeling came over me. It's the feeling where you realize you have to write a *novel*, and not a short story or a screenplay. And a screenplay is, by the way, a very, very difficult thing to write. But a short story or a screenplay is *not* a novel. In a novel, you must be the director, the production designer, the cinematographer, the casting director, the sound man, the actors, the costumer designer, all of it. It's all on your shoulders and, should it fail, there's no one to blame but yourself. It's a trapped feeling when you know it's going to happen. At least, it is for me. I usually spend a year or two alone as I work. In comparison, I often get the first rough draft of a screenplay done in a month of twelve-hour work days, neck-hurting, hands-aching work days. That means relatively quick feedback.

But a novel, well, I was very unhappy to think that I'd have to write a novel about Howard Woods if I wanted to get to know him better, to learn all about his trials and tribulations. (If I was to write a new novel, I thought it would be another Mattagash novel. I now, finally, have one of those in the works.) If I had known in the summer of 1996 that I'd still be rewriting *Running the Bulls* in the spring of 2005, I would have taken that symbolic leap from the nearest bridge. But I didn't know. Characters often lie to their writer so that you'll stick with them, come hell or high water. With screenplays in the works, I found myself knocking out a few pages here and there on the novel. The manuscript grew slowly. As always happens, anything I read in a magazine or see on television or overhear in an airport seems to be suddenly important, as if it's asking for a place in the novel. Not everything is relevant, of course, and my job as author is to pick and choose. But sometimes a bit of information will simply jump out and demand a place. I remember reading in some science magazine about how landfills around the country have been turned into green golf courses and pretty recreational areas above ground, and yet there can be dangerous gases building below, ready to explode. What a metaphor for life! *That* was a keeper.

I usually keep my work to myself until it's finished, rather than talk it out with others and lose the mystery of it. There's an act of discovery that comes with writing in solitude, rather than "talking about writing." If you talk, you often lose that mystery, that indefinable power in letting the characters reveal themselves to you at their own pace. You're no longer an insider, privy to their secret world, once you open the door on them before they are dressed and ready. But this time I let a few people read the first five chapters, including my husband, who bugs me until I throw the pages at him.

Then, in 1997, my mother was diagnosed with cancer. I put the book, now about one half finished, away. She recovered from her operation and there was no sign of cancer for three years. During that time, I should have finished the novel, but I became distracted with screenplays and agenting books for friends. Way led on to way. When my mother's cancer came back in the autumn of 2000, I went home to take care of her. She wanted to die in her own bed, in the house she and my father had built in 1946, on the banks of the river in northern Maine. And she did that. She died late one evening, December, 27, 2000. It was snowing that night. As we waited for the hearse to come from thirty miles away, on that same old road that follows the twisting river, I couldn't help but think of how she had given birth to me in that same house, also on a cold winter's night. As the hearse was leaving, red taillights in the snow, I put on the hanging porch lights, something Mama liked very much. I told myself that I may never write again. I knew there was going to be a death in *Running the Bulls,* and I knew that it would be difficult for me to write the scene. I also knew that the big themes of life and fiction would now be so painful that I couldn't imagine myself ever tackling them again.

Time heals somewhat, or so it seems. But it took a couple or more years before I could think of writing any novel again. Novels insist that you go down deep, down to where the pain lives. Yet, and surprisingly, instead of avoiding the writing about death, I found myself embracing it. I was especially interested in what happens *after* we die. But I still avoided *Bulls.* Instead, I wrote another book, also under a pseudonym and about reincarnation. I then finished an old book I'd started years earlier, again on reincarnation. I suppose I was seeking answers in any and every place I could look. And then, after three more screenplays, the albatross was still sitting there, waiting for me. I decided I should either say goodbye to *Running the Bulls* forever, or finish it. I finished it. Friends had been very supportive, writing me lovely letters and telling me that it was time I wrote another novel. I think that friendship and love are two things that make living worth the arduous journey. I am very lucky to have found both. My good friend, the poet Wesley McNair, mentioned that I should send the book to John Landrigan, at UPNE. Wesley finally e-mailed and said, "Shall I send it for you?" There are some offers that come your way like little birds, winging. This was one I couldn't refuse, and one that I greatly appreciate. Well, that meant it was either sink or swim. I certainly hope I swim.

An Interview with Cathie Pelletier

This is your first novel as Cathie Pelletier since Beaming Sonny Home, *but in the meantime you have published two novels under the pseudonym K. C. McKinnon. What distinguishes a Pelletier novel from a McKinnon novel? When do you know whether a book is one or the other?*

This is very easy for me to answer, and it's also very difficult. The easy answer is the difference in the *sense of humor* that appears in each book. My Mattagash books, and other Pelletier novels, tend to be darkly comic before they take a more tragic turn. The McKinnon books (while I hope a reader smiles here and there) tend to be more serious. No quirky humor. And while I hope that I take on the very same themes in a McKinnon book as I do in my Pelletier books, I only allow the "interrogation" of the theme to go so far in the McKinnon books. I hope that they are smart and thoughtful books, since that's certainly my intention. But my intent is also to "tell a story" and to entertain the reader. I rarely think of the reader when I write a Pelletier book. It's my own little journey of discovery. In the Pelletier books, whether I like it or not, I tend to pull off the scar tissue and start mining the emotional past. I'm very much closer, personally, to the kind of characters I write about in Pelletier books. The sarcasm that I give Howard Woods (and certainly Fred Stone in *A Marriage Made at Woodstock*) is mostly stuff I've personally said, and then rushed to write down for my characters to also say. The McKinnon characters are far nicer people than I am. But here's where the two types of books overlap: I often find my love of nature coming up in all of the books. So, they are both different and yet alike.

How was the experience of writing this novel different from (or similar to) your earlier novels? Do you find that your novels inform one another from one to the next? Or is each its own separate experience?

It's different in that I've never taken so long to write a novel. This has certainly been the longest gestation period. And then, *Running the Bulls* is not a Mattagash novel. I find the Mattagash novels tend to be closer to the world I knew growing up as a child in remote northern Maine. My other novels (*Running the Bulls; A Marriage Made at Woodstock; The Bubble Reputation*) allow me to explore the world I discovered *after* I left remote northern Maine. I suppose each novel grows out of the previous only in that the author is also growing, after having written each one. My Mattagash trilogy is more likely to inform one another, although I do hope the books also stand alone.

Critics consistently praise your ability to combine humor with poignancy. What are the challenges of walking such a line? Do you believe it is important for a novel to include both, and if so, why? Were there particular challenges in maintaining that balance in this novel?

I'm glad we're not referring to the critics who *don't* believe this!

I think this is my own Irish sense of humor, which I picked up not just in my DNA (my mother was an O'Leary) but from the fact that my hometown was mostly full of Irish-descended folks who enjoyed, and still do, a comic sense in their daily lives.

It's important to me that my novels do both, since I have always seen the humor in the tragic. So it's inevitable that this combination of humor and seriousness turns up in my work as a writer since it's in my personal life. But you can't please everyone. Just as I sometimes sit across a dinner table from a person and think, "Please, *please,* let this be over soon so I can escape from this joyless human being," people enjoy a different sense of humor, depending on their backgrounds, whether ethnic or geographic. Maybe that person I thought hopelessly dour was sitting there thinking the same thing of me.

You have referred to *Running the Bulls* as a "coming-of-age" novel about a sixty-three-year-old retired college professor. What was it about this notion that appealed to or inspired you?

It's often said (and I think it's true) that we writers don't always know what we feel about a certain subject unless we write about it. I suppose I would have to say that I've undergone a change myself, just as Howard did. In December of 2000, my mother died. I am the baby of the family, and I'm still dealing with this loss of a parent who was very close to my life and even my career. I was a rebellious child, the youngest of six, and my mother and I had a very unique relationship. I once read an interview in which Joyce Carol Oates said that her career doesn't mean as much to her anymore, now that her mother is gone. I understand this. Just as Howard's life takes a turn with the death of someone close to him, I think my mother's death was my own coming-of-age catalyst. Two years after she died, I turned fifty years old, and that's another unique life experience to go through for any woman, a time when the body begins its own journey, whether the mind likes it or not. Perhaps this is how I identify with Howard. And yet, tomorrow I will say and do something that will immediately reduce me to an immature and insecure twenty-year-old. Go figure.

Ernest Hemingway is a significant presence in this book. What made his work particularly appropriate for your story? How do you relate to his work? Was there a particular appeal in engaging such an icon of hyper-masculinity?

In the summer of 1974, when I was still a very young woman and living in Toronto, I came home to Maine and signed up for a summer class at the local college. It was called, simply, *Hemingway*. By the time it was over, not only was I drinking more beer and shooting more pool than any college student should, I wanted to slap almost every girl in my class. The "angst du jour" was how Ernest was a sexist, a macho bastard, and a killer of animals, given the big game he was constantly bagging in his books and in his life. That last one hit home with me, too, since I have been concerned with animals and animal rights since I was a child. But I felt the book deserved to be judged by its own artistic merits, and not by my personal beliefs. Added to this, no one seemed to mention that this novel had been written in the 1920s, a very different time in America, and in the world. My argument back to them was that literature is fiction, no matter how much it relies upon the author's real life experiences, and therefore a novel should be treated as its own world. Leave the real world out of it, and leave your own personal grievances out of the reading of it. Thankfully, the professor agreed with me. Fiction has the amazing ability to teach us the truth about ourselves because, unlike real life, fiction has *all* the answers. A novel is a complete world, a total universe, so it can supply us with everything we need to know about that world. Real life can't do it.

It was my summer of discontent with what was obviously becoming the Politically Correct Literary Police. This was about the time it was also becoming unpopular on campuses to admire Hemingway for his craft. I was still too young to fully appreciate his work, although we dashed through a few novels in three weeks time. (But I do think I became a better pool player that summer.) It was twenty years later, when I was living yet again in Toronto, that I reread *The Sun Also Rises*. I would take the novel and stroll down Queen's Quay, on the lakefront, and take the elevator up to the revolving restaurant on the 30th floor. This was just across the street from the *Toronto Star*, a paper Papa once wrote for. I'd order a red wine, and I'd sit and read the novel while the restaurant spun around and around. I was so taken with the book. And humor? I laughed out loud in so many places, and yet, I don't remember even smiling when I first read the book in 1974. This is what John Irving means when he says we should reread good novels every ten years or so, as we ourselves grow more experienced. I suppose all these old emotions and experiences were waiting to come out, and so, when I wrote *Running the Bulls*, there was Papa Hemingway.

Most of your novels are set in Maine and exhibit a strong sense of place. What does Maine mean to you as a writer? Does it offer narrative opportunities that other settings might not? How do you maintain your connection to the state?

I'll quote Eudora Welty when she said that writers tend to write out of the first ten years of their lives. I suspect this is very true. In 1837, my maternal ancestors came in pirogues from New Brunswick, Canada, and founded our little end-of-the-road town in Maine, a place called Allagash. I was born at home, in the midst of January cold, in the house my father had built a few years earlier. My mother died in that same house, and I was there then, too. She and I went through birth and death together in that house. Those are old and deep roots for any person, no matter what the profession. The St. John River was my playmate. I almost drowned in that river when I was very young. The old birch tree in our backyard, until it died a few years ago, was like one of the family. It was old and tall in 1945 when my father and mother first came there to raise a family, on the banks of the St. John. All of this is so ingrained in me that it's impossible to forget my roots. I often find myself asking people if they'd go back to childhood if they could. About 90 percent or more quickly say, "No!" But I would go back in a heartbeat. My childhood, remote and safe, was an electric place where older brothers worked on their fast cars as they listened to the latest hits on the radio. Older sisters were learning to jive and wearing poodle skirts. I was safe, watching from a distance, with Daddy teaching me how to drive the tractor, cut hay, or bridle a horse. And Mama was cooking wonderful meals and planting a big garden each year and decorating the house for every holiday. Of course, I'd go back!

For all the years I've been gone, I always answered, "Maine," whenever someone would ask where I was from. I'd follow it with, "But I now live in the South," or "I'm living in Canada now." I plan to move north again soon, but until then, I often visit my family and friends in Maine. It's home. The house is like a haven for me. So perhaps this is my way of recapturing northern Maine, by putting it in my novels. There is always a sense of safety and hope at the end of each Mattagash novel.

You have set at least one earlier novel in Bixley, Maine. What was it like to return to that landscape? What are the advantages and drawbacks of revisiting the same locale in more than one novel (as you have also done in your books set in Mattagash, Maine)?

People tend to think that if you're from Maine, you know the ocean. But I was born and raised eight hours north of Portland and five hours north of Bangor. I don't think I even *saw* the ocean until I was about nine or ten years old. And to this day I have never even *tasted* lobster. I was definitely a river kid. But as an adult I had spent a bit of time in Portland and thought it might be interesting to explore a new part of the state, one that's very different from northern Maine. So I set my novel *A Marriage Made at Woodstock* in Portland. When I accidentally made a one-way street into a two-way street, I heard about my *traffic faux pas* from at least one indignant critic. I wanted to say, "Hey, listen, Keats had Cortez gazing with eagle eyes at the Pacific when it was really Balboa who had the eagle eyes, so cut *me* some slack!" What can I say? Some folks became prostrate that I'd set a novel in Portland without having lived there. You learn a lesson from this: *Ignore such people.* But I knew I wanted to build a Maine town that I could revisit when I didn't want to do a Mattagash novel. So, in *The Bubble Reputation*, I gave Bixley a population of 25,000. That's unheard of since there is no town north of Bangor that large. And I got some flack for it in Maine. More prostrate critics, in pain over my geographic shortcomings. I kept wanting to ask, "Don't you think I *know* this?" And I kept trying to explain that Bixley didn't exist except in fiction. But, again, the Gendarmes of Political and Geographic Correctness walk among us, untethered. There is a great discussion on this and I've talked about it with other authors. How factual does our fictional place need to be? Again, this is fiction. And, like Alice Munro once said, fiction should take some "starter clay" from the real world. But that's all it need do. I had to have a town large enough that I could be more expansive in scope than Mattagash allows me. Mattagash gives me history and roots. I wanted a place with restaurants and movie theaters and a sense of "city." Now, of course, cable TV with 200-plus channels has changed all this. The outer world has found the inner world. My fictional Mattagash now has satellite dishes. Progress is everywhere, unless you move to Easter Island, but I suspect there may be a Starbucks in the works there too. Nonetheless, for me to keep setting novels in Maine, which I wanted to do, I had to create a place where there was no ocean, but a place with "large town" sensibilities. I went back to Bixley for *Running the Bulls*, and it's got a population of 25,000 and it's not Bangor or Portland, and the Population Critics will just have to live with it.

Advantages? I suppose that it's familiar terrain. Drawbacks? Well, it's the same old terrain, isn't it? How to make it seem new? I've lived most of my adult life in the South, and yet I'd never set a novel in the South unless it was the story of a Yankee coming to the South. I wrote only one such book in all these years (not published yet—it's one of the pseudonymous ones) in which a Boston travel writer moves to Nashville. How can I possibly know what it's like to grow up as a true southerner? I can't. But by writing about Maine from here in the South, or in Canada, I get distance, and perhaps also freedom.

You have extensive contacts in the country music world. What has been your involvement with that scene? How has it informed your writing? How does that aspect of your life intersect with your writing life?

I started writing as a poet, or at least that was my intent. I published a first volume at the age of twenty-two. It was during that time that I started traveling around Canada with my musician boyfriend, and I started writing songs. My writing prof, when I got back to college, said he saw an improvement in my work, due to the year I'd spent songwriting. Again, the literati will cry foul, but I can understand this very well. Ezra Pound once said that, without music, "the poetry withers and dies." He may not have had Billy Ray Cyrus or Dolly Parton in mind when he said that, but cadence is cadence in any language, in any genre, and in any era. (Okay, maybe Ezra *did* have Dolly in mind.) On another aspect, I lived with a country musician/singer for many years and through that relationship I traveled the world for free. That kind of world experience is a great asset for any writer.

You have written original screenplays and you have adapted your own novels for the screen. How is the experience of writing a screenplay different from writing a novel? What are the challenges of adapting your own work in order to create a screenplay?

The biggest difference is that I don't find myself wondering how much a gun costs when I'm writing a novel. A screenplay, as tough as it is, is really just a blueprint for a whole lot of people to take up and then make their own. It's maddening, frustrating, infuriating. But it can also be terrific, as in the experience I'm now having with a director I hope will do *The Funeral Makers.* Terrific, because he knows my Mattagashers better than I do. But it's also maddening in that it's no longer just *my* vision. A novelist is used to working alone, after all, in solitude for months at a time. And then, writing a screenplay, you have to reverse what it is you do as a novelist: You don't *show.* Well, you do show, but you have to learn to rely upon pictures more than words. I don't like adaptation. I'd much rather discover stories and characters anew than try to be true to a novel. Again, the *literary police* will hate this, but I did not reread *The Funeral Makers* to write the screenplay based upon it. I have changed almost everything about the book. Why? Because it's a *novel* I wrote in my late 20s/early 30s, before I'd written a lot of novels, and I've grown up some, and the characters themselves have grown up some. (Amy Joy was 14 in *The Funeral Makers,* and she's now 56 in this fourth Mattagash book I hope to finish in a year or so.) I'm always changing, and the characters are also growing. A novel should stay safe, as its own entity, one that no one can touch or change. A film is born out of that idea that was the novel.

Can you say a bit about your own writing practice? Do you write every day?

I write all day long on some *thing*, whether it's a novel, screenplay, book idea, proposal for myself or someone else. I dance all around when it comes to projects, so I'm never bored. But when I settle on a project, I really settle. This means aching neck and aching hands, since I work many hours a day. But I do stop and walk the dogs on my land here (thirty-five acres surrounded on three sides by creek), and I always make sure I have a glass of wine for the sunset. (It sets far too early in winter.) I'm slowly becoming the old woman I once wrote of in *The Bubble Reputation* (and writers do, amazingly, strangely, often write down the *future*), the woman whose hair goes wild as she grows more and more a recluse until she dies and no one remembers her, there in the house overrun by thorns. I often don't get in an automobile (or even go down to my mailbox) for five months at a time. When I have to leave the house and land, usually to visit my father in northern Maine, a car going thirty-five miles an hour seems to me like an Amtrak train hurtling me towards my certain death. Even a tiny supermarket is Piccadilly Circus, what with all the colors and sights and sounds. I have been quite gregarious throughout my life, so how this is happening amazes me. What my computer and the Internet have taught me is that I now prefer to be gregarious at a distance. Friends do come to visit me, and Tom and I have the twelve rescued animals, and fires at night, and stars and planets. In all, I have lots of company. But my lifestyle nowadays is most difficult for my European-born, cosmopolitan husband. He loves our farm, but he also misses the city.

Have you ever owned a Ford Probe?

Yes, and in truth, I loved it. I wish I hadn't sold it. It eventually became a "Take the Dogs to the Vet" car. What I didn't love is that my Probe GT came with birth defects, thanks to the Ford Motor Company. It was dark blue, as is Howard's car. And when I found out too late that it was a *lemon* (I had taken it new and moved to Canada, where, in their opinion, all of America is in a state of *lemon-hood*) it was too late. I missed the lemon recall sent out by Ford. They paid for some of the repairs, such as when the muffler dropped off one sunny day, in Toronto traffic, when the car was still very new. But mostly, I was past the lemon recall time period. For years after I sold it, however, I kept getting letters from the Ford dealership in Nashville where I bought the car (despite the awful things I had said to them over the telephone) trying to entice me back, offering everything from "a free lube job" to "a Thanksgiving turkey." I kept all these letters in my file for *Running the Bulls*. I hope they sit in purgatory for a long, long time, the people who sold me the Probe GT, along with all those girls who hated Hemingway.